DELUDED

LYNN STEINSON

PublishNation
www.publishnation.co.uk

Dedication

For my mother, who loved books and music.

*Libera me, Domine, de morte aeterna in die illa tremenda
Libera me.*

*Deliver me, Lord, from eternal death on that awful day
Deliver me.*

Libera Me, Requiem

Contents

1

PROLOGUE

Cry me a river

Far below, through a gap in the trees, Judith glimpsed the stone wall where Martin's body had been found. As she approached the edge of the woods she recognised the broken timbers that marked the site of the old bridge. She would never forget it.

The police had brought her there the day after the flood. Then the muddy waters were still angry, whipped into a fury by a cold easterly wind. Only the tops of the stone walls were visible. Fields had been swallowed, trees were standing in water, and footpaths led into a deadly swirling torrent. She had been there when they had found the dog. He was wedged against a wall in the tumbling water, his golden fur sodden. It had taken three men to dislodge him. She had wondered how many men it had taken to carry Martin out. Had he been face down in the water? Had he been trapped against the wall like the dog?

She remembered returning to their house later that day. When she had opened the front door the warm, comforting smell of home had enfolded her. Sheltered her. It was indescribable, but totally familiar. Their own unique scent, the notes of their marriage. Each day the scent had diminished. Her own presence was now dominant. Martin's had outlasted his death, lingering on a jacket or scarf, but she knew he was drifting away. This morning, before leaving home, she had held his scarf to her nose and breathed deeply. He was almost gone.

The coroner had recorded that Martin's death was by misadventure. But now the narrative of events that described her husband's last moments no longer made sense. Niggling doubts she

3

had ignored while she was reeling from the shock of unexpected grief were now consuming her. She stopped. Only the startled cawing of hidden birds broke the stillness.

Aching to escape the conifers' gloomy embrace, she quickened her pace, springing through the pine needles towards the grassy valley. In the distance, a dipper bounced along the line of the river as a grey-faced rook flew across its path. Taking steady breaths to check her dizzying anxiety, she inhaled the scent of cedar. As the sun shone through the gnarled, skeletal branches of the trees along the riverbank, casting sunbeams on Martin's final resting place, she felt a deep chill. She drew the scarf closer. She turned.

'What are you doing here?'

STANDING
IN THE
SHADOWS OF LOVE

One step beyond

Friday morning
'Judith. Judith.'
Martin was never far away. He interrupted her thoughts and infiltrated her dreams, calling through space and time, lest she forget. Her head was cradled by a pillow. The ice-blue cotton duvet was wrapped around her body like a straitjacket. Her bed was no sanctuary. Although it was still early, she knew that if she lingered her thoughts would wander back to her past and a dark weight would descend, crushing her chest, pinioning her to the bed. She was determined to beat the demons that always lurked nearby and which could, if she chose to indulge them, imprison her for the day. She headed for the shower and stepped around a plump feather pillow, almost separated from its cotton case, that lay on the bedroom carpet.

She sat at the French-style dressing table as she carefully made up her face. She checked the reflection of the back of her hair in the three-way mirror, teasing the curls around her ears, then she picked up a framed photograph that stood alone among the bottles of perfume and make-up. She caressed the twisted pewter frame as she examined the familiar portrait. It captured the essence of him, smiling and welcoming, yet there was also something hidden, unknowable, too. Those dark eyes, gazing into the distance, sometimes seemed to follow her round the room.

She put the photograph down, quickly tidied the bedroom, and headed for the kitchen. She had taught herself to look forward to the small pleasures that commenced the day. They were a reason to leave her bed and face the world. She switched on the radio then sat at her computer. She always listened to Radio Four over breakfast, not that she usually noticed what the presenters and guests had to say. It was the comfort of hearing voices in conversation that she enjoyed. She opened her Facebook account and scrolled through the newsfeed.

She had decided to set up the fake identities when she thought that she was going to have an embarrassing absence of friends

7

displayed on her Facebook pages, although now she had acquired far more 'real' friends than she had ever anticipated. She had created a whole social life for herself through its pages. Each fake friend had their own page in a red spiral-bound notebook that described their character traits. She had even devised a grid that showed the friendship links of the fake friends.

They all had their own email address, registered with five different email providers. She used pictures of strangers she copied from Google images and invented names by combining the first and last names of personalities in the headlines. Some of the characters had even established friendships between themselves. A particular favourite was Jeremy May, who routinely posted rants about the state of the economy. She had given him the profile photo of a young Simon Cowell she had found while browsing one day.

She had half a dozen so-called friends from an archery interest group she had once joined. But she did not actually know them, had never met them, and never would. Some of them lived in Europe and one was in Australia. She had enjoyed the initial excitement of communicating with new people and relished their sympathy and kind words when they heard how she had tragically lost her husband, Martin. She had soon got bored when they wanted to chat about archery. Her interest in toxophily had been short-lived. In fact, her fictional friends seemed more interesting than some of these virtual real friends.

Now, though, she had friends who knew her, although she would like more. There were Merriam and Simon from the history of art MA, and Rob and Lisa, but not Keith, from the pub quiz. The lady captain of the golf club was a surprising devotee of Facebook, although they had not had much contact recently. Becca, from the Nail Boutique, had seemed to be on a mission to acquire a record number of friends. She had even befriended Jeremy May and maintained a lively but short correspondence with him.

She checked the notifications listing. Lisa had posted a link to a quiz:

Which character would you be in Game of Thrones*?*

Time for breakfast.

She savoured the aroma of the fresh coffee as she hulled and sliced strawberries. The smell reminded her of Europe. A lunch in Luxembourg, a dinner in Barcelona, an espresso at Geneva Airport. It was the smell of hope. She was not sure why she associated the smell of coffee with hope, but she did, and it made her feel better.

~

Lisa had been overwhelmed with anxiety during the week. It had loitered at the back of her stomach, sneaked behind every thought, and even infiltrated her dreams. She had spent hours researching Bergers and their clients. Yet, whenever she had practised the answers to imagined interview questions, a string of disconnected phrases would stumble clumsily from her mouth. What chance would she have against her colleague, the self-assured Olivia? The previous night, before she had drifted to sleep, Lisa had brooded that the interview might mark the end of her career in advertising.

As she stirred, a dream was still playing in her head. It was so vivid she felt like a viewer in the cinema, watching herself, poised and professional, fielding the questions at her interview. She desperately tried to clutch on to the fleeting fragments of her reverie, to make sense of this convincing other Lisa, as she scrambled around getting ready. She scrutinised her eyes in the looking glass as she rubbed away a smudge of kohl that had touched her cheek. Green flecked with golden brown. They were a trifle smaller than she would like. Rob, however, seemed enchanted by them. He said they were ever-changing, like a chameleon. She looked at her whole reflection: cobalt blue designer suit, new smart haircut and dazzling highlights, exotic, enchanting eyes. Forget the competition. She *was* the new account executive at Bergers. She smiled at herself.

Believe it. Believe in yourself.

Friday evening
The Mancunian sky hung low and heavy, casting a grey pall over the city. The iciness that accompanied the fall of dusk was just beginning to edge its way into the consciousness of the shoppers, causing the lifting of a collar, a search for gloves, a quickening of pace. As the cold inveigled its way through coats, hats, and scarves, Lisa

9

sauntered down Deansgate with a beaming smile on her face and a jaunty stride, as if she were enjoying a glorious spring day. Warm in the aura of success, she was indestructible, unassailable. She wanted to high-kick like a cancan girl. She smiled. Olivia. They had picked her over Olivia. Yes!

'Lisa, darling. How are you?'

'Judith. What are you doing here?'

'You look happy. Have you just won the lottery? Or perhaps you got that job after all?'

As Judith moved to kiss her, Lisa grabbed her shoulders and jumped up and down.

'Yes, I did. Woohoo! I did it. I beat O-liv-i-ah.' Then Lisa stood back, smiling at the older woman. Judith responded with a wide smile. Her eyes were accentuated by a subtle dark grey, which melted at the corners into laughter lines. Dark blonde waves fell on to her red cashmere jacket. She was, as ever, immaculately dressed.

'I knew you would,' Judith said, a touch uncertainly. 'Did my question come up?'

'Well, one quite like it. Thanks for the advice.'

'Right then, it's time to celebrate and you can tell me all about it. Let's go to the champagne bar round the corner. My treat. It's gone five, so it's not too decadent.'

Lisa had no hesitation in accepting the offer. What a fortunate coincidence to bump into Judith like that.

Lisa and Judith perched on tall bar chairs, their glasses fizzing with champagne. A bottle was resting in a silver ice bucket next to Lisa's handbag, which occupied most of the table.

'That's a lovely suit, Lisa. Not your usual style. Here's to your new job,' Judith said, lifting her glass towards Lisa. 'Tell me about it. You're still in the same office, aren't you?'

'Well, yes,' said Lisa, gulping a mouthful, then holding the glass stem to her chest as she wriggled on the bar chair. 'But I'll be working for Andy directly now – everyone loves Andy – I've always got on really well with him. I'll manage two graduate trainees to start with. One's based in London and transfers here next week when Sonia starts work.'

'Sounds like it will be fun,' Judith said, her eyes straying around the bar.

'Oh, yes. I love working in a team. I will make sure they get the support they need and develop them, to get ready for their next career move. In Bergers, of course.'

'You're not being interviewed now.' Judith laughed. 'It's not always easy, you know. It's balancing the personalities that can cause you headaches. Not everyone wants to work hard. I learned that at the museum.'

'Well, I think at Bergers you will be out unless you do, and it's so competitive that only the most ambitious people get in, anyway,' Lisa said.

'Really? And what about, what was her name, your rival?'

'Olivia. I didn't see her afterwards. She had rather thought that the job was hers, that it was her natural right, as she's been there longer than me.' Lisa shrugged as her phone pinged. She looked down. 'It's just my flatmate, Maya, saying, "Well done".'

'Did you tell Rob?'

'Oh, yes. He's thrilled. We're meeting up.' Lisa put the phone in her bag. She glanced around the bar, which was now almost full. There was an invigorating buzz in the air as Friday transformed into the weekend. 'I could get used to this. Thank you, Judith. Cheers.' They clinked glasses.

Lisa toyed with her glass.

'So, what are you doing in town, Judith?'

'Just window-shopping, really.' Judith sighed. The beat of a jaunty samba rhythm was getting louder as Lisa rummaged in her bag for her phone.

'Lisa here. She said what? Hah! Thank you. Byee. Sorry, Judith. Which shops?'

Lisa's phone pinged.

'Hah. It's Sally in the office. Olivia's not happy.' Lisa took a gulp of champagne and began texting.

Judith rested an elbow on the bar table and put a long red fingernail to her lips. Finally, she lightly placed her hand on Lisa's.

'You seem to have a lot of friends to tell,' Judith said.

'Yeah, I do.' Lisa stopped texting abruptly. 'I'm sorry.'

11

'I was just looking forward to hearing about your day.'

'I'll put it away.'

The phone beeped again.

'Oh, God, that's Rob. I'll go outside.' Lisa started to get up.

'No, please stay,' Judith said. 'Take that call. He needs to know where we are.' She caressed her glass as she contemplated the bubbling potion.

'Thank you. Hi, babe. I need to be quick. Thank you. I know you did. You know the champagne bar near St Ann's Square? See you soon.' Lisa put the phone back on the table. 'Rob's already left. He'll be here soon. Business is quiet.' Lisa grinned, sipping more champagne, visualising a wonderful night ahead with her boyfriend. Rob had endured her views on Berger and Berger's marketing strategy throughout the previous week and had cajoled and encouraged her when she had despaired at her own attempts to communicate her ideas in a convincing manner. He deserved to enjoy the celebrations.

'I thought he was rushed off his feet the other week,' Judith said, staring at the mobile which now occupied the space between them.

'He was. Business is always crazy in January with all the package discounts, which makes February a dead month. He prefers it busy, otherwise he has too much time to wonder why he's working in a travel agency when he could be in some sunny country using his Spanish.' Lisa picked up her phone, switched on the silent button, and put it in her bag.

'Martin was always very good with languages. He spoke excellent French and we always intended to holiday there,' Judith said.

'Oh.' Lisa was no longer embarrassed when Judith mentioned Martin. However, she still often felt at a loss for something appropriate to say. 'You must miss him.'

'Yes, I do. And Ben, my golden retriever. They just disappeared, swept away in a torrent of dirty water. All my hopes and dreams drowned that day ... You know, Martin and I were a great team. At work, as well. We won a national prize. Not easy to win, I can tell you. But I had to leave the museum in the end. Too many memories. Not that they stayed there.'

'I'm sorry.' Lisa fiddled with the strap of her handbag. 'Will you be going away on holiday this year?' *Damn, what a tactless thing to ask. Who's she got to go with?*

Lisa repeated her question as Judith strained to hear over the clatter of the scraping chairs on the wooden floor.

'Holiday? I don't know. Bunters, our cat, always makes a fuss if I go away, so I feel guilty.' She paused. 'But maybe I should ask Rob for some advice about a short minibreak. What do you think?'

Lisa was suddenly hanging in the air. Two strong arms were grabbing her, spinning her round. Rob let her drop to the ground. She inhaled the cold February evening on his scarf and the faint smell of aftershave on his collar as he kissed her. She held his eyes for a moment.

'Well done, Lisa. Didn't I tell you? The brightest star of the bunch.' He turned, running his fingers through his almost black unruly locks at the same time. 'This is a wonderful surprise, Jude. Again.'

Judith, stepped off the stool and hugged Rob, then signalled to a waiter and pointed to her glass.

'Judith's been very generous, babe. I'm afraid I've not been much fun, though, texting and taking calls,' Lisa said.

'I'm glad to witness the beginning of a glittering career.' Judith smiled at Lisa.

'I think we'll have another bottle of that,' she said, as the waiter arrived with an extra glass and emptied the bottle. 'Don't worry, you two. I'll get it. I hope you don't mind, Lisa, but while you were on the phone I reserved a table at San Carlo for eight o'clock. We can carry on celebrating there.'

'Crikey, Jude, you're pushing the boat out. But we can't—' said Rob.

'You're not going to abandon me, are you?' Judith said, touching Lisa's hand and laughing.

'That's a fantastic idea, Judith,' said Lisa. 'I've never been there. We might even see some footballers. Pizzas on me.'

'So you've trounced Olivia, then, Lise. How's she taken it?' asked Rob.

'I think it can safely be said that O-liv-i-ah is not happy.' Lisa

13

mimicked an upper-class accent. 'She has told everyone in the office that they have made a dreadful mistake.'

As Lisa returned from the ladies she noticed that a young woman, wearing a purple silk blouse that revealed much tanned cleavage, had moved next to Rob. The girl's face was framed by a mass of tousled ash-blonde hair. Her large eyes, heavily made up with layers of mascara, were fixed on Rob as he shared a joke with Judith. A blade of jealousy cut through Lisa, but then she noticed that a young man with a dark quiff, dressed in an expensively cut grey coat, had positioned himself near Judith.

When Rob and Judith slid off their bar stools the couple scrambled past to claim the vacant seats. Babe threat terminated. Lisa turned to leave, almost colliding with a woman who was carrying a bucket of champagne and three glasses.

'O-liv-i-ah,' Lisa said, mimicking her rival's accent through recent habit and tipsiness. 'I didn't think *you* would be here.'

'Lisa.' Olivia put the bucket and glasses down and kissed Lisa on the cheek. 'I think I could say the same. I thought pubs were more in your comfort zone. Congratulations. You have done very well today.' She smiled stonily as she patted her dark brown French pleat. 'Tasmin, Jeremy, let me introduce you to Lisa.'

'Well done, Lisa,' Jeremy said, offering a warm hand.

'We were just talking about you,' Olivia said, exchanging glances with Tasmin. 'I was explaining that Andy had told me that there was going to be an opening in the London office shortly, a key role, clearly just right for me. They wouldn't want to have to go through the whole interview process again in just a few months' time.' Olivia began to fill three glasses with champagne.

'Well, actually, O-liv-i-ah, Andy also mentioned that to me, and he said there should be no reason why I shouldn't apply,' Lisa said.

'Really?' Olivia frowned. 'Don't you think that the people who work there are the company's high-fliers?'

'Yeah, I do. That's why I'll be applying,' Lisa said.

'Tasmin will be upset if she loses her manager so quickly. That would be very unsettling.'

'Sorry?' Lisa said.

14

'Tasmin's your direct report. She starts on Monday.' Olivia smirked. 'We go back a long way.'

'I am so very pleased to meet you,' Lisa said. She wished she were sober. 'Tasmin, this is my boyfriend, Rob, and my friend Judith. Olivia and … and Jeremy.' They exchanged awkward handshakes.

'Nice to meet you, Tasmin. I'm sure we'll be meeting again,' said Rob.

'Oh, please call me Taz. All my friends do.'

'How do you know Lisa, Judith?' asked Jeremy, politely.

'The Sun pub quiz,' said Judith.

Olivia snorted as the champagne tickled her nose.

'You should come on Tuesday,' Judith said, looking pointedly at Olivia. 'Unless, of course, you're afraid of being shown up.'

'That sounds like a challenge we can't refuse, Judith,' said Jeremy, grinning flirtatiously.

'"We go back a long way",' Lisa mimicked, following Rob and Judith as they pushed their way through the Friday revellers. '"We were just talking about you". Nightmare.'

'Well, Taz would probably rather not work for her mate. Give her a chance,' Rob said, as he ushered Lisa in front of him through the door. 'That was quite a sharp retort to O-liv-i-ah, though I wouldn't advocate having almost a bottle of champagne every time you take her on.'

'How do you mean?' Lisa said.

'Saying you could go for that London job. It put her off her stride. Very inventive.'

'Well, not really. It was true.'

'True?' Rob stopped, seizing Lisa's arm. 'You're thinking of going to London?'

'Rob, that hurts. No, what Andy said was true. You're putting words in my mouth. Forget it. I've just got the job here, remember?'

Lisa was paying the bill as a white saloon cab crawled to a halt outside the restaurant.

'Look, it's Keith, after all,' Rob said, waving through the

15

restaurant window.

The cab driver touched his cap in acknowledgement.

'He wears that cap everywhere,' Judith said. 'I don't think I've ever seen him without it.'

Keith opened the rear door as Lisa lurched on to the back seat, followed by Judith.

'You did well getting a table here tonight,' Keith said. 'Thought they'd be booked up for weeks.'

'There's room for three at the back,' Judith said, as Rob sank into the front passenger seat.

'Three's a bit of a crowd,' Rob said.

'I don't think I need ask if you got that job,' Keith said, glancing at Lisa through his mirror. 'Congratulations. Did they ask my question?'

'Very similar,' Lisa slurred, 'but I answered it a lot better than I did at the quiz. I'm people-centred now, you know.'

'I hope that job's not going to stop you coming on Tuesdays,' Keith said. 'We have a good team now.'

'Only now?' Lisa said, as they headed down Oxford Road towards the leafy suburbs.

'Well, we've added at least four points since Judith joined. We might even beat those cheating Terminators.'

'We gotta beat everyone. There's no point playing if you don't want to win,' Rob said. 'Lise, we're here. Keith, this should cover all of it.' Rob pressed a note into Keith's hand. 'Take care, Jude. Thanks for a lovely night.'

'I was lucky to bump into you, Judith. Thank you so much for helping me celebrate.' Lisa climbed out of the cab, toppled over the kerb, and lurched into Rob's embrace.

'At last I've got you to myself,' Rob said, as they walked unsteadily towards the door of Lisa's apartment. 'One bottle of champagne and you're anybody's. I was beginning to think you were more interested in spending Valentine's night with Judith than me.' He glanced at his watch. 'There's forty minutes left. You're going to have to make it up to me.'

Games people play

The mail thudded on to the doormat as the letter box clattered shut. The brown envelope from HM Revenue and Customs that was addressed to Ms Judith Crayvern would be dealt with later. The two envelopes addressed to The Householder would go straight in the bin. The white square envelope looked far more interesting. She held it to her nose, then pressed it between her fingers. A card with a letter folded inside, she deduced. She turned it over. Disappointment followed. The envelope was addressed to her octogenarian next-door neighbour, Mr Baker, who now resided for most of the year with relatives in Norwich. The address had been carefully written in a flowing but unsteady blue script. A birthday card from an elderly friend or relation, she supposed.

As she placed the brown envelope on the hall table she caught a glimpse of herself in the art deco mirror and stopped to inspect her reflection. Her cheekbones were not quite as high as she would have liked, her grey eyes might be slightly too wide apart, and her full lips might be a little too broad, but all her features seemed to work well together, she had always thought. And her eyes still sparkled. Her dancing eyes, Martin had said.

She returned to the comfort of the kitchen and Verdi's *Requiem*, casting the junk mail and Mr Baker's birthday card into the newly polished swing bin. Outside, the bare arms of the ash tree bobbed up and down. Black-and-white feathers twitched on the viburnum. Sharp beaks pecked at the redwood. The wagtails flitted from bush to bush, advancing towards the kitchen. A solitary robin hopped across the patio flags, then perched on the handle of a tall green bin. Bunters, her grey-and-white striped cat, nuzzled her legs as she watched the impromptu garden party. She stooped down and stroked his soft fur, then pulled open the French windows.

'Go, Bunters, get them,' she said, closing the doors. She smiled as the winged scavengers swooped away, then resumed her ironing.

17

Dies irae, dies illa calamitatis et miseriae; dies magna et amara valde.

The first time she had heard Verdi's *Libera Me* was shortly after Martin had died. Then, though captivated by the music's manic power, she had sensed only the dark terror of death. Now she found the haunting voices intoxicating and comforting. The music lifted her spirits as she smoothed the creases from the Egyptian cotton sheets and sprayed a soft mist of lavender over the white fabric. The sound system was a good one. The speakers, so small they could scarcely be seen, delivered a clear sound in all the rooms downstairs. She was fortunate that she could afford the best.

She preferred to wash the sheets on a clear day. She would dry them on the line in her back garden where they absorbed, she liked to think, the rays of the sun, and then iron them while they were slightly damp. The mundane task was worth it. At night the crispness of the freshly laundered sheets cocooned her body, and their scent often transported her into a dreamless sleep.

Peace was not always so easily achieved. Many nights she had lain tormented in a sleepless bed. But last night was not dreamless. She had dreamed of water. Rushing brown water. She had woken in the darkness. Outside a solitary bird was warbling through the winter night. Soon the nightmares would end, recede like the floodwaters had done.

She must believe that. She must hang on.

There was a clunk, then a fluttering and a thumping by the kitchen door cat flap.

'Oh, Bunters, why him? He's the only one I didn't mind.'

The robin's brown feathers twitched on the kitchen floor, his vermillion breast camouflaging the bloody blow the cat's claw had delivered. She picked up a plastic freezer bag and put her hand in it to shield her skin, then grasped the bird and twisted the bag inside out. Gingerly, holding it at arm's length, she walked into the garden and dropped the light parcel on the patio. She would have to put him in the bin. But was he dead? If he wasn't he was unlikely to live. The cat walked over to the bag, sniffed, and jogged down to the bottom of the garden.

'Leaving it all to me are you, Bunters, as usual?' she said, as she surveyed the flower bed. She stared intently at the fragile package, looking for a hint of life. Perhaps the red breast was trembling. A black eye stared at her forlornly.

She delivered the fatal blow decisively, smashing a rock on to the polythene shroud. Well, now he was definitely dead.

~

Berger and Berger occupied the fourth floor of an award-winning city centre office building, an iconic unsymmetrical tower of concrete, granite, aluminium, and glass. As Lisa crossed the sleek, spacious reception area her spirits rose, just as the architect had intended.

'Congratulations, Lisa,' called the receptionist. 'I hope you enjoy your first day as an account executive. You seem happy enough.'

'Morning, Sally. Yeah, I'm really looking forward to it.' Lisa paused by the reception desk to chat to the radiant Sally, then walked towards the door of the general office.

'Good morning, Lisa,' Olivia said, without looking up from her mobile. She was standing just in front of the door.

'Morning, Olivia. How are you?' said Lisa. 'Did you have a good weekend?'

'Yah, good, thank you.' Olivia continued to text.

'Did you spend the weekend shooting again?' Lisa said, absently stroking her cardboard coffee cup, hoping that Olivia would move just a fraction to one side to let her pass.

'Shooting?' Olivia made an exaggerated sigh. 'The season ended weeks ago,' she said, as she pushed back some errant hairs that had escaped her chignon.

'Excuse me,' Lisa said, as she squeezed past her colleague, and opened the door with her security card.

'It's just up to you now to show you're up to the job, to prove that they haven't made the most dreadful mistake,' Olivia said, as she followed Lisa through the door. 'Of course, I'll be right behind you.'

Keep cool, keep cool, Lisa counselled herself. *Don't be flustered. In fact, that is probably what Olivia wants. Calm, calm.*

'Thank you so much. Have a nice day,' Lisa said, almost under her breath, as she smiled frostily. She turned to the right towards a bank of giant fig trees and miniature palms that screened a group of closely packed desks. She tossed her empty coffee cup, which was now squashed into a mangled cardboard ball, into a litter bin.

At 9.29 a.m. Lisa walked to Andy's office, a glass room in the left corner of the floor. It had sweeping views of the city on the outside wall and ceiling-to-floor narrow wooden slatted blinds on the inside walls, which unashamedly flouted the architect's intention to foster transparency and break down hierarchies.

'Lisa,' Andy said, smiling and beckoning her in. 'I've just explained to Tasmin and Sonia that they will be reporting to you. I have to make a conference call now, so perhaps you could brief them further about the graduate training programme, as we discussed?'

'Certainly. I'd be delighted.' Lisa held her hand out to shake Sonia and Tasmin's hands. 'Let's do this over coffee. What would you like?'

'So that's about it,' Lisa said, as she completed the briefing session, checking that she had covered all the points on her list. 'Sonia, you'll be working with Barry in human resources.'

'Poor you, Sonia. I was in HR in London for a few weeks. Boredomsville,' Tasmin said.

'I'm sure you'll love it there, Sonia. You'll learn a lot of stuff you'll need to know for when you're a manager. Tasmin, you'll be working with me on a couple of new accounts. Then next week you'll both go to London for a training course.'

'Brill. Thanks. And who gets our train tickets for us? For when we go to London,' said Tasmin.

'You need to see Sally, the receptionist, for that. Have you both managed to find decent places to stay?' Lisa asked, relaxing as she reflected that the meeting had gone well, and that the girls seemed to be getting on with her, and each other. Sonia was strikingly pretty. She was a trifle reserved – shy, perhaps, in contrast to the blonde-maned Tasmin, who seemed to project confidence. However, despite Lisa's fears, Tasmin did not seem to share Olivia's cool arrogance. On the contrary, she seemed warm and outgoing.

'At the moment I'm staying with an auntie, but I think we both probably see that as a short-term thing,' said Sonia.

'I'm in a flat-share, with someone from uni,' said Tasmin, 'and I see quite a bit of Jeremy – a friend with benefits, you might say.' She raised an eyebrow. 'Nothing serious, though.'

'I share with a uni friend as well. I met Maya at and we just clicked,' said Lisa. 'She's often away, though, as she's in sales. Then Rob, my boyfriend, and I have the run of the place.'

'Aah, Rob. What does he do?' asked Tasmin.

'He's the acting manager of a city centre travel agency, for now. He should get it permanently, when they finally get round to the interviews. He's a language graduate. Fluent in Spanish and Italian. Oh, and Catalan.'

'A linguist ... how very interesting,' said Tasmin, thoughtfully, as her tongue traced the outline of her top lip. 'How long have you been together?'

'We met after he came back from Spain, just after I started working here two years ago.'

'You don't live together, then?' Tasmin said.

'Well, no,' Lisa said. 'We are serious, though,' she added, anxious to signal to Tasmin that Rob was not available for any extra 'benefits' she might be seeking.

'Which uni did you go to?' asked Sonia.

'Durham,' responded Lisa, relieved that Sonia was now fielding the questions.

'Durham?' said Tasmin. 'The university?'

'Yes, of course the university.'

'Oh. You know, Lisa, I would really have liked to go to that pub quiz but I think I'm out every night this week,' Tasmin said.

'What a pity,' Lisa said, unconvincingly.

Tuesday evening
Lisa stretched lazily across the almost cream sofa, listening attentively to her flatmate while gorging on a chocolate creme egg. Maya looked elegant and stylish in a lemon crocheted dress which just skimmed her knees, as she animatedly described how she had dumped her last date. Lisa would look matronly, like her mother, in

21

the same outfit – something she knew to be true because she had once tried the dress on and, hurriedly, taken it off. Maya could make a pile of rags look attractive. Her long, glossy raven hair, wide eyes, fine bones, and bronzed skin enhanced any outfit.

'So, how have your first two days as Boss Lady been?' Maya said, settling into the brown leather armchair.

'Oh, all right, really.'

'All right, really?' Maya said. 'Methinks you sound a bit doubtful. The bubble's not burst already, has it? I can see you're going to go all introspective again.'

'Oh, just Olivia being Olivia. Trying to wind me up.'

'Well, that's not always too difficult. Don't let her. She's bound to be peeved. Give her space and avoid her. She'll soon have other irons in the fire.'

'I don't really see her very much, but she's best friends with Tasmin.'

'And?'

'And nothing. Well, they do seem a bit similar, that's all,' Lisa said, sighing.

'Two days and you already have problems with your team,' Maya said.

'No, no, not at all, I don't have any problems. Sonia's great. Not that I've seen her since yesterday morning. Tasmin's very eager. I like her. A lot.'

Maya frowned.

'I hope you sound more convincing when you're with her.'

Lisa grimaced, then sat up as she glanced at her watch.

'Oh my God, it's later than I thought. I'm going to have to run. Rob's going straight to the quiz.'

'Keep cool. I'll give you a lift on my way to the gym. It will only take two minutes. I just need to change.' Maya disappeared into bedroom. 'You seem to be seeing a lot of him at the moment. Must be serious. What's happened to your treat 'em mean, keep 'em keen strategy?' she called. 'Not that I recall you've ever implemented it very well.'

'Rob's different. Though I'm worried he thinks I'm not committed to the relationship. Some stupid thing I said about a job in

London. I was pissed. I was just winding O-liv-i-ah up. I didn't mean to wind Rob up as well.'

'What? It's obvious to everyone you're besotted,' Maya said, waving her car keys.

Lisa groaned.

'Really? I don't want to scare him off. He's quite ambitious. I'm not sure he's a settling down type of guy.'

'So that's what you want, is it?'

'Don't tell him, Maya.'

'Depends if you make it worth my while.' Maya laughed. 'Come on, we need to go. I'll tell you all about my new Tinder date en route. He's a barrister from Northampton and he's hot.'

~

Judith Crayvern
Webmaster
History of art
Hazelton

She frowned at her new photograph as she reviewed her Facebook profile. Earlier that day she had taken many self-portraits from various angles with both her webcam and her iPhone, but none of the photographs pleased her as much as the one she had just replaced. She wondered if Tasmin or Jeremy were on Facebook, or even Olivia. She did not know their surnames, though. She searched for 'Taz' and received an immediate response.

Taz Browne. Rob Granville is a mutual friend.

She sent a friend request immediately. Perhaps that would lead her to Jeremy as well. Perfect.

She glanced at the clock on the screen of the MacBook. She knew she would have to get ready, or she would be late for the pub quiz, but she could not resist clicking on the glowing globe at the top of her page.

Rob Granville likes your photo.

Perhaps she would keep the new photograph after all. She ignored the Google alert in her inbox and closed the lid of the computer. Her high heels clicked as she walked over to the American-style fridge-

23

freezer which, like all the other appliances, was camouflaged behind a duck-egg blue Shaker-style wooden door, and took out a carton. As she poured the milk into a bowl some droplets splashed on the black polished slate tiles. Bunters circled round her legs.

'I wonder if our new friends will be there tonight?' she said, picking him up and rubbing her face in his soft fur.

Judith always walked to the pub quiz, whatever the weather. Tonight it was dry, but there was a sharp nip in the February night. It was under fifteen minutes' walk, and a pleasant enough stroll, through leafy residential roads and then a brief hike up the main road. She enjoyed the excuse to wander past her neighbours' houses and share a glimpse of their everyday lives through their open curtains. She lingered occasionally at a garden, judging the merits of its design and planting. She stopped by a recently laid shale forecourt. A *For Sale* placard had now been crossed with a *Sold* sign. She shuddered. A family moving on, a new one moving in. A simple sign still had the power to remind her of memories that should have been buried years before.

As she approached the main road, she frowned at the display in the last house's garden. A collection of tall plastic bins crowded the front door, their owner's house number boldly proclaimed on each bin in gaudy gloss paint. Thank goodness she did not have such lazy neighbours. In Judith's opinion Mr Baker was the ideal person to share a garden fence with.

As she arrived at The Sun she smiled, acknowledging a solitary smoker who was drawing on a cigarette as he always did at this time on a Tuesday night. She walked through the front door, searching the familiar seats and tables for Keith. He was always first and she usually arrived just before Rob and Lisa. She beamed as she walked across the room, acknowledging admiring glances with a flash of a smile, as if she were a film star on the red carpet.

The Sun had not changed much over the years, despite the brewery's efforts. Bookcases of never-to-be-read books had replaced the cigarette vending machines and the chairs were now upholstered in red velveteen, but the customers remained the same. It was still the meeting place of choice for the local Sunday league football teams and, on Tuesdays, it presided over the biggest pub quiz in the city. Long-standing locals jibed with sojourning students between rounds, their edgy banter barely concealing a mutual contempt. Aspiring young professionals who had settled on the edge of smart, leafy suburbia rubbed shoulders with the tradesmen who inhabited their neighbourhood during working hours.

As Judith walked across the lounge bar, cradling a glass of sparkling water, she noticed two young women and a man divesting themselves of their outerwear as they took possession of three chairs and a round table. The woman, in a fuchsia, low-cut jumper was waving at her.

'We have taken up your challenge. I hope you've been swotting up. Game, Set, and Match don't like to be beaten. We play to win.'

Judith immediately recognised the eager face and braying tones of Tasmin.

'I'm profusely sorry. I have a terrible memory for names,' Tasmin said, putting on a sad face.

'Judith.'

'Yah, Judith, of course. How could I ever forget that? I'm Taz. You've met Jeremy and Olivia.'

Olivia nodded as Jeremy held out his hand and shook Judith's.

'I thought Lisa and Rob would be here,' said Tasmin.

'Oh, they'll be here soon,' said Judith. 'They don't always come together. They're both free agents.'

'Judith, there's only three of us. Please, please do us a terrific favour and join us,' Jeremy said.

Judith smiled.

'Thank you, Jeremy, but I couldn't possibly let my team down. We are on a mission to win.'

'Judith, the daring and beautiful widow. On second thoughts, we would certainly be ill-advised to tempt you into the enemy camp. Who knows what you might do?' said Jeremy, winking at her.

'Sorry?' Judith was taken aback. Why did he say she was a widow? Had Lisa been talking about her?

'The Book of Judith? I would have thought you would be very familiar with your namesake's story. She used her charms to ingratiate herself with the enemy of the Israelites, Holofernes, but

25

while he was in a drunken sleep she decapitated him.'

'Oh, yes, of course.'

'Come to think of it, you do look rather like the Judith in Caravaggio's *Judith Beheading Holofernes*. A wonderful painting. The embodiment of a beautiful and powerful woman. Seductress and assassin.'

'Well, I wouldn't agree. I'm far fairer than her and, for that matter, I certainly don't look like Gustav Klimt's Judith, nor Franz Stuck's,' she said, taking off her hat, letting her hair shower over her shoulders in a cascade of blonde waves. 'Jeremy, I'm simply not dark enough to be Judith.'

'Touché,' said Tasmin. 'Jeremy just likes to show off. He doesn't normally meet his match.'

'Let battle commence, then.' Judith laughed as she made her way across the bar to the table that Lisa and Keith had occupied.

'Hello, everyone,' said Judith. 'Your work colleagues are here, Lisa.'

'What?' Lisa said, urgently scouring the room. 'Tasmin said she wouldn't be able to come.'

'Well, she's most definitely here. Aren't you going to say hello? I'll hold the fort.' As Judith unravelled her scarf she recognised Rob at the other side of the bar, embracing Olivia and then Tasmin.

'Thanks,' said Lisa, making a move out of her chair with newly found urgency.

Judith watched as Lisa edged into the space between Rob and Tasmin. Mission accomplished, Lisa gripped his arm.

'Good evening, Ladies and Gents. Welcome to The Sun, where it's always warm and friendly, even in darkest February. If you haven't registered yet … Get a move on, you lazy s— so-and-sos,' announced the quizmaster, a self-proclaimed wit who found his purpose and beer money from testing the customers' knowledge of trivia each week.

'I didn't see you at the park today, Keith.' Judith said. 'I hope Scamp isn't ill.'

'Heavens, no. He's fitter than me.' Keith stroked his stomach and laughed as he spoke of his brown-and-white Jack Russell terrier. 'I just got a spate of bookings, and a very lucrative one, from the airport this afternoon.'

'Phones away. We'll have no cheating from Prime Suspects again this week.' A bulky man with deep-set eyes, his tattooed arms and neck exposed beneath a short-sleeved polyester shirt, glowered at the pair. Keith scowled and looked earnestly at his pint of Guinness.

'Always the joker, Brian.' Judith flashed a smile. 'We always play fair and square. You know that. There're no mobiles here.'

'Now I might believe that of you, but not him,' Brian replied, nodding in Keith's direction. He waddled back to his seat, from where he commanded a view across the bar. Brian Cordon always sat there, surrounded by his acolytes who made up The Terminators.

'He's such a charmer,' said Judith.

'He's been a bully since he was five. Always flips the truth. He'll never change. You wouldn't believe he once had all the girls after him, would you? That's a long time ago. Age hasn't been kind to him.' Keith smiled.

'Will Val Cordon from The Terminators please come back for her sheets?' the quizmaster announced. 'Wake up, Val.'

'Or her,' Keith said, as a woman wearing a bulky jumper and a short miniskirt, which emphasised the shapelessness of her legs, walked back to the bar, her face red, her hand over her mouth.

'I've registered us,' said Lisa, as she put down the answer sheets and collected the pound coins from the table.

'Oh, no, I'm too late,' said Rob, arriving behind her, carrying two bottles of Peroni. 'I had the perfect name. The Yah-Yah Sisterhood.'

'You can't do that. They will know,' said Lisa, aghast. 'Come on. We need to get on with the photo round. The Dispossessed and that table of students have just about finished it,' said Lisa.

Rob picked up a pen.

'Come on, team, let's go.' Rob, Lisa, Keith, and Judith focused their attention on the photocopy of famous people's faces.

'Hey, look at this one. It's Judith. You're a dead ringer. I always thought you were a bit familiar,' said Rob.

'Michelle Pfeiffer ... You're right,' agreed Keith.

'Well, I have been likened to her a few times but, I have to admit, I just can't do the accent,' Judith drawled.

'Mobiles off. Are we ready? Round one: general knowledge,' the quizmaster announced.

'Focus,' said Rob.

'We have to beat The Terminators,' said Keith.

'And the Yah-Yahs,' said Rob winking at Lisa. He took a gulp of Peroni and then picked up the pen. 'Any spelling mistakes are down to the brewer.'

'Are you ready? Question one,' the quizmaster announced. 'We're starting off with some culture this week. Who wrote this?

Out flew the web and floated wide
The mirror crack'd side to side
"The curse is come upon me," cried
The Lady of Shalott.'

'Alfred, Lord Tennyson,' Judith said, without hesitation.

Keith began to recite,

'And they cross'd themselves for fear
All the knights at Camelot
But Lancelot mused a little space
He said, "She has a lovely face
God in his mercy lend her grace
The Lady of Shalott."'

'Blimey,' said Rob. 'I didn't realise I was in such highbrow company.'

'No, I don't suppose they teach you classical poetry at school these days,' said Keith. 'I bet you've never heard of it, have you?'

'No. It's amazing what they used to teach you just so you could show off at quiz nights,' Rob said.

'I have a painting by John Waterhouse which is inspired by that poem,' Judith said. 'The Victorians loved all things Arthurian. The Lady of Shalott is only supposed to look at the world through a mirror, but when she sees Lancelot she is captivated and looks out through the window. The mirror cracks and the curse begins. She glides down the river in a boat to Camelot, but dies before she gets there. When Lancelot sees her she's already dead.'

'Sounds very jolly,' Lisa said, not looking up from the quiz sheet, and relieved that she had not volunteered 'Agatha Christie' as the answer, which she nearly had.

'She's still alive in the painting. There's some beautiful detail. I think it's exquisite,' Judith said.

'You'll have to give us a guided tour of your art gallery, Jude, with a poetry recital by Mr Keith Sharpe here,' Rob said.

'I'd be delighted to, Rob,' Judith said, placing her hand over his. 'You must come to Camelot.'

'There's no way The Terminators beat us fair and square,' said Keith. 'I reckon they had seven in that team. At least.'

'At least we've beaten Game, Set, and Match,' said Lisa.

'They haven't done too badly with only three. They'll be contenders if they get one more in their team,' said Judith. 'Oh, before I forget, I was in town today, Lisa. I thought you might like this. It's just a sample.' Judith held an amber glass phial between a crimson-tipped index finger and thumb.

Lisa grasped the small gift and unstopped the tube. She held it to her nose.

'Mmm, sort of woody. Spicy, too.' She inhaled the exotic fragrance. 'Thank you.'

'Base notes of cedar and amber. Martin always loved amber. It works, don't you think? Rob?' Judith raised her wrist and then placed it under Rob's nose.

'Yes, seductive. Very potent,' Rob said.

Lisa watched as the older woman's gaze moved from Rob and settled on her. She felt as if Judith was assessing all her weaknesses, but was too polite to articulate them. She brushed her fringe away from her hazel eyes as she watched Judith's hand finally move away from Rob.

'It could make the plainest girl seem alluring,' Judith said. 'Not,' she added, as she touched Lisa's wrist, 'that you need any help, darling.'

Early Wednesday morning

Lisa swung her legs on to the bedroom rug and stole out of bed. She felt the silkiness of her bathrobe beneath her feet, lying where it had fallen several hours before. She gathered up the robe and quickly put it on, tying the sash around her waist as she moved to the window.

She glanced at the gently snoring body of Rob. One arm had escaped from the sheets and was dangling over the side of the bed. He had not stirred for hours, even as she fidgeted restlessly beside him.

She peeked through the gap in the curtains. The moon was almost full. The road was totally still, like a photograph. She felt like she was the only person awake on the planet, observing a world asleep.

The sky was starless, reflecting the soft amber lights of the city. She surveyed the familiar road below. Although many of the houses were converted into flats quite a few remained as large family homes, providing fashionable abodes for the middle classes. She wondered how the original owners of these homes had made their fortunes and acquired the trappings of wealth when so many others were imprisoned in a hand-to-mouth existence.

She mused that the houses that had been the grandest were now callously dissected into small apartments, their gentility lost forever. Now it was the smaller houses in the road which were most sought-after – prized by their owners for their postcode, which could fast-track their offspring into the most highly regarded schools in the area. These were aspirational homes her parents would never have dared dream of buying. She glanced down the road. Even some of the cars were worth more than her parents had ever managed to save.

The road, though wide enough during the day, was reduced to a single carriageway at night as vans, four-wheel drives, and smaller cars jammed every inch of the roadside. Lisa had been lucky that night and had parked her small white Fiat almost under her apartment, although she had not intended a wheel to be perched so perilously on the side of the curb.

She felt suddenly resentful of her environmentally friendly car, bought partly for ethical reasons but also for fun, which was dwarfed by the gas-guzzling wagons she scorned – the urban trophies, the must-have accessories for the school run. Was she embarrassed by what it said about her? That she was principled, but also frivolous and small-minded? Some people had to get to the top of the career ladder. Why not Lisa Clarkson from the council estate? She had taken her chance, and they had chosen her, not Olivia.

'Break from the past. Believe in yourself, Lisa,' she muttered. 'If you don't, no one else will.'

She was distracted for a moment as a black-and-white cat trotted purposefully through the lamplight, its shadow slinking alongside like a dark accomplice. She watched as it disappeared into the darkness of the Victorian houses opposite. Across the road she noticed the glow of an interior light in a car. As she peered in the car she thought she detected the shape of someone. Was it a burglar, a getaway car? She looked more closely. Perhaps she would need to remember the description, but she could not quite tell the colour of the car as it was beyond the range of the street light. She recognised the vehicle, though. An Audi convertible.

A taxi passed slowly down the road. For a moment its headlights caught the features of the occupant of the stationary vehicle. The driver's eyes were gazing up at Lisa's bedroom window. Lisa gasped. Surely not? She screwed her eyes in the darkness and pulled the curtains further apart, then quickly went to her dressing table and fumbled for her glasses. When she returned there was no sign of the car. She suddenly felt weary and flopped under the sheets.

It seemed only minutes later that Rob was gently shaking her, reminding her that she had better get up. She walked to the window and pulled back the curtains. Had she just had a vivid dream? The black-and-white cat was sitting on the wall opposite, staring directly at her. There were quite a few spaces in the road now. Her car was perched unsteadily on the edge of the curb, just as she remembered.

It was odd, though. The driver had been the spitting image of Judith.

Just to see her

Tuesday morning
She tapped 'Judith Crayvern' on to the keyboard of her MacBook, added her personal details, then read the instructions for the assessment test while she savoured the aroma of a mug of Columbian coffee.

You should not discuss your job application, other than with your partner or a close family member.

Well, she would have no problem with that. She had always been cautious – guarded, even – and there was no partner nor any close family member to tell. The door creaked open as Bunters walked across the pristine kitchen floor and sat in front of the French windows. She left the kitchen table and crouched down to stroke the cat's silky fur. Bunters's grey ears stiffened as a sparrow hopped on to a large plant pot on the patio. The weather, however, was too inclement to entice him away from his mistress's parlour.

'Perhaps they won't mind if I tell you, Bunters. What do you think? Aren't I just the sort of person they're looking for? Intelligent, perceptive, and discreet.' She stood up, and gazed into the garden. Although it had stopped raining, pearls of water still ran down the windowpanes. Three wood pigeons sat motionless in the bare branches of the ash tree at the bottom of the garden.

'I wonder which of you has won the mate, and who must fly away on their own and search for love again. Or perhaps the contest has yet to be decided,' she brooded. 'Not like you two lovebirds.' She looked with distaste at the yellow-beaked blackbirds hopping along the grass, then turned sharply away. Oh, to be somewhere sunny, without the deadly sound of birds singing. She returned to the computer.

She completed the questionnaire but hesitated as she was about to press the submit button. An image flashed through her mind. She was sitting in a large leather chair surrounded by colourful tropical fish, with Bunters on her lap. No, she chastised herself. Wrong side. The man with the cat was the villain. She had been imagining a new life, complete with undercover assignations in exotic locations, sipping Martinis while protecting Britain's national security. These questions, however, seemed to imply a lot of sifting of boring information, arguing with colleagues for resources, and reprimanding lazy subordinates.

The feedback was almost instantaneous:

Your responses suggest that there are a number of areas where your approach may not exactly fit the role of an intelligence officer in the Security Service.

She instantly dismissed her future career in MI5 as a flight of fancy. But she was bored. What could she do? She didn't want to work in a museum again. She was tired of writing essays. Being the webmaster for the antiques dealer had filled her time, but it was hardly fun and not at all sociable. There was barely any work to do now. A permanent office job wasn't very appealing. Perhaps temping, though, working when she wanted to, only choosing the places where she wanted to work ... Now that might be fun.

Tuesday evening

'Last chance to register. If you're not here in five you're out,' announced the quizmaster, grinning from the side of the bar, microphone in his left hand, pint of bitter in his right. 'I just want your money.'

'I'll register us,' said Judith, sliding the pound coins on to her palm. 'In the absence of any suitable alternatives, I propose we stay as Prime Suspects.'

'Rob doesn't like that name. You know that,' said Keith, as Judith left.

Lisa gazed round the bar. Tasmin was in London at head office on a course. Olivia and Jeremy would be unlikely to come on their own. There was no sign of them, and all the tables seemed full. Good.

Brian Cordon was in his usual seat, surrounded by a group of heavyset men. He was staring at Judith, who looked striking in her short red wool jacket and tailored grey trousers. Lisa glanced over towards the bar. The quizmaster was leaning against the counter, chatting to Rob. A shard of intense desire ran through her as she watched her boyfriend run his fingers through his hair.

'Striking woman,' Keith said, pushing back his glasses. 'Always immaculate, even on a rainy day in the park.' He took a sip of Guinness and wiped his moustache with the back of his hand. 'Judith, I mean,' he said, as Val Cordon squeezed through the gap between the seats nearby.

Lisa gave him a questioning look, then resumed her survey of the customers in the bar as she massaged some hand cream, a present from Judith, into her skin.

Keith shook his head.

'No, I'm not interested. Don't think I ever will be again.' His moment of melancholy turned to laughter as he added, 'And she wouldn't be interested in the likes of me.' He paused, then lowered his voice. 'You know, she has a lot of guilt, that one. A lot of guilt.'

Lisa gave Keith her full attention.

'Guilt? About what?'

'Her husband, Martin. When my Sandra died, though it was quite sudden, we had a bit of time knowing. But I still feel I never told her how much she really meant to me. I feel guilty about that. Three years later and I still feel it. But you know, I don't think you ever would have enough time to say everything you could.'

'I am sorry, Keith.'

'Martin died in an accident, so she had no time to say anything to him,' Keith said, scratching under his cap. 'Nothing at all.'

'Yeah, it must be hard. She told me how he drowned in the floods at Hazelmere,' Lisa said.

'That's right. He was trying to save their dog. He was her whole life. They even worked together.'

'That was at Hazelton Museum.'

'That's right, love. She had too many memories there so she moved here, only an hour or so away, but a whole lifetime too.' Keith raised his voice. 'All right, Judith?'

Judith placed a sheaf of papers on the table and sat down.

'Wait until Rob's back,' she said, holding down the picture quiz as Keith tried to pull it away. 'You know how he likes us to do it together, as a team.'

'Here he is. You're keeping us waiting, Rob,' Keith said.

'Now, before we start,' the quizmaster said, sternly, 'I want to

34

remind you that no team should be bigger than six. If there are seven of you then you make two groups of three and four. No cheating.'

'Have you been having a word with the authorities then, Keith?' Judith asked.

'Well, it's about time they enforced the rules. We'd have won last week if they had,' Keith said.

'Keep your eye on The Terminators, Jude. You're nearest,' Rob said, nodding over to the table where Brian Cordon was giving a finger in the direction of the quizmaster, then he nodded to his right. 'The Dispossessed are a bit dodgy, too.'

'Question one,' said the quizmaster. 'What, or who, is Medusa?'

'A Gorgon,' Keith whispered. 'Rob, I can't believe you can't spell that. It's G-o-r- g-o-n. I thought you were a graduate.'

'I write perfect Catalan,' Rob said.

'We will just have to take your word for that, Rob,' Judith sniggered.

'Get your answer sheets back,' said the quizmaster. 'Then bring them up here. On the double.'

'Kevin Costner, you let me down. And don't say you knew it was Don Johnson, Rob, 'cause you didn't,' Keith said, as Rob held this palms in the air.

'Fair enough. But I knew it wasn't Kevin,' Rob said, as he swapped the marked answer sheets with Dead Ringers.

'They're all correct, for once,' Keith said, checking the ticks and crosses. 'We'll not be among the winners, though.'

Lisa nudged Rob.

'Have you asked Keith?'

'Keith, can you help me out? This job's gone to Lisa's head already.' Rob rubbed his hand against Lisa's thigh. 'She's already double-booked me on Saturday.'

'Well, I don't get the chance to see my sister very often,' Lisa said.

'So I've a spare ticket for the match. Yours, if you want it.' Rob smiled expectantly at Keith.

'I've not been to a match since my Sandra died. We went to every home game,' Keith said. He took a handkerchief out of his pocket and began polishing the lenses of his glasses.

'Really?' said Judith, leaning back. 'How strange, sitting out in the cold. I've never been one for self-sacrifice.'

'We had our ritual,' Keith continued. 'A flask of coffee and pies when we got there.'

'Fascinating,' Judith said, rolling her eyes.

~

Lisa's laptop was cradled on Rob's knees. He tapped steadily at the keyboard as Lisa snuggled next to him on the sofa, peering over him to view the screen.

'Look, that's the photo I meant,' said Rob, opening up his album of holiday photos on Facebook. He wanted to settle an argument which had begun at The Sun earlier that evening. 'The Shrine of Our Lady of Guadalupe.'

'I remember it now. It was near Mexico City, and we passed all those shanty towns on the way,' Lisa said.

'That's right,' he sighed. 'We've been there. We should have known the right answer. We had no excuse.' He looked away from the computer towards Lisa. 'That was an ace holiday. You know, I'm getting pissed off with organising everyone else's while managing the office on a scummy acting-up allowance. I wish they'd do the interviews. At least I'd know it was permanent. I have so many ideas, but I can't do anything at the moment.'

'Don't worry, babe. Things will work out. It's just taking longer than you thought. Your figures are great. They're bound to appoint you.'

Rob grunted.

'Won't Tom Graham be on the panel? He'll support you, won't he?' Lisa touched Rob's wrist as the computer emitted a pinging noise. 'What's that?'

'It's Judith. She wants to chat,' Rob said.

'Judith? I didn't know you chatted with her.'

'Well, not often. Just sometimes.'

'What times?'

'I don't know. Now and again.'

36

'She's always texting you.'

'What?'

'Tonight, on the way to the pub.' Lisa said, her back arching as she looked closely at Rob. 'What do you say when you chat to her?'

'Say? Well, when I've been on updating my status she goes, "Hi, Rob," and I go, "Hi, Jude," back, and we just have a banter.'

'A banter about what?'

Rob shrugged.

'I can't think. Music. Yesterday she was asking what music was in the charts. Last week she was asking me about minibreaks. Your idea, I think.'

'What?'

Ping. A message filled the chat box.

I knew it wasn't Lourdes, Rob.

'A banter about me giving the wrong answers?' Lisa said, pointing her finger at the screen.

'What? No, no, that's a first,' he said, frowning. 'I'll have to reply. She'll know I'm online.'

'You should block her,' Lisa said, folding her arms and looking at her lap as she breathed in deeply.

'Block her? Why? Why should I do that? It's just harmless … chat.'

'I mean, just block her so she doesn't know when you're online.' Lisa lifted her head up.

'How do I do that?'

'I thought you were the techie. Look, I'll show you.' Lisa moved towards the keyboard.

'Look, Lise, it's late. Another time.' He closed down the computer. 'You can do it then. Let's just crash now.'

Friday afternoon

'I'm absolutely exhausted. The train didn't get in until nearly eleven last night. They really put us through our paces at HQ,' said Tasmin.

Lisa had been wondering why Tasmin had been so subdued since she had returned from London, but now realised it was just tiredness.

'I went on the course last year when I first joined,' said Lisa. 'It was great fun, I thought. I met lots of people and learned loads too.'

37

'Oh, yes, I learned loads,' Tasmin said, shaking her hair away from her face as the wind whipped it against her mouth. 'Loads. Do you get a report about me?'

'I'm not sure,' Lisa said, as she pressed down hard on the brass latch. The cafe door jolted open with a fierce rattle. Fashionable long white lampshades hung from the ceiling over each wooden table, casting as much shadow as light.

Lisa peered into the back of the room. A dark-haired woman in a black pea jacket and stylishly knotted scarf stood up and caught her attention. Lisa and Tasmin walked to meet her, footsteps echoing on the bare floorboards as they passed the gleaming chrome of the coffee maker and the neon-lit carrot cakes and muffins.

'Della,' said Lisa as she shook her hand lightly. 'I'm glad you found the cafe all right.'

'I did. Thanks, Lisa. It's a great location. I need to be on the four o'clock train or I'll be in trouble with Lorna, my daughter. It's her school play tonight.'

'My pleasure. Let me introduce Tasmin, who's working with me. She recently joined us as a graduate trainee.'

'Hello,' said Tasmin, shaking hands.

'Right, let me arrange the coffees and then we can begin,' Lisa said, signalling to a waitress as she sat down.

Forty-five minutes later, Lisa and Della were exchanging cards.

'Well, I certainly like your outline proposals and your passion for them, Lisa. So perhaps when we meet next time you could bring along the detailed treatment. It's been a pleasure meeting you both,' Della said, shaking hands. 'Thanks for running the meeting so efficiently. I've plenty of time for the train.'

'If there's anything further I can help you with please contact me,' said Tasmin, breaking her silence as she offered her card to Della.

'Thank you, Tasmin,' Della replied, taking the card.

Lisa was pleased that her first meeting with a client had gone so well, although Tasmin had seemed distracted until now.

'That seemed to be a success,' Lisa said, as she sat down, watching Della walking to the door.

'Yah? Really?' said Tasmin. 'I thought she seems a bit, well, uncommitted.'

'Uncommitted? What on earth do you mean?'

'Leaving to get home so early.'

'Well, she explained why. Family's important. It's her kid's special day. She will certainly put in the hours at Taylors.'

'Mmm,' said Tasmin, disapprovingly.

'You know, Tasmin, perhaps it isn't such a good idea to be looking at texts when we're having a business meeting,' Lisa said. 'That doesn't seem like *you're* committed.'

'She didn't say anything. I was just checking there were no texts relevant to the meeting.'

'Really? It's best to give the client your full attention, I think. Anything else might be seen as rude.' *Bad choice of words,* she thought the moment they left her lips.

'Rude ... *You* are accusing *me* of being rude? Well, I don't think you should have introduced me as the graduate trainee. It's very patronising. That's rudeness,' Tasmin said, looking down at her phone and then putting it in her bag.

'But that's what you are. You are a graduate trainee. That's what I was called when I was in your position.'

'Just because you put up with it doesn't mean it can't change. I think you should just refer to me as your colleague,' Tasmin continued.

'If that's what you want.' *No arguments, listen to her point of view, and compromise.*

'And I was certainly not rude to a client,' Tasmin said, expressively. 'Are you saying I was?'

'I'm sorry,' Lisa said. 'I didn't intend you to take offence.'

'Well, I did,' said Tasmin. 'Perhaps I could go early too, as I've had an exhausting week.'

'Now?'

'Thanks, Lisa. See you Monday.'

Friday evening

'Yay, Lisa Clarkson, Berger and Berger's *première* fashionista. I didn't think I'd find you shopping in here.'

Lisa was standing opposite a full-length mirror in Kendals,

39

holding a mustard and red playsuit against her chest, as the reflection of Maya appeared next to her. Lisa smiled.

'I hope you're not checking up on me, Maya,' Lisa said.

'I thought you were an eBay addict these days,' Maya said. 'That blue suit you got for your interview was quite a coup.'

'There's nothing like a bit of real-life retail therapy. That's my vice: stroking the cashmere coats, a quick sniff of the cotton sheets. It even beats the thrill of the last few minutes of an eBay auction.'

'I do worry about you sometimes,' Maya said. She stood next to Lisa, looking in the mirror.

'I'm just killing time before I go to the cinema. We're going to see that new thriller everyone's raving about.'

'The colour's not too bad, but I'm not so keen on the pattern. What would you wear it with?'

'Well, I was thinking my cork wedges.'

'I'm thinking black tights and pumps.' Maya scrunched the fabric between her finger and thumb and screwed her nose. 'Cheap polyester, methinks. No, I really don't think I should allow this. This would suit you so much more.' She held a lime green silk shift dress in front of her flatmate.

Lisa had to admit the dress suited her colouring. It was understated and not so much fun, but she did look classy. It felt good too, although maybe it could be a bit shorter.

'Yay, very modish, Lisa,' Maya said, as she held up a cream lace blouse.

'That will look good, Maya,' said Lisa, as Maya examined her own reflection in front of the mirror.

'Shoes this way, Lisa. Come on. How's Tasmin?' Maya said.

'Fine,' Lisa said, sighing as she followed Maya to the shoe department.

'More problems, I see. I thought you looked distracted. In a world of your own,' Maya said, as she walked in front of Lisa in a pair of towering red patent platform shoes, posing like a catwalk model as she admired her reflection. 'Just be firm. Believe in yourself.'

'True enough. I just need to prise her away from her mobile when we're having meetings with clients … and be more assertive.'

'Just tell her. Don't shilly-shally. Who's that over there, Lisa?'

'What? Where?'

'There was the reflection of someone in the mirror. I thought someone was watching us when we were looking at the dresses.' Maya peered round the stands of shoes.

'I didn't see anyone. There're so many mirrors here, it could be anyone's reflection,' Lisa said.

Maya leaned on to Lisa as she took the shoes off.

'Now, that's my vice: killer heels. The higher and sassier the better.' Maya picked them up. 'I think these will earn their keep.'

~

Lisa strode into the multiplex, relieved to escape the uncertain weather. She was searching the foyer for Rob, but it was another familiar figure she saw.

'Judith, what a coincidence.'

'Lisa, darling.' Judith touched her arm and kissed her cheek. She smelled of expensive perfume, delicate jasmine with a hint of spice. Lisa stepped back.

'No coincidence, Lisa. We're all going to see the same film. Rob asked me to come along.'

'Oh.' Lisa pulled a tissue from her pocket and blew her nose.

'You don't mind, do you?'

'No, of course not.' Lisa forced a smile. She felt like an unkempt, gauche schoolgirl next to Judith. 'He should be here soon.'

'He's just gone for the tickets. You're the one who's late, not him. The main feature starts in two minutes,' Judith said, through her perfectly lipsticked smile, then turned, beaming, as Rob walked towards them.

Lisa gave him an icy glare. He could have texted. She glanced at her mobile. Perhaps he had.

'Right, mission accomplished. Tickets, ice cream,' Rob said, as he offered cardboard tubs and tickets to Lisa and Judith. He put his arm around Lisa and blew in her ear. 'You don't mind, do you?' he whispered. He squeezed her with his spare arm. 'Brrr, you're cold. She really wants to see this film and had no one to go with. Mmm, I love that perfume.'

41

'No, I don't mind, *I suppose.*' Lisa kissed him back on the mouth, darting a glance at Judith as she did, prolonging the kiss just a moment longer than she might have done.

'Lead the way, Jude,' Rob said.

They followed the signs to Studio 4. Judith proffered her ticket to the usherette's torch and they mounted the stairs, which were barely illuminated in the dim beam of the torch. The theatre was almost full.

'This is it. Row G. We're the three down there,' Judith whispered to Lisa.

'After you,' Lisa said.

The occupants of the row stood up, leaning against the chair backs to let the latecomers squeeze past. Judith was about to walk down the row but pulled back into the aisle.

'What is it?' said Lisa, urgently.

Judith opened her bag and started fumbling.

'It's OK. You two go. I think I just need to—' Judith said.

Ahead Lisa could see a row of impatient faces turned towards her, their arms clumsily holding bags, coats, and popcorn as they waited. She started walking along the row.

'No, it's OK. I've found it,' Judith said, slipping in front of Rob as she followed Lisa along the row. 'I'm so very sorry to disturb you. We didn't mean to be so late.' She sat down. 'I am so looking forward to this film,' she whispered to Lisa, as she pulled off the lid of the ice cream tub. 'I haven't seen a good thriller since *Fatal Attraction.*'

'Sit down,' a voice from the row behind instructed.

Rob sat down next to Judith.

'Thanks for the ice cream, Rob. I'm going to enjoy this,' Judith whispered, leaning towards him.

Lisa looked anxiously over Judith, who seemed settled in her seat, towards Rob.

'Well, Judith, do you think—?' Lisa began as the censor's certificate lit up the screen.

'Shush,' said Judith. 'It's about to begin.'

~

42

'Did you see that scar on her wrist? I saw it on Tuesday. But it was absolutely clear in the torchlight,' Rob said, closing his eyes as Lisa stroked her fingers round his temples.

'I have permission to talk about Judith and the cinema again, do I? No, I haven't been honoured with the opportunity to inspect her wrist.' Lisa hit Rob with a pillow.

'Well, I wondered, you know, if she'd tried to cut herself or something.' Rob tapped her back with the pillow. 'And there's something else. She seems sort of familiar. I've racked my brains but I just can't place her.'

'I'm pretty sure I'd have remembered her, if I'd met her before. You said it yourself. She reminds you of that film star.'

'Mmm, maybe. Just massage my back, will you, Lise? My shoulder's been niggling all day. Wish I'd never taken up the arrows sometimes.'

Lisa ran her hands over Rob's back, kneading his muscles.

'That's good,' he said. 'You know, sometimes she seems so vulnerable. That's why I wondered if she had, you know— Ouch. Careful.'

'Sorry. I don't think she's the sort to self-harm. She always seems in control. But it's hardly surprising if she's sad. Losing Martin like that. And her dog. But vulnerable? No, I don't get that.'

'It's more than sad. Sometimes, for a fleeting moment, you just get a glimpse of another Judith, who's lost, fragile.'

'Sad, yes. Fragile? No. That's not how I see her. Look, why are we talking about her again?'

Saturday morning

Bunters peered into the kitchen through the French windows. He caught his mistress's eye and then continued circumnavigating the outside of the Edwardian house in an anticlockwise direction, as he did most fine mornings. He would strut round his mistress's home and then the identical home of the absent Mr Baker, jumping effortlessly over the front wall and then ducking through a hole in the back garden hedge as he returned. Like Keith, the cat was a creature of habit.

She closed the MacBook. The day would yawn endlessly ahead

43

unless she took control of it and did something useful, kept herself busy. She fastened an apron around her waist, put on some latex gloves, and set to work on the kitchen tiles. As she rubbed the cleaner along the grout an image of a placard, the type estate agents put up when a house is for sale, drifted through her mind. It was a fragment of the previous night's dream. There had been many signs in the dream, falling on top of each other. She could not remember very much more, but a feeling of dread lurked in the pit of her stomach as she brushed the toothbrush head fiercely against the grouting.

She stopped to contemplate her work, then impulsively she opened her MacBook and typed 'Hazelton Museum' into the search engine. She went straight to the museum's home page. The logo had changed. In fact the whole website had been completely revamped since she had worked there. She searched for her own name on the site. Nothing. All trace of her had been erased from history. Martin, too.

Louise Pyatt was still there. Her claims to lead a 'nationally recognised award-winning museum' were absurd. There had been no more awards since Martin had died, not even a commendation. She glanced at the list of staff. Helen was still there. Lovely Helen who always saw the best in everyone, somehow avoiding engagement in the internecine feuds that had developed over the years, even when they caught her in the crossfire. Paula and Marsha, of course, had not moved on. Who would have them? It was a miracle, really, that she and Martin had won any awards, with those two on the team. She snapped down the lid of the computer, angry with herself for letting curiosity get the better of her. It was history.

Saturday afternoon

The dusty Victorian door creaked open, allowing the late sun to creep inside and expose the shabbiness of the interior. The pattern on the deep red carpet had almost disappeared, and the paintwork was chipped and grimy. Rob had rented the ground-floor flat intermittently since he had been a final-year student, keeping his things there even when he was working in Catalonia. Now only his sister, Heather, shared the kitchen, bathroom, and one of the three bedrooms of the divided Victorian house. The students and graduates who had lived there officially and otherwise over the years were now fading memories.

'What's this about you and Keith boozing in the Bergers corporate box with Tasmin? How did she manage to get an invite, Rob?' Lisa demanded, as she brushed past him, heading for the kitchen.

'Is that my starter for ten?'

'Here's the milk you wanted. Heather out?'

'She's at Karl's. They'll be back later.'

Lisa put the carton on the battered wooden worktop. The kitchen had survived many parties and late-night fry-ups, but was now unlikely to outlast Heather's demands of the landlord for a radical makeover.

'Brrr, you're still cold.' Lisa moved her hands under Rob's wool jumper as he switched on the kettle. She hugged his back. 'I've been trying to get an invite for months but the seats are like gold dust. She's only been here two weeks.'

'So you've had your spies out on me again?' Rob turned round, feigning a stern face.

'I've just seen Keith in Tesco.'

'I thought you were boycotting Tesco.'

'Well, it was only for a pint of milk.'

'That's all right, then.'

'It was raining.'

'You enjoy your lunch with your sis?' Rob stroked her back.

'Great, thanks. She sends her love and kisses. We must try La Rioja one evening. There's a great atmosphere.' She frowned. 'The boys done good, then.'

'Yep, we're safe from the drop now.'

'As we're in the top three that would be pretty hard.'

'If any team could do it we can.'

'How do you think Tasmin wangled it?'

'No wangling. She's not interested in footie. She said she was a last-minute replacement for someone whose kid was ill. Olivia had something to do with it. I think she was helping Livvie out, really.'

'That explains it, then. Definitely not Olivia's scene. But she

45

wouldn't have asked me, even though she'd know that I really wanted to go.'

'But you couldn't go, anyway.'

'No, but she didn't know that. Who were the clients?'

'It was a charity do. Taz was helping host Age Concern. They seemed to have survived her, just about. She spotted us when we were leaving. I think everyone else in the stand heard her shrieking.' Rob reached into the cupboard for the instant coffee.

'Keith seemed quite taken with her.' Lisa spooned the coffee into two mugs.

'Well, he would be.' Rob filled the mugs from the kettle.' He had two Guinnesses and a whiskey in your company's box while watching a replay of the goals, placing a bet on the gee-gees, and winning fifty quid.' Rob passed Lisa the milk. 'And he was chatting up the old dears and giving away his cards for his taxi. So I would say he's very fond of Taz. Unlike you, it would seem.'

'She's all right. She just gets a bit too … I dunno.' Lisa said, pouring the milk into the mugs, then taking them into the high-ceilinged living room.

'Let me help … Up herself.' Rob sprawled on the cracked leather sofa.

'Yeah, definitely. Well, I couldn't have gone, anyway. It should be my turn next time, when we're entertaining clients, not doing our bit for charity.' Lisa flopped on to the sofa next to Rob.

'Good. That's what I like to see. Positivity. That's what gets you on in the world. Whatever you might say about Taz, she's certainly positive, full of life,' Rob said.

'Not all the time. She's addicted to her mobile. Didn't you notice?' Lisa said.

Rob shrugged. Lisa hesitantly explained her altercation with Tasmin in the cafe.

'It's quite straightforward, Lise. You want to change her opinion about something, so you just need to be clear about what your objective is. Think through what you want to achieve, what you're going to say, and how Taz is likely to react. Will that achieve your desired outcome? No one likes to be told they're in the wrong, or rude. You were bound to annoy her.'

'Yeah.'

'And I guess a bit of humour never hurts, or empathy. Come on, stop being so sensitive.'

Lisa nodded. Although Rob seemed to enjoy giving her advice she decided it would be wise to change the topic of conversation.

'Where do you want to go tonight? Into town?'

'Taz was saying how good The Soaphouse was last week. Fancy it?'

Lisa wriggled, making more room for herself.

'Could do ... or Coimbra. That's supposed to be up-and-coming.' She looked round. 'What's different in here?'

'Different?'

'The room. It's brighter.'

'Heather's been behaving oddly. Spring-cleaning. Even brushing the cornices.'

'Very odd. It's usually you who does the cleaning, or so you keep telling me.'

Rob bounced a cushion off her, narrowly missing her mug of coffee.

'She seems very taken with Karl. It's changed her personality. She just wants to stay in all the time now. Which is a great pity, because he's a knob.'

Saturday evening

Tasmin's familiar theatrical gestures were unmistakeable, even at a distance across a crowded bar. Jeremy seemed to be enthralled by her performance. Lisa glanced at Rob. He had not seen Tasmin.

'On second thoughts, I think your idea to go to The Soaphouse might be better,' Lisa said, turning to the door and tugging on his sleeve. 'Come on. It'll take too long to get served here. I'll text the others to let them know where we're going.' There was no problem, no danger, but being risk-averse seemed a good strategy. Keeping Rob away from Tasmin seemed to be a desirable outcome.

As Lisa reached the top deck of the bus she could see the triumph on Rob's face. He had a childish enthusiasm for sitting in the front seats that never seemed to diminish. He seemed to enjoy the bus journey

47

more than the buzz of the city's trendiest bars. She slipped into the window seat and peered through the front window. There was little to see, as a veil of condensation obscured the view. In the centre of the window fine droplets of moisture clung more densely to marks left by the palms of long-gone passengers, eerily marking out their misty handprints.

Lisa watched as the raindrops meandered down the window outside. She put her finger against the cool glass as she had done when she was a small girl, willing one raindrop to stop and the other to get to the bottom of the pane first, betting against herself. She watched as one droplet found the path forged by another, picked up speed, and then raced down to the imaginary finishing line, overwhelming a smaller raindrop in its path.

'I'll race you,' said Rob, leaning over her. 'This is mine. Which is yours?'

Lisa put her finger on a droplet that was level with Rob's finger, and traced its tremulous path. As the bus jolted to a halt Rob's finger touched hers as the rainy tears merged and they traced its final descent together. Silently they nestled into each other as the monotonous purring of the idling engine changed and the bus moved off, accelerating through the gears.

'We're here. Wake up, Lise,' Rob said, standing up abruptly.

Lisa opened her eyes, unsure for a moment where she was. Anonymous handprints stood out like limbless phantoms against the darkness, jostling for her attention. She shivered. For a moment unidentified terrors seemed to lurk ahead.

'You look like you've seen a ghost,' said Rob.

She jumped up. Beyond, the street lights illuminated the road, banishing the night. She laughed and grabbed Rob's hand as they ran down the stairs.

'Just a crazy dream. I felt that someone was calling me, wanting my help,' Lisa said.

'Who?'

'It was so very real for a moment, but every fragment of the memory has almost vanished. But I think … I think it was Judith.'

The prettiest star

Tasmin stopped typing.

'Are you seeing Andy today, Lisa?'

'No, he's away this week, skiing. He's back next Monday.'

'Oh.' Tasmin returned her attention to her computer. 'It was good to meet Rob at the football match. I guess he told you?'

'Yeah, of course. It sounds like you enjoyed yourself.'

'Does he go every week?'

'If we're at home. I usually go with him but my sister was in town for lunch, so I didn't.'

'He's fun.' Tasmin laughed, tossing back her hair. 'You're lucky.' She looked at the screen again, then added. 'Keith's a sweetie, too.'

'Yes, yes, and yes.' Lisa said.

'Rob's very competitive, isn't he? You'd think he'd actually scored that last goal, he was so happy.'

'Have you finished that analysis of the Taylors clients, Tasmin?'

'Almost. I can't say I really get football ... Rob was telling me about his job. I hope he gets that promotion.'

Lisa stopped analysing the spreadsheet which had preoccupied her for most of the morning. *What had Rob said to Tasmin?*

'I guess he won't want to stick around if he doesn't. It sounds like he had a great time working in Spain ...' Tasmin said. Lisa gave Tasmin her full attention.

'Judith's had a tragic life, hasn't she, Lisa?'

'Judith? Yeah, she has. How do you know about that?'

'We met her on Saturday evening. Just after you and Rob left. You should have come over.'

'Sorry? Left where?' said Lisa, reaching for her coffee and taking a sip of the cold dregs.

'Coimbra. Jeremy saw you.'

'Really? It was just so busy we couldn't see anybody. We decided to go to The Soaphouse. We met the gang there.'

'It's fab there, isn't it? Anyway, she was telling us about how her husband drowned. She's so brave. Starting her life in a new city, with just her cat for company. It can't be easy.'

'Who was she with?' Lisa said.

'She was waiting for a friend. They were going to have drinks but he was late, so in the end she decided to meet him at La Rioja.'

'You didn't meet him, then?'

'No. Why?'

'No reason.' Lisa realised she was frowning and that Tasmin was looking curiously at her. 'I just wondered if it might be Keith. That's how we met her. She was Keith's friend. They met when he was walking his dog. Then, just before Christmas, he brought her to the pub quiz. I just wondered if there was anything between them.'

'Really?' Tasmin pulled a face. 'He's a sweetie but I don't think he's in her league.'

~

The golf ball landed with a thud on the frozen grass. Judith smiled contentedly as she trailed it. Her shadow, elongated by the low sun, preceded her on to the green. She was about to remove the pin as the shape of a long, thin four-legged creature crossed the ghost of the flagstick, then it was suddenly gone as a cloud eclipsed the sunbeams. The dog barked excitedly. Judith frowned. She disapproved of dogs on the course.

'Well, fancy seeing you here, Judith,' said Keith.

'Well, perhaps it's not so unusual, as this is my club and I often play on Monday mornings.' She responded a trifle sharply as she turned, her breath vaporising in the cold air. She placed her club back in the bag and leant over Scamp, fussing and petting him. Her disposition warmed as she felt the heat of the little brown-and-white terrier's fur. She sniffed his head. Perhaps a little company would be preferable to a solitary round of golf after all. She shivered in the iciness of the early morning and smiled at Keith.

'I hope you're not following me.' She laughed. 'What brings you to these parts?'

'Oh, we like to get about and try different places.'

'I always thought you were a creature of habit.'

'Not at all. Don't let me stop you.'

Judith started walking, pushing the golf trolley ahead as Keith and Scamp followed her.

'Your golf partner's not turned up, then?' Keith enquired, as he increased his pace to keep up with Judith.

'I haven't got one. I used to play with one of the students from my course, but when he moved I had to play with these strangers. They seemed to get hung up about the rules.' She shrugged her shoulders. 'Now I prefer to play alone.'

'Golf ... Yes, they have some archaic rules.'

'Yes. You must not exceed the permitted number of clubs in your bag at any time, you know, or you lose two strokes.' She stopped and looked at Keith.

'Oh, did it cost you a game?'

'Not me,' she said, laughing. 'It was the lady captain's bag. You would have thought she would have known the rules. She claimed it was an oversight, her husband's fault.' Judith raised her eyebrows. 'I ask you! You have to watch out for these things, you know. Although she wasn't too pleased that I did.'

'Well, I guess she would have been the first to let you know if it was the other way round.'

As Judith teed up her ball, Keith pulled on Scamp's lead to distract him from sniffing at her golf club.

'Exactly. Rules are rules.' Judith struck the ball firmly and it arched magnificently down the fairway. Their eyes followed the flight of the ball in silence until it plopped just short of the green.

'You're a dark horse,' said Keith. 'I didn't realise you were that good.'

'And why not?' Judith turned and looked him in the eye.

Keith looked at his shoes.

'Rob and I had a good time at the match on Saturday. We won, you know?'

'Yes, I did hear. Pity your top striker's out for the next few matches after his fifth yellow card,' she said, as she placed the driver back in her bag.

'You are well informed. I thought you hated football.'

51

'I don't know enough to hate it. It was never Martin's game. I'm just curious to understand its attraction.'

They walked along a cinder path, parallel to the fairway, towards the ball.

'We're through to the next round in Europe. I'll be going with Lisa and Rob. I'm getting the tickets.'

Judith looked at him. She thought he sounded a trifle smug.

Keith scratched under his cap.

'We won't have such grand surroundings as we had on Saturday,' he laughed. 'We bumped into Tasmin and she took us to a hospitality suite. What a girl.'

'Taz? Oh, she's good fun, though rather full of herself.'

'That's her. She's quite a handful. Took a real shine to Rob.' He laughed.

'Really?' Judith said.

'Don't you put two and two together and make five. He only has eyes for one girl.'

'And who would that be?' Judith took her pitching wedge and putter from her bag. She left Keith on the path, then she chipped the ball just short of the hole. She easily putted the ball home and rejoined him to walk to the ninth tee.

'Well done,' Keith said.

'It's just a question of concentration, the mind and the body in perfect harmony. If you believe you can do something, you can.'

'Lisa's a lovely lass,' Keith said.

Judith puckered her brow and squinted at him in the sun. Keith was determined to have his say about Lisa. He was quite taken with her.

'She can be vivacious, but sometimes she can be a bit earnest, can't she?' said Judith, carefully. 'I guess that's an intriguing combination. But, you know, I think Rob is only spending so much time at Lisa's because his sister has a new man. He's just giving Heather some space. He's really not ready to settle down. By the way,' she continued quickly before Keith could come to Lisa's defence, 'you know you once said you would help me with any jobs I might have?'

'Oh, yes, anytime.'

52

'Well, would you mind putting up my kitchen blinds tomorrow?'
''Course not, love,' Keith said, touching his cap.
'Judith,' she smiled, icily.
'Eh?'
'My name is Judith.'

Tuesday afternoon

Through the kitchen window, Judith could see the bare, red branches of the dogwood and flowering viburnum shrubs twitching. She looked more closely. A family of blue tits were delving for grubs. One bird sat alone, balanced on the top of a fist of early pink blossom, its azure and yellow feathers plumped out as it chirruped merrily. She glanced at Bunters, who was asleep in a sheepskin-lined basket in the corner of the kitchen, then back at the garden.

Her heels tapped as she crossed the gleaming black slate floor and opened the French windows. She grasped the wooden clothes pole from the side of the house and poked at a cluster of twigs and moss that had been twined into the dogwood branches to make the base of a nest. She had to prod persistently before it broke up and fell on to the flower bed. She picked up the twigs from among the sodden dead leaves.

Don't even think about building it again, she thought, as she threw the detritus in the green bin.

'Forgotten about me, have you?' a voice asked.

Judith turned sharply.

'I didn't hear you,' she replied, leaning the clothes prop against the wall.

'I've been knocking and ringing your front doorbell for the past few minutes. I was just about to phone you.' Keith pushed his glasses further up the bridge of his nose as he peered up the drive towards her.

'Sorry, Keith. I was just doing a few chores. Come in through the back door and I'll show you the blinds. Tea?'

Bunters squinted through one eye at the stranger and stretched out a paw, as Judith explained how she wanted the venetian blinds to be put up. While Keith got on with his work Judith prepared a pot of tea. Bunters jumped on a worktop as Keith stretched over from a

53

stepladder to take a measurement. He sniffed inquisitively, then licked Keith's hand. Keith patted the chubby cat on the head, smoothing its soft fur affectionately and stroking his ears.

'Bunters, down,' said Judith, as she picked him up and set him on the floor. He meowed, sulkily.

'He's all right, Judith. Quite a friendly chappie.'

'Sometimes,' she said. 'He doesn't always do as he is told, like his mistress,' she laughed.

'How did he get that tear in his ear?'

'Turf wars. Fighting with another cat. He won. That was when we still lived in Hazelton.'

Unconsciously she rubbed her arm.

'And what about that?' Keith said, pointing at the white scar that crossed a vein near her wrist.

'An old war injury, delivered by Bunters when he objected to being sent out in the rain. I locked him out for two days after that. Then I gave in. I just couldn't bear his crying any longer. We agreed an easy truce. No more claws, no more rainy excursions into the garden.'

Keith sat at the table, opposite Judith, admiring his workmanship. He had a mug of tea in his hand, and a slice of parkin on a side plate in front of him.

'You could feed a family of eight in here, Judith,' he said, looking round the kitchen admiringly as he took a large bite of parkin. 'This cake hits the spot. Scrumptious.'

'Thank you. I like the space,' Judith said.

'So, you do lots of entertaining then?' Keith asked.

'Sometimes. I was wondering if you could get me a ticket for the football. It's not too late, is it?'

'You do surprise me. I will if you like. They aren't on sale yet.

'I'm just curious, that's all. Don't tell the others, though. It'll be a surprise for Lisa and Rob.'

'Are you sure surprises are always a good thing?' Keith asked.

'I don't know what you mean.'

'Really? You just spent yesterday criticising Lisa.'

'Criticising?'

'Yes, very subtly, of course,' Keith said, softly.

'No, you misunderstand me, Keith. I think she's a lovely, kind girl. She just seems to be a bit too focused on her career sometimes. She's a bit inward-looking. No, wrong word. Self-absorbed. She could have more fun. Like Tasmin.'

Keith pointed to a fading colour photograph of a girl with long blonde hair. It was standing on the dresser in front of some larger framed portraits of a smiling man. Martin, he presumed.

'Is that you when you were a teenager?'

'No, that's my sister Kathryn. Or Kate, as she calls herself now. We did look alike, I suppose. She emigrated to Australia years ago. I haven't seen her since she was seventeen.'

'Pretty girl.'

'She was five years older but we always got on. She'd let me try on her make-up and clothes, listen to her records. She was my idol. She was also a constant worry to my parents. She would rather be at a coffee bar in town, with some boy my mother deemed unsuitable, than stay in and do her homework.'

'What happened?'

'David Bowie.' She grinned, picking up the photograph. 'It was all his fault – oh, and his wife, Angie. Kathryn spent all day getting ready for a David Bowie concert. Shaved off her eyebrows, transformed her blonde hair into a spiky peroxide crop, and made up her face to resemble Angie Bowie. My father, who had banned her from going to the concert, was beside himself when she arrived home. It was after midnight. He thought she was drunk or on drugs, or both.' Judith was getting quite animated in the telling of the story.

'But she was just excited. Kathryn boasted that she'd caught David Bowie's ring. He'd thrown it deliberately to her, she'd said, and she vowed, rather melodramatically, that she would never take it off and would die wearing it. My father snapped, pulled the ring off her finger, and threw it on the floor. Then he slapped her. I saw it all through a crack in the living room door.'

'I bet he regretted that,' Keith said.

'Kathryn came in my bedroom early the next morning. I was barely awake. She said she was getting the bus to the railway station and going to London. She said she'd write. I never saw her again.'

55

She put the photograph down.

'And did she write?'

'Yes. I think my parents guessed where she was working from her letters. They read them first, of course. My mother went to London a few times to persuade her to come home. The last time she went there seems to have been some sort of altercation in Miss Selfridge.' Judith was silent. Keith took his second slice of cake. 'It happened in front of the customers so, of course, she was deeply upset. A public humiliation.' She laughed, but her mirth was hollow, her eyes vacant.

Tuesday evening

Lisa was getting dressed while Rob was taking a shower.

'Will you be ready soon?' she called, as she buckled the belt round her jeans. 'It'll take us a good fifteen minutes to get to The Sun.'

'No worries,' he shouted. 'Oh, I nearly forgot to tell you, they've had to delay the interviews because Tom Graham's been admitted to hospital.'

'Tom? I hope he's OK.'

'I think so. They're just being cautious, doing some tests. You know, I don't think they've even shortlisted yet.'

'That's odd. You would've thought they'd have done that by now.'

'Suppose. There was some talk about possible restructuring, as well,' Rob said, as he came into the bedroom barefoot, his shirt undone.

'Well, even if they restructure they won't close your place, will they? It's far too successful. Besides, it's saving them money, with you running it on a pittance,' Lisa said, pulling him towards her. She felt, at that moment, that going to the pub was the last thing she wanted to do.

'That's too true. Mmm … Come on, Ms Clarkson, I thought you were worried we were going to be late.' Rob said, pushing her down on the bed. She giggled as she smelled his fresh cool skin against hers.

~

'Are you sure you've added the score for that round up correctly,

Lisa?' Judith said, peering at the answer sheets. 'You know how angry Brian Cordon gets if anything is wrong.'

'Yes, I am sure and I know,' Lisa said, trying to ensure that her voice did not betray her annoyance. Judith had been quite irritable all night. She had admonished Lisa and Rob for being late. Although they had been later than usual, they had not, in fact, been late.

'We should never mark their papers. We should have exchanged with The Dispossessed. What's come over Rob today?' muttered Keith.

'I make it seventeen, not eighteen,' said Judith.

'He just said there were two marks for question five, so it's eighteen,' Lisa said.

'Oh, I am sorry. So that's settled, then.' Judith looked across at Keith, who was looking gloomily into his pint.

'Do you approve the final score, then, Judith?' Lisa said, presenting Judith with the answer sheets.

'Yes, I do,' said Judith, without looking.

Lisa got up and returned the sheets to The Terminators. As she came back she craned her head to view the far side of the bar. She wondered if Rob might have taken a detour from the gents to be sociable with Game, Set, and Match but was relieved when she him saw him talking to one of his football mates. She had scarcely got back to the table when Brian Cordon slammed the papers down between the glasses.

'Who marked this? March 1 is the official birthday of all those who were born on February 29. He should know,' Cordon said, pointing at Keith. 'Though his mum didn't. He was the only kid in the class who never had a proper birthday. Cheating again, are we?'

Lisa turned round to face Cordon, moving her hands to her hips.

'Sorry, my mistake,' said Judith, before Keith or Lisa could intervene. 'I marked that sheet, not Lisa. So here's one more point for you.' She beamed at the growling man as she added another point to the total score. 'There you are.' She flirtatiously cocked her head to one side. 'I think you tied with us. We both got two music questions wrong. We'll have to wait until next week to thrash you now,' she said, sweetly, dismissing him with a wide smile.

'We got Harold Macmillan and Rotterdam wrong as well,' said

57

Lisa.

'What did Cordon want?' asked Rob, returning to finish the last drops of a bottle of Peroni, as the bulky Cordon waddled back to his team.

'Oh, just complaining that a mark was wrong. He was right, for once,' said Judith. 'But now we know why Keith got the leap year's day birthday right. It was his birthday last weekend. What did you do Keith?'

'Well, I came in here,' Keith said gruffly.

'But you do that every night, Keith,' Rob said.

'Not every night I don't, not Sundays,' Keith said.

'That's because you're here at lunchtime.' Rob laughed.

'I only come if I'm not working,' Keith said. 'Or after.'

'What's your favourite food?' Judith asked. 'What would your last meal be?'

'Oh, that's easy. Chicken madras, naan bread, rice, and onion bhajis. And popadums, of course, with all the dips.'

'And which is your favourite Indian?' Judith said.

'Well, me and my Sandra always went to the Gate of Bengal.'

'Right, that's settled. We're going to celebrate your birthday this weekend, Keith. Rob, Lisa? Can you make it on Saturday, eight o'clock? I'll book,' Judith said, resting her hand gently on Lisa's jacket sleeve.

'Yep, I think so,' Rob said, looking on his phone. 'Maybe seven thirty rather than eight, though? Lisa?'

'Yeah, I can do that,' Lisa said.

'It's settled, then,' said Judith. 'On Saturday we'll make up for all the birthdays you never had at school, Keith.'

'He was just making that up. I had one every four years,' Keith said, as he sipped the last of his Guinness and wiped the creamy froth from his moustache.

It was the first time he had smiled all night.

Wednesday evening

The tiers of the dark, mammoth stadium soared into the night skies as Lisa and Rob walked down the concrete steps. The high-tech adverts pulsed around the perimeter of the football pitch, as if in

58

competition with the main event, reminding the spectators who was bankrolling the performance. The pitch at the night match seemed greener, more vibrant than that of the afternoon game, as if the floodlit grass had been preened specially for the television cameras.

'Where exactly was it you wanted me to get the tickets?' Lisa asked, as she and Rob took their seats.

'Over there,' Rob pointed to the stand opposite. 'I just thought it would be different. Just because this is where we got our seats the first time we ever came, it's no reason why we should come to the same place every week. It's not as if we know anyone.'

'There's Chocolate Box Woman,' Lisa said.

'Exactly. We don't even know who she is,' Rob retorted.

'No, but she gives us chocolates. It's just sort of familiar. Anyway, they didn't have any other seats, except on the very top. I prefer lower down so we can see their faces,' Lisa said. Rob had seemed quite keen to move, she thought, but there seemed no real reason for it. She watched the spectators as they made their way down the steep aisles.

'Did that man wink at you?' Lisa said, catching Rob's arm.

'What?'

'That man with the tattoos. I'm sure he winked at you,' she said, firmly.

'Why would he do that?'

'Chocolates, love?' Chocolate Box Woman offered Lisa and Rob an open box of Quality Street.

'Mmm, thanks. I'm Lisa, by the way.'

'Good evening, Lisa,' Chocolate Box Woman said, as she unwrapped a chocolate.

Lisa unwrapped a green foil-covered triangle and nibbled slowly on the sweet milky chocolate as she wondered if she was imagining the furtive wink and Rob's denial. But had he actually avoided denying it? And why did he want to move to the other side of the ground? Lisa quickly looked up towards the Bergers box. She could just see some shadowy figures in front of a flickering television. Some day she would be in there, and she would be entertaining her own clients.

'It's the Champions League soon, Rob. Did you remember to get

59

the tickets for the home match?'

'Keith's getting them. You don't mind him coming, do you? He really enjoyed Saturday. Sorry, I forgot to mention it.'

'That's fine. Your warm heart is one of the things I love about you.' Lisa flicked a lock of shiny brown hair away from her cheek. She gave Rob a sideways glance and realised he was staring at her.

'What is it, babe?' she asked.

'Oh, nothing,' Rob said, as the crowd roared and they rose to cheer the players out. He grabbed Lisa's shoulder and hugged her.

Why did she always have to feel so suspicious? There was no evidence. It was all in her head.

Stuck in a moment you can't get out of

Thursday morning

'Judith, I think it's time for a little Latin passion,' she said to herself, while pressing the play button on the remote control. '*Olé.*'

Within seconds the silence of the kitchen was succeeded by the searing chords of a flamenco guitar and a raw, anguished masculine voice. She could almost see the *cante* as it soared overhead like a secular call to prayer. Although the meaning of the words was unknown to her, she recognised their sensuality. It seemed to vibrate through her, connecting at a primal level.

She still used the mechanical scales her mother had used when baking. The heavy basin was scuffed now, but the large clock face still accurately measured the weight of the ingredients. She no longer needed to look at the exercise book in which her mother had carefully written out recipes in her neat script. The book was now redundant, languishing at the back of her kitchen drawer where she kept her red book and memorabilia. She had no desire to throw it away, even though she was unlikely to attempt any of the other recipes that had been served for family teas. They weren't events she wanted to remember. Especially after her sister left. Her father had seemed to retreat into himself and communicated very little with her, or her mother.

The treacle and golden syrup melded with the butter and sugar over a warm heat, while she carefully measured spoonfuls of spice. She inhaled the rich aroma of ginger, cinnamon, and nutmeg as they fell into the bowl with the flour and oats. And then she stirred all the ingredients together with a wooden spoon, as she did every Thursday.

Even though she had endured Keith's company for far longer than was desirable, she had watched with great pleasure as he devoured the ginger cake. Usually only two small squares were eaten each week, treats she reserved for the weekend.

61

The rhythmic hand clapping and foot stomping became more urgent and intense as she vigorously beat the mixture round and round.

'I love you, Judith. I love you, Judith.'

Martin's last words repeated endlessly in her head, whirring round and round like a spinning prayer wheel. As the glorious, aromatic mixture glooped into a cake tin the singer wearily ended his heartbroken song.

Friday afternoon

'Please can I go now, Lisa?' Tasmin scooped her lion's mane of hair off her shoulders and stretched her arms.

Lisa was so engrossed in the paperwork that she almost missed Tasmin's request. She had worked closely with the younger woman that morning, patiently showing her exactly how to set up an Excel spreadsheet, and she was now catching up on her own work. She was determined to get on top of things for her Monday morning meeting with Andy.

'Please can I go now, Lisa?'

Lisa glanced at her watch.

'But it's not four o'clock yet.'

'Yah, but it's such a drag to get the late train. You know it's hell getting through London on a Friday. It's Daddy's birthday this weekend. It will make all the difference if I make the early train and I can surprise him. I was in early this morning … You did say that you thought family was important when we had that meeting with Taylors.'

Lisa was uncertain whether Tasmin had been in early that morning or not. What had Rob said? She should think about what she was going to say, how Tasmin would react, and what the desired outcome should be, though perhaps not in that order.

'Have you finished all the work for my meeting on Monday?' Lisa asked, smiling. What would Tasmin have to do for the next hour that was so urgent?

Be reasonable. Treat others as you would like to be treated. It's a special occasion. Tasmin should just have cleared it earlier.

'Yah, it's all on my desk, and saved where you told me to, with a

62

backup copy,' said Tasmin, getting up.

'Next time—' Lisa began.

'Lisa, thank you. You're amazing. I do like working for you,' Tasmin said, picking up her coat and diving for the gap between the fig trees. 'I'll see you on Monday.'

'OK. Enjoy your dad's birthday,' Lisa said.

She buried her head in her papers for a few moments and then decided that she really ought to check that Tasmin's work was where it was supposed to be. Having retrieved it, she decided to familiarise herself with the figures for Monday, only to discover that the spreadsheet contained several significant errors.

'I was just looking for Taz.' Olivia stood between the plant pots. 'Any idea where she might be, Lisa?

'Sorry, Olivia, I didn't see you there. She's gone to catch the early train to London,' Lisa said. 'It's her father's birthday.'

'Her father's birthday? It looks like she left in haste.' Olivia let her eyes rest on the cluttered desk that belonged to Tasmin. 'I hope she caught the train. Never mind, I'm sure I'll catch up with her later. I can always text her. You don't mind if I do that, do you, Lisa?'

Friday evening

'So, Lisa,' said Maya, sitting cross-legged in red tartan pyjamas on her leather armchair, 'what precisely is it you see in Rob Granville? Is it a: his brown come-to-bed eyes? Is it b: his wit and intelligence? Or is it c: his culinary skills?' She put the glossy magazine down.

'None of those,' replied Lisa, as her spoon delved deeper into a pint of Häagen-Dazs vanilla ice cream. 'We have chemistry. He makes me laugh and I trust him.'

'Trust him? It was only the other week you were obsessing about his last girlfriend. Who was that? Bex?'

'Becca.'

'Then last weekend you were peeved because he'd been at some football match and bumped into Tasmin. Oh, and you were annoyed because Judith turned up at the cinema. And now you're wondering why he wants to change his seat and doesn't want to sit next to Chocolate Box Woman any more. Or perhaps you suspect he shares a murky secret with the tattooed man. Correct? And you say you

63

trust him?'

'Mmm.'

'Methinks it sounds like a serious case of besottment,' Maya said, grinning and tucking a lock of long black hair behind her ear, 'and it's making you jealous. You're seeing every woman as a babe threat.'

'Don't let him know,' Lisa said, as she licked the spoon, savouring its velvety, sticky sweetness.

'You think he doesn't?' Maya tilted her head inquisitively.

'I hope not. As soon as they know they have you hooked the game's up, and they want out. The thrill of the chase is gone.' Lisa stroked her finger through a drop of ice cream, which had fallen on to her pale blue dressing gown, and licked it.

'They? Don't base all your views on James. He was completely different.'

'Yes, you're right. He was a complete tosser,' Lisa said, with conviction.

'Yes, he was, but you didn't think that at the time, I seem to remember. Besides as it took him three years to ditch you, you must have played a very long game, Lisa.'

'I'll never forgive him.' Lisa blamed James, her boyfriend throughout university, for ruining her graduation day by finishing with her on the morning of the awards ceremony. She had been devastated, shell-shocked, as she watched him parade around the college reception with Hayley Bridges in tow.

'He said he had nothing in common with the hunting and fishing set and I believed him,' Lisa said, still sounding surprised by her ex-boyfriend's deception.

'James was a jerk, and, as I told you then, you're well rid. He and Hayley only lasted three months, anyway,' said Maya. 'He always was a liar. And, as I've also said before, not all men are the same. Certainly not Rob.'

'I just don't want to be hurt again. I know Rob's not like him, but he's very outgoing. He likes to be the centre of attention. I hate James for making me so, so insecure.' Lisa paused. 'Tasmin seems quite taken with Rob.'

'Well, he is hot. I bet he was a babe magnet in Barcelona.'

'You've never said that before.'

'Oh my God, the girl's going to get suspicious 'bout me now. Well, you two will have plenty time alone next week. After Monday I'm out on the road, so you and Rob will have the place to yourselves. Then I'm off to Glasgow for the weekend for a wedding.'

Maya pointed at the ice cream.

'I don't think you were eating quite so much of that stuff before you took on the new job. Three pounds a carton, all on the hips.' Maya laughed. 'When was it you said you last went to the gym?'

Lisa guiltily put the spoon down.

'Maybe I've been a bit obsessive about my work. I'm just worried about how to deal with Tasmin. She's very, very forthright, and I'm sure she reports everything to O-liv-i-ah.'

'Who cares about Olivia? Stop imagining things. You're being introspective again, and it's getting boring.'

Saturday lunchtime

Lisa carefully closed the book and put her pencil and notepaper aside. She had been gathering some background information to support her pitch for the Lloyds account. She was going to impress Andy at the Monday morning meeting with her knowledge of the company and its role in the development of the city. She had lingered far longer than she had intended in the library and way beyond her usual lunch hour. She checked her Facebook newsfeed then changed her status to:

Finito. Let the weekend commence.

She leaned back from the carrel, stretching her arms, and looked out of the window across the courtyard to another wing of the neo-Gothic sandstone library. As she glanced up she saw a face staring at her through the mullioned windows across the courtyard. A pale face, a shock of blonde hair, and a fur-collared red jacket. Judith?

She looked back again. The window was empty. She felt uneasy. Maybe she was daydreaming, but the image had seemed so real. She decided to return the books and get some lunch.

As she emerged from the lift she saw some children fooling around in the foyer cafe. A girl, about ten, with blonde hair and a red

65

jacket and black scarf was playing tag. Lisa had been convinced she had seen Judith, but why would Judith be watching her? How would she have any idea she was there? Perhaps it was a coincidence. More likely, though, it was the girl with the blonde pigtails. Nothing to do with Judith at all.

Lisa bought herself a cup of coffee and a cupcake and went to sit by the window. She surveyed the plaza and the road beyond. There was no sign of Judith but, walking across the road arm in arm and swinging designer carrier bags, were Tasmin and Olivia.

Saturday late afternoon
Judith was sitting at her dressing table, deliberating what to wear for the evening ahead. She pressed the purple plastic button on the top of a small phial. It was a sample of a new fragrance, but the perfume seemed familiar, and transported her back to her sister's bedroom. She remembered lounging on Kathryn's bed, while their parents were engrossed in front of the television. She had made up her eyes with her sister's Biba eye crayons, then she had inspected her sister's amber Aqua Manda perfume bottle. She had inhaled its mysterious, spicy scent as she twisted the art nouveau stopper. Even its cardboard box, decorated with oranges and flowers, had been considered cool. Though she could not be sure if the word 'cool' was in use back then. What would she have said instead? Groovy, hip, trendy, far out?

The year before, she had meticulously digitised all her vinyl records. She still had the originals, of course, but now she could easily switch to her favourite playlist in the car, in her bedroom, or in the kitchen. She selected David Bowie's album *Aladdin Sane* and stretched out on her bed. The velvet throw felt silky against her skin. She smiled as she listened to the jaunty opening chords of 'Time'.

Instinctively she imitated drawing on a cigarette, then she started singing the words that she had memorised all those years ago. She was sure that her teenage self would have had little understanding of the lyrics. She laughed at the memory of herself. Yes, she had been twelve and cool when she held the embossed amber bottle under her nose and David Bowie, dressed as the androgynous Ziggy Stardust, had pouted from the opposite wall. As he sang to her from the record

66

player she had waited for her sister to return home. Although, once she did, life was never quite the same again.

~

'That isn't the best Indian around, you know. You should try the Darbar,' said Maya, bringing the ironing board into the kitchen.

'I know, but it's Keith's favourite. It's his birthday. Judith's coming too,' Lisa said. 'Her idea. We won't be staying too long. We're meeting up with the gang in town later.'

'Champagne bar Judith? She seems loaded,' Maya said.

'Very. She's a widow, so I guess she must have inherited some money. She can be fun, but she tends to monopolise Rob sometimes,' Lisa whispered.

'Stop it. You're being jealous again. She's a lonely widow, old enough to be your mother,' said Maya, sliding the ironing board into a cupboard. 'I thought it was you she brought the little gifts for. This state of besottment is making you act strangely.'

'She's most definitely nothing like my mother, nor yours,' said Lisa.

'My mother is like no one else,' said Maya. 'Except my gran. I think they've done all the housework they're going to do now.'

'I was hoping they were going to do the windows.'

'No. They're finished,' Maya said, peeping round the door. 'They've been distracted by your boyfriend. Rob can charm the birds off the trees, can't he?'

'He certainly can. I'm amazed you've let him sit in *your* chair,' Lisa jibed.

'By the way, if my mum asks, you know the sassy red shoes with the killer heels?'

'Yeah.'

'They're yours.'

'Madeira,' said Rob. 'I would definitely recommend Madeira for an early holiday. Beautiful scenery. Warm, but not too hot. Pleasant walks. The botanic gardens are known for their rare orchids. Then there is a really high standard of hotels, so it's good value. Not cheap, but good value.'

67

'Well, that sounds like the sort of thing we like,' Maya's mother said to her mother. The ladies were sitting on the almost cream sofa drinking tea, while Rob lounged on Maya's armchair. Lisa collected the empty side plates.

Maya's grandmother nodded in agreement as she rubbed her fingers over the ancient stains on the sofa.

'Value we like. Cheap we don't. It attracts the riff-raff.'

'Come in next week and I'll give you some brochures. If you can't see me I'll be in the back office. Just ask for "Sir".' Rob smiled as the ladies laughed.

Rob loved to know he'd put a smile on someone's face, Lisa thought, to make someone's day a little brighter. It was what made him tick.

'We'll do that,' said Mrs D'Souza. 'We'd better go now. We don't want to delay you and your girlfriend. She certainly has an interesting taste in shoes, doesn't she?'

'What?' said Rob, as the women chuckled.

'Shiny red stilettos. A real temptress.'

Saturday evening

'Keith, I didn't recognise you,' said Lisa, waving as she walked carefully across the dimly lit restaurant in her black platform shoes. Keith was staring uneasily into his Tiger beer.

She peered at his bald pate which, surrounded by a semicircle of brown and grey hair, gave him the look of a medieval friar.

'I've never seen you without your cap before, Keith. Happy birthday!' Lisa placed a card and a box of chocolates on the table next to Keith. 'Sorry it's a week late.'

'No, I don't think I have, either,' said Judith. 'Belated happy birthday, Keith. Another year older, but we improve with age, just like vintage wine. That's what Martin always used to say.' She leaned over and kissed Keith on his cheek, then handed him an envelope and a wine bottle-sized carrier bag. She took off her jacket, with the panache of a model, to reveal a clinging royal blue silk dress. It looked expensive.

Keith grunted his thanks and took a large sip of the beer. The cream head clung to his moustache. He smoothed it away with the back of his hand as Lisa sat next to him.

'I take it you'll have another of those?' said Rob, signalling to the waiter.

'I'm not sure it's worth celebrating a birthday at my age. I'm past it. That's what I think when I look in a mirror.'

'Don't be ridiculous,' said Judith. 'You have years left in you. It's not as though you're overweight. Though you could lose a few pounds.'

'Maybe try some new glasses,' said Lisa. 'Those big metal-rimmed ones aren't so fashionable any longer.'

'Grey hair isn't exactly flattering,' Judith said, 'And that Tom Selleck moustache is a bit dated. It's up to you to make the most of yourself. You have potential.'

'Potential?' muttered Keith. He stared at Judith for a moment. 'Is that a compliment?'

'And women are supposed to be the gentler sex,' said Rob. 'God help us.'

'I think as it's your birthday you can be assured it is.' Judith laughed coquettishly. 'I certainly wouldn't be saying that to Brian Cordon, or Val.'

Keith grinned.

As the drinks were replenished Lisa was already deep in conversation with Keith. She detected that he was feeling quite lonely and had found it quite difficult to adjust after losing his wife, especially as his children only paid an occasional visit. She began to feel a little guilty about how often she saw her own parents.

She was glad when Keith lifted his mood by telling her some funny stories about some of his punters, as he called his customers, but she could not resist having half an ear on Rob and Judith's conversation. Rob was laughing as Judith related how she had managed to lock herself out of her house the other week. Lisa suddenly felt a kick of jealousy as she noticed Judith whispering in Rob's ear.

When Keith had finished his story Lisa made her excuses and went to the ladies. While she was washing her hands Judith came in.

'What a great guy Rob is. I bet you can't believe your luck that you've snared him,' Judith said, leaning against the wall and looking at Lisa in the mirror.

'Snared him? That's not how I'd put it,' Lisa said, as she smoothed her short lime green dress.

'Well, no, probably snared is the wrong word.' Judith paused and gave Lisa a long look. 'Have you put a little weight on? Your face is a bit fuller, but maybe it's this bright light. It never highlights our best features, does it? No, snared is probably not the right word. What I mean is that there must be competition. Don't you think Becca still holds a light for him?'

'Becca?'

'Yes, Rob's ex, Becca. She's quite a stunner.'

Lisa wondered how Judith knew what Becca looked like. Lisa didn't. She studied their reflections in the mirror. Was Judith the person she had seen in the library? She just could not be sure. It was hard to connect the ghostly glimpse of the face in the window with the vibrant, blue-clad woman next to her.

'She's no competition. He's moved on. He has no contact with her,' Lisa said.

'Really?'

Lisa did not respond. The question mark was still hanging in the air as Judith, smiling at her own reflection in the neon-lit mirror, dabbed some scent on her wrists. Lisa decided against touching up her make-up and left, pulling the door very firmly behind her.

Keith was sitting on his own at the table. Lisa sat down, feeling hollow inside.

'She clearly adores your man,' Keith said, as Judith walked towards the table looking radiant. She was followed by the stares of several customers and a waiter carrying an iced cake that was sparkling with candles.

Not me, though, Lisa thought.

'You don't need to worry,' Keith said. 'Rob only has eyes for you. Anyone can see that.'

PRIVATE
INVESTIGATIONS

Would I lie to you?

Sunday morning

Lisa had suspended her routine of pains au chocolat, coffee, newspapers, and political television in favour of a healthier regime. Her preference for the physical challenges of the gym, over the sedentary pleasures of the sofa and Sunday morning television, had been reinforced when Rob had dragged her out of bed and left her on the cold kitchen floor beside her gym bag. Then he had sprinkled icy drops of water over her giggling body before he had left to play football. She had driven to the gym, but with little enthusiasm.

A slim, handsome woman approached Lisa the moment she entered the changing room.

'Lisa, long time no see. I thought maybe you'd left the area. Welcome back.' Gemma had the smooth, unlined face of a young woman, but her almost white hair gave the impression of someone much older. She was of indeterminate age. Lisa's spirits changed immediately in response to the enthusiastic welcome and, after chatting for a few minutes, she made her way to the Zumba class Gemma had recommended. The class promised more fun than the lonely contests against the fitness equipment. Soon Lisa was totally engrossed in the samba beat.

'Forward, two, three, four. Pivot, two, three, jump,' the elfin instructor called into her wireless headphone. Lisa obeyed, jumping on the fourth beat. As she pivoted round to face the large window that overlooked the studio she caught sight of Judith. She turned and jogged forward again.

'Forward, two, three, four. Pivot, two …'

Distracted, Lisa jumped up before the rest of the group then, as she pivoted again, she searched the window. There was no one there.

Judith was nearing the end of the tour of the state-of-the-art gym equipment when her guide, skilfully balancing on her high heels, stopped outside a yoga class.

'I just thought it would be more sociable to go to exercise classes.

73

I enjoy pushing a few weights with John Fashanu or Davina McCall but a video's not as rewarding as interacting with real people,' Judith said, interrupting the sales executive.

'As you can see, we have a wide range of activities, suitable for all ages, including those who prefer gentler exercise,' the tightly miniskirted woman continued.

Judith stiffened.

'Usually, anyway.'

'And next door we have the Zumba class. This is very popular with our ladies.' The sales executive pointed her long, sparkly acrylic nails towards the window of the dance studio. Judith was admiring the symmetrically choreographed moves of the women when she saw Lisa jump up above all the others. She gasped. She did not remember Lisa mentioning she came to this gym, or any gym, for that matter. Perhaps she was new, too. For a moment she felt rather guilty for suggesting that Lisa had put on a few extra pounds although she had, of course, been very diplomatic.

Despite taking a dislike to the sales executive, especially her cheap hair extensions, she could imagine coming here. There was even a beauty salon in the same building and a very comfortable coffee bar.

Judith was finishing a coffee in the lounge, browsing the leaflets about membership, when she became conscious that someone was standing over her.

Judith looked up.

'Lisa, this is a—'

'What are you doing here?'

'Sorry, what ...? I could say the same to you. How long have *you* been coming here?'

'This is my gym.'

'You never mentioned that you came here,' Judith said.

'I've been a member for at least a year. Perhaps even longer. What about you? Why have you decided to come here?'

'I just got bored working out at home, so I thought I'd have a change. I didn't think I knew anyone here. But I'm so glad I do. Although I have the feeling you aren't too pleased to see me.'

Lisa looked embarrassed.

'I'm sorry, I wasn't expecting to see you here. I was just surprised. It was very nice of you to organise Keith's birthday yesterday. We really enjoyed it. Can I get you another coffee?'

Judith accepted the offer graciously.

Lisa returned from the self-service bar with two large lattes.

'Oh, I have something I meant to give you last night. I have a voucher for a new Spanish restaurant. I wondered if you would like it. You can take Rob.' Judith offered a brightly coloured card to Lisa. It was a two-for-one voucher for La Rioja. 'It was a promotion,' added Judith. 'It didn't cost me anything, but I won't use it. There's probably an expiry date.'

Lisa looked on the back.

'Why don't you use it yourself?' Lisa said, turning the card over, offering it back. 'You could take Keith.'

Judith put her coffee cup down so firmly on the table that coffee spilled over the sides and into the saucer.

'Keith?' Judith said, folding her arms.

There was an awkward silence, then Lisa said,

'Thank you. It's very thoughtful of you. You're joining here, then?'

'I think so, on a three-month trial. I'll probably come during the day, when it's quieter. When everyone else is at work. I'm fortunate that I can do that.' She laughed and paused, dabbing her saucer with a serviette. 'You and Rob seem very much the happy couple.'

Lisa fixed her gaze on the contents of her coffee cup.

'It's lovely to see. He's obviously smitten,' Judith continued. 'You know, I didn't know Martin was my soulmate immediately, but when it suddenly hit me, there was no turning back,' Judith confided.

'Really? How did you meet him?' Lisa asked, stirring her coffee again.

'Work. I loved my job, but I'd had a difficult year. A serious relationship had broken up very suddenly and then my mother died. I felt very much on my own – my father had died some years previously.'

Lisa murmured her sympathy.

'I had so much to deal with,' Judith said. 'You know, selling the house and all the stuff that has to be done when a generation expires. Martin was the director of the museum, so obviously we saw a lot of each other. He invited me out one evening to talk about the museum's plans. We were leaving the museum, then ... Then I realised that the accidental meetings in the corridor were not coincidental, the lingering glances were not just concern. It was as if I'd been waiting all my life for that moment. We fell head over heels in love. It made all previous relationships I had look like shadows of the real thing.'

'Mmm, I know what you mean,' Lisa said, putting her cup down on the low table. 'I had a boyfriend all the way through uni. He ditched me on the morning of the grad ceremony.'

'How awful.'

'My graduation photos are awful. I look spaced out. Every time I go home to mum's I have to look at that awful photo of myself over the fireplace. One moment I had a certain future, the next it was completely unknown.' Lisa opened her hands expressively. 'I was heartbroken at the time, but with Rob it's so different, so real. We have chemistry. Real chemistry. James Strather is an also-ran in comparison.'

'James Strather?'

'That was the name of my ex. I'm just amazed I spent so much time grieving over that loser,' Lisa said. 'James Strather, RIP.' Lisa raised her coffee cup. 'Oh, I'm sorry. I didn't mean ... Of course it was nothing like losing ...'

Judith pursed her lips and tried to smile. She did not doubt that Lisa was over James Strather, but she could see his memory still cast a long shadow. Lisa, on the other hand, had no idea what it meant to grieve for someone.

Judith drank her coffee quickly. She knew Rob would not be coming to the gym. He always played football on a Sunday from eleven until one, then went down to The Sun with his teammates and Keith.

Monday morning
Lisa carried her file back to her corner of the office after her meeting with Andy. He had been very pleased with her work, but was clearly

unimpressed with the report he had received from London about Tasmin. How was she going to deal with this?

Intended outcome: Tasmin admits waywardness and agrees to change her whole personality. Fuck.

'Hi, Lisa,' Tasmin said, as Lisa walked through the jungle foliage. 'How was the meeting? Is he pleased with our accounts?'

'Yes, Andy's extremely pleased with the way the Lloyds and Taylors accounts are going.'

'So, my spreadsheet was really useful last week.'

'Well ...' Lisa put her file back down on her desk and pulled her chair up opposite her colleague. Tasmin stroked her hair behind her ears and blinked repeatedly.

'Are you all right, Tasmin?'

'Slight contact lens malfunction. I'll be fine.'

'Andy mentioned he's had a report from head office about the training course. It must have arrived while he was on holiday.'

'Oh.' Tasmin bit her bottom lip.

'You know, I remember having a great time on my course. The last night we all went out and got hammered. I was a bit late in the next morning.'

'Oh, God, yah. We had a fantastic night.'

'Well, me too, but it was just the once.'

'Oops.'

'Do you want to tell me what happened, Tasmin?'

'Well, I guess.'

'Perhaps you could also include what is meant by "inappropriate use of mobile phone".'

'I'm sorry, Lisa, I suppose I was acting like it was a jolly.' Tasmin said. 'I bet Sonia's report was a bit shorter than mine,' Tasmin said, as Lisa tried not to show any emotion.

'There are a few other things as well. Perhaps you'd like to explain why you left early to catch a train to go to London for your father's birthday but didn't actually go there?' Lisa took in a deep breath.

'Oh.'

Lisa said nothing as she waited for Tasmin's explanation.

'Have you been watching me?' Tasmin said.

'No. Why would I do that? I let you go early because I trusted you.' Lisa scrutinised Tasmin's face.

Tasmin bit her bottom lip. She looked guilty and contrite.

'I did fib. It was because of Jeremy,' Tasmin said.

'Jeremy?'

'I was worried. I thought he was taking someone else out for early doors. I wanted to get round to his office before he left work.'

'I thought you weren't that keen on him. I mean, that it wasn't that serious.'

'Well, I changed my mind. And it all worked out fine, and then this weekend everything was amazing. I'm sorry if I fibbed. I'm really grateful you let me go, because it worked out.'

'Why did you fib? Why didn't you tell me the truth?'

'Well, you were a bit tetchy the other week, after Della left. I didn't think I could tell you the truth.'

'If we're going to work together, we have to trust each other. Can you promise me you will be truthful in the future?'

'I apologise, Lisa. I shouldn't have fibbed. I promise. It's just … just you seem a bit … a bit remote sometimes.'

'Oh.' *Tetchy, remote? Fuck.* 'Well, I'm sure we can work these things through. One other thing, though, Tasmin. That spreadsheet was completely and utterly wrong. I'm sorry.'

Tasmin groaned.

'Oh, God, Lisa. I've always been hopeless at anything like that.'

'Graduate trainees have to be competent in basic IT skills …'

'I just can't get my head round it.'

'We'll do it again. We'll do it until you can get your head round it. I want you to succeed.'

If you don't, thought Lisa, *neither will I.*

~

Monday evening

'Shush, I'm watching.' Maya was curled up in the leather armchair in front of the television, watching a recording of *The Apprentice*. 'There's only five minutes left, so don't you dare tell me who gets

78

fired, Rob Granville, like you did last time.'

Rob sat down on the sofa next to Lisa. He fidgeted as he drank from a mug of tea and flicked through some magazines, but remained quiet.

Prokofiev's *Dance of the Knights* signalled the end to the programme as the credits rolled.

'All yours now,' Maya said, as she threw the remote to Rob.

'Have you ever thought of applying, Maya? I would have thought you would have a good chance of winning. I can't imagine anyone crossing you in the boardroom, not even Sir Alan,' Rob said.

'I bet Karren Brady would have a whole new wardrobe by the end of the show,' Lisa said.

'Now, there's a thought, but I don't think I could abide being holed up with those no-hope wannabees for a few months. It's far more fun living here, seeing what madness you two allow to happen. And I think I have managed to train you quite well,' she winked. 'Even the tea is made properly these days. Anyway, Rob, you'll be in the boardroom soon, won't you? Have you heard when your big interview for the manager's job is?' Maya asked.

'Not got it,' Rob mumbled.

'What?' said Lisa.

'Not got it.'

'Not got the job? When did you have the interview?' Lisa asked.

'No, there was no interview,' Rob said.

'Why didn't you tell me? When did you find out?' said Lisa, as Maya picked up her mug and slipped out to the kitchen.

'Friday. I found out on Friday. Head office rang up, just before I left work.' Rob averted his eyes from Lisa and stared at the television screen.

'Friday! When were you going to tell me?' Lisa turned sharply.

'Soon,' he mumbled.

'When?' Lisa said.

Rob said nothing.

'But you've exceeded the targets. You are doing the job,' said Lisa.

'Yes, I know, but they don't want me. End of.'

'What did they say?'

79

'Tom's secretary rang to say they weren't interviewing me. There's nothing more to be said. Let's watch the film. That's all I want to do at the moment.' He turned up the volume and stretched out his legs as he settled into the corner of the sofa. 'Maya, it's about to begin. Hurry up. Bring in a couple of beers, will you?' Rob yelled to the kitchen.

Lisa knew there was no point in delving further. She had spent most of the weekend with him and he hadn't mentioned the interview once, nor tried to communicate his feelings to her. Rob deflected any attempts to share his unhappiness. She watched the familiar figure slumped at the far end of the sofa. Tonight he seemed no more than a stranger.

We're all alone

Tuesday lunchtime

Lisa took the last bite of her Pret a Manger sandwich and finished the bottle of orange juice. She had bolted down her lunch in ten minutes and was reluctant to return to her spreadsheet. She had thought she had chemistry with Rob, but was she just fooling herself and blaming James Strather for her insecurities when the real reason was her fragile relationship with Rob?

She googled herself. She was pleased to see details of her appointment were in the Bergers online magazine. She wondered if Olivia was mentioned. No. No mention at all, but then there was no reason why Olivia should be. She googled Olivia. She had far more results than Lisa, mainly due to her sports clubs. The only other result Lisa had was on her university alumni site. She supposed all her contemporaries had an entry there. She searched for Maya D'Souza. Yes. Who else? James Strather. Yes, he was there. Same year, course, and college.

Lisa googled him. He was working for an international consultancy in London. The career he had sworn he would never choose, but the one his parents had mapped out for him. Quelle surprise. She looked up the other results. He was in a sailing club, and on the board of a charity for children with disabilities. He always did have a caring side to him. That had attracted her to him. He wasn't as bad as Maya said. He didn't seem to have taken up any of Hayley Bridges's interests, but then Maya said they had finished long ago. It had just been a fling.

There was a video among the search results. Lisa opened it. He looked just the same. Blonde hair and boyish grin, athletic build, just smarter. Dazzling smile. It seemed to be an online presentation for a job in Hong Kong. She laughed as she heard him describe himself as 'an experienced, globally mobile professional with excellent management and organisational skills.'

She listened intently, feeling guilty for eavesdropping at the same

81

time. She wondered how many times he had made the video before he could perform without laughing. He had presented his experience as a student social committee representative as if he were some international entrepreneur. Just like him to be careless and to leave the presentation online, for all the world to see.

She wondered if James had got the Hong Kong job and was surprised that she felt downcast at the thought that he might be half the world away. She could always find out. He was on Facebook and LinkedIn. It was a good thing people couldn't tell you were googling them, she thought, as she switched back to the Berger and Berger report.

Tuesday afternoon
Judith smoothed the sheets as she ironed while the soprano's grief filled the kitchen.

Requiem aeternam, dona eis, Domine, et lux perpetua luceat eis.

She glanced at the photograph of her sister that Keith had admired. Next to the photograph a small dish held a solitary copper ring. The firstborn often claim that they fight the battles with their parents, trailblazing a path into adulthood on behalf of their siblings. That's what Kate would have said, but in fact her sister's actions seemed to have constrained Judith's own choices. She remembered how excited she had been when she was offered a post at the European Court of Justice in Luxembourg, using the language and office skills she had developed at the local college. She had been excited, filled with romantic expectations.

She had almost finished packing for her new life when her father had his first heart attack. The job was put on hold for a short time but, after her father died, she did not have the heartlessness to abandon her inconsolable mother. Instead of taking an apartment and leading the life of a bilingual, cultured European she took a small flat in Hazelton four miles from the family home, where her widowed mother now lived alone. She went to work as a secretary for an auctioneer, where she was treated like a member of the family, and worked there for years before she applied for the job at the museum. She had been there for almost a year, loving every moment, when suddenly, without any warning, her mother died and everything changed again. That was nearly ten years ago now.

She had not witnessed her sister's reaction to the solicitor's letter explaining the terms of the will. Kate was to receive £10,000, while her younger sister inherited everything else: the house, the shares, and the two student flats her father had astutely acquired in the early 1970s. She had felt it unfair herself at first, she remembered. In fact she had been quite shocked, and had even wondered about asking the solicitor to vary the will in Kate's favour. There were her nieces' and her nephew's futures to think about now. However, Kate's bitter phone call – the first and last, accusing her of conniving and deliberately turning Mother against her – had convinced her to do nothing. After all, she was the one who had shouldered her mother's grief for almost twenty years, done her duty. Maybe Kate deserved what she got. She reflected for a moment about whether she would swap her wealth for the love of her sister but decided that she would not.

She neatly folded the crisp cotton sheets and placed them in the laundry basket before stowing the ironing board. She picked up a photograph from the worktop of her sister aged seventeen, beautiful golden curls cascading over her shoulders, just before she had shorn and bleached her hair. It had been taken not long before she left home.

Yes, she thought, *I would have liked to have had a relationship with my sister, but not with the selfish, vindictive woman she became.*

She put the photo down with a thud and walked away from the memory of a family she no longer had.

Tuesday evening

'New perfume, Lisa? It suits you. An intriguing blend of patchouli and vanilla, I'd say.' Judith was sitting in a haze of cedar and juniper as she sipped a white wine spritzer.

'A present from Rob, a Valentine's Day present.' Lisa swigged a Peroni. She wondered if Judith had any more gifts to offer her. She had been annoyed with herself for revealing so much to Judith at the gym.

Have I allowed myself to be bought? she wondered. Maya was right. Some things just needed to be forgotten, and James Strather was one of them. She was not going to confide in Judith again, nor accept any more gifts.

'I liked your gym wear, Lisa. I don't think I have anything that's so fashionable,' Judith said. 'You will have to let me know where to shop.'

'Well, I think you just have to wear what you're comfortable in. I got mine at Asda,' Lisa lied. 'Why don't you try there?'

'Martin really wasn't a fan of the big supermarkets. He always preferred to support the little guy. I've always tried to do that, too.'

'Good if you can afford to, though I didn't think John Lewis was one of the little guys,' Lisa countered.

'Rob must be disappointed about Frieda Smithson.'

'Frieda Smithson?'

'Yes, his new manager. She starts in a month's time. She's coming up from Exeter. I thought you would know. He must have been devastated not to have got the job. It will relieve the pressure, though.'

'Rob has no problem with the pressure. If anything, he thrives on it,' Lisa said. 'I don't think you understand what makes him tick.'

'Don't I?' Judith said, twiddling a lock of her hair and smiling as Rob sat down next to Keith.

'Come on, everyone, let's see if we can get this picture round done before the first round,' Rob said. He pushed a CD towards Judith. 'As promised. You'll have no excuses now, Jude.'

They scrutinised the photocopy of famous people's faces and called out suggestions while Lisa wrote the answers in her neat script.

The quizmaster called for attention.

'Mobile phones off, please. Round one, question one. Who is the youngest sibling of the late Michael Jackson?'

'Who was in The Jackson 5? Is it Marlon? Randy?' Rob whispered, picking up the pen.

'Answer the question. It's the whole family,' said Keith.

'Janet or La Toya,' Lisa said.

'La Toya? Never heard of her,' said Judith

'Janet or La Toya? Quickly,' Rob said, urgently.

'Janet,' said Lisa.

'Shush. Does everyone agree?' said Rob taking his pen.

'Well, yes,' said Judith, 'but I am quite happy to admit that I don't know the answer.'

'Agreed,' said Keith. 'Lisa's our pop expert.'

'Two. In which city would you see Picasso's painting *Guernica*?' Rob said.

'Oh, I know. Madrid,' said Lisa.

'No, no, it must be the Guggenheim in Bilbao,' countered Judith.

'Madrid. I've seen it,' said Lisa.

'It's about the massacre of the Basque people. It must be Bilbao. It makes sense.' Judith took a sip of wine.

'But I've seen it. Have you seen it?' Lisa asked, gripping her Peroni glass tightly.

'No, I've only been to Barcelona. Precisely where did you see it?' Judith probed. 'Which gallery?'

'Quickly decide. Final answer?' Rob said.

'Bilbao.'

'Madrid.'

Keith looked to the ceiling, opening his palms out and abdicating any responsibility.

'Well, Judith is our history of art expert, so I will write Bilbao.'

'Thank you, Rob,' said Judith, touching the CD.

'Thank you, Rob,' said Lisa, tapping her pen noisily on the table.

Lisa began the argument as soon as they left The Sun.

'I told you I'd seen *Guernica* in Madrid and you believed *her*.'

'You know the team rules. If there's deadlock then the person whose specialist subject it is makes the decision. Hers is art. Yours is music. You had just had the final say on the Jackson family.' Rob said.

'Yes, but no one was disputing that. Eyewitness evidence should take precedence over the specialist subject. Then we would have won, beaten The Terminators. You took her side.'

'I don't believe you.' Rob stopped in his tracks.' It's only the other week you were all over her. We even spent Valentine's night with her because you asked her to join us. What's changed? She seems just the same to me.'

85

Lisa had to admit he was right. Until recently she had actually looked forward to meeting Judith at the weekly quizzes. Now she bridled whenever she thought of her. They walked on in silence.

Lisa finally erupted.

'She's so artificial. All that hair, perfect make-up, carefully enunciated vowels. The click, click, click of her high heels. Underneath, she's ... she's just not what she seems. She's fake. That's what she is: fake.'

'She's just putting on a brave face. She's had a hard time. She's still up to her eyes in grief for that husband of hers. You never have a conversation without her going all misty-eyed over Martin.' He paused. 'It sounds like you're jealous.'

'Don't be ridiculous.'

They walked on in silence.

'And you confide in her more than me,' Lisa said.

'What?'

'Telling her about your new boss. When did you tell her that?'

'We only heard about her today. I don't know how she knows. I didn't know she did.'

'And the other week ... oh, nothing. And that disc ... what was that disc you gave her?'

'Just some music. She said she felt out of touch – I'm sure I told you the other week – so I just did a playlist of stuff I thought she wouldn't have heard.'

'I would have thought you would have referred that request to the music expert.'

'Look, Lise, I just feel sorry for her. Don't you think she's a bit old for me? Crazy girl. I'm going to go now and catch the bus,' Rob said. 'I need to pick up my football things. I'll be going straight from work tomorrow,' he said. '*Adios, bonita.*'

~

Lisa tossed under her duvet, tired but unable to sleep. She was supposed to have the flat and Rob all to herself this week, but instead she was sleeping alone. What did he mean by, '*Adios, bonita*'? He never said that, and he didn't go home after the quiz.

She pinched her stomach. Not really much more flesh to grasp hold of than usual. She had already spent a good ten minutes inspecting her face in the bathroom mirror. It seemed just the same as ever. Maya had warned her about the ice cream, though. She hadn't got annoyed with Maya, so why had Judith riled her?

Rob was right. She had enjoyed Judith's company until recently. Now she was suspicious of her. On Saturday Keith had confirmed what she had suspected. Judith adored Rob. Was that a bad thing? Keith, Rob, and Tasmin all saw Judith as a victim, a woman suffering in her bereavement. Why couldn't she see that too? She tried to picture how she would feel if she never saw Rob again, but the bleakness was too much.

Rob had favoured Judith's answer, but he was right about the team rules. It was just a quiz. Was she just a very jealous person? Maya had hinted at it. Rob wouldn't talk about MedTime and what he was going to do. But had he confided in Judith? He said not. Judith was just trying to make her think he had.

If she was honest, the Judith she liked was the one who had ingratiated herself by always giving compliments, and champagne and gifts. The Judith she didn't like wielded her tongue like a stiletto, furtively throwing barbed comments when she thought no one else was listening.

She remembered how she had warmed to Judith the moment they were introduced. Judith had mistaken Lisa's perfume for one of her own favourites. They had the same base notes of amber and lotus, she had said. Now Lisa thought about it, that was something else that had changed about Judith. She used to wear a fresh, aquatic fragrance. Now her perfume was heavier, more woody. Sensual. Yes, it wasn't her imagination. Judith was changing.

Don't let go

Wednesday morning

'Judith … It is Judith, isn't it? Don't you remember me? Gemma Barker. We used to go to the same Spanish class.'

Judith recognised the slender, white-haired woman immediately. As she walked across the studio floor to greet her she caught sight of herself in the mirror. She liked her new gym wear.

'Of course, Gemma, I do remember. Do you still go?' Judith kissed Gemma on both cheeks.

'No, I gave up shortly after you left,' Gemma said. 'I got fed up with all that homework, and I had no one to chat with at the break. Look, have you time for a coffee? We can catch up, properly.'

Between sips of lemon and ginger tea, Judith listened half-heartedly to Gemma's assessment of the new Zumba teacher. She tried to make enthusiastic noises while she analysed Gemma's appearance. Gemma had good skin but her hair, cut quite short and straight, was now almost white with just a few hints of dark grey. She could be described as handsome, Judith supposed, but she could look a lot better, with a bit of effort. Why on earth should she want to let herself go au naturel? Judith's gaze followed the progress of two men who were walking though the lounge on their way to the tennis courts. She was contemplating whether taking up tennis might be a good idea when Gemma asked her a question. She realigned her gaze to meet Gemma's eyes.

'Lisa, how do I know Lisa?'

'Yes, I saw you talking to Lisa Clarkson the other day,' said Gemma.

'She's a member of my pub quiz team. How do you know her?'

'She goes to some of my classes. Although I hadn't seen her for ages until last Sunday.'

'Yes, I think she was worried she was putting on weight.'

'She's done very well, getting promoted. She's an account executive now, she was telling me.'

'Yes, she did very well, getting that job. There was fierce competition. Fortunately for her, she's *very* friendly with Andy, the managing director.' Judith looked at Gemma and lowered her voice. 'He's even got her lined up for a job in London.' Judith almost winked. 'Yes, she loves Andy.'

'She's got a young man, hasn't she?' Gemma asked, guardedly. 'Rob.'

'Well, Gemma, Lisa's very ambitious. I don't think she would allow anything, or anyone to stand in the way of her career. Rob's a lovely guy, though. It's sad when you see couples who aren't right for each other. Time wasted. He, of course, will be the one who's hurt.'

'I would never have thought it of her.'

'No,' Judith smiled sadly, then raised her voice again. 'It's the anniversary soon. Five years since Martin died.'

'Of course. You must miss him so much. It must be hard on your own.'

There was a silence before Judith asked,

'Are things all right between you and Mervyn now?'

Gemma flushed.

'Yes, we've forgotten all about our difficulties, put it all behind us. *She* has left the company. Works at John Lewis now. I never shop there any more, of course.'

Judith touched her arm.

'I'm so sorry. I'm glad everything else is back to normal.'

'Well, not quite. I can't bear for him to touch me, or for me to touch him.'

'Oh, dear. I hope that's not for good. Are you on Facebook? We can keep up to date, meet up here again.'

'Let's just swap phone numbers. I don't have anything to do with all that stuff. You never know where it might lead,' Gemma said, with great authority.

Wednesday afternoon

Judith googled 'Gemma Barker' as Beethoven's *Ninth Symphony* blasted through the downstairs rooms of her house. The woman had no Internet footprint at all, although her husband, Mervyn, seemed quite active in a local railways interest group. She wondered if he had used his hobby as a cover for his affair. She couldn't imagine things were really back to normal. Mervyn would soon be looking elsewhere again, seeking someone who would touch him.

She sometimes ached for Martin's touch, the way he had stroked the nape of her neck. She still tingled when she remembered it. That's how it had begun. The rest of the staff had gone home and they were about to leave the museum by the back door. Martin had gently, but deliberately, touched the back of her neck, as he helped her with her coat. The next moment they were in a deep embrace next to the exhibition case that held the collection of Egyptian cat mummies. Nothing was the same again. But it was the past. The present beckoned.

Now, Lisa Clarkson, let's see just how much you can resist the pull of the past. James Strather, let's start with your university.

She quickly discovered a result from James Strather's student rowing days.

So, that's definitely the right name. Judith went to get her red spiral-bound notebook from a kitchen drawer, pausing by the French windows before she returned to her MacBook. She sat back at the kitchen table and opened the notebook. She wrote 'James Strather' at the top of a page.

About half the pages of the red book were adorned with her precise handwriting. The perfectly formed letters were joined to each other with a slight forward slant, making neatly shaped words which cascaded tidily across and down the pages. She turned to the section headed 'Emails'. There was a list of over twenty email addresses, all structured in a similar way: a first name, a full stop, a surname, and three digits, although they were registered with different email providers. Most of the codes followed sequentially. One was for her sister, Kate. The last one was Sarah.Roper 312@gmail.com. She logged into Hotmail then set up an account for James.Strather313@hotmail.co.uk. She carefully noted the details in her notebook alongside the passwords and security questions she had used to create the electronic addresses of around twenty of her Facebook friends.

So, let's see what you're doing now, James. She worked

methodically through the Google search tools, carefully noting any information she gleaned about him. She found his CV and a video presentation for a job overseas. He was still in London, though. He did seem rather pompous, she thought, not at all like Rob. Ambitious, too. He had lots of friends on Facebook but not Lisa, nor Maya.

She stopped. This was going into new territory. Apart from her sister she had never faked real people. What if Rob or Lisa found out? But there would be no link back. How could there be? Wouldn't they think it was more likely someone from university if they suspected something? She began to feel uncomfortable. She was not sure why.

When in doubt do nothing.

The house was unusually silent for a moment, resting between the last movements of Beethoven's *Ninth Symphony*, when the doorbell rang, echoing in the silence. No one was expected. The sticker on the door advising hawkers and canvassers they were unwelcome was effective. At least she thought it was, as she rarely received any callers. The door knocker echoed loudly and impatiently. She opened the front door a fraction and eyed the green-clad courier through the crack, then opened it fully. He was holding a card envelope.

'Judith Crayvern?' The man offered a hand-held terminal to her and a cheap pen. She removed the cap to write her electronic signature.

'No, don't take the cap off,' he warned. 'You'll get me in trouble with my boss if I get ink all over the hand-held.'

She scrawled *Judith Crayvern* over the LED display and exchanged it for the packet. She doubted whether anyone could prove that was her signature in a court of law or not. It was just a shaky collection of joined-up letters. Someone must have decided this system worked, though.

Ode an die Freud.

'I know that,' said the courier, turning an ear towards the sound of the strings which seeped from the kitchen. 'We had it at our quiz night,' he said, then began to sing.

'Duh duh duh duh, duh duh duh duh, duh duh duh duh, duhhh.' He grinned. 'It's the European anthem, *Ode to Joy.*'

91

'Friedrich Schiller wrote it before anyone had thought of peacefully uniting Europe or leaving it. Thank you.'

She took the package and dismissed the tone-deaf courier politely. The anonymous tenor sternly welcomed her back to the kitchen as she eagerly pulled the brown cardboard envelope apart.

Her new passport.

Ja - wer auch nur eine Seele,
Sein nennt auf dem Erdenrund!

She waltzed around the kitchen holding the small maroon booklet as she sang Schiller's eighteenth-century chorus. She had once read the translation but could no longer remember its meaning, but she enjoyed the Teutonic resoluteness.

Was den großen Ring bewohnet,
Huldige der Sympathie!
Zu den Sternen leitet sie,
Wo der Unbekannte thronet.

She stopped and opened the passport. Well, she was no more impressed with the photograph that was now mounted between the embossed, laminated sheets than she had been when she had submitted her application. It was a pity that even the slightest smile was prohibited. After all, that had always been one of her best assets. Her smile and her eyes. No matter how tired she was, how wretched she was feeling, smiling would light up her face. She knew that. She just had to remember to do it.

She could not control her eyes so effectively, though. Martin had always referred to her dancing eyes. They twinkled even in the dark, he had said. She looked at her eyes in the mirror sometimes, willing them to twinkle and dance, but often she did not like what she saw. Her eyes, like dull black embers, stared back at her, accusing her.

She opened the kitchen drawer where she kept her notebook and placed the passport on top. It was reassuring to have, even though she had no imminent plans to travel.

Wednesday evening

'Four seasons pizza with jalapeños,' said Rob. 'It's what you chose last time. I got the coleslaw and potato salads as well.'

'You are spoiling me,' said Lisa, settling down on to the leather sofa and taking a slice. 'Where are Heather and Karl?'

'Flicks. Karl seems to have lost his interest in football recently.'

'Hah, yes. They don't seem to be coping very well with their early exit from Europe.'

Rob put a bottle of white wine and a glass on the low coffee table, squeezing it between the cartons and open pizza boxes and cans. He sat down and took a slice of pizza.

'I'm sorry, Lisa.'

'What?' Lisa put her pizza slice down and turned towards him. Her stomach churned. 'I'm sorry' often heralded a conversation that had an ominous ending. Rob was concentrating on the topping of his pizza.

'I'm sorry for not sharing with you.' He glanced at her.

'Oh?' Lisa failed to catch his eye.

'About what happened at work. I should have told you properly, not when Maya was there.'

'Oh.' Lisa munched on her pizza crust.

'I felt like I'd been kicked in the stomach. I didn't want to think about it. You'd been doing so well … things had been going so well, I didn't want to burst the bubble.' Rob turned up the sound of the television.

Lisa heaped some coleslaw on to her plate. She had to ask, not take the coward's way out.

'Did you tell Judith?'

'What?' Rob frowned. 'No, like I said, you were the first person I told. I have no idea how she knew the new manager's name. It's a mystery.'

'Rob, don't you think she tries to monopolise you sometimes?'

'How do you mean?'

'At the Indian, she was all over you.'

'I think she just enjoys the company.'

'Well she seems to enjoy your company over Keith's and mine. That's all I'm saying. What are you going to do now at MedTime?'

'Shush, they're coming on,' Rob said, topping Lisa's glass up. 'We can talk later. Let's hope we win, then the home leg will be a cinch.'

Tuesday morning
'Hello, hello.'

Judith turned to see Keith standing by the garage. She was filling the hanging baskets with blue and yellow spring flowers.

'Oh, you did startle me.'

'I just had a drop opposite. Mrs Jones. Perhaps you know her?'

Judith shrugged her shoulders.

'I don't think so.'

'Old lady. Seemed to be friendly with your next-door neighbour, Sam Barker.'

'Oh, her? Nosey busybody. Always wanting to know your business. I have no time for her.'

'She seems to think you're quite the party girl. Off gallivanting day and night, she said.' Keith said. Judith glowered. Keith shifted his weight from one foot to another uneasily. 'I was just wondering if you had any jobs that needed doing, as I was passing.'

For a moment Judith looked appalled by the idea, then changed her mind. She got hold of the clothes pole.

'I've been trying to dislodge the makings of a nest in the gutter. I think they're the ones that were in the dogwood. But I'm just not quite tall enough. Do you think you could do this?'

'Well, I don't know. It seems a bit high even for me,' Keith said, scratching his head under his cap. As Keith surveyed the gutter, Bunters pranced up the garden towards him and sat at his feet.

'I am sure you could if you tried,' Judith said, smiling warmly as she held her hand to her chest, her bright eyes shining. 'I have a ladder.'

'Mmm,' Keith said, finishing his second piece of ginger cake. 'That was scrumptious. I'll be back here for more jobs tomorrow,' he joked, 'just for the parkin.'

'I wouldn't advise it. I don't think that would be good for you at all,' Judith said, collecting the side plate. 'You should watch your waistline.' She could not help thinking he looked remarkably like a grey Coco the Clown every time she saw him without his cap.

'I don't think I've had such lovely cake since my Sandra's.'

'My Sandra?' said Judith, turning round from the sink. 'What do you mean, "my Sandra"? Why is it always "my Sandra"? You didn't own her. Which century do you live in?'

'It's just a manner of speaking, like you might say "my cat".'

'Well, Bunters *is* my cat. I'm his owner. You, however, did not own your wife.'

'No, I know I didn't, but I don't think anyone owns your cat. Bunters has his tea every day with Mrs Jones. I've just seen him.'

'He told you that, did he? I think you will find you are quite mistaken.'

She watched Keith's eyes wandering to look at the photographs behind the one of her sister.

'That's Martin. It's the anniversary of his death soon. Five years.' She sighed.

'Anniversaries are hard.'

'Every day is hard,' she countered.

'Yes. It takes a long time. I mean, you have such guilt when you lose a loved one.'

'Guilt? Why should I have guilt?'

'Well, for me, I never had time to say all I really felt. I feel guilty that I never told my Sandra how much I really loved her. The things I wish I'd done differently and all that. I thought everyone felt like that,' he said, quickly.

'Oh, I see what you mean. I thought you meant—'

'Meant what?'

'Well, that maybe it should have been me.'

'No, Judith, no. I didn't mean that.'

Judith looked at him with a wild, haunted look in her eyes.

'Ben and Martin were swept away. I was the only survivor. Why not me as well?' she said.

'Why would —? I guess I was just talking about me, how much I wished I could have made everything up to my Sandra, how I—' he stammered. 'I only found out afterwards that she knew.'

'Knew? Knew what?'

'That I hadn't always been, you know, well, faithful. But it was only the once. It was a big mistake.'

Judith gazed into the distant garden. Keith moved uncomfortably on his chair. She continued to stare into the distance, lost in her

95

thoughts, giving no sign that she had witnessed Keith's great confession.

Tuesday evening
Judith was engrossed with her mobile when Rob sat down on the bench next to her.

'I've left the others chatting with Taz,' Rob said. 'And how have you been?'

'Well, not so great. It's the anniversary this weekend.' Judith looked up into his eyes. 'The weather doesn't help – all the rain. I try to keep myself busy, though.'

'Chin up, Jude. Look forward, not backwards.' Rob put his arm round her back and squeezed her briefly.

'How's your job search going, anyway? Any luck?'

'I've decided that the only way I'm going to get another job is by starting my own business. I'm inviting myself to a second interview,' he said.

Judith laughed.

'Something will come up.'

'Yeah.'

'Look, I've bought myself a new toy to play with.' Judith showed Rob the phone. 'Top of the range. The camera's almost better than my digital camera.' She quickly took a photograph of Rob. 'Look at the resolution.' She showed him the snap. 'It's really fast on the Internet, too. Here's Willow Tree Avenue, and there's my house on Street View.'

'A red door ... Does that reflect your football allegiance?' Rob said, frowning.

'Martin was a rugger man. My father, too,' Judith said. 'What's the postcode for your house, Rob? It should be on Street View, too.'

'I hope you'll be putting that mobile away,' said Brian Cordon as he passed, three pints between his hands. 'I'll be watching you.'

'So in joint second place we have The Terminators and Prime Suspects with eighty-two, and in first place, The Dispossessed with eighty-four. So would the winning team collect their prizes, please?' the quizmaster said.

'Nearly,' said Keith. 'Next week.'

Rob high-fived Keith, then Judith, then Lisa.

'Well done, team,' he said. 'I reckon it was Max Bygraves that did for us on the music round. Next week we win. Right, Lisa, let's make "good show" comments to the Yah-Yahs, then we're off. See you on Wednesday at the match, Keith.'

'Thanks for the tickets, Keith. See you next week, Judith,' said Lisa.

Wednesday morning

The yellow beak was pecking. Pecking up and down, side to side. Pecking in time to a staccato beat. Judith looked away from the window but could still see the blackbird from the corner of her eye. That beady eye was always looking, judging. Sneakily stealing a glance, singing a cocky little tune, piercing the peace. Those others, flitting among the branches, infesting the bushes. Always watching, knowing.

There he goes again, hopping. Hopping up and down. Feathers like death. Stop it. She put the iron away and grimaced. *Just be still. Be still.* The garden was alive, teeming. It seemed possessed.

'Bunters, Bunters,' she called urgently. 'There you are. Time for some exercise. Yes, and no consorting with Mrs Jones.'

The cat trotted towards her and sat comfortably in front of the refrigerator. Sometimes he looked like he was smiling.

'No. Come on. Out. Just ... just go and do your stuff, frighten that lot off,' she commanded. The cat tilted its face towards her, paused as it looked her in the eye, and then languidly stretched its legs across the kitchen tiles before exiting through the cat flap. She observed the abrupt retreat of the unwelcome garden guests to the higher reaches of the trees with satisfaction. The blackbird flicked its wings on the topmost branch of the linden tree as it rattled a communal warning. Bunters sat upright on the lawn, surveying his prey patiently.

She sat at the kitchen table, lifted the lid of her laptop, and immediately accessed her emails. Nothing too much of interest, although there was a Google alert informing her that there was a result for MedTime Travel. She would look at that later. The

97

information about Rob's new manager had been very useful. The look on Lisa's face had been priceless.

She paused and looked at the still, silent garden then returned to her workstation and continued. She ran a quick search on Lisa Clarkson. She had found little of interest when she had googled her in the past, but now Lisa had actually made news in the Berger and Berger online newsletter as a newly appointed account executive. But she had learned more about the company at the pub quiz than she had from the Internet, and about Lisa, too.

Economics graduate, Durham University. Brought up by a single mother, errant father, one sister. Current boyfriend, Rob Granville. Clingy. Self-obsessed. Shares flat with Maya, whom she met at university. Wears skirts too short and too much make-up. Poor choice of hairdresser. Not a bad choice of perfume, though. Likes music and has encyclopaedic knowledge of the most banal trivia, but also inclined to be too serious. Supports any environmental cause that's in the news but also adds to the city's pollution by driving a car, although she usually leaves it behind so she can drink. A peculiar combination of vacuousness and dull earnestness. Enemies were Olivia and Tasmin, aka Taz. Rob called them the Yah-Yahs, for some reason.

She went to her Facebook pages. She hit Taz's link and went straight to her profile, which declared her to be an account executive at Berger and Berger. She clicked on the wall icon and read her recent status messages.

I am now a reformed character. True, m' dears.

Me rude? Rude? How dare she?

Loving being back in London. Party party time.

She wondered if Lisa knew that Tasmin was Rob's friend. Though Rob didn't seem to have noticed she was a 'friend' of his ex, Becca. With over 1,500 Facebook friends it was not surprising. Lisa, however, only had 220. *No posts from Rob. How disappointing.*

The cat flap creaked, announcing Bunters's return. He padded along to the refrigerator, where he meowed pitifully.

'Yes, you do deserve some milk now,' she said, opening the fridge door. She poured milk into a red plastic bowl. 'A job well done, I think. Next time, though, get him next time.' She picked up the cat and hugged him. The cat fought back, his eyes remaining fixed on the bowl, which seemed to be receding from his reach. She allowed him to break free and guzzle the milk.

'Just you and me, Bunters,' she sighed. 'We can't trust anyone.'

Wednesday evening
The black cab was slowly crawling through the dimly lit streets. A commentary of the match was playing on the radio. Lisa fidgeted in the back, repeatedly checking her watch and her text messages. Doing so was having no effect on the sluggish progress to the football stadium. She wished she had decided to walk when Metrolink had announced – with regret – that, because a car was stuck on the tram tracks at Holt Town, there was no service.

She took off her quilted jacket. Earlier, on her way to head office when she was crushed on a crowded underground train, she had regretted her decision to wear it. Now, as she squinted through the clunking windscreen wipers, she was glad she had. There was nothing much worse than spending ninety minutes watching a football match when all you could think about was the cold. As she rooted in her bag for her jumper and scarf there was a groan from the radio commentator.

'One goal down already,' said the driver.

Lisa could not see his face, but she knew he was smirking.

'I'm surprised they've got this far. They have no team spirit. All money and no commitment,' he continued.

Lisa wondered if the cabbie was deliberately choosing a slow route to sabotage her attempt to watch the match. That would be just typical, she thought, as she transformed from smart city girl to warmly dressed football fan. She had managed to call Rob to tell him the train from London was running late and to go straight to the ground, but now, when she tried to text and phone again, there was no response. Network overload.

It was a good thing Keith had given her the match ticket on Tuesday, otherwise everyone would be waiting for her, or perhaps she wouldn't be going at all. How long would Keith and Rob have waited before they would have decided to go inside and abandon her?

99

Lisa waited until the taxi driver found every penny of the change he owed her, then hurried into the pulsating stadium. As she walked through the almost empty food courts, past tributes to the heroes of old, there was a massive roar. When she stepped into the tiered seating area everyone was on their feet, cheering and dancing. She walked down the steep staircase towards row E. Her seat should be about three seats to the right but she could not see a gap. She scoured the backs of the spectators, then she saw Keith's cap, Rob's beanie, and then, where there should be a vacant seat, a tumble of wavy blonde hair.

She felt like an icicle had stabbed the pit of her stomach. Rob and Judith were jumping up and down, their arms around each other. As she watched they turned round and saw her. She was sure she saw a look of triumph in Judith's eyes. Rob grinned and waved then muttered something to Keith, who nudged the woman next to him and they moved along. Lisa took her seat next to Rob, holding her laptop bag tightly between her feet.

'Brilliant, eh? We're going to win this,' Rob said, hugging her.

'We thought we'd never see you tonight,' said Chocolate Box Woman, leaning across Keith and offering a box of chocolates. 'Your man was getting quite concerned when his phone wouldn't work.'

Lisa smiled weakly as she dug into a box of Celebrations. She tried very hard to concentrate on the game, but realised, as the crowd rose to celebrate a second goal, that she didn't even know which direction they were playing in.

As the crowd's chants ebbed and flowed with the tide of play, Lisa's head was filled with a jumble of images from the previous few weeks. The gym, the cinema, and celebrating her promotion – which was, of course, on Valentine's Day. Then the face in the library, the car outside her flat. Surely they were not all coincidences, figments of her imagination? Were they not just as contrived as Judith's appearance tonight? Lisa flinched as the caramel found a sensitive spot. What next?

Thursday morning
Lisa was in a better mood as she arrived in the reception of Bergers

just as the town hall clock chimed nine. Rob had been in great spirits as they had left the ground, and they had immediately got the bus to her flat, leaving Judith with Keith. The thoughts that had taunted Lisa during the match quickly melted away, as she had realised that Rob was clearly eager to spend time alone with her. Certainly there was no reason why Rob shouldn't have celebrated the goal with Judith. After all, that's what he did, with whoever was next to him. She had decided not to dwell on the reasons for Judith's surprise appearance. She was not going to be oversensitive any longer. But it was definitely odd.

Lisa was about to say 'Hello, Sally,' as she did every morning.

'Good morning, Lisa.'

Lisa stopped and stared. Judith, expensively attired in a grey trouser suit, was standing behind the reception desk.

'What are you doing here?' Lisa said.

'I'm covering for Sally. She's away for a few days. The agency I work for has asked me to cover. I think I will like it here.'

'What agency? Since when have you worked for an agency?'

'Didn't I tell you? I was feeling rather idle, even with the distraction of the gym, so I thought I would do some temping work. If I have too much time on my hands I just get so anxious about everything, especially at this time of year. I decided things must change.'

Judith twirled her pen between her fingers, conveying an air of confidence and authority.

'Isn't it a coincidence that this job was the first they offered me?'

Lisa sat down at her desk and swigged a large gulp of hot coffee.

A coincidence? A coincidence? How can it be? But it must be a coincidence that Sally is off, and the temping agency just happened to have her on their list.

Well, only partly a coincidence. She could have found out which temping agency Bergers used. She also knew enough about the company to convince them she would fit in here. But why would she want to? Was Judith stalking her?

Friday lunchtime

'Did you get a choice, Judith, or was it a complete surprise when they told you that you would be coming to Bergers?' Lisa asked, sliding the plate with the remains of her chicken sandwich to one side.

'It was a complete surprise, darling. I had no idea at all,' Judith said. 'Aren't you going to eat that salad, Lisa? It's a pity to waste good food.' Lisa shook her head.

'Well, we're all so very glad you are here,' said Tasmin.

'Delighted,' Olivia said as she beamed at the older woman.

'Is it just while Sally's on holiday?' Lisa asked, as Judith picked at the cucumber and tomato that Lisa had left on her plate. Judith munched on the salad, unable to answer, nodding.

'Of course, when Sally's on maternity leave they'll have to arrange cover. You might be able to work here for months,' Olivia said.

'Well, Andy did mention it, when we had lunch yesterday,' Judith said.

Lisa's heart sank. She had wondered where Judith had been the previous lunchtime and now she knew. Ingratiating herself with Andy. This morning Tasmin had seemed quite surprised when Lisa had accepted her invitation to lunch with Judith and Olivia. Lisa was well aware it was made as a polite gesture rather than out of a genuine interest in her company. After all, they spent most days working and chatting together behind the fig trees. But, even though it meant tolerating Olivia's company during her lunch break, she was intent on discovering why Judith's presence was so pervasive in her life. If, as she had suspected, Judith was seeking Rob's attention why was she working here, not at MedTime?

'I'm glad to be fully occupied this week,' Judith said. 'It's the fifth anniversary this weekend. It feels like all my efforts to move on are being tested. I find myself trying to shake off this black cloud that follows me around. Andy was very understanding when I told him what had happened to Martin. He's delightful, isn't he?'

'Andy is lovely,' said Tasmin. 'Very fair.'

'Yah, he's a decent guy but he doesn't suffer fools gladly, either,' said Olivia. 'He's no pushover. You might be allowed one mistake, but not two. He's got a very sharp business mind, but he's charming with it.'

'Like his wife,' added Lisa.

'You're really doing well, Judith,' Tasmin said. 'Whatever you might feel, you look radiant. You seem very confident behind reception already,' Tasmin said.

'Very confident,' said Lisa, forcing a smile. *Or like the cat that got the cream, and is planning on seconds*, she thought as she reminded her colleagues of the time.

'Don't look so glum, Lisa darling,' Judith said, standing up and following Olivia to the cafe door alongside Lisa. 'Really, looking miserable is no way to motivate a team. Smile. It's not as if you have anything to be worried about.'

Hanging on the telephone

Saturday morning
Lisa was on a mission to lose seven pounds. She had been pushing weights in the gym for the second time that week and, instead of lazily savouring melting chocolate and sweet buttery bread, was on her way to a Zumba class. She was quite impressed with her own activity, and the scales showed that her effort was proving worthwhile. She was sitting on a bench tying a shoelace as Gemma Barker came through the changing room door.

'Hi, Gemma,' Lisa said.

'Hello, Lisa. And how are *you* today?' Gemma said, with the demeanour of a stern schoolteacher reprimanding a naughty pupil. She walked to the other side of the changing room and sat down.

Lisa glanced over at the older woman, who was deliberately looking away from her. She felt very uneasy. Perhaps Gemma had been having a bad day. No, that's just making excuses. Gemma had intended to snub her. What had she done wrong? No, what did Gemma think Lisa had done wrong? She did not really know her well enough to ask.

She couldn't possibly mention this to Rob. He would think she was becoming paranoid. Was she? She wished Maya were back so she could get some advice. Maybe she should text.

Saturday night
Judith woke up, tangled in the sheets, thinking she was choking. The tinkle of rolling glass pierced the dull whooshing of the wind as beads of rain buffeted the windows. She tensed, gripping the pillows. She felt as if unwelcome memories were battering against the glass, trying to invade her sanctuary and consume her. The dim table light, which could make the room look cosy, offered no comfort.

She turned up the volume of the radio. A BBC correspondent gloomily described the suffering of refugees in East Africa. She switched to her music app. The fourth movement of Beethoven's *Ninth Symphony*, the chaotic *Ode to Joy*, boomed through the bedroom. She got up and walked through the upstairs rooms, switching on all the lights. Her home seemed strange and alien. There seemed to be nowhere she belonged. In the spare bedroom she picked up a set of newly laundered sheets and held them against her bare chest, inhaling their fresh, dry scent.

She stared through the shimmering rain as it washed down the windowpane, and at the neat, cultivated gardens, which were now oblongs of dark sodden turf and tumbling dead leaves. The trees played like recalcitrant members of a wild, discordant orchestra, each swaying to their own rhythm as the wind conducted their movements. The wooden skeleton of the ash tree swayed and groaned, while the bare copper beech, defrocked of its rich foliage, jigged to a syncopated beat. As the rain hammered against the glass, she was transfixed by the anarchic dance.

She returned to her bedroom and pulled off the old sheets, dropped them in the linen basket, then she smoothed the new crisp ones around the corners of the bed. She slid between the sheets then, oblivious to the sound of the radio, switched on the DVD player, and watched the images flick across the television screen on the wall opposite.

In the morning she awoke feeling cold. She was curled on the slate tiles of the kitchen floor under the heavy table. Her hands were entwined around a chair's leg and her knees were pulled up to her chin. Mud, pink petals, and leaves were smeared on the floor and clinging to her skin.

Not again.

She could hear an urgent meowing in the hallway. Her arms stiff, her body shivering, she crawled out from her refuge and opened the door for Bunters. She ignored his pleas for attention as he buffeted his head against her calves. Instead, she went upstairs and stepped into the hot, steamy water of the shower.

The only way she could get rid of the ghosts haunting her head was to go back. To be there. The lake was drawing her back.

Sunday morning

Rob was standing on the pavement studying the pairs of immaculately groomed houses. He leaned into the open window of

105

the car and casually scraped a lock of dark brown hair from his forehead. Lisa stretched across from the driver's seat to meet his eyes. A stray glance, a careless, familiar gesture, still had the power to make her heart race.

'This is definitely the road she showed me the other night on her mobile. Willow Tree Avenue.' He smiled, revealing just a hint of nervousness. 'Perhaps it would be better if we left the car here and walked.'

Lisa nodded as she closed the windows. Rob's unexpected telephone call from the changing pavilions, nearly thirty minutes earlier, had interrupted her plans to spend a leisurely morning reading the newspapers while half-watching the television. The combination of a hangover and the memory of Gemma's unwarranted frostiness had quashed any desire to return to the gym, and she had effortlessly returned to her Sunday morning routine. Rob, however, had never missed a Sunday morning football match, whatever unexpected pleasures he had enjoyed the night before. He loved every moment on the pitch and had strong opinions, which he was keen to share, about the characters of unreliable teammates.

Rob's voice had carried an edge, an anxiety, she had never heard before. She had felt apprehensive as she rummaged in the laundry basket for her jeans and long navy blue sweater. Despite her urgency, she had still made time to highlight her eyes with a line of kohl, dab her lips with gloss, and squirt on a spray of Juicy Couture before driving, on the cusp of the speed limit, to pick up Rob at the playing fields.

The car locks clunked as Lisa activated the remote control. She screwed up her eyes for a moment in the glare of the sun. A solitary blackbird's song, intermingling with the dull judder of a lawnmower and a distant peal of bells, confirmed the arrival of spring. Overhead an aeroplane packed with holidaymakers silently soared away into the milky blue sky. As she joined Rob on the pavement, she felt a single light stroke of his fingertips on the back of her neck. It felt like a kiss.

They walked in an easy rhythm past the rows of semi-detached houses, looking for some distinguishing feature that marked out Judith's home from the rest.

'This is it,' said Rob, as he pointed at a double-fronted house. A large silver birch tree that almost shrouded the bay windows, still resplendent with their original stained-glass panels, overlooked it. Rob opened the single gate and walked up the footpath. He repeatedly rang the doorbell, and then impatiently knocked on the red front door. Lisa peered through the window into the living room, which was furnished with two large navy blue sofas. Empty.

'You said she sounded very agitated on the phone,' Lisa said.

'Yeah. Kept rambling about Martin and how she couldn't cope. I hadn't heard her like that before. Did she try to call you?'

'No.'

'I tried calling her back when I arrived at the football ground, but her phone just went on to voicemail. That's when I called you. Perhaps she's in there. Perhaps she's tried to … you know …'

'She's probably gone shopping.'

'No, really, the texts and phone calls I've had recently … They've been quite, quite dark.'

'She looked fine to me on Friday.' Lisa decided not to ask the questions that crowded her mind, and said, instead, 'Let's look round the back.'

They walked along the path that skirted the front of the house to join a long tarmac driveway, then followed the drive towards the garage. At the bottom four tall plastic bins stood upright, like sentries, at the entrance of the garden. A Cheshire brick extension jutted on to a patio, beyond which was a flawless, deep green lawn. Baskets, filled with trailing cascades of blue and yellow spring flowers, hung from the wall. Lisa squinted through the semi-glazed back door, trying to focus through the dimpled glass. Rob looked through the kitchen window.

'Are you sure this is Judith's house?' Lisa said.

'Yes, this is definitely it. She showed me on her phone at the quiz. And there's the supporting evidence.' Rob pointed at the bottom of the back door. 'The cat flap.'

Lisa knocked loudly on the door.

'Judith!'

Rob joined in, beating heavily and shouting,

Jude! Jude! Judith!' He stepped back, frowned, and turned to

Lisa. 'Perhaps we need to go in.'

'Isn't that a bit drastic?' said Lisa.

'We have to do something.'

Why? Lisa thought, but said, 'We could dial 999.'

'What would we say? They might not take it seriously. It could take too long.'

'Not necessarily.'

'It could be too late. We have to do something.' Rob looked around the garden. 'What was it she said?' he muttered. 'I know ...' He walked across to the nearest hanging basket and felt blindly with his hands among the flowers, finally retrieving a key. 'It's not breaking in with this.'

'How did you know that was there?'

'Elementary, my dear Watson.' Rob's demeanour lightened a little. 'Well, actually, she mentioned it at the Indian. She told me she was determined not to lock herself out again.' He turned the key in the lock.

'She's very trusting. Is there anything she doesn't tell you?' Lisa asked, thinking that she had managed to rid her voice of any hint of resentment.

'Why shouldn't she? I'm a very trustworthy guy.' He swaggered, relaxing for a moment as the door opened. He replaced the key in the hanging basket and, wiping his hands on the back of his tracksuit pants, followed Lisa into the kitchen.

'Judith,' Lisa called. 'Judith.' She looked around. Gleaming, oiled beech worktops, polished black slate floor tiles, Shaker-inspired pale blue kitchen units, and a bank of brushed-steel ovens. Not a pot or a pan in sight. The humming of a large American-style refrigerator only emphasised the silence. In the centre of a large oak table, surrounded by eight chairs, was a closed MacBook. The only evidence of habitation was an empty cat basket and a red bowl on the floor.

'It's more like a kitchen showroom than a working kitchen. Who on earth does she entertain here?' Lisa said, as she walked over to the worktop next to the fridge. She picked up the largest of three framed photographs.

'This must be Martin. Not bad at all,' she murmured. 'There's no sign of her, Rob. She must have gone out. Maybe we should go.'

Rob looked at the photograph briefly and frowned.

'She didn't seem in a fit state. Perhaps she's upstairs,' he said. 'She'd have heard us.'

'Not if she's comatose. Maybe she's tried to do something stupid.'

For a moment, Lisa saw panic in his eyes as he tried to articulate his fears. Rob turned and moved out of the kitchen into the hall, which was immaculately carpeted in peacock blue.

'What did she say to you? Tell me exactly what she said.'

'It was on voicemail. She said she had gone over that wretched day in Hazelmere so many times. She was weighed down with the ghosts haunting her. She couldn't bear it any longer.'

Lisa followed Rob as he quickly looked into the main living room. Two dark blue chenille sofas were angled on a television. A digital camera and a remote occupied a glass-topped table. A monochrome print of a pair of flamenco dancers hung above the fireplace. A faint trace of rose potpourri drifted in the air.

'Judith,' Rob shouted again. He looked up the stairwell, which was hung with several large gold-framed Victorian prints. He pointed at the first, at the bottom of the staircase. 'Look, that's the painting from the quiz night. *The Lady of Shalott*, just as she described it.'

Lisa stopped and touched the picture frame as she studied it. Rob was breathing heavily next to her, as if he was gulping the air. A woman, dressed in cream medieval-style robes, her face a deathly pallor, and her long hair unkempt, was staring out of the painting as if in a trance. She was sitting in what looked like a grand canoe, drifting down a river.

'Exquisite,' said Lisa, dryly, 'but very contrived, staged.'

Rob bounded up the stairs, two steps at a time. Sunbeams filtered through the leaded glass, brightening the dim stairwell, as he reached the corner landing.

'What's this?' he said, squinting at the carpet and bending down. He picked up two delicate pink petals between his fingers. He stroked the carpet. 'That looks like mud, part of a muddy footprint.'

He took the last three steps in one leap. Four glossy white doors, all slightly ajar, led off the square landing. Rob headed for the first one. Lisa trailed behind, watching, as he quickly looked around the gleaming chrome and ceramic bathroom and checked there was nothing in the bath. A little condensation clung to the window.

'Not here,' he said.

Lisa followed as he pushed open the door of the farthest room. It was empty, apart from a large mirrored wardrobe, a television, and some exercise equipment. Lisa watched as Rob opened the wardrobe doors to reveal shelves of neatly folded bedding.

'Nothing,' he said.

Lisa grimaced and moved on round the landing to the adjacent room at the back of the house. She slowly opened the door and peered inside. The room was decorated in shades of aqua. Green and cream thick drapes bordered the window. A large bed, covered in a silky, sea green quilt was positioned against a wall in the centre of the room.

'Aagh. What's that?' shrieked Lisa. Rob rushed up behind her.

'What? What is it? Is she dead? Is there a body?'

'Something touched my leg.' Lisa grabbed Rob's hand tightly, and together they scanned the room. Something made a lightning leap on to the window ledge and sat upright, its gaze fixed on the garden.

'The cat,' said Rob, holding on to Lisa's shoulder. 'Thank God, it's only the cat.'

Bunters turned his head, looking over his shoulder at the interlopers, then renewed his interest in the garden. His tail wagged fiercely from side to side.

The quiet of the room was disturbed abruptly by the rising sound of *The Dam Busters* theme. Rob pulled his phone from his pocket.

'It's Judith,' he whispered.

'Judith? No.'

'I can't answer.'

'Why not?'

'Why not? This. All this! I'm in her house. In her bedroom.'

'Tell her that. It will make her day ... I'll answer. We need to find out what she's up to.' Lisa took the phone and a deep breath, 'Hello, Judith. Judith, where are you?'

There was silence for a moment, then Lisa heard the muffled

voice of Judith, far weaker and sadder than she had ever heard before. She understood why Rob had been so worried.

'She says you've been trying to call her,' Lisa whispered, needlessly, as she was using the mute button on the phone. She released the button and raised her voice. 'It's Lisa, Judith. I have Rob's phone. He's gone to the football. Yes, he forgot his phone so I, er, answered it ... Yes, I always do ... Yes, he trusts me. Where are you?' Lisa listened, looking at Rob, who looked anxious and uncomfortable.

'She says she's in the car at the lake where Martin died. She says it's the last time.'

'Christ, why didn't I think of the lake?' Rob muttered. 'What does she mean when she says, "the last time", Lisa?'

Lisa watched Rob as he moved over to the window and absently stroked the cat's grey-and-white fur. He looked out over the cat's head then turned around abruptly, gesticulating towards the back garden.

'She's here,' he whispered.

'What? "She's here." What do you mean?' Lisa mouthed.

'Her car is here, on *her* drive, with *her* in it. Look. There.' He pointed between the curtains.

Lisa forced herself to concentrate on the voice in her ear.

'Why is that, Judith?' Lisa said, as she walked over to join Rob by the window. She could see a red Audi parked at the end of the drive in front of the garage and inside was the unmistakeable, perfectly coiffed head of Judith. Below she could hear the soft rumbling of the car engine. The same sound echoed faintly in her ear. She pressed the mute button again.

'Let's confront her,' Lisa said. 'I've had enough of these games.'

'How do we explain the fact we're in her house? In her bedroom? We need to go. Keep her talking.'

'We could tell the truth. We've done nothing wrong. We were worried about her, or you were. And we could also ask *her* to tell the truth,' Lisa added ardently, then returned to the mobile. 'Why do you think Hazelmere is so comforting, Judith?' Lisa was almost mimicking Judith, desperate for something to say. She switched the mute button again.

111

'The truth could be seen as breaking and entering,' Rob responded, in an edgy whisper. 'How do you think that story would go down at Bergers? We need to go.'

Lisa pictured Judith sitting with Olivia and Tasmin, recounting her version of Sunday morning, while a police officer waited at her desk. That would be just like her.

'Do you think she's lured us here?' she asked Rob.

Rob lifted his eyes up to the ceiling, then shook his head.

'We need to go. Keep her talking.'

Lisa nodded apprehensively, desperately trying to think of something to say.

'What's happening there, Judith?' She thought she detected a trace of petulance in Judith's voice. The sadness and despair had gone.

Bunters bounded down from the window ledge and through the bedroom door. Lisa followed him on to the landing, where he stopped at the top of the stairs. The open door of the remaining unexplored room beckoned. Lisa pushed it open as Rob closed the other bedroom door.

'What are you doing? We've got to go,' Rob said, as he began to descend the stairs. Lisa swung the door wide open. The heady scent of amber and cedar hung heavy in the air.

'I just thought we might have to hide,' Lisa said, turning towards him.

'We don't want to hide. We'll be trapped. We want to get out before she comes in. Front door.' Rob started running down the stairs. 'Then it will be like we were never here. Keep her talking.'

'It might not ... Fuck, Rob. See this ...'

The curtains were closed, but the bedroom lamp softly illuminated the room in shades of violet. A large double bed, draped with a purple velvet throw and strewn with cushions, was set against the back wall. Next to it was a bedside table, crammed with a radio alarm clock, a lamp, a remote control, and some framed photographs. Opposite the table a large flat-screen television and small pile of DVDs rested on a chest of drawers. A large angled triple mirror, perched on the dressing table, eerily replicated the photographs which hung on the opposite wall.

'Now come on. Come on. Do as I say.' Rob went back up the stairs and pulled on Lisa's hand as the cat shimmied down the stairs in front of them. 'Keep her talking.'

'Yes, yes, I'm still here,' Lisa said, softly. 'It's not the best connection.'

They crept swiftly down the stairs as Lisa made sympathetic noises into the phone.

'Yes, I will tell him. As soon as he's finished football, I will tell him you called. He'll see you at the quiz on Tuesday, too. We'll both be there, looking forward to … to winning,' Lisa continued, her voice flat and emotionless.

'Aagh, you bugger,' Rob yelped, as he stepped into the hall. 'Lise, come on.'

'Shush, what is it?' she mouthed.

'That cat. I think it's drawn blood.' He turned the latch on the front door. It opened with a click. He swung the door open and looked up and down the road. He gestured for Lisa to follow.

'Bye, Judith,' Lisa said, and closed her mobile without waiting for the reply.

Lisa's head was resting on the steering wheel of her car. Rob had rolled up his tracksuit bottoms and was examining his calf.

'That cat whacked me with its paw,' he said. 'It was waiting at the bottom of the stairs.'

Lisa looked up.

'Let me see,' she said, brushing her hand across his leg. There was a small droplet of blood and a wafer-thin red scratch beneath the black hairs which sprawled across Rob's olive skin. 'It's just a scratch. I think it's unlikely to be terminal.'

'It's made a hole in my trackies.'

Lisa looked in her mirror. She could see the cat in the distance, surveying them from the gatepost.

'Maybe you could ask her for compensation when you phone her after the football match you're playing in is over. You have an hour.'

Rob grunted.

'Do you think we're safe here?'

'I can't drive at the moment. Give me a few minutes.'

113

'Thanks for coming over, and for being so brave,' he said. They held each other, exhausted.

'What did you see in that room?' he asked.

Lisa groaned.

'It was her bedroom. That other room must have been the spare one. It was beautifully decorated, in sumptuous shades of purple velvet and satin and photos. Lots of photos everywhere. It was like … like she'd made a shrine.'

'A shrine? A shrine to Martin?' said Rob.

Lisa remembered the portrait smiling at her from the wall, and the mirrored images tessellated above the dressing table.

'No.' She took a deep breath. 'Not to Martin. A shrine to you.'

Don't look back in anger

Late Sunday morning

Judith did not go straight into her house. Instead she left the keys in the lock and her handbag and groceries on the doorstep while she returned to the garage. She carried out the patio furniture, a round table, and two stacks of chairs. They were bulky, but easy enough to lift. She rolled the heavy parasol base under the table and slotted in the sun umbrella, although she did not unroll it. Not quite sunny enough. Then she opened the door as Bunters dashed between her legs and into the kitchen, where he positioned himself patiently in front of the fridge. She filled a shelf with packets of cat food as Bunters nuzzled her legs with his face.

Irritated by the cat's incessant meowing, she dispensed the contents of a packet into a bowl and put it on the floor before preparing her own fresh coffee. Damn. She remembered she had met Keith in the supermarket when she was buying the cat food. What if Lisa found out she hadn't been to Hazelton? Well, she would just deny everything, make Lisa think she was imagining things.

She opened a kitchen drawer and took out a pair of oversized Prada sunglasses, picked up her coffee cup, and went out on to the terrace, as she liked to call the Yorkshire stone patio. Bunters lay on his back, twisting from side to side as he peered down at his chubby, furry belly. The garden was quiet and still, apart from two cackling magpies resting in the overhanging branches of Mr Baker's trees.

She sipped the hot coffee while looking admiringly at her refection in the kitchen window: shades, crisp white shirt, and well-cut jeans. Although it was not quite the south of France, it was very pleasant when the sun was out. Unconsciously, she pursed her lips as she replayed the morning's events in her head. She had been so relieved when Rob's phone had finally been answered. When she had called earlier that morning it had switched to voicemail. Again and again. She had left messages at first, but then she had just hung up when there was no answer.

She had been dismayed when Lisa answered, lost for words at

first. Lisa had no right to answer Rob's phone. It was an infringement of his privacy, and her own. She wondered if Lisa's right to answer Rob's phone extended to eavesdropping on his messages as well. Lisa had seemed very intrusive, asking her lots of probing questions. But she had not betrayed her thoughts, despite her disappointment.

Of course, Rob would have been playing football. She had known that, but she had quite lost her sense of time that morning. Lisa, clearly, had not gone to the gym, and was taking the couch potato option again. For a moment she had worried that Lisa might decide to visit her, so she had said that she was at Hazelmere, which had almost been true, since she had been on her way there an hour before.

She had intended this to be her farewell visit to the lake, having decided that she had to let her memories go, not nurture them. She had been about to join the dual carriageway when she had seen the signpost to Hazelmere next to one pointing homewards. It was an epiphany. She had to change now, not tomorrow, and had driven all the way back round the roundabout. By the time she was driving through the suburbs again she had felt a sense of achievement. She had already started to put the past behind her, for good.

Five years had gone so very quickly. It seemed only yesterday that the police had dropped her at home, after questioning her. They had been very kind and had arranged for her car to be brought home, so she did not have to go back to the Hazelmere car park to collect it. She had rebuffed their offer to contact a friend to comfort her. She could not think of anyone she had wanted to see. Finally, she had told them she would call her sister, later, when she would be back home from work, and ask her to come round.

After the police had dropped her off she had opened her door to a deathly stillness, so profound it seemed animated. She had picked up the empty dog bowl and cradled it in her hands and then carried it to the bin. As she had opened the lid with her foot she had stopped, and set the bowl down on the granite worktop. Not too soon. He might be found alive, unlike Martin. There had been no mistake. His skin had been icy cold. He had looked like a wax mannequin, white, lifeless. A stranger, no one she knew, most definitely dead.

116

She had gone to work on Monday. She had not known what else to do. Doing nothing at all was unbearable. Her colleagues had seemed to tiptoe around her, treating her like fragile glass, offering her cups of coffee, speaking almost in whispers. No one had asked her about Saturday and Hazelmere, or Martin.

She remembered returning home from work later that week. Bunters had looked down at her from the landing, like a haughty grey-and-white sphinx, his ears tense and alert. In a flash he had leaped down the stairs, meowing urgently, trailing closely at her heels as she had walked into the kitchen past the wicker cat carrier. He had rubbed his head against her calves, his mewing growing louder and louder. She had poured food into Ben's bowl and watched while the cat devoured it urgently. Finally, she had picked him up.

'Oh Bunters, Martin has gone. I'm sorry. Martin won't be coming back. We have to look after each other now.' She had clung on to the cat, stroking his fur over and over again. Unusually, the cat had tolerated her desperate embrace.

Alone that night she had sobbed until she was gasping for air, her throat tightening, her heart pounding. She had felt totally alone in her grief, gulping as if she was drowning. The door had creaked open and Bunters had bounded on to the top of the bed, strolling up the duvet until he was sitting next to her face. Then he had softly placed a paw on her cheek. She had put her hand around his warm, silky body. Somehow that had kept her going.

She surveyed the garden. Small green leaves that had unfurled in the sun nearly hid the red branches of the dogwood. There was hardly a trace of the storm. She felt calm now. Last night was behind her. Bunters jumped on her lap and started kneading his paws into her trousers.

'No claws,' she said, firmly, stroking the back of his neck, feeling his bones beneath the soft fur. 'I have to make this work, Bunters. To live a new life.' She was looking to the future, like Rob said she should. He would be proud of her. But he hadn't phoned. He hadn't phoned because dull little Lisa hadn't told him she'd been calling. That was why.

~

Rob was sleeping heavily, lying across the almost cream couch. Lisa had been awake for ten minutes. Although the drowsiness had gone, every muscle in her body felt heavy with fatigue. She had got up without disturbing him and had tiptoed into the kitchen, where she had poured herself two glasses of water – which she had gulped back one after the other. She filled one of the glasses again, carried it back into the living room, and sat on the edge of the couch. She looked at her watch. It was only one o'clock.

Rob stirred.

'Jesus,' he laughed, without any humour. 'Jesus. What was that all about?'

He smiled, but Lisa felt there was an uneasiness about him, a vulnerability she had not seen before. Rob was good at smiling. He could smile and joke even when he was worried. He used his wit like a suit of armour to deflect any attempts to reveal his true feelings. She offered him the water, which he guzzled greedily.

'That was an Oscar-winning performance,' Lisa said. 'Meryl Streep had better watch out. I knew Judith had film-star looks, but I didn't realise she had such accomplished acting skills as well.'

'You're wicked.' Rob pulled at her hand and pulled her closer. 'She's a sad woman.'

Lisa pulled back.

'No, she's a liar. Whatever she said to you, she's a liar. She's just manipulating us. She's always turning up unexpectedly. Then she lies about where she is. I wouldn't be surprised if she'd lured us there. And don't forget that room, full of photos of you. She's crazy.'

'Are you sure it was me?'

Lisa looked at him. He was being deadly serious.

'You are unbelievable. It was unmistakeably you. There was a photo of you playing football, one with your jacket over your shoulder looking into the distance. One of you smiling, top off, cocktail in hand, with a blue sea in the background. I can't remember them all – it was a bit gloomy – but it was you. Yes, she certainly likes to go to bed thinking of you,' Lisa said. 'So tell me, what exactly has she been texting and phoning you about?'

'How she always felt very depressed around the time of Martin's death, swamped by all the memories.'

'Nothing new there, then.'

'And she kept saying how much she missed him over and over again. How it was all a tragic accident. She felt as if the lake might be calling her back. Then she said how she couldn't sleep at night, that the past seemed to be more real than the present.' He was gazing up at the ceiling, his face expressionless.

'And she texted all this?'

'Mostly. Sometimes there were some phone messages, too. And chat, though not so much of that.'

'Why didn't you tell me?'

'I wanted to, but you were so anti-Judith last week I thought I'd better not. I felt sorry for her, Lise.' Rob looked at her and touched her hand. 'She seems so fragile at times. Can't you see that?'

'What exactly did you say?' Lisa said.

'I said she should look to the future, that she had a lot going for her. I just tried to get her to be positive, but I just got more and more messages. Heather said I should ignore her.' Rob sighed. 'So I stopped replying, but then the texts and calls became increasingly desperate, dark. One said she couldn't go on, there was no point, she was drowning under the weight of the past. No one would miss her.'

'She seemed very positive and in control when I saw her at work on Friday,' said Lisa. 'She didn't mention any of this to me.'

'Perhaps she thinks you're not approachable.'

Lisa eyed him.

'I see a calculating bitch who has got the object of her desire around her manipulative little finger.'

'I think you've got it wrong. Don't you see that haunted look in her eyes sometimes? She has no one. I couldn't just abandon her. I wanted to tell you, you know. But after she started working at Bergers and you, well ... I didn't.'

'Because I'm unapproachable, I'm cold. Are you saying I'm part of Judith's problem?'

'Come on, Lise. Don't you think it would be awful to lose a lover like that? I can't imagine how I'd feel if I suddenly lost you.' Rob stroked her face.

'It's not Martin's photos she has in her bedroom. It's yours.'

Rob moved uncomfortably. He didn't believe her because he did

119

not want it to be true, she thought. Her heart was racing again, but this time there was a heaviness within her as well. She felt she needed to do something. She picked up her laptop from the coffee table and sat back down on the sofa with it resting on her thighs.

She looked up at him.

'Right, I want to know more about Judith. Let's start with Martin. I think Keith said he died about five years ago. How do you spell her surname?'

'Her surname?'

'You're always chatting with her on Facebook. Doesn't she use her surname on that?'

'Let me think. Yes. Crayvern. C-r-a-y-v-e-r-n.'

'Let's see if Google can reveal anything.' Lisa typed on the keyboard. 'Yes, here we are. *Tragic hero and dog die in storms.* That must be him. *Martin Crayvern, 45, Director of Hazelton Museum, drowned as storms lashed the country. On Saturday afternoon Crayvern was walking near the River Hazel when the river broke its banks, destroying the footbridge near Hazelmere. The Director bravely tried to save a dog that was stranded on the shattered bridge but he and the golden retriever were swept away when a violent torrent of water swept down the valley engulfing them.*

Crayvern had transformed the museum since his appointment five years ago. He was a popular figure locally and recently received a prestigious award for the museum's educational programmes. Crayvern is survived by his wife, Judith, 46.

Two more people lost their lives in the storms which swept through Britain this weekend.'

Lisa looked up.

'It's what she said. And I recognise him from the photo in the kitchen.'

'What a surprise,' said Rob.

The silence that followed was suddenly broken by the rising chords of *The Dam Busters.* Rob pulled his phone from his pocket, glanced at it, then threw it on the sofa. The music eventually stopped. Moments later an upbeat Latin rhythm began to play. Lisa looked at the display on her phone.

'Don't even think about it,' he said, tensely.

120

Lisa set the computer back on the coffee table and pushed it away.

'Did you block her chat?' Lisa asked.

'No.'

'Why not?'

Rob shrugged.

'It didn't seem important.'

'Rob, what have you been doing to make her so, so enamoured of you? No, obsessed. That's what she is.'

'Nothing.' He got up. 'Look I'm going to The Sun to buy the lads a drink to make up for letting them down.'

'You're not going to block her, then?'

Rob took the computer and logged on to his Facebook account.

'Be my guest. You're me now. Block anyone you want. I trust you not to dishonour my name.' He kissed Lisa's cheek and picked up his jacket.

She heard the front door slam.

Lisa studied Rob's Facebook page. She felt both triumphant and guilty, like an invisible spy. No, an agent provocateur. With a few taps of the keyboard she had the power to influence events, not merely observe them.

A list of notifications was displayed next to the photographs of some of his 1,532 friends. Most were comments from his football mates, comprehensible only to the team members of Western Blues. She was about to click on Judith's name when she noticed a familiar photograph: Tasmin holding a Martini glass, as if toasting the photographer. Lisa felt a surge of resentment, although she was not sure whether it was against Tasmin or Rob. Perhaps it was both.

What have they been saying to each other? she wondered.

She tapped on Tasmin's name, which took her to her colleague's page. She tapped on the relationship history tab. Nothing. Well, Tasmin would have just sent a friend request to Rob and he would, of course, have accepted, just as he had done to hundreds of others. Why not? She felt warm towards Tasmin again. They were getting on well, now. Then she saw a comment that Tasmin had written several weeks before on her wall:

Me, rude? Rude? How dare she?
Olivia had commented:
She's the rude one. Forget it.
Fuck Olivia, Lisa thought.
The computer pinged. Lisa started. At the bottom of the screen she read:
Judith is typing.
Hola, Rob!
She typed, *Hola, Judith!* then deleted *Judith* and retyped *Jude.* Motionless, she sat looking at the screen, trying to decide whether to hit the send key or not. She continued to type and reread her message:
Hola Jude! Get out of my life, you lying bitch.
Her finger hovered over the send button as Rob's words repeated in her head:
'You're me now. I trust you not to dishonour my name.'
As she reread the words she had typed on the screen she realised she was holding her breath, as if the slightest sound would make Judith aware that she was eavesdropping. Then she deleted her typing and restricted Judith's and Tasmin's access to Rob's Facebook pages and messages.
She was just about to log off when she remembered that she could read all the history of Rob and Judith's chat. It was all flippant banter, she realised, mainly prompted by Judith. Then she saw a message from Rob:
Adios, bonita!

Beyoncé was singing 'Crazy in Love' on the music channel as Lisa was flicking through the Sunday papers, although she could not remember anything she had read. Something was preying on her mind. Something other than Rob's affectionate use of Spanish, but she could not work out what it was. She folded the newspapers and piled them in the corner of the room, then puffed up the cushions of the sofa.
She had just opened her laptop when the doorbell buzzed several times. Rob hugged her as he came through the doorway. Lisa could sense tension in the tautness of his shoulder muscles. Although the

freshness of the drizzly spring evening was still clinging to him, she could smell the rancid tang of beer on his breath and a hint of a cigarette.

'*Hola, bonito,*' she said smiling.

Rob gave her a puzzled, oblique look.

'Were they all there?' she asked.

'Yes, everyone. They gave me a ribbing, as I expected. Keith was there as well.' Rob said, throwing his coat on to the armchair. 'He'd seen Judith.'

'Oh?' Lisa sat down, as Rob paced the room.

'Yes, he'd seen her in the supermarket buying cat food. She'd been quite upbeat, he said. She'd been on her way to Hazelmere but had decided to come back home. She'd decided it was time to escape her past, he said.'

'Drama queen,' Lisa muttered. 'What time was this?'

'About half eleven. About the time we arrived at her house.'

'Oh, and what does that mean?' Lisa waited for a reply, as Rob flopped on the sofa.

'It means are you sure she said she was at Hazelmere?' Rob asked.

'What?'

'I mean there was a lot going on. Perhaps you misheard her.'

'You don't believe me? Oh my God, you don't believe me, do you? You are unbelievable, after all that's happened. How can you not believe me?' Lisa yelled, then said, quietly, 'Was it Judith's dog that died?'

'What?'

'Was it her dog that died?

'Yes. No. I don't know.'

'She had a dog called Ben that died in the floods. At least, that's what I thought. Did you, Rob?'

'Yep. I think so, I suppose it was Ben who died. I guess that's what I always thought.'

'So you believe that?'

'Well, perhaps it wasn't. Look, I've never really liked to delve too much in the details of what happened at Hazelmere, like you. I just respond when she wants to talk.'

'That newspaper report … it implied that it wasn't Martin's dog,' Lisa said.

'Well, maybe it wasn't. So what? You know the newspapers. You're the one who's always saying they can't be trusted.'

'Why do you call her "*bonita*"?' Lisa said.

'What? Do I?'

'Yes.'

'It's just a word I use sometimes.' He shrugged. 'It's a term of endearment.'

'Exactly. Do you think she's got the wrong idea?'

Rob looked at Lisa, furrowing his brow.

'I must have called hundreds of clients *bonita*, and I really don't think any of them have got the wrong idea.'

'Are you sure of that? I thought you were the cool guy every girl wanted to hang out with when you were in Spain. In fact, I thought you were quite the shag monster when you were in Barça.'

'I really don't recall ever saying that. Look, I'm going to go. I'm shattered. I'll call tomorrow,' Rob said. He picked up his coat just as the door opened.

'Hi, Lisa, Rob!' Maya came through the door, pulling an overnight case and holding a bunch of pink tulips. 'Rob, you're looking as gorgeous as ever. You always had a flair for fashion. Got your finger right on the button,' Maya teased.

Rob laughed. He was unshaven and still wearing his tracksuit. He usually showered and changed after playing football before he went for a drink, but having a drink was the only normal thing he had done that day.

'How are your folks, Maya?'

'Still reeling from meeting you, Rob. You can charm the birds off the trees, Granville, you badass,' said Maya. 'You've even managed to captivate Lisa. Quite a tricky task, I can tell you,' Maya added in a half-whisper, looking at Lisa. 'She tries to pretend she doesn't care, but she does really.'

Lisa glowered at Maya. At the moment she definitely did not feel charmed, nor won over. Damn Maya.

'Well, I'll let Lisa tell you about our adventures today, Maya.' He pecked Maya's cheek. 'See what you make of it all. Don't forget to mention the cat, Lisa.'

As the front door slammed, Maya unwrapped the flowers and headed for the kitchen.

'You are smouldering, Lisa,' Maya said, as she returned with a vase.

'I am not fucking smouldering.'

'When Rob does it, it's quite attractive, but it doesn't become you. You just look sulky.'

'When have you ever seen Rob smoulder?'

'When the referee sent off his favourite player, Companion.'

'Kompany.'

'And he was smouldering just now,' Maya said. 'What's happened?'

'Well, perhaps burning might be more accurate.' Lisa fiddled with the tulips Maya had put in the vase. 'Lovely colour.'

'I'll make some tea,' said Maya, 'and you can tell me all about it while I'm ironing. Don't forget the cat.'

'Well, what do you think?' said Lisa, as she finished telling Maya about the morning's adventures and Rob's doubts about what she had seen and heard.

Maya put the iron down.

'I think she's a drama queen getting emotional sustenance from the men around her. Rob mainly, but Keith, too. She's like a vampire, draining everyone of their emotional energy.'

'Yes, that's her. But don't forget she was following me, and now she's working at my office.'

'She needs you to get up close to Rob. She's probably hoping she can get in a position where she can dispense with you.'

'What do you mean? Dispense with me?'

'Socially, I meant, not murderously. But she must also be quite lonely, so you can see why she might behave like this, if she's still grieving.' Maya picked up the iron again. 'I'd like to see what you say to her when you meet her at the Bergers reception tomorrow morning. You need to set the boundaries.'

'How, exactly?'

'Well, basically, I'd tell her to fuck off. Of course, you could do nothing and put up with it.' Maya smoothed a red dress on the ironing board.

Lisa pulled a face.

'I can't believe Rob doubts what I saw in the bedroom. It was so clear it was him. And she definitely said she was at Hazelmere. Why does he believe her, not me?'

'He doesn't want to. It's far easier for him to believe that you're mistaken. He's just not facing up to things. Again. He's just a big kid, isn't he?'

Lisa squinted at Maya from the sofa.

'What's different about you, Maya?'

'Do you like my shoes? I'm just wearing in the killer heels.' Maya kicked a slender leg up and rested her foot on the ironing board.

'Well, they certainly make you look taller. But will you be able to walk in them?' Lisa glanced back at her laptop.

'I'm getting picked up from the hotel tomorrow, so I'm not walking anywhere.'

'Who by?'

'Third date with the glam barrister at a very expensive restaurant. This could be the one.'

'Well, be careful,' Lisa said, looking up. She felt unusually maternal for a moment. Then she returned her gaze to the computer screen.

'He seems to be checking out OK. Safer than your average quiz team member, methinks.' Maya hung the red dress on a hanger and hooked it over the door.

Lisa typed 'Judith Crayvern'. A similar article appeared to the one she had read earlier about Martin. She typed on the keyboard again.

'Martin's death got quite a lot of coverage at the time,' Lisa said. 'There's a photo of Judith, the tragic hero's widow. It doesn't look much like her, though. She must have decided to glam up after Martin died. Amazing what money can do.

'Fuck, I wasn't expecting that,' Lisa said.

'What is it?' Maya said. 'You're looking very weird.'

'Listen to this, Maya. *Running heroine death riddle*,' Lisa read.

126

'Judith Crayvern, 48, was found dead in the waters of Hazelmere, where her husband, Martin, tragically drowned. The popular teacher was an enthusiastic runner who raised thousands of pounds for local charities.'

'Now that is weird,' said Maya. 'That's a real mystery. I have to confess, I thought you were being very conspiratorial, maybe making a mountain out of a molehill, but this is something else.'

'Look, there's more. *Tragic widow's anniversary death puzzle. An inquest recorded death by misadventure on Judith Crayvern, the widow of the museum boss who drowned two years ago. Husband Martin was swept away by flash floods as he tried in vain to rescue a dog. His widow's body was found by a lone walker in the River Hazel on the second anniversary of the tragedy. It is thought that Crayvern might have fallen down a muddy slope and was knocked unconscious before slipping under the water.*

'She was found by seventy-five-year-old Lawrence Bignall. The frail old-age pensioner had spotted her body in the water and bravely pulled her on to the riverbank. There was no phone signal in the valley so plucky Lawrence climbed up to the car park to call an ambulance. Friends of the family gave evidence that Crayvern had been very depressed following her husband's death. She was found at the exact spot where her husband disappeared. Verdict: Death by misadventure.'

The flatmates were silent for a few moments.

'Go to the police,' said Maya.

'What would the police do?'

'Investigate. This all looks very suspicious. Why steal a dead woman's name? That can't be legit, surely?'

'Rob and I have been in her house, remember? That won't look good.'

'No one will ever know that,' said Maya.

'She's crafty. She always manages to be the one who looks good. I'm going to find out who she is first. Then there's proof.'

'If you don't go to the police, just back away.'

'It's only moments ago you were telling me to confront her. How can I back away? I'd have to leave my job, my gym, stop going to the football, and the quiz nights. Stop doing everything that was part

127

of my life before I ever met her. She has wheedled her way into my life. All of it. She has secret texts with my boyfriend, and chats to him on Facebook. Like you said, it's Rob she wants, not me. And I'm not going to leave him as prey for her to feast on,' said Lisa.

'Well, it all sounds a compelling reason for going to the police.'

'What she's done isn't illegal, though, is it?'

'We don't know. We have no idea who she is, why she—'

'Well, I can't believe the police are going to make it their priority to find out. I'm going to put a stop to her. Then Rob will have to believe me.'

Heroes and villains

Monday morning

'Good morning, Judith. I do hope you're feeling better today.' Lisa scrutinised the expression on Judith's face as she listened to the response. There was not a hint that the older woman was being disingenuous.

'I am very well, thank you. Who could not feel good on such a beautiful day?'

Lisa looked in her eyes, and said,

'Hazelmere must have worked its magic.'

'It always does. I have a message for you,' Judith said, handing over an envelope. 'I think Andy tried to call you, but—'

'Thank you.' Lisa snatched the envelope and went straight to her desk, exchanging greetings with Tasmin before she sat down. She tore the envelope open. Damn. Andy wasn't going to be in until later and her meeting was rescheduled for late afternoon. She opened the drawers in her desk, looking for her battery charger.

'Would this help, Lisa?' said Tasmin, offering her a tangled cable.

'Thanks,' said Lisa. 'Did you have a good weekend?'

'Yah. Excellent, thank you.' Tasmin yawned. 'I hope this week's going to be as much fun.'

Monday lunchtime

'I didn't think I'd enjoy the quiz,' said Olivia, 'but really it's quite fun. I'm amazed how well The Dispossessed do for such a small team. They got all the music questions right last week, and they're so old.' She sipped a herbal tea.

'Jeremy loves it, don't you, hon?' Tasmin said.

'I went to a quiz every week at uni. We used to win, too. Now I just want to beat those cocky students. They're hopeless on the arts,' said Jeremy.

'Martin and I used to be in a quiz team. We were quite good, but we never actually won. Did I mention that it was the anniversary of

129

his death this weekend?'

'Yes. We're very sorry, Judith,' Tasmin said. 'It must be so hard. Was he your first love?'

'No. We met when I got the job at the museum. I'd been working at an auctioneer's before that. I did all the admin. It wasn't my original choice, but I'd stayed in Hazelton to be near Mum when Dad died. My sister was in Australia by then. We aren't in touch. I was in a long-term relationship with a guy called Peter. He helped me get the job at the museum, so I should be grateful for that. I wasn't grateful when he dumped me without any explanation and left Hazelton for London, though.'

Tasmin and Olivia made sympathetic noises. Jeremy squeezed her hand.

'Martin was my soulmate, though. Definitely. In fact that's what we called our quiz team. Soul Mates.'

'Aah, how lovely. Finding a decent team name's the hardest thing,' said Tasmin.

'I don't know why we chose to be Prime Suspects,' Judith said. 'We intend to change it every week but no one ever has a better suggestion. Lisa has a wicked sense of humour, and she has some bizarre suggestions. I'm sure they are intended without malice, though ...'

~

Lisa was engrossed in her private investigation on the Internet, despite her intention to work on the Taylor account. She glanced at her watch. It was almost two o'clock. She had better start work instead of googling 'Judith Crayvern'. She had now discovered that Judith had been a popular secondary school history teacher who had moved to Hazelton with her husband. She had been forty-eight when she had come to an untimely end in Hazelmere. She had met heroic would-be dog rescuer, Martin, at Sussex University. Lisa had discovered a couple of images, taken mainly at charity runs, in which the heartbroken widow had selflessly continued to compete to raise funds for children's charities. Lisa was surprised not to come across a story headlined with the words *Saint Judith*.

The real Judith Crayvern had a sinewy, lean physique, short, cropped dark hair, and black-rimmed glasses. She was not at all like 'Fake Judith', as Lisa now dubbed the current incumbent of the receptionist's desk at Bergers. If she could discover Fake Judith's identity, then surely she would have the key to the woman's obsession with Rob. Fake Judith did talk about the museum a lot. Perhaps she had met Martin there? She googled images of Martin. Quite a few, but only of him. She tried searching 'Hazelton Museum', which brought up lots of images of a Georgian building.

Perhaps there was no reason. Perhaps Fake Judith had randomly borrowed someone else's life. No, there had to be some link. What else did she know?

Awards. Of course, Hazelton had won the National Museum awards. She quickly brought up the website. It must have been over five years ago. Yes, there it was, six years ago. Woohoo! Martin, holding the award, surrounded by five smiling women, one of whom was most definitely a member of Prime Suspects. *Gotcha.*

Lisa was just about to resume her work when she realised there was a Facebook friend request waiting for her. She clicked. James Strather. She was stunned for a moment. She would look at that later.

'There's an amazing Greek deli just round the corner,' Tasmin said.

'Kounos?' Lisa said. 'Yeah, it's good value. Very friendly.'

'We had lunch with Judith,' Tasmin said, as she sat back at her desk.

Lisa involuntarily stiffened on hearing the name of her nemesis. 'We?'

'Yah, Jeremy and Livvie,' Tasmin said.

Lisa could imagine Judith holding court to the three of them.

'Judith's had a tragic life, hasn't she? Her sister's in Australia. She seems to have no one. Jeremy's going to take her to the Holman Hunt exhibition at the weekend. It's not my sort of thing, so it's good he's found someone else to take, don't you think?' Tasmin said.

'He's taking Judith?' Lisa was surprised that Tasmin seemed to be genuinely interested in her opinion.

'Yah, I think he's quite fascinated by her. She's quite a magnet for men, isn't she?' Tasmin continued, looking subdued. She heaved a sigh, then fumbled with her pen and after a pause said,

'Lisa, you know, I need to say this. I really don't think you should call Olivia and me the Yah-Yahs. Olivia was hurt she didn't get your job, but she is trying to like you. Really. And I thought that you and I were getting along amazingly. I really don't think you should talk about us like that. I was very disappointed.'

'But I didn't, I don't, I … Rob …' Lisa could feel anger rising. *Calm. Be calm. This is the reaction Fake Judith wants.* Everything Fake Judith said is contrived. She is actress, director, and stage manager. *You need to take control,* Lisa told herself, *or fuck knows where Fake Judith's performance will lead to next.*

'Look, Tasmin, I am really sorry. I have never called you and Olivia the Yah-Yahs. Judith is mistaken. Do you believe me?' Lisa said.

'Yah,' Tasmin gave her a smile and then laughed. 'OK, I believe you.'

'You are right, we do get on … amazingly, and I hope we will in the future.'

'Lisa, could you come into my office?' Andy asked, putting his head round the gap in the greenery.

Lisa picked up her papers.

'No, that can wait until four. This is just a quickie, I hope,' he said.

Lisa followed him to his office.

'Sit down, Lisa.' Andy motioned to Lisa to sit on an aluminium-framed leather chair in front of his large dark wood desk. His usually smiling face was a mask. 'Barry from human resources has been to see me,' he said.

Lisa's heart sank.

'He has had a rather unusual request from you this morning, Lisa. Although it sounded more like a demand, the way he put it. Would you like to tell me what you said?'

'I said I had reason to believe that the temporary receptionist, Judith Crayvern, was not who she said she was. I asked him to check out her credentials with the agency. I would have asked you if you had been here, but you weren't. It was a request. I didn't mean it to sound like a demand,' Lisa said, her confidence faltering.

'I had thought Mrs Crayvern was a friend of yours.'

'Yes, well, an acquaintance,' Lisa said. After a silence she added, 'She has been following me, and she's obsessed with my boyfriend.'

'Following you? Have you reported this to the police?'

'Well, no.'

'Have you asked her to desist?'

Lisa shook her head.

'Mrs Crayvern—' Andy began.

'But she's a—'

'Mrs Crayvern has done very well in the short time she has been here. I would certainly ask for her if we ever need a temporary member of staff again, which of course we will once Sally starts her maternity leave. It would be helpful, Lisa, if you would support rather than try and undermine her position.' Andy stared ahead as he waited for Lisa to answer.

'Yes, sir, I mean, Andy,' Lisa said, feeling like a schoolgirl being reprimanded by the headmaster.

'I'm very surprised and disappointed in you, but let's put the matter behind us now.'

Lisa reddened and left the office, almost bumping into Olivia, who was standing directly outside the door drinking coffee.

'Oops, sorry,' said Olivia, as Lisa almost knocked her over.

Lisa decided silence was her best strategy or she might betray the tears that were welling inside her. She sat at her desk, staring at a blank piece of paper. She could hear tap, tap, tap as Tasmin furtively texted on her mobile.

'I'll just be a mo,' Tasmin said.

Lisa unplugged her phone from the charger and texted Maya. As Tasmin returned Lisa's phone vibrated. She read the text.

Deed Poll. M xxx

'Ha ha,' said Lisa.

'Are you all right?' said Tasmin.

'Absolutely fine,' said Lisa. *I'll show them*, she thought. She checked her diary. She was free tomorrow. She would take a day's leave and continue her investigations at Hazelton.

Monday evening

She was surprised with herself for mentioning Peter at lunchtime. He had long been consigned to the dustbin of history, or so she had thought. She had been in a long-term relationship with him. That was true enough. But he had never left his wife. Because. Because. Because. There was always an excuse.

She had been working at the museum for about a year when Peter had called her at work, which in itself was unusual. He had announced abruptly that he was leaving. Leaving the area. Leaving her. Starting a new job in London. With his family. And then he had put the phone down. When she had tried dialling back it was engaged.

She had gone straight to his house. Empty. A *For Sale* board stood in the front garden, slashed across with a *Sold* label. The next-door neighbour had told her they had left two days before. The whole family had gone to London. Tough time for them, with two teenagers and a new baby. A baby? No, no forwarding address.

She still felt a burning anger, but now she directed it as much against herself as Peter, a married man who had never had any intention of leaving his wife for her.

Impulsively she opened her MacBook and typed 'Peter Holbeck' into the Google search engine. She scrolled through singers, teachers, and plumbers of that name. Then she came to the minutes of a London Borough Council meeting, just a month before. That must be him. *Peter Holbeck, Deputy Director of Planning*. He had not achieved his ambition to run a department, then. Good.

She returned to the search results screen and scanned it again. There was a photograph album for a Peter Holbeck on Picasa. She clicked on the link, not expecting it to be her former lover, but it was. A whole series of photographs unfolded before her. Christmas with the family, a holiday in Marbella, a son's graduation. He was fatter, greyer, and balder. She looked closely at a family photograph. Did he look happy? She could not tell. She did not want him to be happy.

She looked at the other family members. The boys were young men now. The lanky girl must be 'the baby'. The woman in the photograph did not look like his wife, though. She switched back to the Marbella album. The brunette woman was obviously his partner.

134

He had left his wife for someone else.

She snapped down the lid of the computer, angry with herself for letting her curiosity get the better of her. It was history. What would she have done, she wondered, if she had been able to use the Internet to track him down all those years ago? She shuddered. It was probably fortunate for Peter that that had not been an option.

Libera me, Domine, de morte aeterna in die illa tremenda.

The soprano's voice, like a shard of glass cutting through the melancholy chanting, awakened her from her reverie. As the haunting notes of the requiem finished abruptly she collected the laundry basket and glanced at the photograph of Martin on the beech worktop. She must have knocked it when she had picked up Kate's photograph. It was slightly askew, not exactly where she normally placed it. She held the frame in the palm of her hand and scrutinised the photograph. She would never forget him. But she had to move on, without him.

She took the linen basket upstairs to the spare bedroom, stopping to straighten the frame of the John Waterhouse print on the way. She pushed open the spare bedroom door. Until recently it had been the master bedroom, but she had impulsively decided that the aqua colour scheme was dated. She had redecorated the larger front bedroom in warmer colours and moved most of her clothes in there.

She put away the ironing, grimacing at a chipped, varnished nail. Now, something felt strange about the room. She could not put her finger on it.

Faint notes of patchouli and vanilla lingered in the air as she closed the bedroom door.

~

Lisa had the flat to herself. She had been googling for over an hour and felt she needed to talk to someone. Not Rob, though. She called Maya.

'Hi, Maya. Are you ready for your date?'

'Yeah, got the red dress and killer heels on. Just waiting to be picked up. Are you seeing Rob tonight?'

'He says he needs an early night, so I'm sleuthing. Did you know that 300,000 people have changed their names by deed poll?'

'Really? I didn't, but I've been doing some investigating myself. I remembered I know someone who knows someone who changed her name. She changed just about everything. Her passport, her bank account, and even her national insurance number to her new legal name. I think the only thing she couldn't have changed was her birth certificate.'

'I thought there would be a register somewhere that lists all the name changes but there isn't,' Lisa said.

'It seems like it's a great service for villains as well as victims,' Maya said.

'So any trace of Fake Judith's real identity has just disappeared.'

'Well, it looks like legally she is the real Judith Crayvern now. Be careful. Methinks she errs on the side of villainy. Aah, here he is. I have to go.'

'Well, give me a ring when you get back, so I know you're safe,' said Lisa.' I'm taking the day off tomorrow and going to Hazelton. Fake Judith's caused me enough upset today. I'm going to find out just who she is.'

'Well, you be careful. She might have left for a good reason. Got to go. If I'm really late I'll call tomorrow.'

Lisa opened her laptop and looked at the photograph of the award-winning museum staff again. One face seemed to be taunting her. The woman was malicious – like a virus, a worm. Lisa wondered what havoc she had wreaked on her co-workers. The prospect of seeing her cover Sally's maternity leave filled her with dread. She decided that the best place to continue her research was on Judith Crayvern's Facebook site.

She started to look at the list of friends. There were about thirty names.

Some of these people must know who she really is, she thought. She glanced through them. Becca Parlick, Rob's ex. How had they ever become friends? She immediately clicked on Becca's profile. After a few minutes she had surmised that Judith had met her at the Nail Boutique, Becca was pregnant, and Franklin was the father. Becca loved taking photographs. Interesting to see Heather on there, but no Rob. Babe threat terminated.

She scrolled through the other friends. She wondered if Kate was the sister Judith had mentioned to Taz. She checked her out. It looked like she lived in Brisbane, Australia. There was even an email address. She copied the address. She could contact Kate if she needed to. She trawled through a few more. Not many of them seemed to be active users of Facebook.

She stopped at Jeremy May. The photo looked quite familiar. She had a closer look. He only had a few friends. She clicked on them. They all seemed to be friends of Judith. She checked out Merriam. She seemed to have been on the history of art course. She copied the email address. The next friend seemed to be a politician, and the next was an archer. She carried on copying all the email addresses, then looked at her list. Apart from fourteen of the addresses, including hers and Rob's, the structure of the email addresses was very similar. There was also a surprising number of her friends who were only friends with each other.

She looked closely at the photograph of Jeremy May again and enlarged it. Using Google, she took a snap of it with her phone. It immediately returned the name from its image library: Simon Cowell. She snapped another suspicious profile picture, which instantly retrieved the photograph of a D-list celebrity.

'Aha,' said Lisa, aloud. 'I've got you. These are your fake friends. Fuck, even your sister's made up.' She divided the list into two. 'And I guess these are your real friends.

'So, Fake Judith, just who are you?'

Secret love

Tuesday morning

Although the sun had touched the city, painting its trees vibrant shades of green, the woods near Hazelton were dark and brooding. Tired daffodils, battered by a rainstorm, were the only hint of colour in the drab palette of muted greens and browns, but the sky was blue and clear.

Lisa was feeling optimistic as she drove up the long driveway to Hazelton Museum. She turned into the gravel car park. Empty. She got out and walked, apprehensively, to the grand doors of the Georgian building. Closed. Fuck. She hadn't expected that. She looked at the information notice on the wall.

Opening hours:

Sunday: 11.00 – 4.00.

Tuesday – Saturday: 10.00 – 4.00.

As she walked back to her car, she remembered that she had forgotten to check if Maya had left a message. She looked at her phone. Nothing. No messages because there was no signal. Fuck. Fuck. Fuck. She had been so careful the previous night: plugging her mobile in the charger, checking it was switched on and, in the morning, that it was fully charged. Then, this morning she had completely forgotten about Maya. She had an hour to kill. Well, she had plenty of time. She would drive the few miles down the road to Hazelton town centre.

Lisa was the only customer sitting in the shabby but highly priced cafe. She sipped coffee as she read her texts. The flavour wasn't bad, but she wished she'd asked for a coffee to take away, as she was now used to the taste of coffee from a cardboard cup. Fuck. Maya hadn't sent any messages, and her phone was diverted to voicemail. Perhaps there was a problem with Maya's mobile. Lisa posted a comment on Facebook:

Please confirm red shoes safe and sound.

She would just have to hope Maya saw the message.

138

Lisa had discovered a lot in just a few days. She had been right to believe in herself, even when it seemed everyone else doubted her. She could quite understand why someone might fall for Rob, but Fake Judith's obsession wasn't a harmless crush. Or was it? she wondered. Hadn't she only googled James Strather herself the other day in an idle moment? She had to admit that once she'd started discovering snippets about his new life she had found it was difficult to stop satisfying her curiosity. However, she could not imagine, under any circumstances, filling her bedroom with his photographs. She glanced at her mobile and smiled with relief. Maya was safe and well.

Shoes did their job well. Very late night!
Lisa replied,
Excellent choice, Maya! See you later.
She drank the last of the coffee while she deliberated her strategy for the museum. She was feeling nervous, like she had before her job interview.
Believe in yourself, Lisa.

~

Paula was filing her nails under the reception desk while reading a gossip magazine. She was sucking on a chocolate Minstrel. Caramel eclairs used to be her favourite morning distraction, but chewing toffee and answering visitors' questions seemed, unfortunately, to be incompatible. She had not appreciated why this was so until it had been carefully explained to her for the third time.

She glanced at her watch. Fifteen minutes until the first of the school parties arrived. Then it was one after another. She sighed. The powers that be who agreed these things never had to deal with the consequences. She looked up as a smartly dressed woman in a blue suit came through the doors, then looked down again to continue reading. She took another Minstrel from a large bag that was stashed with her nail varnish under the counter.

'Good morning ... Good morning,' said Lisa.

Paula looked up, moving seamlessly from the minutiae of Gwyneth Paltrow's private life to a welcoming smile.

'I'm Lisa Clarkson.'

Paula stood up and awkwardly shook the hand which was offered

139

to her. She glanced at the business card that Lisa had placed in front of her on the counter.

'Welcome to Hazelton, Lisa. What can I do for you?'

'I wonder if you can help,' Lisa said, noting the name on the badge that was pinned to Paula's ample chest, then made eye contact with her. Sharp blue eyes were almost hidden by gold-rimmed spectacles. A short brown bob framed a pale face that was almost unremarkable except for plump rosy lips, which had been enhanced with a generous dose of gloss. She noticed that the cuffs of Paula's pale blue blouse were quite worn. Lisa had to acknowledge, grudgingly, that the temporary receptionist at Bergers had the edge on the museum's receptionist.

'I was trying to get in touch with a couple of people, and I think they have connections here. They were friends of my aunt. I wanted to let her friends know she'd passed away, and ask them if they wanted any mementoes. It was all very sudden.' Lisa held a photograph of Judith Crayvern in front of the receptionist. 'I think Judith was married to the late director here.'

'Judith Crayvern? Why, yes, I did know her. She was Martin, our boss's wife. We used to collect for Christian Aid together,' Paula replied.

'Yes, it was terribly sad that he died so young.' Lisa smiled, looking into the startlingly blue eyes.

'It was. he was a wonderful man. Very caring.'

'Where might I find Judith, Paula?'

'You don't know, then? Well, I'm sorry to have to tell you, but Judith is dead. Martin and Judith died two years apart, on exactly the same day.' Paula paused, and then added in a whisper, 'At the same place.'

'How very sad.' Lisa made a sorrowful face, then responded to Paula's insinuation. 'And what a coincidence. What happened, Paula?'

'Well,' Paula said, 'Martin died a hero, trying to save a dog. It was a pointless tragedy. Judith drowned as well, two years later. At the same place, by the bridge. No one really knows what happened to her. There was a rumour,' she confided, 'that she couldn't live without him. But I never believed it, not at all. She was always her

140

own woman.'

Lisa feigned surprise.

'Oh, how terrible. Their dog as well?'

'Oh, no.' Paula grimaced. 'Not their dog. They didn't have a dog.'

'That *was* tragic, then. Trying to save a stranger's dog.' Lisa persisted, grateful she had met the garrulous Paula.

'Humph,' Paula said, looking down. 'Not exactly.' She mumbled something Lisa did not catch.

'Sorry?'

'He knew the dog. The dog used to come here.'

'Oh?'

'Yes, we all loved Martin. His wife was devastated. Then there was all the gossip, of course.' Paula offered Lisa a Minstrel. Lisa took it.

'There's this lady as well. Do you know her? My aunt was very close to her and her sister Kate. I think Kate's in Australia now.' Lisa leaned forward, replicating Paula's body language, and put another photograph down.

'Denise.' Paula's mood changed. 'Why are you asking all these questions? Why do you want to know?'

Just at that moment a short woman wearing a navy blue jacket and skirt walked over to the desk.

'Five minutes to action stations,' she said, putting a clipboard board down on the top of the desk.

'Marsha, this young lady has been asking questions about Judith Crayvern and Denise Carvel,' Paula said. She turned back to Lisa. 'Are you from the press or something?'

Lisa felt a tightness in her chest. Denise Carvel. That was who Fake Judith really was. She was close to finding out something big. *Keep cool.* She smiled at Marsha.

'Hello, I'm Lisa Clarkson. I'm just trying to find friends of my late aunt. Judith was her good friend at Sussex University. I thought this woman was perhaps Judith's friend, too.' She showed Marsha the photograph.

'That homewrecker,' said Marsha instantly. 'Oh, I'm sorry. I can tell you categorically she was no friend of Judith's, nor mine. I

141

always had my suspicions about her,' she said, eyeing the photograph with distaste.

Lisa decided to be bold.

'You mean she was having an affair with Martin Crayvern?'

'I'm sure they were. Always working late together. He'd never hear a word against her. He was such a kind man, but her …' Marsha exchanged glances with Paula, who looked if she would be ready to dig a hole then pass around stones to any willing passers-by who may wish to dispatch the adulteress who had been among them.

'Once she got her foot in the door she made it difficult for us mere mortals to talk to Martin like we used to,' Paula said.

'It was *her* dog that drowned,' said Marsha. 'She was there when Martin died. Then she comes in to work, bold as brass, on Monday morning, as if nothing had happened, when Martin's body was barely cold. And she wasn't at work the day Judith died. We noticed it, didn't we? Paula was doing the holiday roster at the time.'

'That's right. She took leave on every anniversary of Martin's death. Isn't that right, Marsha?' said Paula. She sounded as if she had been waiting for years to relate her theory to any passing stranger.

'Well, yes, though there were only two anniversaries,' Marsha said.

'Yes, we thought it peculiar, because she hardly ever took her annual leave,' said Paula, with the authority of one who had forensically examined and discussed the relevant evidence.

'It was an open verdict, then, was it?' Lisa probed.

'Misadventure. But I don't think they really knew,' Paula answered.

'Whether she took her own life or not?' asked Lisa.

'What happened at all. I wouldn't put anything past Denise Carvel—'

Paula stopped as a coach drew up outside the door.

'But Denise wasn't there when Judith died, was she?' asked Lisa.

'Well, who can prove she wasn't?' said Paula, with the logic which would have sent many a woman to the ducking stool in centuries gone by. 'But one thing I do know. She stole Judith's cat. Now what sort of woman would do that?'

'You don't know that,' said Marsha.

'I saw it when I was collecting for Christian Aid, just before she left,' Paula said. 'It was outside Denise Carvel's front door. I know cats, and that was definitely Judith's cat. It had a funny ear. Judith had been very upset. One week she lost her husband, and the next week she lost her cat.'

'Action stations,' said Marsha. 'Sorry. We have to go. Brylands' kids are always out of control when they arrive here. I wouldn't bother trying to find that one, though.' Marsha pointed at the photograph of the woman formerly known as Judith, then walked away.

'Yes, she'll only cause you grief,' said Paula.

'Well, actually, I must confess that I have found her, Paula. She plays in my pub quiz at The Sun.'

'Then why?'

'You see, I wanted to find out why she was now calling herself Judith Crayvern.'

'The cheeky bint,' said Paula, her pale face flushing. 'Steals Martin and his wife's name.'

'Paula, Paula,' Marsha called.

'I've got to go,' Paula said, reluctantly.

'Why do you think she's done that, Paula?' asked Lisa.

'Spite,' said Paula, walking away.

'Thanks for your time,' said Lisa. 'You have my card if you—' Her words vanished in the echoing entrance hall as screams of laughter heralded the arrival of dozens of running footsteps.

Being a private investigator was quite easy, Lisa thought, as she walked outside into the spring sunshine. She blinked in the bright rays and took stock of her bearings. Her phone was still dead. The gardens of the museum lay before her beyond the gravel forecourt. A coach driver, prematurely fattened by too many lunches on pensioners' day trips, was walking aimlessly, scrutinising the gravel as he dragged fiercely on a cigarette. He looked up to see Lisa, who smiled at him.

'Hi. It's a glorious day,' she said, then hesitated. 'Do you know the nearest place I can get reception on my phone? My network doesn't like it here.'

'Just a mile up the road on the left. You'll see the car park for the walk round Hazelmere. That should be all right. If not there's a little hill a short distance away. It should work there. Follow the yellow footpath sign.'

'Thanks. This is my first visit to Hazelton Museum. It's a lovely building.'

The driver looked surprised and looked up at the Palladian facade.

'I suppose it is. You know, I've been coming here for years and never really noticed.'

'You must have seen some changes, then?'

'A fair few. The top brass have all changed, and they don't do so much stuff for kids now. The last gaffer won awards. He knew what kids like. Bog men, ancient Egyptian mummies. Dead bodies. Kids love death and torture.'

'That would be Martin and Denise?' Lisa said. 'Sad about Martin. I wonder what happened to Denise.'

'Yes. You knew 'em?' The coach driver inhaled deeply. 'It was all very sad. Denise were a great girl. She always had time for me. Made sure us coach drivers had a cup of tea. She were quite a cracker. I wonder what ever happened to her. Here one minute, gone the next.'

'Martin Crayvern drowned near here, didn't he?' Lisa asked, taken aback that Denise was actually liked – admired, even.

'Yep,' he sighed. 'He drowned in the river just where it joins Hazelmere. It were the worst storm in years. A bridge further upstream had got plugged with a tree, and when it broke free this huge wave of water poured down the valley.' He raised his hands above his head. 'Like a mini tsunami it were, or so they say. He were trying to rescue Denise's dog. She must have been devastated, losing him and the dog … That Ben were a top dog.'

'Martin's wife, Judith, died at the same place, didn't she?' Lisa said. 'That was a coincidence. I heard there were rumours she killed herself.'

'There was talk. Not worth the time of day. A funny place to try and top yourself, if you ask me. In shallow water? I don't think anyone took that seriously. There were a bit of doubt about what happened, though. This old codger found her and pulled her out, single-handedly. But they reckon he might have banged her head doing it. Folks say he might have caused her death, not saved her after all. But you know folks.'

'I thought I heard Martin was going to leave Judith for Denise,' Lisa said.

The coach driver was silent and threw the butt of his cigarette away. He looked at her curiously. Lisa reddened.

'Well, you know more than me, love. He were certainly smitten with Denise, though, you could tell that, and Ben. Who could blame him? She were a stunner. She must have been devastated. But Martin always had an eye for the ladies, and they liked him. Who knows? Why do you want to know, anyway? Are you related?' The coach driver flipped open another packet of cigarettes.

'Related?'

'Yeah, you have a look of Denise about you. It's your smile.'

Ashes to ashes

Lisa pulled into the small car park. There was just one car, a silver Ford Mondeo, parked beside a ticket vending machine. It was unoccupied. She opened her phone. At last, a signal.

She texted Maya.

Fake Judith is Denise Carvel. Lover of boss, Martin. All will be revealed tonight. Glad glam barrister loved shoes xxx

Then she texted Rob.

Hope U having good day, babe. C u later xxx

She had not told Rob she was having the day off. She was looking forward to seeing his face when she revealed that the fourth member of the quiz team was an impostor, an accomplished liar. Lisa got out of the car. She wondered if there was a man in uniform hiding in the bushes waiting to attach a parking fine to a windscreen wiper the moment she left the car park. She fumbled for some change and bought a ticket, then balanced on the edge of the boot as she put on her trainers. It had been quite a good day so far.

The phone vibrated. A text from Maya:

How sad. She must have been devastated. M xxx

Lisa's heart sank. Maya was the one who had said Fake Judith was like a vampire, and now she felt sorry for her. Lisa locked her bag in the boot, then headed towards the corner of the car park to a gate and a gravel path. After a couple of metres there was a signpost. Underneath engravings of a walking man there were two diverging arrows which indicated that there was one footpath down the hill, and one across the top. *But to where?* she wondered.

Lisa chose the path that ran along the top. She soon had a view of Hazelmere, shimmering in the sun. She had heard so much about the lake, but in her imagination it was just a whirlpool of muddy water. From the far shore the slopes of the hills soared majestically, their pale lemon crests gorging on the strong spring sunshine. It was tranquil, but not quiet. She could hear lambs bleating in the fields below and a rush of birdsong, so very different from the noise of the city. Although there was a faint hum of a distant car, the voice of nature was supreme.

Lisa gasped for breath as the path climbed steeply up a hillock. At the top she sat down on a wide bench, grateful to rest her aching legs. *I must go back to the gym*, she thought. She took out her mobile and took a photograph of the lake. At least she could show Rob where she had been. She grimaced. She had confidently assumed that her private investigations and the revelation of Fake Judith's real identity would be enough to put an end to the impostor's entanglement in their lives. Lisa had been eager to accept Marsha and Paula's sour opinions of their former colleague without hesitation, but the coach driver's views made her think that perhaps it was not so simple. Even Maya seemed to be sorry for her. Would Rob? She decided to text him:

Looking forward to quiz tonight, babe xxx

He replied instantly:

Not sure, Lise ☹

Fuck. She had wondered if he might just want to walk away.

What about Keith? He loves it. Can't let him down xxx

She read Rob's reply:

Suppose ☺

Now, what was that supposed to mean?

She had imagined the real Judith as a tragic, innocent figure, and had felt a duty to avenge the theft of her name by Denise Carvel. But why had Martin, who was 'such a kind man', betrayed his wife? How had he become beguiled by Denise? Then again, what did the term 'ladies' man' mean? Friendly, charmer, or shag monster?

She looked across the valley. Getting people to talk to her had not been a problem. But finding the truth? Well, that was clear as mud. Lisa retrieved a battered Twix from the bottom of her jacket pocket and tore off the top of the wrapper. She pushed one chocolatey, chewy finger out from the packet with her thumb and took a large bite. She savoured the melting toffee on her tongue as she texted Maya.

She's poss cat thief as well xxx

'That's Lydia's favourite view, you know.'

Lisa started at the voice behind her. An elderly man wearing a flat cap and blue jacket sat down heavily next to her. Lisa shuffled along the bench.

'Sorry, I didn't mean to alarm you,' he said. He smelled of soap and mints.

'Lydia? Is that your wife?' Lisa said.

The man nodded and pointed at a worn metal plaque.

'Look here. The inscription says: *In memory of Lydia Bignall*. We put this seat up in memory of her and, by heck, I need to rest here now when I come and see her.'

'See her?'

'Yes, we scattered her ashes around here.' Mr Bignall's weather-beaten face smiled as he looked around the knoll. 'In her favourite place, so we knew she'd be where she was happiest and we could talk to her.'

Lisa wondered who 'we' meant, but thought it best not to ask. She looked at the ground as she wondered what Lydia's ashes looked like.

Mr Bignall laughed.

'You'll not see them now. It was over twenty year ago. Lots of folk scatter ashes round here. Most wait till they think no one's looking, but you get to know the signs.'

'There've been a few tragedies here, haven't there? Floods and things,' said Lisa. 'Did you see those floods? Didn't someone drown?'

'No. I was up here in the morning. It was a bit wild, but there was no sign of what was going to happen that afternoon. That was when the museum director drowned. Very sad. No, I saw none of that, but I found his wife a few years after. She'd keeled over into the river. Probably slipped and fell in. She'd have been here because it was the anniversary of his death. People are like that. They remember all the time, but an anniversary's special.'

'That must have been horrific. Where did you find her?'

'By the bridge. They'd rebuilt it by then. She was in a shallow rock pool. I turned her over and pulled her out. I was hoping I'd saved her. She didn't look so heavy. She was thin, but very tall. By the time the ambulance got here she'd gone.'

Lisa looked at the man's face. He looked troubled.

'I guess you don't forget things like that,' Lisa said.

'No. I had to answer a lot of questions at the police station and then at the inquest. I don't think they thought a seventy-five-year-old pensioner was going round murdering people. They just wanted to know if anyone else was around. They just have to do their procedures,' he mumbled. 'They said I'd done the right thing, pulling her out.'

He stood up.

'I hadn't seen anyone else, though. You can see the bridge from here where it happened.' He pointed down the valley as Lisa got up. 'Just before it feeds into the lake. Be careful if you're going down there. They say lightning never strikes twice, but I'm not sure that's true. You've not got a rucksack, though. There are them that say it was Judith's thermos flask in her bag that knocked her out.'

'Well, I'd best be going. I'm going back up. I guess you're going down.'

'Yes, I am. Nice meeting you,' said Lisa.

'You know, they said I was frail. In the papers, like. Would you believe that?' he said quietly.

'Well, they often get things wrong. You're certainly not frail. I'm sure you did the right thing. Bye, now.' She watched the pensioner walk away and took another couple of photographs and then glanced at her mobile.

Denise must have been very lonely. M xxx

Whose side is Maya on? Lisa wondered.

She looked at the view again. Hazelmere was beautiful, truly uplifting. She could see its attraction for walkers, and the pull of the lake. Lisa set off and was soon walking in the pine trees, leaving the warmth of the sunshine and the songbirds. Only the cawing of a crow broke the wood's creepy silence. She looked at her mobile screen for reassurance but realised the signal had disappeared. She was glad when the path finally left the gloom of the conifers, but her disquiet was soon forgotten once she was on the open, lush riverbank.

As Lisa wandered along towards the bridge she stopped by a still rock pool. It was untouched by the current of the main river, which was swiftly carrying its watery cargo to the lake. The stones on the path were quite smooth, knitted together at their edges by moss. The pool was at the bottom of a steep slope and it would be quite possible to slip on a wet day, Lisa decided. The detectives investigating Judith's death must have reached the same conclusions.

Was Judith looking forward to the year ahead just before she took her last breath? Or was she tormented by Martin's death, constantly talking about it, like Fake Judith does? Lisa wondered. Did she know about Denise Carvel? Had she been constantly suspicious of her husband when he was alive, or had she only discovered the affair when he was dead? Or had she a lover and didn't care?

She watched a blackbird chirruping gaily as it hopped along the handrail of the bridge. She had found out lots of information today, but she was not sure what to make of it.

Tuesday late afternoon
She turned up the volume of the music, then braced herself as she switched on the washing machine. After the flood she had been paralysed with fear every time she heard the sound of rushing water. Now, every time she pressed the power button, she registered a moment of her triumph over her fears.

Bunters brushed his warm body back and forth against her calves, mewing quietly, then he buffeted her legs with his head. She felt guilty for neglecting him all day while she was at Bergers. She opened the door and filled the plastic bowl with milk and placed it on the floor. The cat immediately buried his face in the bowl, his white-tipped tail flipping from side to side. She watched him, thinking that dogs were more loyal and less fickle companions.

Late sunbeams crept through the slats of the venetian blinds, highlighting dancing specks of dust, then bounced on to the kitchen floor, emphasising every mark on the glossy slate tiles. She was about to fetch the floor mop, then stopped and looked closely at the dust. Footprints led from the back door to the photographs on the dresser and then over towards the hall door. Not hers. She had polished the floor on Sunday morning, washing away all vestiges of mud, leaves, and petals. No one had visited since. But the evidence showed that two people had. There seemed to be two distinct shoe prints – one large, and one smaller, probably from a woman's boot or shoe.

150

She froze for a moment, then urgently moved to the MacBook. She had set up the security system some months previously but, after the initial satisfaction of successfully activating the webcams, she had rarely looked at the footage. The back door, Bunters, and the occasional bird were the only stars that graced her home movies.

She set the video to play back from Sunday morning after she left the house. She watched as Lisa appeared in a frame, knocking on the back door, then Rob opened the door and they went inside. Rob had responded to her call after all. Images of the out-of-place photograph and the cockeyed picture frame flashed through her mind. The fragrant memory of patchouli and vanilla assaulted her senses.

Lisa has been upstairs. What did she see? She checked the time stamp. They had probably been there when she had arrived home. She tensed. *Think. Think clearly,* she told herself.

So Lisa would have known she had not been at Hazelmere and exactly where she was. What about Rob? What did he know? Why hadn't he been in touch? And what about Lisa? Where had Lisa been today? That was very odd. She had casually asked Andy when she met him for lunch, but he had had no idea. No interest, either. Even Tasmin didn't know. She looked up Lisa's Facebook page. Lisa had posted a message on Maya's wall.

Please confirm red shoes safe and sound.

Judith froze. The message showed Lisa's location when she wrote it. Hazelton. Lisa was not content with trying to make her life difficult at work. Now she was digging up the past.

Lisa was a dark shadow, always getting in the way.

Tuesday late afternoon

Rob was walking through Market Street towards the bus stop. A crowd of women sprawled in front of him, blocking his way. He silenced his phone and watched them, wondering if there had been a fire alarm in the music megastore. But then he realised that the crowd were jostling to get into the shop, rather than escape from it. Most of the women looked as if they had dressed up for the afternoon and had just been to the hairdressers. One woman, wearing a pink cowboy hat, was perched on a litter bin.

Rob wondered if he had inadvertently found his way into the

heart of a large hen party. He looked down on the sea of bodies pressed tightly together, their eyes all trained on the doors of the megastore.

He pushed forward into the mass, curious to find out what was going on. A woman, now relegated to standing behind him, jabbed him with an elbow.

'You need to get a ticket to get in. We've been waiting hours,' she said. He looked over his shoulder at her. Her eyes shone fiercely, willing him to retreat.

'Stand in front of me,' he said, chivalrously. 'You'll get a better view.' He gently pushed her forward.

'Thank you.' The woman smiled. 'He should be arriving in a minute. I waited all night for tickets but they'd sold out. I just hope I get a glimpse now.'

'Tickets?'

'It's a book signing. You need tickets.'

'For who?' said Rob.

'Jayce,' screamed the woman in the cowboy hat.

The call was a signal for the women to transform into an army of amateur photographers, pointing their mobile phones towards the doors of the shop, and scream. Over the heads of the crowd Rob could see a tall, slim figure with a light brown beard walk in front of the shop and wave. Rob flinched as he felt a kick to the back of his knee and a shoe trample on the side of his foot. The star paused while hundreds of mobile phones captured his image for future veneration, turning his body to different angles to ensure that his face could be seen from all sides of the crowd.

As the pack pitched forward, singing, Rob slipped out of the crush and made his way back to work, leaving Jayce to wallow in the waves of adulation. It was alarming that these women could be so passionate about someone they didn't even know. Though, he supposed, they thought they did.

Rob had been the cool one in Spain, the one in charge, the star. He was the one the girls idolised, that they would fight to be around. He wasn't a shag monster, though, not really. Lisa had been very unfair. Sometimes he had benefited from the situation, but the women went home satisfied and that would be the end of it.

Everyone was a winner. No one got hurt.

He really wasn't looking forward to the quiz. It would be so much easier just to not go. But Lisa was right. There was Keith to think of as well. Maybe he could think of a reason to let Keith down gently tonight, maybe find him another team.

Lisa must have been in meetings all day. He had usually had far more texts from her. Maybe her mobile was down. His phone pinged.

See you at The Sun. Going straight there. Don't let Keith down. L xxx

Tuesday evening

Rage and passion propelled Judith towards The Sun. She pulled her cashmere scarf higher, so it covered the lower part of her face against the biting wind. She had fought her demons, moved away from her past, looked to the future. It had been difficult, especially when she had started dreaming again. Dreams? More like nightmares.

She stopped by the pub door and hugged her arms, stamping her feet as she calmed herself. The smoker nodded to her. She was silent for a moment, then took a deep breath and beamed at him with her bewitching smile.

If she wanted to be Judith Crayvern, what was wrong with that? It was perfectly legal. That was who she was, now.

Lisa was sitting on the edge of a red velveteen bench, texting.

'You're early,' said Keith, accusingly, as he put his Guinness down. 'Bernice hasn't been round yet to take the lunch things away.' He slid a condiment set across the table to make room for his glass.

'I came straight from work,' said Lisa, lying. She had come straight from her flat, but had not had time to change, and was still wearing her cobalt blue suit. She had not wanted to be late.

'I've registered us and got all the answer sheets,' she said, holding a sheaf of papers to her chest, as she scanned the room.

'You've not got your drink,' Keith said.

'I'll wait till Rob comes.'

Keith sat down. It wasn't half past yet, and he never had his first sip of porter until a minute past.

'Aah, here she is. Dead on time, as usual,' he said, looking at his watch. 'No change there, then. And the Yahs-Yahs have just arrived, too.'

'Hello, Judith. How did you enjoy your day at work? Tired?' Lisa smiled.

'Oh, I always have work to do. I just don't always have someone to pay me for it,' Judith said, flashing a smile. 'But it has been a very productive day.' She acknowledged Jeremy as he passed nearby, hunting for chairs.

'You only have one more day, don't you?' Lisa said.

'Yes. I'll really miss my new friends. Aren't Taz and Livvie delightful? Very warm and generous. Andy's great company, too. We had lunch today. I'm so pleased he wants me back, even though they're about to announce heavy cuts. Tch. I'm sorry. I wasn't supposed to mention that.'

'Cuts?'

'My lips are sealed. I hope you'll be safe, but you never know, darling. And where have you been today?'

'Out.'

There was a silence. Judith's eyes gazed into the distance as she pursed her lips. Lisa smiled.

'Everything OK, Judith?' Keith said.

'Oh, I'm sorry, Keith, I was just preoccupied. I've just mislaid something. I was so sure I'd left it in a certain place and it isn't there. I can't have had thieves in the house, can I?'

Thieves in the house? What is she talking about? What is missing? Lisa wondered.

'Hello, Rob,' said Keith. 'What's up? You've changed your drink.' Rob was carrying a pint of Timothy Taylor's and a Peroni.

Lisa relaxed. She had not been certain that Rob was going to turn up at all. She was beginning to think that he had no interest in solving the mystery.

'Hello, Lisa. You're looking gorgeous tonight,' Rob said, leaning over and kissing her on the lips. 'Keith, Judith … Glad you seem better, Judith.'

Judith had been moving to embrace him, but sat down as she saw that her intention was not being reciprocated. Rob put an arm round Lisa and whispered in her ear.

154

'Stop canoodling, you two, and pay attention,' Judith said. 'We need to get started on this quiz.'

'Don't flap, Judith. We have plenty of time. I've already got the papers,' Lisa said. 'Here's the picture round.' She placed the photocopy of photographs in the centre of the table, facing Judith.

'Ian Wright, that first one. Definitely,' said Rob.

'That looks like the one we had the other week,' said Keith. 'The one who looked like Judith.'

'Michelle Pfeiffer,' said Rob.

'Yes, that's the one. You're the spitting image, Judith. Strange to have the same answer again,' Keith said.

'Paula,' said Judith, barely audibly.

Lisa studied Judith as she looked at all the images. She had sunk back into her chair.

Keith grimaced.

'This is a hard round. I've no idea who that woman with the short hair is. Must be an athlete of sorts. That looks like Martin ... I'm sorry. I didn't mean to ...' His words trailed.

'What about this one?' said Lisa, patting Rob's hand, which was round her waist.

Judith rose abruptly from her seat, knocking Keith's pint of Guinness on to a vinegar pot which slid, minus stopper, on to Lisa's lap. Lisa jumped up, holding out her skirt, as the black porter began to pour off the table edge. Rob swiftly righted the glass and tried to mop back the stout with some beer mats.

Lisa groaned and shuddered as the cold liquid spread through her skirt and tights. The sour smell of vinegar hung over the table.

'I'm soaking.'

'I'm terribly sorry. It was an accident. I must go home and change. I'm absolutely drenched,' Judith said, swiftly leaving the table, but carrying the picture quiz sheet with her.

Lisa retired to the ladies' toilets. As she walked past Brian Cordon he whooped and conducted The Terminators in a round of applause.

'I really think you need to get out of that skirt,' said Olivia, as she surveyed Lisa in the ladies' toilets.

Tasmin was on her knees, using toilet roll to wipe the spreading black stain from Lisa's skirt.

'Look, you could put it on the top here and soak up the liquid with paper towels,' Olivia said.

'I've always loved that suit,' said Tasmin. 'We need to save it.'

Lisa took off her skirt and shoes and stood in her thick black tights on the terracotta tiles. There was even Guinness in her shoes. She dabbed her blouse with toilet roll, then wiped inside her shoes. She scrutinised her jacket. There were some splashes. She smelled them. Vinegar.

'You're right, Taz. Vivienne Westwood,' Olivia said, with a smidgeon of admiration in her usually disapproving voice. Tasmin gave Olivia an 'I told you so' look as Olivia set to work with paper towels, blotting the liquid out of the skirt.

'Don't put it anywhere near the hand dryer,' Olivia commanded, 'or it will set. Take it to the dry-cleaners, first thing.'

'What was that about?' said Tasmin, as Lisa pulled her damp skirt back on.

'It was just an accident,' said Lisa. 'It wasn't about anything.'

'Are you sure? It sort of looked like she meant it,' Tasmin said. 'Don't you think, Livvie?'

Olivia shrugged her shoulders.

'I didn't see it. Look, we'd better go back to Jeremy. They've just announced the first round. Are you all right now, Lisa?'

'Yes,' said Lisa, still feeling dishevelled and smelly but grateful for her work colleagues' unexpected assistance. 'Thanks. I really appreciate your efforts to save my skirt. You've been amazing. Thanks, both of you.' She went into a cubicle and took off her tights. Tasmin and Olivia, had been, well, amazing. Lisa had meant every word she said.

'I started your Peroni, Lise,' said Rob, studying Lisa's skirt. 'Well, finished it, really. So I got you a white wine. It won't matter so much if it gets knocked over.'

'What? But we need to go. We need to confront her.' Lisa took a gulp of wine. 'Where's Keith?'

'Gone to work. He can't cope with the idea of wasting a pint. I offered to buy him another, but he was adamant he was off. Probably very wise. What do you want to confront her about, Lise?' Rob said, touching her hand.

'This,' said Lisa. She pulled out a copy of the picture quiz from her bag. 'That is not Judith Crayvern. That is Denise Carvel. And that woman there is the real Judith Crayvern.' Lisa pointed at Denise. 'She is an impostor. And here's the proof.'

Lisa put the printouts of the newspaper reports of Judith Crayvern's death on the table as the quizmaster announced round two.

'Fucking hell. Are you sure it's the same Judith?' said Rob. He stared at the papers.

'*Tragic widow of Martin Crayvern. Museum Director. Died trying to save a dog in the floods at Hazelmere.* Yeah, I'm sure,' said Lisa. 'And another thing I'm sure about is that I don't want her working at Bergers and making my life a fucking misery. So that's why we're going round now,' Lisa said, offering her glass to Rob.

'Finish this if you need another drink. Then we're off.'

Do you really want to hurt me?

Judith sat at her MacBook. She had found the images of the museum staff that Lisa had used. Damn that girl. She must have found the reports of Martin's death and her own as well. Just what had Lisa been doing in Hazelton? She must have been to the museum. She sighed. It was highly likely that Paula was still on reception. She was unlikely to give her a glowing reference. Nor Marsha, either.

The security lights flashed on and she heard some banging. She closed the MacBook and opened the back door.

'Trespassing again?' she said. 'I don't know why you're finding my bins so interesting.'

Rob and Lisa looked up, squinting, their eyes caught in the fierce light. Lisa was tossing shards of paper through her hands and back into the blue bin.

'I think you'd better come in, Rob, and bring your melodramatic little friend with you. Lisa's quite an actress. Though not a very accomplished one.'

Lisa followed Rob through the kitchen door.

'So what game are you playing, Lisa? Don't you think asking your boss to check out my credentials is a rather unkind thing to do?' Judith said.

'Well—' began Lisa.

'No, let me finish. I know you tried to get me fired from Bergers, from a job I really enjoy. Don't interrupt.'

'What's this about?' Rob said

'I had coffee with Olivia and lunch with Andy. I know everything, Lisa. No, she didn't tell you that, did she, Rob?'

'You're an impostor. You're not Judith Crayvern. You're Denise Carvel. Judith Crayvern is dead,' said Lisa. 'And … and you stole her cat.'

'Aah, now let me guess who you've been talking to. Paula. Paula, and maybe Marsha. Yes, that's just the petty tittle-tattle they make up and pass on. Am I right?'

Lisa said nothing as she watched the woman who called herself Judith pick up Bunters. He allowed himself to be cradled in his mistress's arms as she buried her face in his fur. She looked up and let the cat jump down and return to his bowl.

'I'm not mistaken, am I? You've been snooping around at Hazelton Museum, haven't you? I can see you don't know about that either, Rob.' Judith walked past Rob, coyly catching his eyes as she looked back over her shoulder. 'I wonder what else she doesn't tell you?' she said, softly.

'Lisa, I hope your shoes are cleaner than last time you came round here. They left some pretty distinctive prints on the floor.' She looked at Lisa and smiled. 'It's all on the webcam.' She opened a drawer and pulled out her passport and handed it to Rob. 'As you can see, this is a valid passport for the United Kingdom of Great Britain and Northern Ireland in the name of Judith Crayvern. The unflattering photograph, sadly, is of me. Don't you agree, Rob?'

'Well, yes,' Rob said.

'Deed poll. Easy to do. Don't be fooled by her, Rob,' Lisa said, then turned on Judith. 'You've shredded them, haven't you? The photos of Rob in your bedroom? They're all shredded.'

'You've been into my bedroom?' Judith turned angrily towards Lisa. 'You crazy, self-obsessed girl, what right have you to snoop around my home, into my life?'

Lisa took a step backwards. Bunters screeched as she stood on his tail and leaped into the air, claws extended.

~

Keith turned the ignition key. The headlights automatically switched on and the windscreen wipers flicked across the screen, providing a steady backbeat to the radio's lonely saxophonist. Keith silenced the music. It resonated too much with his own mood. He searched through the channels until he found a more uplifting tune on a country music channel. Kris Kristofferson. That was more like it.

He hummed along as he pulled down the sun visor and looked into the vanity mirror. He stared back at himself. He wasn't sure he recognised the man he saw any more, although everyone else seemed

159

to think he looked just the same. Except Tasmin. She was the only one who had noticed, even though the others saw him every week.

'Cool new look, Keith,' Tasmin had said as she and Olivia pursued Lisa into the toilets.

He was still not sure what to do with his evening, but he had decided there was no point hanging around in The Sun. He had so much looked forward to the quiz. He had been sure they would win tonight, finally be the champions, but now he had a feeling of foreboding that he would never have the chance. Judith had gone home, and Lisa wouldn't hang about. Poor Lisa. He couldn't imagine that her lovely blue suit would ever be the same again.

The whole thing was odd. It had looked almost deliberate, but then he supposed that most accidents did. Clumsy gestures, lack of concentration, silly mistakes. Really, he was not sure what he had seen. No, he could not swear, on oath, that he had seen Judith deliberately knock his Guinness over Lisa, but it had looked very much like she had. What a waste of a pint. The picture quiz was odd, too. The Dispossessed had had a different sheet of photos.

No, he hadn't observed as much as he should have to be absolutely sure. In fact, most people had been very unobservant tonight, even Rob. He had seemed very wrapped up in Lisa. Rob was usually the show-off, always in the centre of a crowd, never at its edge. A good sort, though.

Rob never had explained why he missed the football on Sunday. That had been quite a talking point. He wouldn't be allowed to forget that too soon. For some reason, Keith thought, Judith was behind it, but no one was telling. Rob always made a fuss of her, but it was all harmless banter. She lapped it up from Rob, from that one, but from no one else, though. If anyone else tried to joke with her, or call her 'Jude', she soon put them in their place. Judith had to be centre stage as well, but tonight she had not got the attention from Rob she was used to.

He looked in the mirror again. He'd moved it so he could see more of his face. The invisible man. He was just wallpaper to their lives, part of the scenery, not the main show. Maybe Judith felt that way as well, not that she would want to be any part of his show. He wondered if he should go round to Judith's and check she had got

160

home safely. After all, who else would? She had looked rather rattled when she left.

He stopped at a give way sign. He wasn't far away from Judith's if he turned right, or he could turn left towards the shops and log on for a night shift. He weighed up the options. Sandra would have told him not to get involved.

'No good will come of it,' she would have said. 'Steer clear of the likes of her.'

And Judith probably wouldn't thank him for calling this late at night. She had done him proud on his birthday, though. He indicated right and continued down the road, and then indicated right again. *Willow Tree Avenue* was displayed on a low street sign. He tapped on the steering wheel as he waited impatiently for a moped to turn slowly into the road, then followed it past a *For Sale* sign.

No, he was not going to Judith's. Sandra was right. No good would come of it. He would carry on and then turn right at the bottom of the road and go on his shift.

Keith reacted instantly, slamming his right foot on the brake. The car juddered and shook as it screeched to a halt and stalled. Keith froze. He looked around. Where exactly was he? Patsy Cline plaintively sang about feeling blue as Keith struggled to find the door handle, which he had opened thousands of times before. Finally, he managed to yank it open and stepped out.

He couldn't see anything. He walked to the front of the car. The windscreen wipers continued to clunk repetitively, like a metronome. The drizzle sparkled in the headlights but he still couldn't see anything. He looked down the road. In the light of a street lamp, he could see what he was dreading. A body. He shut the taxi door and walked towards it. Raindrops trickled down his glasses. He took off his cap and put it in his jacket pocket.

Poor Bunters. The cheeky chappie didn't deserve this. Bunters was still warm, and Keith thought he felt a slight tremor, but he could see blood in the cat's mouth.

If only he'd just been a bit earlier or a bit later or chosen the other direction. He was quivering inside as he walked up the drive. He decided to go round to the back door. He couldn't surprise Judith with her dead cat at the front door. As he approached the end of the driveway, he had to step round two of the bins, which were upturned on the ground.

Foxes, he thought, as he protectively pulled Bunters tightly to him. The back door was slightly open. He could hear raised voices. Through the slats of the blind he could see Rob and Lisa. He stood outside for some minutes, stroking the soft fur.

He could hear Rob talking angrily.

'No, *you* are the crazy one, whoever you are.'

'She's Denise Carvel,' said Lisa. 'She worked at the museum. Whatever this passport says, you're not her. Judith's dead.'

'Judith's not dead. *I* am Judith Crayvern.'

Keith knocked and put his head round the door. The sour smell of vinegar was in the air.

'Who's that?' said Judith, turning to look at him. 'Who are you? Get out of my house. Uninvited guests seem to be the fashion this week.'

Rob and Lisa turned their gaze to the door.

Keith looked at each of them, tongue-tied. Why were they looking at him like that? Rob was standing, holding a passport, looking at him very warily. There were red scratch marks on Lisa's bare leg.

'I'll call the police,' said Judith, wagging a finger towards Keith. 'Get out, whoever you are.'

'You do that,' said Rob. 'I think that could be a very interesting conversation.'

'It will be when they see my webcam video,' Judith spat back.

'My God, that man's got blood on his face,' said Lisa.

'Is this a good time, Judith?' said Keith.

'That man is Keith,' said Rob, pointing. 'What have you done, Keith?'

'I've not done anything,' said Keith, defensively. 'Well, you see, the thing is, the thing is …' Keith pushed the door fully open with his foot.

'That's Bunters,' said Judith. 'What have you done to him?'

'Bunters? But he was just here a minute ago,' Lisa said, looking at her bleeding leg. 'How can that be him?'

162

'There was a motorbike in front of me. He … I found him in the road. I don't think he knew anything. There was nothing I could do.'

All the colour drained from Judith's face. Rob looked up at the ceiling, as if he wished he could be anywhere else.

'No, no,' Judith groaned.

'Are you sure he's dead?' said Lisa, as Judith snatched the cat from Keith's arms.

'Dead? Dead? Of course he's dead, you stupid, dozy cow,' Judith said, turning on Lisa. 'He's squashed. How can he not be dead?' She began gulping for breath, as she smothered her face in the fur. 'This is what dead looks like, feels like. You murdered him, didn't you, Keith? It was you.' Blood was matted in her hair and smeared on her face. Her eyes were red, her skin deathly white.

'No, no, I didn't. Who would want to murder Bunters?' Keith stammered, stroking his smooth scalp.

'You … always coming round here, following me, watching me. And now you kill my cat. My cat.'

Judith started to scream like a banshee and gasped for air as she clutched the cat. Bunters's blood splashed on the black slate tiles.

'Dead, dead,' Judith wailed. 'Dead.' She sobbed until she could not speak, struggling for air. 'Hit me,' she rasped, rocking from side to side.

'What?' said Rob.

'She said, "Hit me",' said Lisa. 'She's hyperventilating. She's going to faint if she doesn't breathe.'

Judith let the cat slip from her grasp. Her eyes were looking blindly upwards. She looked like a cornered wild animal.

Rob stepped forward and gently slapped her cheek.

Judith continued to wheeze.

'Harder. Harder.'

Rob slapped her again.

'Like this,' said Lisa, as she hit her adversary's cheek with more force than she had intended. As Judith fell to the floor over the body of Bunters, Lisa stood back, like a championship boxer. Keith wiped a bloody hand over his bald pate and, through habit, went to pull at his moustache, but instead he grabbed his bare upper lip.

Judith murmured,

163

'He was all I had left.'

'No, Denise,' said Lisa. 'He was all Judith had left.'

~

Lisa's feet were on her sofa, and she was holding her satin robe above her knees, as Rob gently dabbed the wound on her shin with a warm, wet pad of cotton wool. Her stained suit was in a carrier bag against the front door so she would not forget it in the morning.

'Ouch,' she said.

'I don't think it's too deep,' Rob said. 'How does it feel?'

'Not too bad, just smarting a bit. I had a tetanus shot last year, so I don't think there's anything to worry about.'

'It's probably good to let the air get to it, for now. That poor cat. He was a feisty little thing, but he had character,' Rob said. 'Judith must be devastated.'

'Denise. Poor Keith looked so distraught,' Lisa said.

'Yes. When did he do that, shave off his hair and moustache?'

'I'm not sure. He always has that cap on,' said Lisa. 'I'm not too good at sleuthing, am I? I guess I just expected her to be so shocked when she saw the picture of Judith that she would have confessed all. But that's not her style, is it?'

'Well, no harm's done. But, you know, I think in her head she is Judith Crayvern. Well, she is. She has the passport to prove it.' He laughed, pulling at Lisa's hair. 'You still have shredded paper in your hair, from looking in the bins.'

Lisa took the shards of coloured paper from his fingers.

'I bet these are the remains of the photos I saw of you. Once she saw us on the webcam she would have got rid of them.'

'Why didn't you tell me you were going to Hazelton, Lisa?'

'I just wanted to find out the truth. Prove it to you, so you would believe me. Everything about her is fake. Even most of her Facebook friends are made up.'

'What?'

'They aren't real. All their email addresses are very similar. Their photos are ones she's found on the Internet. Some of them are famous people. They're only Facebook friends with each other. Even

164

her sister's a fake.'

'God, this is so crazy. I'm sorry I didn't believe you, Lise.' Rob, held up a DVD case with his photograph on the cover. 'Well, we might not have the photos, but this might prove interesting.'

'What is it?'

'I saw it when she opened the drawer, before she took out her passport and stuck it under my nose, just as Keith arrived.'

'You took a CD from her drawer?' Lisa asked.

'A DVD, I think. As far as I could see it's all about me, so it's my property.'

Rob opened the case, moved over to the television, placed the disc in the DVD player, then picked up the remote. 'You don't want to watch it, then, I presume?' He looked at her quizzically.

Rob settled back on the sofa, one arm around Lisa, the other controlling the remote. She nestled against his chest. The screen lit up, showing Rob at a family gathering, his arm around a tanned, slim girl with long blonde hair. Lisa shuffled uncomfortably and leaned towards the television.

'That's Becca, isn't it? How's she got this? Is this off YouTube?'

'Yep. My sister posted it on the Internet so we could all see it. It's my twenty-fifth birthday, before I met you.'

The images of birthday celebrations played on for some time. Candles, singing, jokes, hugs, kisses, Mum, Dad, cousins, Grandma, girlfriend. Then they faded away. After a few moments a new clip began. In the background there were a few shouts and whistles.

'What about this one, Rob?'

'I don't remember seeing this. It's up at Hough End playing fields. Yes, brilliant goal! You can recognise the trees.'

'Who were you playing?'

'Riverton Rovers. It's odd. I've never seen this.'

'Let me google you.' Lisa picked up the laptop and deftly hit the keyboard. After some minutes she stopped. 'No, I can't find this. I've tried your name, both footie teams, the league, the park. No, it's not on the Internet. But look, the camera seems to be focused just on you, even when you aren't in the play. Fake Judith, I mean Denise Carvel, loves her digital phone. She could easily have taken it.'

'You're right. I'm the star of the show. But ...' Rob looked

165

puzzled. 'Are you sure you can't find it on the Internet? This is strange, very strange. That's our old kit. We met her when? Three to four months ago. Well, that video ...' He swallowed, grimacing. 'That video was taken over a year ago.'

'What?'

'Yes, really. This is absolutely crazy! What's going on?'

Rob stood up and looked pensively at Lisa as he walked in front of the television screen, which had now turned black.

'I have no idea. I really don't remember meeting her before. And I have thought hard about this, believe me. It's all in her imagination. It's all crazy, fucking mad. But now this is really spooking me.'

Lisa went over to him and put her arms round his waist.

'Look, tomorrow ... we'll do some more digging tomorrow. We need to sleep. I have work. She won't be in.'

THE WAY WE WERE

Take on me

Wednesday morning
'Good morning, Lisa.'

Lisa started. She had not expected to see the woman formerly known as Judith behind the Bergers reception desk. Lisa leaned over the counter and looked her in the eye.

'Good morning, Denise.'

'My name is Judith Crayvern, as you know. Perhaps I should speak to Andy again, to prevent this unwarranted harassment,' Judith said, in a low voice. She looked at her watch and said loudly, 'You're late.'

'Everyone who needed to know that I was going to be fifteen minutes late has been informed. I've just taken my very expensive suit to the dry-cleaners. They were not very encouraging about its prospects,' Lisa said. She took a sip of her takeaway coffee.

'That's a surprise. I didn't think you owned a very expensive suit.'

Judith's face was carefully made up and her glossy hair was styled into a neat bun. Lisa looked for a sign of a red slap mark on her cheek but could not see one. She had a barely suppressible urge to hit her again.

'Of course, your little suit is far more important than the death of a living creature,' Judith said.

Lisa walked away. She had felt rather sorry for the cat.

'Tasmin won the bet, I believe. Five pounds, I think it was,' Judith continued.

Lisa had almost reached the office door, but she spun around towards the receptionist.

'Sorry?'

'The make of your suit. Taz and Livvie had a bet. Was it H&M?'

Lisa turned abruptly and walked to her workstation.

'Aw, Lisa, I'm so sorry about your suit,' said Tasmin, putting away

169

her mobile. 'It was lovely, but I think they will be lucky to save it.'

'Yes,' said Lisa, now feeling that she was running on empty. So much for team spirit. 'Thank you for your help last night.'

'My pleasure,' Tasmin said, walking over to Lisa's desk. 'Where did you get it?'

Lisa wondered if the answer to the question was going to make Tasmin more money.

'Harvey Nicks,' Lisa said, as she took a sip of warm coffee.

'Oh. Isn't it absolutely dreadful about Bunters?' Tasmin lowered her voice. 'Judith says Keith killed him.'

'Keith didn't kill him. He found him,' Lisa said. She logged on to her computer. 'He'd been run over.'

'Oh.' Tasmin made no move back to her workstation, but instead rested her thigh on Lisa's desk as she sipped a cappuccino. 'What a night it was. Do you think she knocked that Guinness over you because she found out that you reported her to Andy?'

'What?'

'That's what everyone's saying, that you were questioning her credentials, but Andy likes her. And he was very annoyed with you.'

'Everyone' meaning *Olivia*, Lisa thought. She wondered whether or not Olivia knew what a gossip her friend was. If she did she might be more cautious about the information she shared.

'We tried to poach Judith for our team, but she was very loyal to you, you know. Well, to your team,' Tasmin said.

'Yeah, she would be. Perhaps you should stop listening to everyone, Tasmin. There usually isn't much substance to it. Now, did you do the work on the Lloyds account?'

'Tetchy.' Tasmin walked back to her desk. 'Yah, here it is. I do think she did it deliberately, though.'

'What?'

'Ruined your suit.'

Wednesday lunchtime

'We had lunch with Judith,' Tasmin said, as she sat back at her desk. Lisa involuntarily stiffened on hearing the name of her adversary.

'Olivia and I were already lunching, but we thought Judith might need cheering up after losing Bunters. It's her last day, you know, as

170

Sally's back tomorrow.'

Some good news for a change, thought Lisa. She glanced at her watch. It was already two o'clock.

'By the way, I didn't tell you. We didn't do too badly at the quiz last night. We were in fourth place: eighty-one points,' Tasmin said, lengthening the conversation.

Fuck. I should have asked her before, Lisa thought, guiltily.

'That's a really good score. Well done.'

'I hadn't realised that Judith had known Rob before. I thought you'd just met her at the pub quiz.'

Lisa tensed.

'Yah, she was saying what a fantastic time she and Rob had had at some flamenco club. I hadn't realised you'd all known each other so long – well, Judith and Rob, anyway. She said she would love to go back to Barcelona some day to revisit old haunts. She had an amazing time there.'

'Yeah, I'm sure she did,' Lisa said.

Lisa walked up to the reception before leaving Bergers for the day.

'I know Rob didn't go to the flamenco club in Barcelona with you. He didn't know you then, "Judith",' Lisa hissed.

'Well, that is exactly what I would expect you to believe, darling,' Judith said, touching her chest with her hand. 'But I did know him then, yes.' She laughed, looking Lisa in the eye. 'And yes, we did go to The Bodega de la Casa together. I find his amnesia very amusing, but your gullibility even more so.'

She tapped a pen on the reception desk as she looked, unblinking, back at Lisa.

Wednesday evening

Rob ran up the stairs of the bus but, as he reached the top, felt the same disappointment he had as a schoolboy when he saw that the front seats were already occupied. Grudgingly he sat behind a blonde four-year-old boy who had achieved pole position. The boy was flanked by his young mother, who was holding on to his waistband as he wriggled up and down. She was simultaneously trying to read a magazine and feign interest in her son's conversation.

171

Rob recognised the mother and son from previous journeys. The boy was not averse to using tears to embarrass any adults who had taken 'his' seat. Today he was dressed in a grey hoodie and had a toy sword thrust down his waistband. He held a silver plastic shield in his hand.

Rob watched the queues of commuters being stewarded on to the packed buses to ferry them away from the city. The knight whooped as the bus set off, imitating the engine noise. They flew down the bus lane, then sailed through amber lights before juddering into a lay-by to disgorge some passengers. Another bus swung in front and was reluctantly, or so Rob presumed, allowed in. At least he would have been reluctant to allow him in, same bus company or not. Rob's bus edged up to the bus in front until there was hardly any space between them.

Yeah, you let him know what you think, thought Rob, as the bus set off again.

A trail of BMWs and Audis rolled slowly home to the suburbs. Rob gazed at the new towering geometric apartment blocks skipping by, each narrow balcony giving a glimpse into a stranger's home like an outdoor mantelpiece displaying the treasured effects of daily life. Sun loungers, bicycles, hanging baskets, empty bottles. Strangers drawn together by the city, but living very different lives. He reflected on his assets, or rather his negative equity. No property, a student loan, debts, a set of language skills that were progressively diminishing.

And now Judith, who Lisa said wasn't Judith at all. Why on earth had she become so interested in him? No – face up to it – she was obsessed. He had always thought Judith was slightly familiar. It all seemed to fit when he saw the photo of Michelle Pfeiffer. She really looked very much like her: striking features, large smiling eyes. Charismatic. Almost as good an actress as well, it turned out. But had he done something to mislead her, by calling her *bonita* when he said 'Adios'?

Lisa had suggested that he had been too flirtatious, that he had led Judith on. It had never got him into trouble before. No, never.

And what about the DVD? When had she begun following him, watching him play football? He couldn't remember any strangers

172

videoing the match, but why would he? He never paid any attention to them. Who watched? Some parents, some new girlfriends. After a while they got bored of standing beside a windy football pitch. Lisa had lasted one match.

Lisa had texted to ask if he knew The Bodega de la Casa. Of course he did. He must have been there hundreds of times with thousands of people. During the two holiday seasons while he was in Barcelona, he had dealt with just about every query and trauma that a miscellaneous group of Britons could experience. He had apologised for the inefficiencies of airlines, the vagaries of the weather, and the results of football matches. He had solved clients' problems when they had forgotten their medication, when they had taken too much of the same, when they had got lost, and when they had got arrested. There were so many incidents, so many people. They all blurred into one.

Yes, the British abroad, it could be said, acted very unremarkably like each other. They just wanted to eat, drink, get a suntan, get laid, and see a few sights so that they could use their digital cameras. There were a few extremely unpleasant, loutish holidaymakers and some exceptionally agreeable people he could recall, but not that many.

He had tried to remember every girl he had slept with when he was in Barcelona. That had taken some time, but there really was no one remotely like Judith. Not that he had ever really thought that he had, but he had just wanted to eliminate the possibility. Judith. She wasn't really Judith. But he hadn't slept with Denise Carvel, either. Just what was that all about? He couldn't even bear to think about it.

He was amazed that Lisa was so forgiving, really. He hadn't believed her, probably to avoid facing the truth. At least work was looking up. He had a day off, then it was down to London to see Tom Graham, who seemed to be fit and well again. A change of scene would be good, even if it was a working day. Then he was meeting up with his uni mates. They'd put everything into perspective, even if it had an alcoholic hue.

His phone vibrated. It was probably Lisa. He sighed, wearily, as he glimpsed the sender's name. Not again. He opened the text.

Please call me. I need to talk to you. Judith xxx

Why was Judith still texting *him*? he wondered. He looked up from his phone and into the gaze of the little boy, who was watching him intently.

'Bloody bonkers,' the boy mouthed.

Rob smiled.

'Bloody bonkers,' the boy said, in a whisper, and then again, louder.

'Turn round,' said his mother, pulling him towards her. 'I told you before not to say that. It's always the same after you've been to your granddad's.'

As the bus trundled along, the overhanging trees whipped against the windows. Cascades of branches, their tips hard with spring buds, knocked against the bus roof like wooden timpani.

'It's scary,' said the little boy. Then he started giggling. 'But I like it.' He stood up, thrusting his sword and shield into the air. 'It's an adventure!' he yelled.

Rob got up, bending to avoid touching the ceiling of the bus, and made his way to the stairs. He turned to the boy, who was watching him.

'Bloody bonkers,' he mouthed to the giggling knight.

He went down the steps, jerking against the side of the stairwell, lost in his thoughts. Denise Carvel knew all about him, but he didn't know anything about her. The bus door drew open.

'Thanks, mate,' Rob said.

'Mind how you go,' replied the driver.

Thursday morning

She was sitting at the kitchen table, looking at her MacBook. The doorbell rang. She smiled. She knew he'd come. She walked into the hall and saw a familiar shadow silhouetted in the frosted glass of the front door.

So you're not going to come round the back and use my spare key this time? Very wise. She paused by the mirror in the hall and smiled, turning her head from side to side. Her hair was pinned loosely on top of her crown, allowing a few stray curls to escape. The style enhanced her cheekbones and exposed the nape of her neck. She adjusted the collar of her blouse, smoothed her skirt, then opened the door.

'So you're here,' she said, looking at her watch, then back at Rob. The tip of her tongue touched the corner of her mouth.

'You wanted to see me.' Rob was resting against the door frame. The thumb of his right hand was hooked in the belt of low-slung black jeans. He looked at her steadily.

'Yes.' She scrutinised him. He hadn't shaved. The skin on his face was slack. There were grey circles under his eyes and the sallow skin showed faint pockmarks left by years of teenage acne. She had never noticed the imperfections before. He was wearing a leather jacket, which had seen better days, over a white T-shirt. It suited him. Very Jim Morrison.

'You didn't text me to say what time you were coming,' she said, softly.

'It seemed urgent.'

She stood in the doorway, looking at him.

'Perhaps you could tell me exactly what it is you're up to?' His eyes burned through her.

'What sort of question's that?' She had expected concern or some playful banter. She felt hurt.

'One that deserves to be answered,' he said, looking her in the eye and pushing the door out of her grip. 'Now.'

She detected a slight trace of cigarette smoke as he passed. She moved sharply backwards against the wall as he strode through the hall to the kitchen. As the door opened a throbbing flamenco guitar grew louder.

An empty plastic bowl was on the kitchen floor. Through the French windows a fresh mound of soil marked Bunters's grave. The kitchen smelled of the warm aroma of ginger and freshly ironed sheets. Rob turned round to face her as she walked through the door.

'Would you like a coffee?' She flashed a smile.

'No, thank you.'

'Cake?' She touched her hair, coquettishly. 'It's not long out of the oven. Still warm. Some people prefer to keep it a week or two, but I think it's just as good like this.'

'No, thank you.' Rob looked up at the ceiling. He scraped his hair back with his hand as he looked around the walls.

175

'There's no hidden camera, if that's what you're worried about. The only security cameras are outside the house, to protect me from intruders. The system obviously isn't foolproof.' She smiled broadly, her eyes twinkling.

Rob brushed his fringe aside again. The gesture was so sensual, she wondered if he'd done it deliberately.

'Have you come to offer your condolences?' she said, as she switched on the kettle.

'I've come to find out what you want and who you are.' Rob watched her.

'Bunters has just died, if you remember.' Her lips narrowed.

'It's very sad, and I'm sorry, I really am. But you've been in work since your cat died. I can't imagine you're happy about it, but you're coping.'

She walked over to the sound system control panel. The singing stopped abruptly. The refrigerator hummed.

'How do you know what I can cope with?' She turned and looked into his eyes. 'Losing everything. The man I loved, my gorgeous Ben. Always remembering, every day. Wondering if I should have done something differently, if they could have been saved. Now Bunters has gone. He was all I had left.'

Rob said nothing. His gaze, which had been holding hers, lowered.

'I'm sorry,' he mumbled.

Her heels tapped on the slate tiles as she walked to the kettle and filled the cafetière with water. A newly baked cake was resting on a wire rack on the worktop. She cut a small square. She held it between her crimson fingertips and slowly walked back. She held the morsel up to Rob's mouth.

'Taste,' she said.

He parted his lips as she placed the gingerbread on his tongue. Her finger grazed the tip of his tongue and lower lip as she withdrew it. She watched his eyes as he savoured the cake.

'It excites the palate, I always think. Just teases at first, then all the flavour explodes,' she said.

He swallowed.

'No more,' he said, as she walked back to the cake rack. 'No more.'

She turned and looked straight at him.

'I'm just pouring myself a coffee. Are you sure you don't want one?'

Rob watched her. The refrigerator hummed.

'Who are you? Why have you taken Judith's name?' he asked, finally.

She turned to pick up the cafetière.

'I'm waiting for an answer,' he said.

'It was what Martin had always wanted. What we always wanted.' She turned back and looked at him, meeting his gaze. 'To be married.'

'But he was already married.'

She filled a china mug with coffee.

'It was over. We were known as a couple. It seemed to be the right thing. So I changed my name, in honour of him.' She sat down at the table behind the MacBook, placing the steaming aromatic coffee beside her. 'It was in his memory. Does that make me a bad person, Rob? She had died by then.'

She searched his eyes. Rob said nothing.

'Well, does it? Love's not always as clear-cut as it should be. You know that.' She paused. 'Come round here.'

Rob hesitated, then walked behind the table and leaned over her. He took the DVD case from his jacket pocket and slammed it on the table beside her.

'Why have you been following me? Videoing me?' he said.

'How did you …?'

She could feel the heat in his body inches behind her. She felt that she was in the centre of a magnetic field. Every sense felt alive. His arms rested on the table at either side of her. The air was charged.

'Why?' he repeated.

'We had such a great connection. I knew we must meet up again, but I was shy.'

'Again?'

'After Barcelona, when you came back. It was fate. I'd been here a year when I saw you coming out of MedTime. Then I went to watch you play football – I'd seen your name in a local paper. I left

177

before the end, it was so cold. But I took a video. It was just something to do.' She tried to turn to look up at him, but his arms were almost pinning her to her chair.

'You have a whole DVD of videos of me.'

'There are only two. I just kept them together. I like to be organised. I wasn't expecting you to see it, to steal it from my own home,' she said.

The DVD case fell on the floor. As Rob bent down to pick it up his hair grazed her arm. It felt like gossamer against her skin. The fair hairs on her arm stood upright.

The refrigerator hummed.

Rob straightened his body, then stepped back and turned away gazing into the garden.

'Why did you move here, follow me here?' Rob asked, turning back round.

'Like I told you, I'd already moved here before you came back. I wanted to escape Hazelton to start a new life, get lost in a city. But it's not unusual for people with a strong connection to want to keep in touch, is it?' Judith said. 'I felt compelled to meet you again.'

'When did we first meet?'

'Don't pretend you don't remember.'

'I don't, as incredible as this may sound to you. I'm sorry but, really, I don't.'

She sighed.

Rob said nothing.

She stood up and switched on the music again. The *cante* soared above the rhythmic handclapping as the guitarist plucked a haunting melody.

'Four years ago in Barcelona. And yes, I was Denise Carvel then, but my name now is Judith Crayvern. *That* is my name now. *That* is who I am.'

Rob shook his head, studying the black slate tiles.

'Why did you need to see me today, Judith?'

'I just want what's best for you. I don't think Lisa is. Look at this.' She pointed at her computer. A window was open, showing Lisa's Facebook timeline. 'Who would have thought Lisa and her ex were still friends after all he'd done?' She pointed to a comment by

James Strather on Lisa's timeline.

It would be great to meet up again.

Rob started laughing uncontrollably.

'You really do expect me to believe that, don't you? Well, why not? We believed everything else. You've made it up haven't you? Like all your other fake friends.' He laughed.

'I did not make him up,' Judith said. The sparkle in her grey eyes died. 'But you're right. I do have fake friends, as you call them. I'm sorry you find it so funny. Some might think it's rather sad.'

Rob moved away from the table and towards the door.

'Yeah, you're right. It's rather sad. Very sad. Changing your name isn't going to change your past. You would never have been Judith Crayvern, anyway. You would still have been Denise. None of this makes sense. You need to sort this out for yourself. Just leave me out of it.'

'Rob, but—'

'I'm off. If you want to be called Judith, that's up to you. But, if you want my opinion, it's just plain weird. Denise. There's nothing wrong with Denise. Just be yourself.'

Rob opened the back door. She watched as he pulled it shut, then walked back to the computer. She closed the lid of the MacBook sharply. That hadn't been the reaction she had expected. Damn. And it had all been going so well. Why had she mentioned Lisa? That girl had been the last thing on Rob's mind. It was her own fault. She had been so determined to incriminate Lisa that she had broken the spell.

She walked over to the tray of parkin and cut a small square. She inhaled the exotic spices and then dropped a morsel of cake on her tongue.

But he felt it, too. She knew he felt it, too.

The stomping flamenco guitar was echoing in the kitchen as Rob glanced at the garden and the hanging baskets. He wondered if the spare key was still hidden among the spring flowers. He glimpsed Bunters's grave. It was all very sad. As he walked past the garage he quickly looked in the blue bin. There was a mass of shredded coloured paper. He still didn't know why Judith – no, Denise – had become fixated with him nor where they had met. But he knew he

179

had to get away. He walked up the road to the bus stop, pausing briefly to light a cigarette. That was the second packet that week. Not good.

He felt uneasy. Changing her name still made no sense. She would never have been Judith Crayvern. Bloody bonkers. But it was not what had been said that had really troubled him. It was the atmosphere in the kitchen that had been disturbing. There was electricity in the air, and it felt both part of him and apart from him. He was captivated by its elemental force but repelled by its power. It had the force of a bolt of lightning and was totally beyond his control.

Her spicy heady fragrance had been hypnotic. The fine downy hairs on the nape of her neck had entranced him. Her twinkling eyes had penetrated inside him. He had felt intoxicated, bewitched. *He must keep away.*

I really didn't mean it

Thursday afternoon
Sunbeams, deflected through the frosted glass of the front door, danced on the wall and mirror then abruptly disappeared, draining the radiance from her skin as they vanished. She studied her face in the looking glass. She looked so different in the half-light. Two people. Judith. Denise.

There's nothing wrong with Denise.

She unpinned her hair then moved her head from side to side, inspecting her face from different angles.

Changing your name isn't going to change your past.

Rob hadn't changed since she met him four years ago, but she had. That's why he hadn't recognised her.

The house was silent except for the ticking of the clock and the hum of the central heating boiler. She curled up on the sofa, her head resting on a soft cushion. During the last few years she had been haunted by echoes of her former life but had suppressed the images that had strayed from her past. Now the memories poured down on her. She closed her eyes. She was sitting on the wooden bench that crowned the hillock overlooking Hazelmere. Ben was sitting nearby, preening his golden coat.

Five years earlier
She called to Ben softly, taking out a biscuit from her pocket and holding it above his head. He jumped up and caught it. She laughed as she held the dog's head between both hands and buried her face in his damp, soft golden fur.

'Lydia Bignall, that's it. Lydia Bignall. This seat is erected in the memory of Lydia Bignall. This was her favourite view, Denise,' Martin said, as he finished deciphering the worn plaque on the back of the seat. Drops of rain dripped off his leather bush hat.

'Well, it's very pretty but I don't think it's the best view round here, not even on a sunny day when you can actually see the hills across there.' She pointed at the low cloud that hung over the other side of the lake.

'You're right,' Martin said, getting up. 'Although if you do stand up you can see a lot more. Come and look, Dennie.'

She stood up, splashing in the murky pool which had collected in front of the bench. She tugged on her hood to cover her forehead.

'The sheep don't look too happy today. See, they're all hunched together on that high ground by the wall. Usually they just ignore the rain, like us,' Martin said.

'You know,' she said, her elbow linking with his, 'this is the view Lydia would have seen. Not just the lake, but the river and the bridge, and on a good day the ducks.'

'Well, it's certainly not a good day today. I've never seen the river so full, and the lake looks like a rough, grey sea. Icily cold. Treacherous.'

'Yes.' She shivered as she watched the waves skimming from side to side.

'Warm me up, Dennie,' Martin said, as he put his arm round her and they sat down again. She felt cosy, safe.

'I bet Lydia would be pretty annoyed that they have ruined her favourite spot by putting a seat here,' she said.

'Perhaps she had a row with her husband and he did it to spite her. Just the sort of thing Judith would do,' Martin said. She laughed, then there was an awkward pause.

'You said last Christmas would be the last one we spent apart. So when are you going to leave her, Martin?'

'Soon,' Martin said. 'Don't worry. Soon.'

'Next week?'

'No, not that soon. I still have to tell her.'

'Obviously.' She was silent for a moment, then said, 'You tell her and you move out. It's just one thing, really, not two things done on separate occasions. You just basically have to do it. In fact, you could do it tonight. Well?'

'Well, no, not tonight. She won't be back from her marathon till late.'

'Tomorrow morning, then.'

'We're going to her sister's tomorrow. It's her nephew's birthday. I really don't want to upset their celebrations. Besides, there're

182

arrangements to be made.' Martin looked into the distance.

'What arrangements?' she asked.

'Where I would live.'

'Well, there's no problem about that. You can move in with me. Bunters, too. Then we can buy somewhere together.'

'It's not that easy. You have to think about all the financial implications of a divorce. You don't want me to pay her maintenance forever, do you? Our joint income could be counted. That's what could happen. You could end up supporting Judith.'

'Other people seem to manage.'

'Well, other people aren't us,' Martin said. After a short silence he asked, 'Which other people, anyway?'

'Paula and Tim, for a start. They seem to manage just fine. They're happy. I don't see why that lazy cow can work things out and we can't.'

'Happy? Those two? Paula's part-time and he's unemployed. They have nothing to lose.'

'Maybe I should give in my notice. Then I'd have nothing to lose,' she said. 'Or you could move to one of my student flats.'

Martin pulled on the fingers of his gloves.

'Seriously. The commute won't be too bad. It will be the opposite direction to everyone else. And your cat can move in there, or with me,' she said. The desperation began to well up inside her again. Fear. Even then she had felt fear.

'I like Hazelton.'

'More than me, clearly.' Her voice rose. 'I don't like this situation any more. I don't want to go through another Easter on my own while you play happy families with your in-laws. In fact, I don't want to go through one more weekend of it.'

There was silence. Martin looked away.

'The thing is ... well ... The thing is, she's ill,' Martin said.

'Ill?'

'Yes. I can't tell her at the moment because she's sick. I can't hurt her now. Have some compassion.'

She stood up, flinging back her hood, exposing her face and hair to the rain.

'But you don't mind hurting me, is that it? You're never going to

183

leave her, are you? Come on, Ben.' She pulled on Ben's lead and ran down the footpath.

'Denise. Don't be crazy. You know I want to, but it isn't that simple. Dennie!'

She ran through the pinewoods, desperately trying to expel the fear which had taken her over. How many more years of excuses would Martin want her to endure?

'Denise,' he called. 'Denise, be careful. It looks like a quagmire down there.'

'So what? What do you care?' she cried.

'I care a lot. More than you will ever know, Denise. Come back. Let's talk it through.'

'Talking … You're very good at that, but I don't believe you any longer.'

As she and Ben ran out from the pine trees, rivulets of clear spring water were running through the grass, along the path, pushing away the gravel, relentlessly forging the lowest, fastest channel to the bottom of the valley. The fast-flowing river below was like a cauldron of icy grey water simmering away, ready to boil over. The pair squelched through the grass and on to the wooden bridge. The waters were high, almost up to the bottom of the bridge, bubbling around Denise's feet. Martin had reached the bog that had been the riverside path. He had lost his hat.

'Denise, come back. It's not safe,' Martin shouted over the roaring water.

'I don't care. Nothing matters any longer.' She leaned on the bridge rails. Her hair whipped in the wind.

'You're being ridiculous. Think of Ben,' Martin shouted.

'Am I being ridiculous or am I being strung along? I think perhaps I'm just your bit on the side.'

'I want you, Dennie.'

'Then tell *her* that,' she cried. 'Tell Judith it's me you love.'

There was a rumble, and the bridge split as water broke the riverbanks, tipping her into the icy waters as the dog lead slipped from her fingers. Ben remained on the shattered timbers of the bridge looking into the water, whimpering.

She stood up unsteadily – the water was up to her knees – and

184

looked desperately into Martin's perspiring face. She turned away to see Ben, legs splayed, balancing on the bridge. She tried to move towards Ben, but with every tentative step against the current, she seemed to slip backwards.

'Stay where you are, Dennie,' Martin said. 'Don't move.' He seized a tree branch which had been brought downstream and, with all his strength, held it out. Denise grasped it between her frozen fingers, then slowly waded through the gurgling, fast-moving waters as Martin pulled her towards him and on to firm ground.

'I need to get Ben,' she said, struggling from Martin's grip.

'You're too light. The current will push you over.' He held her for a moment, looked her straight in the eyes. 'Stay here. I'll sort it all out.' He scraped his brown wavy hair from his eyes. 'It's you I love, believe me. I love you, Judith.'

She flinched.

Martin's face contorted as he mouthed 'you' again. He turned and, steadying himself with the branch, waded back towards the remains of the bridge where Ben was yelping. Just as Martin gripped Ben's collar and tried to grasp hold of his body a thunderous roar and a torrent of muddy water cascaded over them. Denise screamed as the edge of a brown wave of water skirted round her. She staggered backwards to the safety of the plantation and higher ground. Saturated, she righted herself and looked towards what had, only moments before, been a bridge and a grey, bubbling river. Now she saw only brown swirling water. No Martin. No Ben.

She had purposefully arrived late for the funeral and had sat at the back, away from her colleagues. At the end of the service she fixed her eyes on a prayer book as Judith had led the mourners up the aisle, behind the coffin. She avoided meeting Judith outside the church, although she scrutinised her from afar. There she was, dressed in black, luxuriating in her widow's grief, fraudulently accepting the kindness and sympathy of strangers. She had her own memories of Martin. A side of Martin that Judith had never wanted to know. Judith had no right to him.

She lingered by the flowers, alone with her thoughts, and when it was quiet had finally departed, leaving behind a single pink rose.

The day after the funeral she overheard Paula, talking, or rather holding court, to her colleagues in the museum's staffroom.

'Back at work already ... The callous bint ... The cheek of her, going to the funeral.'

The room had fallen silent as she had entered. She was an outcast, living on the edge. And all the time echoing in her head were Martin's last words,

'I love you, Judith.'

Late Thursday afternoon

The spring light was fading quickly. Soon the sitting room was nestling in the shadows of the dusk. Her sobs were heard by no one. She inhaled deeply to steady her breathing. The sweet scent of the spring flowers, which drooped in a vase on the fireplace, released another memory. It was one year after Martin had died.

Four years earlier

She stopped by the stone wall and took some freesias from her bag. She left one of them in a crevice in the stones where her beautiful golden retriever had been discovered. She walked over to the bridge where she stood for a few moments, inhaling the heady scent from the last of the blooms. Then she threw them in the river at the spot where she had last seen Martin, before the current pulled him away.

'Until we meet again,' she murmured. She was still daydreaming when she heard a movement among the fir trees. It was probably the old-age pensioner who always seemed to be creeping around. He often seemed to be lurking somewhere nearby, wanting to talk.

She did not want her solitude to be disturbed by the banalities of polite conversation. She deftly took refuge behind some trees. A tallish woman with short brown hair and the sinewy physique of a dedicated runner emerged from the pinewoods. She was wearing a dull combination of earthy hues, as if she had dressed to blend into the landscape. The woman was instantly recognisable as Judith.

She watched as Judith walked quickly towards the bridge and then along the riverbank, stopping directly opposite a bare gnarled tree. Judith took off her rucksack and pulled out a jar, then scattered the contents into the river and on to the grassy bank. Judith finished,

186

knelt down for a moment, then marched briskly back through the woods.

She slowly walked over to the grassy bank. Along the grass was a silvery-grey powder. She looked at it, her body trembling, then bent down and picked up a pinch of the ashes and brought her fingers to her lips, stroking them gently over her mouth. She picked up some more and vigorously rubbed the ash into her face, then ran the tip of her tongue over her bottom lip. She searched for more of the silvery powder, rubbing her hands in the grass and soil, then reached into the water to glean some more.

As she lay sobbing on the riverbank, her face streaked with mud and Martin's ashes, the birds sang a joyful chorus.

Man in the mirror

'I'm sorry, Maya, I thought the glam solicitor was the one.' Lisa put down her mobile and curled up with a cushion on the sofa.

'Barrister.'

'Sorry, barrister.'

'Well, not this time.' Maya took a spoonful of ice cream from a china bowl. 'He said he was too young. He confused lust for love. It does happen, you know.'

'You're wavering,' Lisa said.

Maya was silent.

'He lied to you. I bet he said his wife didn't understand him, as well.' Lisa continued.

Maya sighed. She ran her spoon through the melting ice cream, which clung to the sides of the dish, then licked it very slowly.

'I must say I'm surprised. I thought you'd checked him out,' said Lisa.

'Well, we all make mistakes. I guess I believed what I wanted to. But I'm not wasting any more time on him. I'm taking up fencing.'

'Fencing?' said Lisa.

'Yes, I think that's a sport that will attract lots of interesting people.' Maya put the bowl on the carpet. 'That was good.'

'Do you want more? I've got two more flavours.'

'I do, but I won't. So, how are things with you? Have you declared victory over Judith?'

'Denise. Well, it was certainly a relief going into work yesterday and meeting Sally at reception. And today went very well. Taylors are pleased with everything. So Andy's delighted. Tasmin's happy and I haven't seen Olivia. So everything is hunky-dory. And that bitch is out of my life, for now. I just have to make sure she doesn't come back into it.' Lisa stretched her body along the sofa, arching her back.

'That will be interesting.'

'Keith's the target of her venom now. She's told everyone he killed her cat.'

'Who apparently is not her cat.'

'Exactly.'

'And what does Rob think?'

'Well, he was quite impressed with my sleuthing, but I think he's just put the whole matter behind him now. He won't talk about her. He's in London. He says he has something to tell me. I hope it's good news for a change.' Lisa squeezed the cushion.

'Well, I can't help feeling sorry for her,' Maya said, picking up the bowl and moving towards the kitchen.

'What?' Lisa sat upright.

'She lost her lover and her dog. She probably nearly died in that flood. Then she worked with those bitchy women you met.'

'I don't think I quite described them like that, Maya.' Lisa pulled her knees up to her chin.

'You can recognise the type, though, surely?' Maya put a hand to the side of her mouth, as she pretended to whisper, 'I'm not one to gossip, but between you and me ...'

Lisa glared at her as Maya disappeared through the door.

'That coach driver you met – he had quite a different take on her,' Maya said, as she walked back to her armchair.

'Well, I liked her myself when we first met. It's only when you get to know her that you realise how she takes people in.' Lisa tweaked the corners of the cushion. 'You know, Paula sort of said that she was suspicious about where Denise was when Judith died. She wouldn't put anything past her, she said.'

'Paula doesn't like her, does she? I wonder what axe she has to grind? Just imagine if Olivia got the opportunity to gossip about you, Lisa,' Maya said, picking up the remote.

'Well, I don't think she'd accuse me of murder,' Lisa aimed the cushion at the armchair.

'Aah, but that's what you want to believe about Judith, isn't it? Who's the drama queen, now? Hah!'

Late Saturday afternoon
Although Rob was listening to a Spanish podcast about La Liga and imagining a football match on a sunny day at Camp Nou in Barcelona, he could not help but be aware that he was walking through a crowded, drizzly English city. He nimbly moved his upper body sideways as a shopper's umbrella suddenly tipped backwards. As he dropped his pace, watching vigilantly as the umbrella's dripping spokes whirled erratically from side to side, he saw a familiar figure in a red jacket run down the steps of the art gallery a few yards ahead. She was sharing an umbrella.

Despite their heads being hidden, Rob immediately recognised Judith and Jeremy. He felt a pull in his stomach and a wave of anxiety overwhelm him. Rob quickened his pace and followed them as they dashed down a narrow street. He watched Jeremy open a heavy Victorian door and usher Judith inside, then Jeremy shook the rain from the umbrella and followed her.

Impulsively Rob pursued them inside the bar, veering to the right towards the counter as Judith and Jeremy made their way to a table near the window. He watched through the bar mirror as Judith flirted with Jeremy, then a waiter.

Keep away.

'How are you today, sir? What can I get you?' asked the barman, attempting to give Rob full eye contact, as he polished a glass. 'Sir?'

Rob continued to watch Judith. He was not sure what he was feeling.

'Sir?'

Rob paid for a Peroni and leaned against the bar counter, watching Judith and Jeremy out of the corner of his eye. Judith? No, this woman was Denise.

Keep away.

He checked his watch. As he left the bar and pulled up his collar against the rain he realised what he was feeling.

Jealousy.

Early Saturday evening
'Cheers, Lisa,' said Rob. 'Looks like things are going well at Bergers. Well done.'

Lisa clinked her wine glass with Rob's. The Italian restaurant was humming, packed with wet shoppers, wet football supporters, and wet women out on hen parties.

Lisa looked into Rob's eyes.

'Thank you, babe. Without your support I wouldn't have got the job in the first place, so a big, big thank you. Andy even said that I'd done a good job with Tasmin, influenced her attitude to work and,' she said, beaming, 'that I have the makings of an excellent manager.'

'Brill. How is Taz, by the way? You seem quite pally now. Is she still with Jeremy?'

'Taz has been amazing. A real help. She seems to be quite into Jeremy now. Moved from not caring to being totally besotted in a few weeks,' Lisa said.

Rob looked away and gazed towards the misted windows.

'Is there something wrong?' Lisa said.

'No, nothing. Is she seeing him this weekend?'

'I think they're going to 63 Degrees tonight, the French restaurant in the Northern Quarter. Look, let me show you the photos I took the other day at Hazelmere.' Lisa showed Rob her mobile.

'I took this from the bench where I texted you. There were sweeping views over the hills. It was so peaceful, just the sound of little lambs baaing and birds singing. The whole air was filled with birdsong when I was down by the river. It would be lovely to go for a proper walk there. Maybe we could have a weekend away.'

'Mmm. Very nice, Lise.'

'Look, you can see the bridge that crosses the River Hazel just near the lake. All this would have been flooded with raging water. It was like a mini tsunami, the coach driver said.' Lisa raised her hands above her head. 'It was different to how I imagined it. I guess I'd just pictured how it must have been on the day Martin drowned. But it was so peaceful. Though the woods were kind of spooky.' She swept her fingers across the mobile screen, enlarging the photograph. 'That's where Martin and the dog died. And Judith died just here, too.' She flicked through some more photographs.

'What's that?'

'It's a plaque on the back of a bench. It's in memory of Lydia Bignall. Her husband spends his time wandering round there, to be near his wife's ashes. He's the one who dragged Judith from the water. He was the only one around, he said.'

'Very interesting.' Rob took a large swig of wine. 'It's all very sad, though. I think we need another,' he said, signalling to the waiter.

'That was quick,' Lisa said, diverting her gaze to Rob's glass.

'What are you getting out of this, Lisa? It seems a bit voyeuristic. Isn't it Judith who does the stalking?'

'I'm not stalking.'

'Well, sleuthing.'

'And her name is Denise.'

'Whatever it is you're doing, it's becoming an obsession. A ghoulish one.'

'What?' Lisa gripped the stem of her glass tightly. 'Don't you want to know where she met you? Why *she's* so obsessed with you? Why she might want to take an innocent woman's name?'

'She met me in The Bodega de la Casa in Barcelona. I don't remember. I don't know why she's obsessed. Maybe it's some overgrown schoolgirl crush. Maybe it's post-traumatic stress. I don't know. It doesn't matter.'

'But ...'

'It doesn't matter. It's harmless. Drop it.'

'Your wine, sir,' said the waiter.

'Just pour it,' said Rob. 'I'm sure it will be fine.' He waved his hand dismissively towards the bottle, and then looked earnestly at Lisa. 'You're trying to make her into a villain when she's just a victim. She's a sad, lonely woman. Leave it.'

Lisa glared back at him.

'No harm's come of it,' she said.

'And no good. I won't be a minute,' Rob said, before edging his way through the packed tables to the toilets at the back of the restaurant.

Lisa flipped through the photographs of Hazelmere as she waited for Rob to return. She felt guilty. Maybe he was right. Maybe she did want to prove that Denise was a villain. Maya had said that, too. There was no one about when Judith had died, or so Mr Bignall had said. So how could she have been there? Lisa looked at the photos

192

again, switching from the view she had taken from the seat, to the view of the bridge. How could he be sure, though? If he were sitting on the bench talking to Lydia he wouldn't be able to see the bridge where Judith died.

Rob sat down again opposite Lisa. She smiled and closed her mobile.

'You have a lovely smile, you know, Lise,' he said.

'How did London go yesterday, babe? You wouldn't tell me on the phone,' Lisa said, wondering why she was annoyed that Rob liked her smile. 'I'm very intrigued.'

'Good. Brilliant, in fact. Great night with my uni mates. Kev sends his love, by the way. Well, the reason I never got the interview was because they had other things lined up for me.'

'It's taken them some time to tell you that.'

'It was my own fault. I was so angry when I got the message about the shop manager's interviews I didn't return any of Tom's calls.'

'Great career move.' Lisa pulled at her turquoise dress ring.

'Well, as it happens there may be one on the cards. They see a role in Europe as my next position.'

'That's good?' Lisa looked doubtful as she swirled her wine around.

'No, I'll not be repping.' Rob laughed, shaking his head. 'Ye of little faith. I'll be part of the senior team.'

'Cheers, babe.' Lisa touched his glass with hers. 'About time you had a break.'

'Thanks. That's why they wanted me down in London, to talk about it,' Rob said.

'What? Why didn't you tell me?'

'I didn't want to worry you. I wasn't sure if—'

'Worry me? You never share anything with me. I thought we were a couple: partners.'

'We are. I'm sharing now. It's not definite yet.'

'Well, how will this affect me, if you're running round Europe?'

'I'll still be based here. Of course we're partners, Lise.'

'You don't know what a partnership is. You don't share yourself. Not with me, anyway.' Lisa's voice rose.

193

'What about that job in London? I bet you're going for that. You haven't mentioned that recently,' Rob fired back.

'Well, you were upset last time it was mentioned.'

Rob took another gulp of wine. He turned his attention to the couple on the adjacent table, who had finished their own conversation and were scarcely trying to disguise the fact that they were listening to his and Lisa's. He stared at the man pointedly.

'Can I help you, signor, signorina?' The waiter stood between Rob and the other diners. 'Have you made your choice or would you like more time to decide?'

It's in his kiss

Saturday night
She was certain she had seen him lurking on the street when she had left the art gallery with Jeremy. Later, he had been at the bar drinking a bottle of Peroni. He just couldn't keep away, just as she couldn't keep away from him. She lay on the crisp sheets, her eyes closed, reminiscing. She was in Catalonia four years ago, taking her first break since Martin had died. The memories played in her head like a film.

Four years earlier
The Barcelona boutique hotel was styled very tastefully in understated neutral hues and black. That day, as every day, a well-groomed man in a grey suit was busy behind the reception desk adjacent to a large vase of fresh, lush flowers and a bowl of red apples, which defied the guests to eat them.

'I need to go to *la policía*. My purse has been stolen. I have already tried to find the police station but I cannot find it,' she said, very slowly and deliberately.

'The police station is down the steps behind the fountain or in the subway of the plaza,' replied the receptionist.

'Yes, but where exactly do you mean? I was told that before, but I can't find it.'

'*La mapa*. Here.' He made a circle with his pen on a tourist map, 'And here.' He squiggled a cross about a centimetre away from the circle. 'You go here to here. Is down the steps behind the fountain or in the subway of the plaza,' he repeated, loudly.

'Yes, well, I have looked once.' She was feeling very alone.

'Is down the steps behind the fountain or in the subway of the plaza.' The man spoke even more slowly and more loudly, stabbing with his pen at the circle.

She was afraid she might cry.

'Is there a problem? Can I help?' said a voice in a gentle, friendly northern English accent. She turned to see a smart, dark-haired

195

stranger standing next to her. He was wearing shades, which hid his eyes. The collar of his white cotton shirt was turned up and his casual trousers hung well on his tall, muscular frame.

'Yes, please,' said Denise. 'I've tried to find the police station to report my stolen purse, but I can't find it.'

'It's not far. Just tricky to find. It's just under Plaça de Catalunya. Just follow me. I'm Rob, by the way.' He offered his hand to her.

'Denise,' she grasped his warm, firm hand. She smiled, her confidence was returning already. 'Denise Carvel.'

'*Gracias*, Señor,' said Rob to the receptionist, as he picked up a red apple and took a bite. He turned to Denise again. 'Follow me, Denise. You weren't hurt at all?' He gently touched her on the small of her back.

'No. A young man just slipped his hand in my bag when I was walking down Las Ramblas. I saw him but I couldn't stop him.'

They walked out into the glaring sun and crossed the street towards the hum of Plaça de Catalunya.

'It happens all the time. I sometimes think half my work's dealing with problems caused by pickpockets. Some tourists aren't so lucky as you, though. Fighting back is never a wise move.'

'Your work's what, exactly?' asked Denise.

'I'm the representative for MedTime holidays. Rob Granville.'

Denise followed him down a wide flight of marble stone steps under the Plaça de Catalunya towards the Metro and then, instead of verging left into the subway, Rob stopped and pressed a doorbell on a large glass door to gain access to the police station.

'Easy when you know how.' He grinned.

'I can't thank you enough. You arrived like the answer to my prayers.'

'It must be fate.' Rob laughed. The door opened and Rob led Denise across a large waiting room furnished with large black leather sofas. He stopped at a kiosk, where he murmured something to a policeman.

'Well, Denise, the interpreter will deal with everything here and they will give you a form for insurance purposes. Have you cancelled your cards?' He touched her arm. 'Are you OK for money?'

'Oh, I need to cancel my debit card. I have a credit card in the hotel safe.'

'Which bank are you?' He held out a list of bank telephone numbers. 'Take your pick. Have you got a mobile? A pen?' he said offering her a yellow pen and his business card.

'Yes, I have my mobile. I can ring the bank,' she said, writing down her bank's phone number on the card.

'Cool. Someone should be with you in twenty minutes. You have all my details. Don't hesitate to contact me if you need me.' He pushed his sunglasses on to his head. 'You can keep the pen.'

'Thank you so much. You've been very kind.'

'My pleasure. Be vigilant and enjoy the rest of your holiday. Remember to use MedTime holidays next time. You can be assured of a helpful and charming representative to take care of all your needs.' He laughed. '*Adios*, Dennie!'

She took a sip of Campari and soda as she absently scrutinised her fellow diners, mostly British tourists like herself, celebrating the last night of their holiday. She was sitting at a small round table in a dark restaurant waiting for a flamenco troupe to perform. Although alone, she was content with her own company. She always felt that Martin was not that far away.

She flicked a stray strand of hair away from her face. It had escaped from the unruly bun she had piled on top of her head earlier that evening. She had been pleased with the reflection she saw in the bathroom mirror. Her skin had a healthy glow from the sun and her hair was flecked with more golden highlights than usual. It suited her, she thought, though perhaps the tapas and the sherry had added a few pounds that she could do without.

She had needed a break, to get as far away from Hazelton as she could. Seeing Judith scatter Martin's ashes, then returning to the tyranny of the friendless museum, had been agonising. But she loved Barcelona. She had become enamoured of the architectural accomplishments of Gaudi and captivated by the paintings of Picasso. She had drawn strength just from the foreignness of the place, from her anonymity in a strange city, and had thrived in the dazzling sun that had brightened every day. But at night she had struggled. She had woken up, frightened, tangled in the sheets. The weight of her memories was almost squeezing the air out of her, suffocating her. In the dark solitude Martin's last words replayed like mantra in her head.

'I love you, Judith.'

The performance did not disappoint. Denise was mesmerised by the earthy rawness of the singing and the fierceness of the rhythmic clapping and stamping of the flamenco dancers. She was feeling bewitched by their rhythm and passion, simultaneously wild and controlled, when she felt the pressure of a cool hand on her spine and her turquoise silk dress slipped sensuously across her back. Startled, she turned to her right and just caught a glimpse of dark hair.

'I'm sorry,' a male voice said.

She twisted round to her left and met a pair of dark brown eyes. She felt his fingers at the nape of her neck. It felt like a kiss.

'Your label was showing. I just tucked it in. I hope you don't mind.' Rob smiled.

She beamed, her face relaxing, her eyes creasing in the corners.

'By the way, Dennie, you look lovely tonight,' Rob said, grazing his hand through his brown hair. He touched her arm and she looked into his dark eyes, Martin's eyes.

'Adios, *bonita*.'

Before Denise could think of anything further to say Rob Granville had disappeared through the tables of diners.

The early hours of Sunday morning
She could hear a bird warbling in the night. They never stopped. Never stopped. She turned up the volume on her radio. The newsreader's melancholy reports of murder, rape, and abuse throughout the world resounded around the bedroom. She remembered she had been reading a catalogue in the staffroom at the museum, trying to ignore the conversation around her, when the local news came on the radio. The newsreader had said solemnly,

'An elderly walker discovered a woman's body at a local beauty spot yesterday.' It was three years ago.

'Listen,' Paula had said.

'Shush,' Marsha had said.

'The police have confirmed that it is the body of forty-eight-year-

198

old Judith Crayvern, a local teacher. She was the widow of tragic hero, Martin Crayvern, who died at Hazelmere two years ago. Police have appealed for any witnesses to come forward.'

She had continued reading.

'I told you,' Marsha had said. 'What did I tell you? How tragic is that?'

Marsha's opinion, which she expected the rest of the staff to share, was that Judith had never got over Martin's death.

'They were such a lovely couple. It was a tragedy waiting to happen, like Romeo and Juliet.'

Denise had successfully maintained her own counsel. She was surprised Marsha knew any Shakespeare. She probably didn't. Why on earth did she want to promote this idea that Judith had taken her own life? Judith didn't care about Martin.

'I thought it was an accident,' said Helen.

'Witnesses,' Paula had said, loudly. 'I wonder who they think might be a witness? They must have suspicions. I don't think she'd kill herself. What do you think, Denise?'

She could not remember how she had replied.

She tried, unsuccessfully, to turn up the radio volume again, then threw it on the carpet. It continued to play. She got out of bed to find Bunters, but as she walked across the landing she remembered he was dead. She dropped on to the top step and sobbed.

She was Judith. She could prove it. She wasn't dead.

Patience

Sunday lunchtime

'Keith,' Rob said, 'you're looking good, mate. New look?'

'I had it done last Tuesday. You never noticed.'

'Hey, I have enough of that from Lisa.' Rob laughed, sipping his pint. 'Those glasses are new, too.'

'Yes, I picked them up on Friday. I'm quite pleased.'

'You'll have the women fighting over you. Or is there some woman in your life you've not told us about?'

Keith laughed. Rob could always change his mood for the better in a moment. Scamp reared up on his back legs, keen to let Rob pat and scratch his head. Sunday lunchtime was the only time when the Jack Russell terrier came to The Sun. It was his treat. He'd always get some scraps of the Sunday roast beef dinner that Keith ordered religiously at three o'clock.

'You're buzzing today. Did you win, lad?' Keith said.

'Won? We annihilated them. And I scored,' Rob said. 'These guys, too.' He pointed to a couple of men in replica football shirts who were standing under the large television, their eyes fixed on the screen.

'No bookings this week, then?'

'An absolute clean sheet, mate. Not had one for over a year.'

'That's one for the books. You used to have the worst record in the Sunday league. Lisa must have dampened your ardour. Look, Rob, I'd like a bit of advice. I was just wondering if maybe I should get Judith a cat. A kitten, or a rescue one. You know, to make amends.'

'It wasn't your fault, Keith. I'm sure she'll get over it.' Rob put his hand on Keith's shoulder.

'That cat was all she had and I ran it over. She has no one now. She's lost so much.'

'Well, it's a kind gesture.'

'I'm not sure how she'd take it, though, if it was just from me.

200

Perhaps if it came from the three of us? What do you think? Could you ask Lisa?'

'Yes, I could ask Lisa what she thinks,' said Rob, fixing his eyes on the television screen.

'Everything all right? You seem a bit preoccupied, Rob,' said Keith.

'Everything is pretty magnificent at the moment. I'm the hot favourite for a new job, and one I want.' Rob put his arm round Keith. 'Let me introduce you to someone, though. See that lady over there? The one standing next to Janet, near Val Cordon. You won't recognise her without the hat. That's Chocolate Box Woman. Bea, her name is. She came over before. I'll introduce you again. She'll not recognise the new, cool Keith.'

~

A blackbird hopped across the mound that marked Bunters's resting place. Judith knocked on the French window and successfully cleared the garden of the sound of birdsong. Sunday lunchtime. Rob would be at the pub, and so would Keith. She put her gym clothes in the washing machine. She wondered what Lisa was doing. For some reason she allowed Rob time to himself on Sundays.

She had not seen Rob for a few years after their night in The Bodega de la Casa but she had followed him on the Internet. It had been fate that he'd returned to his home city just after she had decided to start a new life there. She had first seen him again when she was passing by MedTime at the close of business, just as he was locking up. She had recognised him immediately, even from a distance, his gestures were so familiar. She had crossed the road and followed him to the bus stop. She had smiled at him as the bus pulled up, and he had flashed a smile back. The connection was still there, she could feel it. But she was Judith now, not Denise. He hadn't recognised Judith.

There's nothing wrong with Denise.

One lunchtime she had followed some of the football team to The Sun, very discreetly, of course. She had even gone in and bought a drink. She had stood at the far side of the bar, watching him. He was

201

always the centre of attention, surrounded by his mates. One stood out from the crowd, an older man with his dog. *Older man?* She sniggered. Keith was her age. You wouldn't know it, though. She had soon discovered that he walked his dog in the park at roughly the same time every day. It had been easy to contrive a meeting. She was soon on speaking terms with Keith and, eventually, he had invited her to join them at the pub quiz. Fate. She grimaced. She had introduced Bunters to his killer.

Tuesday morning
Lisa's phone vibrated on her desk. There was a message from Rob:
Got the job, Lise. Sun and money. Just need to brush up my Italian. Xx
She picked up her phone immediately and called him but it cut to his voicemail. She texted,
Well done babe. Time to celebrate. C U at Sun. Keith will be pleased for you. Xxx Ciao!
'Rob's got that job,' said Lisa, distracting Tasmin from her work.
'Job?'
'The one I was telling you about. MedTime senior management team. He'll be working in Europe a lot. It's just what he wants – responsibility – and he gets to use his Spanish. Italian, too.'
'Wow. That's good for him, Lisa. But where does that put you, if he's travelling all the time?'
'He'll still be based here. He'll just work in Europe instead of at the shop.'
'Mmm.'
'I guess I'll have lots of exotic weekends away,' Lisa said, as she brushed aside images of beautiful European women seducing her boyfriend. 'We're a partnership, so we'll make it work.'
'Here's the spreadsheet I did the other day, Lisa. I've double-checked it and it's foolproof. The filters work fine. I think I've cracked it. In fact I quite enjoyed doing it. If you've got any more you want doing, pass them my way.'
Lisa looked up and scrutinised Tasmin's face. She was being deadly serious.
'Thanks, Taz.'

Gary Barlow crooned comforting words to her as she washed her hands then sprayed the sink with bleach.

Yes, just more time and I'll be over it, she thought. *Have some patience.* The stench of the chlorine made her nose twitch and revived a memory of Paula, sitting on a stool, holding an ancient Egyptian knife in her latex gloves. It must have been about three years ago, just before she resigned. There were other more striking exhibits in the museum collection, but the copper knife, with the sinister hooked edge, captivated children because of its macabre purpose: dissecting bodies.

Denise had smelled the bleach the moment she had entered the conservation studio.

'What are you doing, Paula?' she had asked.

'Implementing the housekeeping plan, as you instructed,' Paula had said. 'Isn't that what you wanted, Denise?' White gum flicked across her mouth as she spoke.

'I can smell chlorine.'

'The pure alcohol didn't work,' Paula had said, putting the knife down on a bench, and raising two fingers of each hand in the air to mimic quotation marks. 'So I've used "my initiative" and found a better solution. I thought that was what you wanted me to do.'

'Why would I want you to use bleach?'

'Well, I didn't want to fail to meet your exacting standards of cleanliness. I know how important it is that we combat aggressive dust, Denise.' Paula stood up. She was a good six inches taller, even without heels, so had little difficulty in looking down at her. She remembered that Paula's voice had sounded strange, more clipped than usual. She had wondered if Paula was cheekily impersonating her, or merely repeating what she had actually said.

'Although, as visitors are scientifically proven to be the main source of dust, perhaps we should begin by reducing, not increasing their numbers,' Paula had continued, her piercing blue eyes staring back, unblinking. Paula had picked up the knife again.

'You know bleach is corrosive, Paula,' she had responded, transfixed by the sharp blade of the knife which was pointed towards her.

'Do I?'

'Yes, you do. That knife's survived dissecting bodies, grave robbers, and travelled thousands of miles. But it will not survive much longer if it's cleaned with bleach. Just put all that stuff away.'

'I'm sorry. I just need some training.'

'You've just been trained.'

'You don't want me on conservation any more then, Denise?' Paula had placed the knife back on the bench and untied her apron. She had stepped nearer, chewing slowly on a caramel eclair as she waited for a reply.

While she sprayed the kitchen with a linen-scented air freshener she wondered if she had been unwittingly complicit with Paula's plan to get transferred back to reception. She should have been firmer. Helen had far more rapport with the kids. Paula had been almost threatening, though, infringing her personal space, and chewing like she was a gangster's moll. The museum would have been better off without Paula. Her idea of a productive shift at work was to chat all day.

Martin had rarely got involved with staff issues. That was probably why they had all liked him so much. But if she had ever raised any issues about Paula's performance he had always seemed to support Paula. Why was that? she wondered. Now it was almost three years since her last day at Hazelton Museum. The cards that the schoolchildren had made, many depicting exhibits from the Egyptology collection, had especially touched her. Mummies, bound and gagged bog men, disembowelled bodies, knives. Yes, they had certainly been inspired by the exhibition. The new director, Louise Pyatt, although she was not so new now, had made a fuss of her and ensured that her last day 'after years of loyal service' was a pleasantly memorable one. Louise had briefly counselled her against what had seemed to be a hasty decision to hand in her resignation, but had soon agreed that her decision to take time out to study her passion, the history of art, was a good move.

The Director of Cultural Spaces had attended her presentation and personally congratulated her for all her hard work. It was her enthusiasm, he had said, which had contributed to the museum's success at the prestigious national awards. He had taken her aside and personally thanked her for managing the recruitment process for Martin's replacement so efficiently. He knew what a traumatic time it must have been for her. Martin had been a super guy and a great friend of his. He had given her a tap on her backside as he spoke and a quick wink.

She had left the director's office carrying a bunch of flowers, cards, and gifts, and had stopped to repack her overflowing bag at the reception desk.

'Goodbye, Denise,' Paula had said, smiling insincerely.

She had thanked Paula for the present and the card, even though she was sure her contribution was negligible. Then she had said, very softly,

'I am so sorry to hear about you and Tim.'

'What do you mean, Denise?' Paula had replied. She could still recall the puzzled look on Paula's face now.

'You always seemed to be the perfect couple. Oh, I am sorry. When I saw him out with Marsha again at the weekend I thought you must have split up ... They looked so ...' She had enjoyed watching Paula's face. She couldn't resist twisting the knife in a little deeper.

'Look, I'm sorry. I thought it was common knowledge. Maybe I ...'

'What do you mean, common knowledge?' Paula had not been able to hide her anger.

'Forget it. Maybe I got the wrong end of the stick, as usual. Forget it. Goodbye, Paula.'

She looked out of the window at Bunters's grave and smiled as she remembered how Denise Carvel had tripped down the stone steps of the museum for the last time, picturing the impending confrontation between Paula and Marsha, and Paula and Tim. It was amazing what a creative imagination could conjure up.

The kitchen smelled fresh and welcoming again. Now she just needed to banish the memories of the museum as well.

Tuesday afternoon

She watched the distant figure walk along the edge of the pond at the bottom of the sloping parkland. Even though the sun was rapidly setting and a gentle night mist was setting in, there was no mistaking the stooped silhouette and the small dog that tugged on the end of a long leash. He was later today. For a moment she wondered if he had seen her. She turned round and walked back up the hill. She had deliberately started her walk late in order to avoid him, and yet here he was. She really didn't want to listen to any more tiresome confidences. But she had an uneasy feeling that was exactly what he wanted to do.

Queen bitch

'I think I will come,' said Maya. 'I could do with a diversion to forget all about that jerk. You might even win if I join you.'

'I thought you'd already forgotten about him,' said Lisa, wrapping a thick wool scarf round her neck and scrunching her hair under a matching hat.

'Well, yes.'

'We will definitely need a replacement for Denise. I think it's safe to say that she won't be joining us in The Sun tonight. Although, as Sally had a scare today I suspect she's going to be back at Bergers soon. How am I going to get rid of her, Maya?'

'You let things go too far, Lisa. You should have nipped it in the bud.'

'I need someone to complain about her. Get her sacked. You couldn't pretend that—'

'Whoa. You are something else. What's happened to the naive, trusting girl we all loved? No, I will not. What you should have done is to give her a recommendation, so that she goes and works for someone else.' Maya pulled on her leather gloves. She still looked elegant, even in a bulky duvet jacket.

'Someone like who?'

'What about Della at Taylors?' Maya shrugged. 'You need to be wily. Think things through. Then everyone looks good and Judith thinks you're her best friend.'

'You just don't get her, Maya. And it's Denise. Judith's dead. The woman who calls herself Judith is an impostor.'

~

Judith walked along Willow Tree Avenue in the direction of The Sun, as she did every Tuesday evening. It was dry, but gusts of wind were gasping through the branches of the trees. Her hair was piled on to the top of her head, exposing her neck and ears to the elements.

207

She wished she had worn her hat, but decided against returning home to retrieve it. She did not want to risk being too late to join the team. Game, Set, and Match was her target for the evening. They had tried to persuade her to join them before, and she was sure that Olivia would be only too willing to improve her chances of beating Lisa. Although it might be worth spending two hours in the unsavoury company of Brian Cordon just to see Keith's face. Keith would choke if she joined The Terminators.

She listened to *Hunky Dory* on her iPhone as she passed the garden with the *Sold* sign. The house had not taken very long to sell. She fantasised that she could phone a couple of estate agents in the morning and put her house on the market. The agency would soon find her work in London. They had been impressed. She would have excellent references from Andy, of course.

She smiled as she imagined Peter's face, his now fat face, when he saw her. Now where could she choose to engineer their first meeting? His golf club? The planning office? Or perhaps she could befriend his new wife, Eve. That might be fun. She could begin at her yoga class. A little cyber-digging had unearthed a wealth of trivia about their lives. She imagined turning up at the family barbecue as his wife's guest. She could make Peter suffer for his deceit. Some day, perhaps, but at the moment there was still lots to keep her here. Though life would be much improved if Lisa Clarkson was off the scene.

She walked through the car park, squinting in the headlights of the cars that were just pulling up, towards the porch of The Sun.

'Good evening,' she said to the anorak-wearing smoker. He nodded and held the door open for her, like a footman. She smiled graciously as she went in. She quickly looked around, taking stock of who was there. The Terminators were established on a long table that was already overflowing with pint glasses. Keith was at the bar. Tasmin and Jeremy were sitting on a red bench on the far side of the pub. She returned Tasmin's wave. As she did, she saw Rob leaning against the far side of the counter with one arm supporting his weight as he drank from a bottle of Peroni, just as he had been doing on Saturday.

As she took her money from her purse, Janet from The Dispossessed moved away from the bar, thus presenting an unobstructed view of Keith, who was now standing next to Val Cordon. She noticed an exchange of awkward glances. Keith's words echoed in her head.

It was only the once.

As Val left the bar she stepped beside Keith.

'It was her, wasn't it? Val Cordon. You slept with her.'

'Well, this is an unexpected pleasure, Maya,' Rob said, kissing her on the cheek.

'Likewise. It looks like your team needs some help tonight. I understand the woman formerly known as Judith won't be joining you,' Maya said. 'Congrats on your new job.'

'Thanks, Maya. I guess not. It's pretty busy tonight. We haven't got any seats yet,' Rob said, patting down Lisa's unruly hair, which she had liberated from her hat. 'Lisa, I've no idea where Keith is. He's not replying to his phone. The only spare chairs seem to be next to Taz and Jeremy.' Rob took a swig of beer.

'Oh my God,' Lisa said as she turned to wave to Tasmin. 'That bitch has just sat down next to them. Fuck.'

Maya smirked.

'That rather glamorous lady in the red jacket? So that's Judith?'

'Denise,' Lisa said.

Rob groaned.

'I think drinks are required.' He mimed an emptying glass.

'Spritzer, please, Rob. With lots of ice,' Maya said.

'The usual,' Lisa said. 'I'm going to the loo. Make sure my seat's as far away from Queen Bitch as possible.'

'I'll go and introduce myself,' said Maya.

'You must be Tasmin,' Maya said, offering her hand.

'How did you know that?' Tasmin said.

'Who else could you be? Which, by process of elimination, makes you Jeremy. I'm Lisa's long-suffering flatmate,' Maya said.

'Perhaps we should make one team,' said Jeremy. 'Olivia's not coming, and Judith says Keith won't be coming. It makes sense. We

209

can just pull the tables together.'

'That's a great idea. I think it should make a very interesting evening. I'm sure Lisa won't mind. You don't mind do you, Judith? Or,' Maya added in a low voice, 'should I say Denise?'

'It's Judith. No, of course not. I'll go and register us.' She lightly touched Maya's arm. 'I assume you're Maya. We pay a pound each, by the way.'

Maya dropped a coin in Judith's open palm.

'Whatever you want to be called is fine by me, ma'am,' Maya said.

'We're just putting the tables together, Rob,' Maya said, as her thighs shoved a table towards him. 'We're playing as one team. You don't mind do you? I think Judith's next to Jeremy. So if you sit here next to me, and Lisa sits there, it should all work out fine.'

'What about Keith?' Rob said.

'Judith says he's not coming,' Jeremy said.

'Good to see you again, Jeremy,' Rob said, putting the drinks down. 'Is this your idea, Maya?' he whispered in her ear. 'Because it's not a good one.'

'Judith's so thoughtful, isn't she?' Tasmin said, as she unstopped a small phial of perfume and dabbed the fragrance on her wrists. She held the miniature flacon under Lisa's nose. 'She thought it would suit me. What do you think?'

'Hmm.' Lisa inhaled the scent as she looked back at Tasmin through the mirror in the ladies' toilets. Tasmin usually exuded confidence, but Lisa detected a naivety and innocence in the expressive face that smiled back through the smeared glass.

'Notes of neroli and mandarin orange,' Tasmin said.

'Yah, it's very seductive. But just make sure you're the one doing the seducing, Taz,' Lisa said, catching Tasmin's puzzled refection. She moved to the door before Tasmin could quiz her further.

'Hi, Jeremy,' Lisa said, as she got back. 'Has Judith gone?'

'She went to register us. We thought we might as well play as one team. If that's OK with you that is,' Jeremy said. 'Perhaps you don't want to …'

'No, no, of course I want to play with you and Taz,' Lisa said, trying to look enthusiastic.

'I've paid,' said Judith, placing the answer sheets on the table. 'Any more contributions to the pot are welcome.'

Rob pushed a couple of coins in her direction.

'Thank you, Rob,' Judith said, taking the only spare seat, which was next to Jeremy.

Lisa smirked. Rob was wedged between her and Maya. No European kisses for Judith.

'I've just had a text from Olivia,' Tasmin announced, as she sat down next to Jeremy. 'She got the job. She's got the job!'

'Job?' said Lisa, feeling relief that her rival was soon to be out of the way.

'Yes, she's had a second interview for Downhams. She's got it and she'll be moving to London,' said Tasmin.

'Yay, the girl done good,' Maya said. 'Even I know they're Bergers's biggest competitor. Market leader, in fact.'

'She so wanted this,' Judith said. 'She will be thrilled after her recent disappointment. I'm glad Downhams at least recognise her talents.'

Lisa felt a wave of envy as she realised that Olivia now had a job that was superior to her own.

'What are we called, Judith?' Tasmin said, picking up a pen. 'Game, Set, and Match?'

'Well, as we are a completely new team I chose a new name. The first one that came into my head. Judith's Soul Mates. I'm sorry. It's not very creative,' Judith said.

'On the contrary. It's very inventive,' Maya said, as Rob slapped Lisa on her back.

'Are you all right, Lisa?' Jeremy said. 'Perhaps I could get you some water?'

'Sorry. The Peroni went up my nose,' Lisa said. 'I'm fine.'

'Ooh, a picture round. This is fun,' Maya said. 'I'll just get rid of the condiments.'

'What is a "bodega"?' announced the quizmaster.

'Bodega. That's it. That's the club you and Judith went to, isn't it

Rob? I've finally remembered,' said Tasmin.

'Apparently,' said Rob. 'With Judith and a thousand others,' he murmured to Maya.

'The Bodega de la Casa,' said Judith. 'The answer is a wine bar, a Spanish wine bar. Did you get that, Lisa?'

'How did you meet?' said Tasmin.

'Shush,' said Lisa. 'It's the next question.'

'Question two. What creature is a pipistrelle? It is the smallest of its species in Britain. What is it?' said the quizmaster.

'I bet Keith would know that,' said Lisa. 'We need you, Keith. Where are you?' She looked at her mobile despondently.

'Put that away,' said Judith. 'They'll think you're cheating.'

'She's right,' said Rob.

Lisa puckered her lips into a sulk and put her phone in her bag.

'I think I know that,' said Rob. He whispered the answer to Lisa, who had the pen. 'No, not rat,' he said, as Lisa wrote down the answer. 'B,' he mouthed.

Lisa wrote down 'Bee'.

'Not bee. Bat,' Rob said.

'Shush,' said Tasmin. 'The Dispossessed are listening.'

'That's it, definitely,' said Judith.

'I'm impressed with your knowledge of bats, Judith,' said Maya, 'but I guess I shouldn't be surprised.'

'Sorry?' said Judith.

'Next question. Listen,' said Jeremy.

'Which children's book character said, "I have been Foolish and Deluded. I am a Bear of No Brain At All"?' said the quizmaster.

'Pooh Bear,' said Jeremy and Judith at the same time.

'Paddington Bear,' said Lisa. 'Rob?'

'I think Jeremy and Judith are right,' said Rob. 'Winnie-the-Pooh, the bear of little brain.'

'I'll go with Judith,' said Maya. 'I think she's our expert in delusion.'

'Well done, team,' Judith said. 'Who wants the winner's vino? Taz, Jeremy, why don't you take it? Everyone agreed?'

'Lisa, how about popping round to Keith's? I'm worried,' Rob said. 'We'd better be quiet about beating The Terminators, though.'

Lisa nodded.

'I'll see you on Saturday, Jeremy,' Judith said, putting on her red jacket.

'Saturday?' Tasmin said.

'Yes. We're going to the Hockney exhibition,' Jeremy said. 'Judith's very keen.'

'Hockney?' said Lisa to Judith. 'That's not your usual taste. I thought you were more into damsels in distress and chivalrous knights than—' said Lisa.

'I think I might like Hockney,' interrupted Tasmin.

'I didn't think you liked exhibitions, period. You said—' Jeremy began.

'Maybe I'll tag along,' Tasmin said. 'You don't mind, do you?'

'Of course not, darling. Three's a party.' Jeremy kissed Tasmin's cheek. 'Would anyone else like to come? The Sunday papers gave it rave reviews.'

Lisa shook her head.

'Not my scene, guys,' said Rob.

'I'll come,' Maya said. 'It looks like I'll be at a loose end on Saturday. We can all get to know each other better, can't we?'

Rob and Lisa were passing the bar, following Judith.

'See you, Bea. I don't know where Keith is. We're going to find the old bugger. Thanks.' Rob popped a chocolate in his mouth and pocketed a handful as Brian Cordon stopped in front of Judith, barring her way.

'Well done, Judith. You were like a cat on heat tonight. But I think there might have been a little help from a phone by Miss Smarty-Pants behind you.'

'I beg your pardon?' Judith said. 'What sort of cat?'

'Just a turn of phrase love, but if you're ever up for it.' Cordon winked. 'I suggest you drop that twat Keith from your team if you want to beat us again, though.'

Rob lunged forward and aimed his right fist at the bus driver's wobbling stomach. Cordon deftly moved sideways, just avoiding contact.

'Rob, stop it. What's got into you?' Lisa cried. 'We don't want to be barred.' She could see the landlady out of the corner of her eye, signalling to one of her staff.

She pulled on Rob's sleeve.

'Let's go. You don't want a court case looming over you when you've just got promotion. Come on. Now.'

'You're always a liability, Lisa. You're never aware of how things might look. We won fair and square, but now—' Judith said.

'Oh, shut up,' Lisa said.

'Next time.'

'Believe me, Denise, there will be no next time.'

'I can't believe you want to get her a cat,' Lisa said, as they approached Keith's house.

'Do you ever listen, Lisa? *Keith* wanted me to ask *you*. He wants to get it, but doesn't want to do it on his own. Besides, we do bear some responsibility, as the cat ran out after you trod on it and Keith ran it over,' Rob said.

'We? Now you're blaming me and Keith for Bunters's death?'

'No one was responsible. It was an accident. But Keith feels guilty. He knocked him over.'

'No, he didn't.'

'Yes, he did. That's what he told me. Stop twisting things.' Rob stopped at the top of the driveway as he watched Lisa walk towards the front door of the modest semi-detached house, then followed her. Lisa rang the front doorbell. They immediately heard a dog yapping and a scurrying of paws in the hall. The barking got louder but there was no sign of the door opening. Rob looked through the letter box. The door rattled as Scamp thumped against it. Rob stepped back while Lisa looked through the gap in the curtains.

The light was on but there was no sign of Keith. Rob walked down the uneven concrete flags and around Keith's taxi to the garage. It was decades old, a timber construction built by the previous owners. He knocked on one of the wooden doors and put his ear against the door, then walked back to the front door and knocked again.

'Keith, Keith,' he yelled through the letter box. 'You miserable sod, get over to the pub. Bea's in tonight. She was wondering where you were.' Scamp buffeted the door again. 'I fix up a date for you and then you let me down, you old bastard.'

'He's not in,' said Lisa.

'I'm worried.'

'You said he was OK on Sunday.'

'Yes, he was just a bit sad about Judith losing Bunters.'

'Well, perhaps he's gone to the cattery,' Lisa said, her voice heavy with resentment. 'Everyone seems to feel sorry for that bitch. Can't you all see what she's really like?'

'Lay off, Lisa,' Rob said, then angrily pulled her to him. 'What's this about, now?'

'Now? It's what it's been about for ages.' Lisa pulled away, pointing her finger at him. 'You always give her the benefit of the doubt.'

'It was fucking Winnie-the-Pooh.'

'And you don't share things with me. I can't live like this, always feeling suspicious, jealous. You're never there for me. You don't believe in me.'

'Of course I do. I always have. God, Lise, it was only on Saturday you thanked me for being so supportive.'

'And it was on Saturday you demonstrated just how much you don't share with me.'

'Let's talk about this later.'

'No, there's no point. You won't want to talk about it later. I'm not a fool, Rob. You might have been pretending there was nothing between you, but I could feel it. Tonight I could feel it.'

'What *are* you talking about?'

'You and her. I could feel it.'

'I hardly said a word to her.'

'Exactly. Then you go and try and hit Brian Cordon defending her honour.'

'You. I was defending you.'

'I'm sorry, Rob, but it isn't working any longer.'

'Lisa. I can't believe you're saying this. You're the only one for me. It should never be over. We're so good together.' He grabbed hold of her shoulders.

'We were so good together. I used to think about you and I would feel a charge of energy. It would get me through the day. Now I just feel suspicious that you are keeping things from me.' Lisa turned on her heels and ran up the drive.

Rob watched her, then kicked the wall.

Fuck Judith. He leaned on the wall for a few minutes, then hammered on the door one more time, shouting. He pulled out a purple foil-covered chocolate from his pocket and dropped it through the letter box then ran up the path.

Lisa texted as she walked slowly towards her apartment, her head down as she concentrated on typing.

Maya, think I've finished it. Can't trust him. Put kettle on. X

She wasn't sure what she felt. Was it relief? She stopped as she looked at her unread messages.

Sally and Lee announce the early arrival of Zanouska Carey-Waddington. 6 lbs 10 oz Mummy and baby well.

She read another.

We can sort this out, Lise. I'll be round later. Rob xxx

And another.

Up your way soon. Lunch? James Xxx

Lisa texted,

Maybe. L xxx

Then she deleted the kisses.

Love will tear us apart

Judith walked up the main road alongside the pub car park, her head down against the wind. A pair of car headlights shone through the darkness, speeding away from the city centre. While she waited for the car to pass, a distant figure crossed the road behind the car. She hurried across the road and then turned into Willow Tree Avenue, increasing her pace as the wind relented.

Damn Tasmin and Maya. She could do without their company on Saturday. Especially Maya. She did not trust that girl. She was too beautiful, too astute. She had acted like she was Rob's minder in The Sun, whispering in his ear. Lisa had not looked happy at all about that. Rob had been very quiet, edgy. Not himself. He didn't like it when she gave Jeremy all the attention.

Let's see how long he can stay away.

As she passed the garden with the *Sold* sign she glanced at Rob's hip-hop playlist again: *In Da Club, If dead men could talk.* Try as she might, she could not get into rap. She switched from Rob's playlist to her own. The soprano's abandoned interpretation of Verdi's *Libera Me* was far more comprehensible to her than 50 Cent's urban eulogy.

Libera me, Domine, quando coeli movendi sunt et terra; dum veneris judicare saeclum per ignem.

Perhaps it had been inevitable that someone would discover her former identity. No harm had come of it. She needed to think through the consequences, though.

There's nothing wrong with Denise.

As she turned into her drive the soprano's tormented pleas for forgiveness assaulted her ears. She walked along the side of the house, triggering the security lighting. She was overwhelmed with sorrow as the wind whistled round the corner, rattling the lids of the bins, as she glimpsed Bunters's grave.

'Bitch.'

She jolted backwards, yelping as her hair was pulled up brutally by the roots. She could feel hot breath against her neck and the sweet smell of chocolate as a hand slapped her cheek. Her head hit the lid of a rubbish bin. She gulped air hungrily as her hair was twisted round and round, forcing her head to lurch into the unblinking stare of her attacker. As she glimpsed the glint of the knife she tried to scream, tried to claw her assailant with her nails, kick with her feet. But her shriek became a gurgle, as her head smashed against the bin again and again. Then, as her body fell to the ground, her skull crashed against the paving.

Rob was alone again in the darkness. He leaned heavily against the wall, as if its hard permanence could give him shelter from death's performance, just feet away. The hanging baskets creaked on either side of him. Perhaps she was alive. He needed to find out. He did not move. He must find out. He must find out.

Do it. He stepped forward and the crime scene illuminated once more. Hesitantly he touched her delicate wrist.

'Judith.'

Her skin was still warm, but he could feel no pulse of life. He inhaled her fragrance. Earlier it had seemed spicy and alluring. Now it seemed musty and sweet.

'Denise.'

He could hear faint shrieking, muffled sounds seeping from her headphones. He stepped back, taking comfort from the solidness of the wall. He fumbled in his pocket for his lighter and packet of cigarettes. Carefully he moved the cigarette to his mouth and clicked on the lighter. A small flame soared and faded. He tried again. The flame illuminated his hands, red with blood. He flicked the roller on the lighter again and finally lit the end of the cigarette. He watched the tip of the cigarette glow, then hungrily sucked the nicotine from the tobacco.

Jesus. The person who finds the body is always the first suspect. The prime suspect.

His phone vibrated. He reached for it, but it fell from his shaky hand on to the patio. The security lamp lit up the garden. He looked across to the far fence. The bare, slender branches of the linden tree, like long finger bones, swayed together in the breeze. He looked upwards, trying to avoid even a glimpse of the mangled body on the patio. The webcam. The whole thing would be on the webcam.

He breathed deeply and threw down the burning cigarette, glimpsing Judith once more. Her eyes were open, her lipstick was streaked across her mouth, and an unruly halo of long, blood-soaked tresses framed her head. She reminded him of Medusa. He picked up the phone, glancing at the message:

Really sorry, Rob. You don't deserve this. Love Maya xxx

The numbers on the screen keypad shone like jewels in the darkness. Rob pushed his back against the wall, fearful of triggering the security lighting again, and dialled. He stumbled over his words as he responded to the emergency services operator's terse questions.

As Rob heard the distant sound of a police siren, the soft petals of the hanging flowers glanced limply against his cheek. He flinched and stepped forward. Something white was gleaming on the patio beside her. He picked up a business card, averting his eyes from the body.

Lisa Clarkson, Account Executive, Berger and Berger. He turned it over, smearing it with blood. He put the card in his pocket.

He wanted to feel nothing, see nothing. But he could not ignore the screech of the siren, which soon filled the air like a demented banshee. He felt as if the sound had penetrated his skull, was trying to possess him, knock him off his balance. Afraid that he was going to fall, he opened his eyes to see a flashing blue light reflecting on the garage door. The familiar silhouette of a policeman, his high visibility jacket glowing reassuringly, appeared through the darkness just before the garden illuminated again and the drama's leading actress shone in the spotlight for a spectacular, bloody encore.

Denise saw Martin for just a moment. He glowed like an angel as he called her name. Then he was gone, into the darkness, but she felt he was still there. She tried to call to him. She remembered it all now. Watching the blackbird stare at her.

That beady eye.

Always looking.

Judging.

Sneakily stealing a glance.

Singing a cocky little tune.

Piercing the peace.
Always watching.
Knowing.
Telling.
Feathers like death.
She saw flames flickering. Gone, then burning again.
As the final beats of her life ebbed away she tried to call to him again.
Libera me. She merged into the darkness. *Libera me.*

REQUIEM

Don't dream it's over

'That's it. Over. *Finito. Kaput.*' Lisa slammed the living room door behind her, pulling off her hat. Maya looked up from her armchair, interrupting the inspection of her painted toenails, which peeped from under her grey and pink pyjamas. She studied Lisa.

'I don't know why you're looking at me like that.' Lisa threw her jacket, mobile, and bag on the couch and freed her hair from a scrunchie. She took a large gulp from the steaming mug that Maya had left on the coffee table, then sat down heavily. The sofa creaked.

'Thanks, Maya. You're a star.' She took a battered hairbrush from her bag and attacked her locks vigorously. 'It's the right decision. I can't trust him. He never shares anything with me.'

'Judith 1, Lisa 0.'

'What?'

'That's what Judith – sorry, Denise – wants you to do. She has no more need of you now. You're just competition for his attention. Or anyone's attention, I suspect.'

'Well, Rob can confide all he wants with that witch, now. Judith … Denise … I don't care who she is.'

'Rob confide in Judith? He doesn't confide in anyone.'

'He seemed to be sharing a lot with you this evening.'

'What?'

'He wants to come round and talk.' Lisa switched off the mobile. 'There's no point. The sooner he accepts it the better. Then we can both move on and find someone else.' She gathered her clothes and bag and moved to the door, then turned. Maya's gaze had followed her.

'And don't you let him in, under any circumstances, Maya. If he wants his sports bag it's in the hall by the door. I'm having a bath and going to bed. I have a very important meeting tomorrow.'

~

223

Rob watched from the back of a police car as an ambulance set off, its blue lamp eerily brightening the gardens of Willow Tree Avenue and the curious faces of some of its residents. They had hastily wrapped themselves in coats and jackets, some still wearing their nightclothes, as they braved the March night to discover whether some despicable act might have devalued their property.

The car rocked as the door opened and a slim man with brown wavy hair, greying at the temples, got in and sat beside him. He flashed an identity card.

'Detective Inspector Laurie Calvini. Robert Granville? I understand you reported finding Judith Crayvern?'

Rob tried to say yes but made a strangulated grunt as he nodded his head.

'I understand this must be a shock, but could you please tell me when and how you found the body?'

'When? I don't know. Just before I called the police … I called the police straight away, I think. We'd been at The Sun.'

'The Sun?'

'The pub up the road. We'd been at the quiz night. We go every week. I came here afterwards but there was no sign of her. I walked round the back. Then the lights came on. She was there. Is she … is she dead?'

The detective looked at his watch.

'She looked dead.' Rob continued. 'Blood in her hair. It was matted. Blood everywhere.'

'She had been at The Sun, too?'

'Yes.'

'You didn't leave together?'

'No, I left with Lisa, my girlfriend.'

'Where's Lisa now?'

'She went home.'

'Why?'

'We had a row.'

'On the way here?'

'No, at Keith's.'

'Keith?'

'Keith Sharpe. He's a member of the pub quiz team, but he didn't come tonight.'

'What was the row about, Robert?'

'God knows. A cat. Paddington Bear.'

'So you came here alone?'

'Yes.'

'Why?'

Rob shielded his eyes with his hands.

'Why?' he repeated. 'Why?'

~

Scamp seemed more interested in the stranger packing the boot of their car than going in the pub. Keith muttered, 'How do?' as he pulled the dog firmly away, took a deep breath, opened the door, and headed for the bar.

'The usual, Bernice, please,' said Keith, 'and a whisky chaser.'

'You're a bit late, love.'

'Yeah, we got held up.'

'Hello, Scamp. We don't usually see you at night.' Bernice slowly pulled on the arm of the Guinness pump. 'I always thought you were set in your ways, Keith, but I'm going to have to revise my opinion of you – what with your new look, as well. It's good, but it's taken me a bit to get used to it. Here's your whisky chaser.'

Keith smiled glumly.

'What have you done to your neck?' Bernice squinted.

Keith stroked the palm of his hand under his collar.

'Just a new shirt that's been catching.'

'You don't see that so often these days. Well, my dad ...'

'Hello, stranger.' Two hands covered Keith's eyes.

'Bea. Can I get you a drink? You too, Janet,' Keith said.

'Thanks, Keith. I'll have a Malibu and lemonade. Me and Janet were just about to go. We'd given up on you,' Bea said.

'And I still am about to go,' said Janet, bending down to tickle Scamp's head. 'I'll leave you two to catch up.'

Keith leaned against the bar talking to Bea and the quizmaster as Janet waved her goodbyes. As she left two police officers entered and walked up to the counter, surveying the room as they did.

225

'Can we see Bernice Lonsdale?' said the female officer.

'That's me. Can I help, Sergeant?'

'You're the licensee?'

Bernice nodded. Her nonchalant demeanour transformed in a moment to apprehension.

'Perhaps we can have a quiet word?'

'Lucky we got our drinks,' said Bea, as Bernice ushered the police officers to her back room. 'I wonder what they want?'

'They look like they mean business,' said the quizmaster. 'There's another cop car out there. Lights flashing and all.'

'Hey, Janet, I thought you'd just gone,' said Bea, turning to greet her friend.

'I had. There's police everywhere. They've cordoned off Willow Tree Avenue. Won't let you down there at all. Do you think there's some sort of terrorist incident? Anyone know what's going on?' Janet said.

'Well, the police have just gone behind the bar with Bernice,' Keith said.

'Perhaps it's drugs,' Janet said.

'What?' said Keith.

'Well this place used to have a reputation ...' Janet said.

'Idle gossip, Janet,' Keith said.

'There's no smoke without ...' Janet continued.

'Well, well, well. Judith's Soul Mates did all right tonight.'

Keith turned. Brian Cordon was standing next to him, smiling. His wife was four steps behind him, studying the carpet.

'They obviously found the winning formula. Drop the twat.' Cordon laughed.

Keith looked past the bully towards Val Cordon, who continued to scrutinise the floor. He gripped Scamp's lead tightly. The tannoy crackled.

'Ladies and gentlemen, it's Bernice, your landlady. The police sergeant here would just like to speak to you. I'd be grateful for your kind attention, sir,' she said, glowering at Brian Cordon, who simply said,

'Ma'am.'

'Ladies and gentlemen,' said the police officer, taking the

226

microphone, 'I'm Sergeant Lindsay Metcalfe. We are investigating a major incident in the area. I'd be grateful if, before you leave tonight, you could make sure that you have given your names and addresses to the officers here and answered any questions they may have. There's nothing to worry about. It's just so we can eliminate you from our inquiries. Thank you for your cooperation.'

'We're still serving, by the way,' said Bernice, grabbing the microphone.

The hush of the pub changed into a frenzied hum, as the customers realised that a policewoman was blocking their exit and they were all now helping with a major police investigation.

'What did they want, Bernice?' Keith said.

'CCTV,' the landlady whispered, looking out of the corner of her eye as a policeman spoke to the quizmaster. 'But we didn't have it on. They weren't too happy. They're very interested in the pub quiz, though, especially who was in Judith's team.'

Keith looked across the bar as two more police officers entered, weighed down with body armour and weapons, their radios crackling. One stood by the door. The other went to confer with her sergeant and then drew Brian Cordon aside.

'Number 23 Willow Tree Avenue,' said the quizmaster. 'Just had a text from me mate. There's an ambulance outside and police everywhere. Must be serious.'

'Then it's Judith,' said Keith.

'The looker?' said the quizmaster. 'By the way they're acting it looks like we're all suspects in a murder investigation. Better get us alibis sorted.'

'Don't worry,' said Brian Cordon, as he grasped Keith's shoulder. 'I've already let them know you were missing tonight. And your mate Rob was fired up, trying to take a pop at me. They were very interested.' He winked. 'Always pleased to help the bizzies.'

'Are you all right?' said Bea, staring closely at Keith. He lifted up Scamp, buried his head in the dog's coat, and wiped his tears against the short, springy hair, as his shoulders shook uncontrollably.

~

227

Lisa had just fallen asleep when Maya banged on her bedroom door.

'Lisa, it's Rob. He's been trying to get hold of you. It's urgent. Listen to me.' The handle rattled. 'Lisa, why have you locked the door?'

'Maya I told you, I don't want to see him again, under any circumstances. Just tell him from me to fuck off. Just do that for me.'

'Lisa, you'll regret this.'

'Please.' Lisa turned up the volume on her headphones but was immune to Pharrell Williams's entreaties to be happy as she buried her head under her pillow, sobbing. Even Maya was against her. Being strong was hard, but she must follow her head, not her heart.

Suspicious minds

'So he got his bag, then?' Lisa called as she picked up her car keys. 'Maya?'

Maya walked into the living room, wearing jeans and a sweatshirt. Her hair was pinned in a topknot.

'Make me a tea. It's the least you owe me,' Maya said.

'I'm sorry, but I've got to go. Thanks for giving him the bag. Did he say anything?'

'I took it to the police station.'

'What?'

'He rang me. He needed it.'

'What? Why did he ring you?' Lisa drew closer. 'Why? What's happened? Tell me.'

'He was being questioned.'

'About what?'

'They took all his clothes for forensics.'

'Maya, why didn't you tell me?'

Maya folded her arms and sucked in her cheeks.

'Judith's dead.'

'What do you mean, dead? She can't be dead.'

'Murdered.'

'What do you mean, murdered?'

'Killed outside her back door. Knifed, I think.'

'What? Is this some kind of weird joke?'

Maya arched one eyebrow.

'So why question Rob? Not Rob? Surely not.'

'Of course not Rob.' Maya turned sharply away.

'Where is he? I'll phone him.'

'He has no phone. The police have it.'

'They think he did it?' Lisa took a step closer to her flatmate.

'They're eliminating him from their inquiries. After all, he found her. I took him home. Heather's with him now. She'd been at Karl's.'

229

'Where did he find her?'

'I told you. Outside her back door. On the patio.'

'God.'

'I've got to go.'

'But I need to know—'

'I'm late already and I still have to change,' Maya said. 'You're not the only one who has important meetings.'

~

Lisa shot past the empty reception desk and went straight to her desk.

'Oh, Lisa, have you heard?' Tasmin shrieked.

'Something's happened to Judith. What do you know, Taz?' Lisa said, sitting on Tasmin's desk.

Tasmin wiped her nose. Her cheeks were wet and her eyes red.

'The police are here. Plain-clothes officers. They went in to see Andy. They've been speaking to him for about ten minutes. Olivia heard them say they were leading a murder inquiry and they had questions to ask about Judith.'

'They'll want to talk to us next, I bet. Find out what we know,' Olivia said.

'She left around the same time as us,' said Tasmin. 'I guess they'll want to talk to Jeremy and Rob as well. And you, of course, Lisa. All Judith's team. And Keith, even though he wasn't there.'

The office phone rang. Lisa answered.

'They want to see me.'

'Good luck,' said Tasmin, giving her a nervous but encouraging smile. 'By the way, I'm glad the dry-cleaners saved your suit.'

'Yes, of course I'll help you as much as I can, Detective Inspector Calvini,' Lisa said, glancing at his ID. She felt unnerved by his penetrating gaze and wondered why she was feeling guilty.

'When did you last see Judith Crayvern?'

'She's dead, isn't she? How did it happen? Do you—?'

'I'll ask the questions, Lisa.'

'Sorry. I last saw her at the pub quiz last night. We go every week.'

230

'The same team?'

'No. Keith wasn't there, so we teamed up with Tasmin and Jeremy.'

'We?'

'Me and Rob. My boyfriend. And my flatmate, Maya.'

'Oh, yes. Maya.'

Lisa paused, irritated. Had Maya been interviewed? She hadn't mentioned it.

'And Judith joined us. And we won. Afterwards Rob and I went to Keith's to find out why he hadn't come but he wasn't there. Just his dog, Scamp, was. Then I went home.'

'Why did you go home alone?'

'I don't live with Rob and I have a busy day today.'

'So what time did you get home?'

'Time? I don't know. Maybe eleven o'clock. Is this important? I sent a text just before I got home.' She took her phone out of her pocket and glanced at it. 'I texted at 11.12. That was just before I got home.'

'Do you mind if I look?'

Message to James at 11.12.

'Why did you text then?'

'I'd just checked all the messages I got since 7.00, which was the last time I looked.' Lisa felt uncomfortable as the detective read the messages. 'I was in the pub quiz then.'

'What time did you leave Rob?'

'I guess about twenty minutes before I got home.'

'Where did Rob go after you left?'

'To Judith's.'

'Why?'

'I don't know. That's what Maya said he did. When I last saw him he was still at Keith's.'

'Even though Keith wasn't there?'

'Yes.'

'Why?'

'Perhaps you should ask him that,' Lisa said. Calvini tapped his fingers on the table. 'Sorry,' Lisa continued. 'Rob was concerned. It was unlike Keith to miss the pub quiz. He likes his routine.'

231

'But you weren't that concerned?'

'I was concerned. But I couldn't think of what else we could do.'

'Why did Maya come to the station with Rob's clothes, not you?'

'I asked her to. Well, I didn't know she would be taking the bag to the police station, obviously. Just returning it.'

'Why?'

Lisa paused.

'We had had an argument. We sort of split.'

'So your relationship with Robert Granville is over?'

'Yes. No.' Why had she finished with Rob? When he had needed her and asked for her help Maya had been there instead.

'Does he know that?'

'I suppose. I don't know if it is over. Perhaps it was just a tiff.'

'About James?'

'No. No.'

'What was your relationship with Judith, Lisa?'

Lisa hesitated.

'A friend, sort of.'

'Sort of? Didn't you like her?'

'Well, she could be charming. She used to bring little gifts.' What had Andy said about her and Judith? Had he mentioned their spat? Or perhaps Maya had.

'For whom?'

'For me.'

'She sounds very thoughtful.'

'They were freebies she had picked up, mainly. It made her look generous, caring, thoughtful.'

'Was she?'

'She was thoughtful, but in a manipulative way.'

'What was it she wanted, do you think?'

'I don't know.'

'Did you socialise with her outside the quiz?'

'Sometimes. Not so much recently.'

'You don't sound too fond of her, Lisa. Why did you say to her that there would be no next time?'

'Sorry?'

'As you were leaving the pub, when Judith mentioned the next

232

quiz you said that there would be no next time.'

Lisa could feel her palms sweating. Had Rob said this?

'She had another side. She could deliberately misconstrue things, to make other people look bad. And she wasn't—'

'Which other people?'

Lisa chewed her thumbnail.

'Me, I suppose.'

'Sorry?

'Me. She tried to make me look bad.'

'What was the reason for your argument with Rob?'

'I felt he kept things from me. He didn't share things with me. I felt he shut me out of his work life.'

What had Rob said? Had he told them about her sleuthing? How would that make her look? It was best to say as little as possible. She didn't want the police to think she had a grudge. *And Andy. What had he said?*

Calvini leaned back in his chair.

'Lisa, were you jealous of Judith?'

'Do you think they'll keep our fingerprints on the police computer for ever?' said Lisa, twirling her empty cardboard cup.

'I certainly enjoyed that part, where he put his hand on my fingers. How can anyone fingerprint someone so sexily? God, he's so drop-dead gorgeous, isn't he?' said Tasmin. 'Those deep brown eyes. Though, judging by the accent, more Mancunian than Italian, I'd say. Clever, too. I even admitted I was jealous of Judith's attention to Jeremy.

'Oh my God, do you think that makes me a suspect? Oh, no, they might suspect Jeremy.' Olivia raised her eyebrows as Tasmin's voice got higher.

'Why Jeremy?' Lisa asked.

'I'm sure they're just keeping all their lines of enquiry open at the moment. It could have been a random killer,' said Olivia.

'Oh my God, what if it's a serial killer? I might be next, or any of us,' Tasmin said.

'You are being melodramatic now, Taz. It's usually someone the victim knows,' said Olivia. 'I just can't process it. It seems unreal.'

233

'Then perhaps we know him,' said Tasmin. 'They gave Andy quite a grilling. Maybe he's a suspect. He's had lunch with her, more than once. Shit. Mummy is going to be so freaked. They were worried enough that I was coming here because of all the drugs, but now I'm in the middle of a murder investigation. Murder. Can you believe it?'

'It's often the one who found the body,' said Olivia.

'It's not Rob,' said Lisa.

'Rob found the body? Oh my God. I didn't know that. Where?' said Tasmin, holding her hand over her mouth. Olivia looked at Lisa with renewed interest.

'At her house. Outside the back door.'

'How did she die?' Olivia asked.

'That's all I know. Rob's a bit worn out.' Lisa sat back in her office chair, looking at the ceiling.

'Did you ever find out where Keith was?' asked Tasmin.

'No ... Look, you're not saying it's Keith?' said Lisa.

'Of course not. He's a sweetie. Anyway, it was Judith who had the motive for killing *him*, after he killed her cat,' said Tasmin.

'It was an accident,' said Lisa. 'Keith found Bunters.' *But Rob had said Keith had confessed to running him over. That was how the whole argument had started last night.*

'What about the bully boy with the tattoos?' said Olivia.

'Brian Cordon,' said Lisa. 'I think he quite liked her.'

'Exactly. It could be a sex crime.' Tasmin looked at her phone. 'They're going to interview Jeremy. At least he has an alibi. Me. And he's mine. Livvie was on a train with hundreds of people. What about you, Lisa? Do you have an alibi?'

'Well, I don't know exactly what time it happened. Can texting be an alibi?'

'I guess it depends how she was killed. Could you text and strangle someone at the same time? No. But you could hit someone over the head with a lead pipe in between texts,' said Tasmin.

'Motive. It's all about motive. Sex. Money. Revenge. Blackmail,' said Olivia. 'They will be putting together a profile of Judith then the killer. Like in *Cracker*.'

'Who has the best motive, then?' said Tasmin.

Lisa felt uncomfortable. What if the police started asking her friends what she thought of Judith? They would soon conclude that Lisa hated her, if Detective Inspector Calvini hadn't formed that opinion already. Tasmin and Olivia were looking at her.

'You don't think I did it, do you?' said Lisa.

'Of course not, Lisa. But I think you're in shock,' said Tasmin. 'You don't look well at all.'

'Poor Judith. She had a tragic life,' said Olivia, passing a card and a pen to Tasmin. 'Can you sign this for Sally's new baby?'

'By the way, Lisa,' said Tasmin, flourishing the pen. 'What exactly was Rob doing at Judith's?'

Lisa mechanically signed the card as she thought about how much she needed to get in touch with Rob. His home number was permanently engaged. How long would it take for them to find out that they had the body of an impostor? Fuck. Could they charge her for withholding evidence, obstructing a police investigation? Well, she had wanted to tell Detective Calvini but he hadn't been willing to listen.

'Lisa?'

'Sorry, what did you say?'

Wednesday afternoon

The blue-and-white tape marking the boundaries of the crime scene fluttered in the breeze. After lunch the cordoned-off area had been reduced to the immediate vicinity of 23 Willow Tree Avenue. A policeman stood on duty near the open gates, surveying the groups of journalists, photographers, and cameramen who were jousting for pole position on the opposite pavement, occasionally scurrying towards a passer-by in the hope of a new sound bite. Keith held Scamp's lead tightly as he strained to see down the driveway. At the far end he could see two figures wrapped in white protective suits. They seemed to be wrestling with the plastic refuse bins.

'Did you know the lady?' asked a gaunt man with deep lines etched into his world-weary face. He threw the butt of a cigarette on the ground and stepped on it with the sole of a scuffed desert boot.

'What?' said Keith.

'Did you know the deceased?' The man bent down and stroked

235

Scamp's head. His jacket flapped open, revealing a paunch that seemed incongruous against his otherwise slender frame. The dog growled. 'She'd just won the pub quiz, hadn't she?'

Keith ignored him and moved away, grateful to see a familiar figure at the gate opposite the crime scene. He smiled at Mrs Jones. She had a silk scarf tied around her head, from which two regal white curls protruded.

'Do I know you?' Mrs Jones said.

'Keith, the taxi driver.' He touched his cap. 'I pick you up from the hairdressers sometimes.' She looked at him suspiciously. 'At Three Lane Ends.'

'You look different.'

'New glasses. Did you see anything last night? Do you know what's happened?'

'First I knew was when the police turned up, and then an ambulance. I had to go outside. It was so loud I couldn't hear the telly. Blue lights flashing all down the road. I saw them take that young man away. Put him in the police car, like they do on TV. Hand on his head as he gets in. I always wonder why they do that.'

'Which young man?'

'I've seen him at hers a few times. Tall, dark hair. Says hello sometimes. I don't know him.'

'When was that?'

'Before midnight. The police arrived during *Newsnight*. I always knew she was trouble. What sort of woman ends up dead in her back garden? I told them,' she said, nodding towards the gaggle of journalists.

'Who'd have thought that young man was a murderer? Someone said he was in her quiz team. My father was right. No good comes of public houses. Teetotaler, he was. Took the pledge.'

'You be careful what you tell them,' said Keith, gruffly. 'You can't trust the press. Judith was a fine lady. And Rob is certainly no murderer.'

'Who's looking after her cat? The grey-and-white one? I called him Smokey,' Mrs Jones said.

'I've got to go,' said Keith.

Keith approached the journalist he had snubbed before.

236

'Who are you? Which paper are you with?'

'Dave Dawson. I'm local, mate. Freelance. Often string for *The Courier* and the Sundays.' The journalist smiled revealing crooked, discoloured teeth. He took out a pen and a notepad from his pocket.

'Well, I'd just like to tell you about Judith,' said Keith. If he couldn't make amends while she was alive, at least he could give her a decent epitaph. Then he'd call the police.

~

'Rob, sit down in my chair. You look dreadful,' said Maya.

'Thanks, Maya.'

'I bet you've not eaten. I'll get you a sandwich.'

'It's OK. Heather made me eat some eggs on toast. I feel like I've lost my balance. My head's spinning.'

'Have some biscuits, then, with your coffee. Keep your energy up. No sleep won't have helped.' Maya put down a large, steaming mug as the front door rattled.

'Oh, babe. How are you? I've been thinking about you all day.' Lisa swept through the doorway and threw herself around Rob's neck. 'What happened? I tried to contact you at MedTime. Are the police going to interview you again? They've been hanging round Berger's all day. Have you seen Keith?'

'Steady on. Too many questions, Lise,' Rob said.

Maya put a packet of biscuits on the coffee table.

'If you want a drink, Lisa, you're going to have to put the kettle on and make it yourself.'

'I'm good, thanks. What happened, Rob?' Lisa said, sitting on the floor opposite Rob. Maya stretched out on the couch.

'Are you sure you want to talk about it, Rob?' Maya said.

Rob nodded.

'I need to. I went to her house after I left Keith's.' He glanced at Lisa. 'There was no one in. I couldn't understand why she wasn't at home. I went round to the back. The security lights came on as I walked down the drive. For a moment it was pitch-black as I turned into the back garden. Then the garden lit up. It was like a scene from a play. Her body was stretched out under the spotlight. I thought maybe she'd fallen awkwardly. Or, I don't know, that maybe she was playing a practical joke and she'd get up.

'I don't know what I thought, but I didn't think she was dead. I mean, it's not what you expect. I leaned forward and touched her, then I realised there was blood everywhere. Soaked in her jacket, in the grass, in her hair. I called her name. She was warm but limp, lifeless.'

'She was gone?' said Lisa. 'Already dead?'

'You touched her?' said Maya.

'Yes, I touched her. It was like her energy was seeping away.' Rob took a cigarette out of his pocket and flicked his lighter several times. His hand was shaking. He looked into the distance.

'She didn't look like Judith. Her hair was matted, like snakes. She looked like Medusa. There was a huge gash across her throat. I don't know how long I was there for, just standing in the darkness praying that light would not come on again. Then I called the police. This copper arrived and asked me some questions and then they put me in a car and this smart-arse Calvini arrives and takes me down the station just "to eliminate me from their inquiries". So they take my clothes, my phone, question me all night.'

'What did they ask you?' asked Lisa.

'What time did I find her? When I'd last seen her. How I knew her. Did she have any enemies? What I thought of her. Why I tried to hit Brian Cordon. Did I see anyone?'

'Did you?' said Lisa.

Rob shook his head.

'I don't know what else. It's all a blur.' He shut his eyes briefly, then gagged and spluttered out his tea.

'Have either of you mentioned Denise Carvel?' Maya asked, dabbing a tea cloth on Rob's jumper and carefully collecting his fallen ash into a saucer.

'No.' Rob hunched his shoulders wearily. Lisa shook her head.

'Have they interviewed you, Maya?'

'Yes, last night. They wanted to know my movements after the pub quiz and when I saw you two.'

'What did you say about us?' said Lisa.

'As little as possible,' said Maya. 'When do you get your phone

238

back, Rob?'

'God knows.'

'You need another, so you always have someone to call. I'll go to Tesco now and get a pay-as-you-go one.' Maya said, picking up her car keys. 'That, by the way, Rob, is the first and last cigarette you smoke in here. But what I want to know – and what Lisa will not ask, even though she really wants to know – is why you went to Judith's in the first place.'

Rob looked from Maya to Lisa.

'I don't know,' he said. 'I don't know.' Then his eyes closed, his chin fell on to his chest, and he slept.

'I'm sorry about last night, babe,' said Lisa, running her hand across Rob's arm. She looked up at the ceiling of her bedroom. Rob had been gazing at it for most of the last hour, his eyes open, his body tense.

'No, don't touch me. I feel like the world is spinning. Like I'm drunk. Just knowing you're here is a comfort,' he said.

'I was jealous. She always manages to wind me up just by being there. Never mind her sly cracks.'

'That won't happen again. She is most definitely past tense.'

'I overreacted. I'm sorry.'

'Lisa, there's something I need to know.' He turned towards her. Can you explain why I found your business card by her body?'

'What? No. No, I can't.' Lisa lifted her body weight on to her elbow and looked in his eyes. 'Where is it?'

'In my jacket pocket, which is in an evidence bag at the cop shop.'

'Why?'

'I didn't think it was evidence that would do you any good. But I'll guess they'll find it now.'

Lisa lay back on the bed and looked at the ceiling.

God, he thinks I killed her, and he's covering for me.

~

Keith sipped his tea as Detective Inspector Calvini watched him

239

closely from the chair at the other side of the dining room table.

'So, Mr Sharpe, would you mind telling me again your whereabouts on Tuesday evening?'

'I went to The Sun for the quiz,' said Keith, 'but then I wasn't feeling so good so I came back home.'

'And what time was that?'

'I guess about 7.25. Then I went back at 10.50. I knew I still had time to get in a pint, maybe two, before they stopped serving. It's only five minutes' walk. I walked up the road and through the pub car park.'

'Did anyone see you? Did you see anyone?'

'There was someone in the car park. I had to pull Scamp away. I just said, "How do?" I didn't know them. They were putting something in the boot of their car.'

'What sort of car?' Calvini made a note.

'I don't know. Just a car. A dark saloon car.'

'This wasn't what you usually did on a Tuesday, was it?'

'No. Usually I get there before 7.30. Meet the others and stay for the quiz.'

'Who are?'

'Lisa, Rob, and Judith.'

'So why not last night?'

'Like I said, I wasn't well. Headache. Then when I got home I had an accident. I fell, you see.' Keith hesitated.

'Where did you fall?'

'Here.' Keith pointed to floor in the centre of the room beneath a hole in the plaster where the ceiling rose had been.

'I was lying on the floor when I heard Rob at the door. He was banging really hard.'

'How long had you been there?'

'I don't know.' Keith stroked the red, roughened skin around his neck. He could barely utter the words but he had to, to give Rob an alibi. 'You see, I'd tried to top myself. It was a moment of madness. I couldn't even do that right.'

'And why had you tried to do that?' Calvini said sharply.

'Just feeling guilty about my Sandra. I could have made her happier.'

240

'Sandra?'

'My late wife. My princess.'

'And then, after failing to kill yourself, you decided to go back to the pub?'

'Yes, I guess I thought I needed to pull myself together.' Keith rubbed his neck. 'Rob was knocking for ages.'

'Was Lisa there too?'

'I don't know. By the time I'd got myself to the door Rob had gone. I saw him crossing the road but I couldn't say anything. I couldn't see Lisa. He'd left a chocolate on the doormat. One in a purple foil wrapper. It was like a sign to carry on. Look to the future.

'Rob's a good lad. Salt of the earth. Cares about everyone. I felt I owed it him. And to the little fella.' Keith nodded towards Scamp. He searched the detective's face for empathy but found none.

'Did you see Judith Crayvern on Tuesday?'

Keith shook his head.

'She was in The Sun, but I didn't speak to her.'

'How often did you usually see her?'

I used to see her in the park sometimes, or take her in the cab on a few errands. She didn't like parking, or buses.'

'Where did you take her?'

'The Nail Boutique, Hills Solicitors, Kendals, Harvey Nichols. Sometimes I'd go round to her house, do odd jobs, and have a brew and some parkin. But I hadn't been to hers for a bit.'

'Keith, when was the last time you saw Judith Crayvern before the quiz night?'

'A week last Tuesday, when I killed her cat.'

Watch that man

Thursday morning

'He's been a long time with Louise,' Paula said.

'Who?' Marsha said.

'That copper. DI Calvini, he said he was.'

If Marsha leaned against the back of the reception desk chair she could just glimpse into the director's office through a narrow inner window. She sat up smartly and swivelled the chair round as the door opened.

'Marsha, have you got a minute? Detective Inspector Calvini would like to speak to you, then Helen and then Paula.' Louise Pyatt nodded at her colleagues as they tidied the leaflet displays beside the reception desk. 'He will explain why,' she added as she hastened towards the grand double doors. 'I'm going to County Hall. They know I'm running late.'

'But why would they care?' Marsha muttered, as Paula settled down in the reception chair and reached for a chocolate.

'What did he want, Marsha?' Paula snapped, as Helen took her turn to meet the detective.

'We're not allowed to talk about it, but he asked me about Judith Crayvern's death and what I knew about Denise Carvel,' Marsha whispered, looking furtively around. 'He's very thorough.'

'What did you say?'

'I just said Judith had been depressed after Martin died, a bit reclusive. How popular Martin was. How we all missed him. What a tragedy it was.'

'And?'

'And I said I hadn't kept in touch with Denise after she left. He wanted to know why. He had a way of making you talk. I hadn't meant to say so much.'

'Why, what did you tell him?'

'I said we had nothing in common. She had no real qualifications to do the job. She just knew the right people. She was a trouble-

242

causer. I was glad she'd gone.'

Helen gently closed the door of the director's office behind her.

'Your turn, Paula.'

'What did he ask, Helen?' Marsha said, as Paula left.

'I'm not supposed to say,' Helen said.

'Go on. Denise and Judith?'

Helen nodded.

'Go on.'

'I said I didn't know Judith. I'd liked Denise but I'd not heard about her since she left.'

'You liked her?'

'Yes, she was always fair to me, though I wished she'd let me do more on reception.'

'It must be an important investigation,' Marsha said. 'They've not used the local cops.'

Helen shrugged.

'Look, you've got a customer. I'll get out of your way.' She looked over to the museum entrance where a tall, suntanned man wearing a padded bomber jacket and stonewashed jeans was looking intently at the display of staff names and photographs. Marsha forced a smile as the man ambled towards the reception desk.

'Marsha, I was just wondering if you can help?' The man grinned a toothy smile as he leaned against the desk. 'Didn't Judith Crayvern live round here?'

'Are you a cop as well? They've already asked us about Judith Crayvern and Denise Carvel. Get your act together.'

'Well, it's not every day that folk get murdered.' A piece of white gum flicked through the man's mouth.

'Who's been murdered? Denise?'

'Judith Crayvern.'

'Nah. Judith's already dead. It must be someone else.'

Helen walked urgently into the reception area.

'I'm sorry to interrupt,' she said, thrusting her iPad in front of Marsha. She whispered, 'I googled Judith. She's been murdered again. At least, someone with her name has been. They said she comes from Hazelton.'

'Well, you don't get murdered twice, do you now?' said the man.

243

'This must be a case of mistaken identity. So who do you think it might be? Seems to me it sounds like Denise Carvel.'

'Why would anyone want to murder her?' said Helen.

'Plenty,' murmured Marsha. 'That slapper had no shame.' The door of the office opened and Paula emerged, followed by DI Calvini.

'Now, isn't this interesting?' Calvini said, standing in front of the reception desk, staring at the man, who returned his gaze coolly. 'I hope you've not been speaking to Mr Dawson here, ladies. It's the police, not the press you should be talking to if you have any information.'

'I'll be on my way then,' Dawson said, smiling in turn at each of the three museum administrators. 'I've got some googling of my own to do. I'll just leave my card if you want to call me, though. You've been very helpful.'

'Scumbag,' said Marsha. 'Keep it.'

'What did you say to him, Marsha?' said Paula, flushing.

'Nothing,' mumbled Marsha.

'Marsha's been very helpful, love. I always like to keep up with the DI here.' Dawson took a leaflet from the display stand. 'Pity. I'll have to leave the Egyptology exhibition for another day. Seems there's a bigger story here than I was expecting. Sounds like the body on the patio had quite a lot of explaining to do.'

Thursday lunchtime

'You wouldn't think it was the person we knew,' said Olivia, folding the newspaper and putting it back in the news rack at Kounos. 'Who on earth is Margaret Jones? I wouldn't call Judith a party girl.'

'I was surprised Keith talked to the press,' said Tasmin. 'I didn't think he was the sort.'

'I bet the flattering bits came from him,' said Lisa. 'He never had a bad word to say about her, even though she could be quite condescending to him at times.'

'And Brian Cordon, I bet. She had him round her little finger,' said Tasmin. 'Do you think there will be a police reconstruction? You know, at the pub quiz?'

'They might, you know. That's a good point,' said Olivia. 'I supposed I'd have to not be there. What a drag.'

'Can you remember everything you did that night, Taz? It's a bit blurry to me already,' said Lisa. 'I think I want to forget.'

'We arrived just before 7.20 and got our drinks and a table,' said Tasmin. 'Then we saw you and Rob come in with Maya. While you were at the bar Judith came and sat with us and asked if she could be in our team. She gave me some perfume that she thought would suit me. That was so sweet. She was always so thoughtful and caring. Then she went to the bar,' Tasmin said.

'Nothing of any import to the crime there,' said Olivia.

I wouldn't be too sure, thought Lisa. *Calvini would think I was jealous.*

'I bet they would want to know why she wanted to swap teams,' said Olivia.

'Well, how would we know that?' said Lisa.

'You do know, Lisa, though. There's no point not being honest with the police,' Olivia said. Lisa sucked on an olive, annoyed at Olivia's forthrightness.

'Livvie's right. They will want to know why you didn't get on, Lisa.'

'I think the police already know how I feel about her. Calvini has a way of making you talk about things you didn't even know you had buried deep down,' Lisa said, responding to Tasmin's concerned expression.

'What happened next?' said Olivia.

'I don't know what happened after that because I went to the lav and met Lisa there.'

'When I got to the table you had already agreed we were all playing together,' said Lisa.

'Yes, we'd been chatting to Maya and agreed to play as one team. You agreed, though you looked *very* tetchy. When I came back Judith told us she had registered us as Judith's Soul Mates. You nearly choked.'

'Who suggested playing as one team, Taz?' Lisa said.

'I'm not sure. Maya, I think, or it could have been Jeremy,' Tasmin said. 'Then we played the quiz, swapped answer sheets with The Dispossessed, and we won! Judith said Jeremy and I could have the bottle of wine. You said that was fine. So we collected that and left just ahead of her. She seemed to get delayed in the pub, because we had to wait for her to come out to say goodbye.'

'Yes, we were behind Judith. Rob spoke to Bea – Chocolate Box Woman – the lady who gives us sweets at football. She gave Rob and me a handful of Quality Street. Then Brian Cordon made some lewd remark to Judith in his own inimitable way. I think he thought it was a compliment. Then he had a go about Keith – called him a twat – and then called me a cheat.'

'A cheat?' said Olivia.

'Because I had my phone out during the quiz. I was just going to check up on Keith. I wasn't going to cheat.'

'Oh, I remember now. Judith got very annoyed with you,' Tasmin said.

'Then Rob flung a punch at Cordon and missed. I thought we were going to get barred,' Lisa said.

'Wow. I didn't know that. I can't believe we missed all this. That's a reason to murder Brian Cordon, though, not Judith,' Tasmin said.

'I don't think it's a reason to murder anyone, to be to be fair,' said Olivia.

'Rob didn't murder anyone, Taz,' Lisa said.

'Sorry. I know that, Lisa. So we said goodnight when Judith came out and turned left. She turned right. That was the last time we saw her. She was in good spirits, I thought. Oh, yes, and Jeremy said, "See you on Saturday," as she turned away.'

'We turned left through the pub car park, then up Cromwell Road to Keith's. It's not far: about five minutes,' said Lisa.

'They'll want to know the timing,' said Olivia.

'I got home about 11.14. I know that because I sent a text at 11.12,' said Lisa.

'We got to Jeremy's about 10.40, I think. Then we opened the wine,' said Tasmin.

'So, Lisa,' said Olivia, 'How do you account for leaving the pub at 10.30 and arriving home at, roughly, 11.14? That's forty-five minutes to make a ten-minute round trip to Keith's and fifteen minutes home. That's twenty minutes to be accounted for.'

Lisa drank most of her half-empty glass of water in one swig.

'We were outside Keith's for what seemed an age. Then I left Rob and I was texting on the way home.'

'I would say,' said Olivia, 'that while you, Rob, and Keith have partial alibis for one another they aren't very convincing. Not that I believe that any of you murdered Judith, of course, but you don't have any proof that you didn't.'

'What about Maya?' asked Tasmin. 'Where was she?'

'She was last out of the pub, I think. She was already home when I got back. So she can vouch for me,' said Lisa.

'And who can vouch for her?' said Olivia, embracing her role as armchair detective.

Thursday evening

Rob was sitting behind the boy with the golden curls. The boy was studying Rob over the back of his seat.

'Bloody bonkers,' mouthed Rob. The boy mimicked him silently and laughed, then turned round as the bus set off.

'Bloody bonkers,' said the boy as the bus cranked up a gear after it rounded a corner.

'What did I tell you?' said his mother.

Rob gazed blankly as the houses raced by. He could not think about the past without being submerged by waves of nausea, and the future was too bleak to contemplate. There was only the present. The bus journey had been the only pleasant part of the day, the only place where he felt safe from DI Calvini's suspicious mind and cynical questions.

'Oh, no! They've murdered all the trees,' the boy yelled, pointing. 'Look.'

Just at the point where Rob expected to hear the branches knocking on the metal roof there was only the sound of the bus engine. The trunks of the trees stood forlornly along either side of the road, their upper branches brutally lopped off, their silhouettes like giant desert cacti. The road ahead had completely changed.

'Who's done that?' cried the boy. 'Murderer!'

~

p'What are you doing, Lisa? You're looking very serious,' said Maya.

'I'm writing out key contact names so I have a manual record of them and I'm not dependent on my mobile.'

'Why don't you just back them up to the cloud? Then you can get them on your laptop.'

'What if I lost that as well?'

'Why would you do that?'

'Who knows what the police can do? They have powers. They could come in here and search everything, even your room. Take our computers, if they wanted.'

'Why would they want to do that? You think you're a suspect, don't you?'

'Well, I had a motive. I hated her. Or maybe they think Rob did it. They always suspect the person who found the body.'

'You are obsessing too much about this. Let's go out. A few drinks in The Sun, maybe?' Maya rarely suggested spending a whole night in a pub, but this week had been like no other.

'Good idea. Let's go now. I can't be bothered to change.'

Although The Sun car park was sparsely populated, inside the locals were queuing at the bar three deep. As Bernice pulled pints from the bar she fired questions at Lisa about what Rob had seen on the night of the murder. Lisa evaded giving any direct answers and reassured the landlady that Rob would be able to tell her himself next time he came in, but for now he was having a quiet night at home. As Lisa picked up their drinks she saw Tasmin and Olivia beckoning, and squeezed past the familiar faces she had last seen on Tuesday.

'It's like a quiz night,' said Tasmin. 'Everyone's here, except Keith and Rob, of course. It's like a wake.'

'No one's here to celebrate her life,' said Lisa. 'They're just here to gossip.'

'Like us, you mean,' said Maya.

'That's not fair,' Tasmin said. 'I was just wondering ... When do you think the funeral will be? So we can pay our respects. Who do you think will organise it?'

'I suppose her sister will. She'll be her next of kin, won't she?' said Olivia.

'Has she got a real sister? Aren't all her friends fake?' said Lisa.

'What do you mean, Lisa?' said Tasmin.

Maya groaned.

'Oh, here we go. No respect even for the dead.'

'I'm only telling the truth. A lot of her Facebook friends aren't real. They are fake. Like her.'

'How sad,' said Olivia. 'You mean there might be no one to organise her funeral? What d' you mean, fake?

'Excuse me, and you are?'

A tall man placed a half-full glass of lager on the table.

'Terrible, just terrible. I'd just like to pay my respects to Judith's teammates. Lisa ... It is Lisa, isn't it? You must be in shock.'

Lisa looked up at the stranger. A packet of cigarette papers protruded from the breast pocket of his blue striped shirt. A flash of white chewing gum glinted in his mouth.

'Excuse me,' said Lisa. 'I don't know you. Did you know Judith?'

'By two degrees of separation, shall we say, love?' he replied.

'So who do you know, *love*?' said Maya.

'Well, Keith. He's a great guy.'

'How do you know Keith?' said Lisa, sharply.

'Well, he's a regular here, isn't he?'

'But you're not. You're definitely not. Who are you?' Lisa said.

'Dave Dawson. Pleased to make your acquaintance.' He proffered his hand but no one took it. 'You girls must be wondering if it's safe to be on the streets now there's a killer on the loose.' He moved his hand over his belly, which spilled over the top of his jeans.

'Goodbye,' said Lisa.

'Sorry, love?'

'Goodbye. We have nothing to say to you,' Lisa said. Maya waved her hand, as Tasmin followed suit.

'Well, if you ever want to put the record straight on Denise, just let me know.'

'Creep,' said Tasmin. 'Some people love bad news. Who's Denise?'

'What does he know?' Lisa whispered to Maya.

'Ignore him, Lisa. Going back to Facebook,' said Maya, 'she does have some real friends. I looked today but no one's posted anything, so they can't know. The body hasn't been formally identified yet.'

'We really should announce it, you know,' said Tasmin, 'So people can leave a tribute.'

'I bet they're monitoring her Facebook. Do you think they're in here tonight, eavesdropping undercover?' said Maya.

'I can't see DI Sex on Legs,' sighed Tasmin.

Maya giggled.

'He's hot. I was hoping I could remember some crucial evidence so I could see him again.'

'I'd confess anything to him,' Tasmin said.

Brian Cordon approached their table. For a moment Lisa saw in him the younger version of the man, the blue eyes and aquiline nose, a firm chin in front of the sagging jowls.

'Nasty do,' he said. 'Judith was a lady. You don't get many of those these days. Where are the police up to?'

'They've interviewed everyone at work,' said Tasmin.

'Yes, I think they've seen everyone who was in here on Tuesday, asking the same questions. Did they see her leave? Who else left at that time? Who was she friendly with? Never seen so many bizzies at once. Nearly give me a heart attack,' Cordon said.

'What did you say?' said Lisa, quickly.

'I said she was a smasher, always had a good word for everyone. The lowlife who did it should swing.'

'They've eliminated you from their inquiries, then?' Lisa said.

'Yep, I've got a cast-iron alibi. I was here all the time with the missus and the rest of The Terminators. Keith hasn't, though, has he? And he's changed his appearance and run over her cat.' He made a slitting throat sign, then winked. 'They'll soon have the case closed.'

'I hope you don't mind I told them you were outside when I left,' said Lisa, 'having a sneaky fag. Maybe you nipped up to Willow Tree Avenue and back.'

'What are you up to, lady? I don't even smoke these days.' He drew his face level to hers. 'Careful, girly.'

'Just my joke,' said Lisa.

'That wasn't very wise, Lisa,' said Maya, as Cordon walked away.

'Have you seen Keith yet?' asked Tasmin.

'I spoke to him on the phone. He fell asleep on Tuesday and then he came here. He just missed us.'

'I thought you went to see him,' Olivia said.

'We did. We heard Scamp. He was in the loo.'

'No alibi. Not good,' said Olivia. 'Why didn't you walk back with Rob? Why did he find Judith on his own?' Olivia pressed, as she exchanged glances with Tasmin.

'I wanted an early night. We were supposed to have the Taylors meeting the next day,' said Lisa.

'So why did Rob go to Judith's?' said Tasmin.

'I think that's for Rob to tell,' said Maya. 'Olivia, I think it's a great idea to write something on Facebook.'

'OK,' said Olivia, opening her tablet. 'What shall I write on Judith's wall?'

'Make sure it's clear she's not writing it,' said Tasmin. 'Announcing one's own death is rather gross.'

'How about this?' Olivia suggested.

Dear friends of Judith,

We are afraid we have some sad news. Judith died suddenly and unexpectedly on Tuesday night.

After some discussion Olivia read out their final statement.

She was a flurry of elegance and fun, kind and generous. Her sense of style and wit lifted the spirits of those around her. Despite the tragedy she had experienced in her life she always tried to be positive and help others. She will be greatly missed.

'We should put *tragedies*,' said Tasmin. 'She lost Bunters and Martin, and the dog. We should put all our names on it. Is that OK, Maya … Lisa?'

Maya concurred. Lisa reluctantly agreed as she scanned the bar.

'You're blushing, Lisa. What's wrong?' said Tasmin. 'Are you going to faint? Ooh, it's DI Sex on Legs. He probably thinks we're concocting some sort of story.'

'We are,' muttered Lisa.

'Evening, ladies. It's my lucky night. Mind if I join you?' Calvini put a half pint of lager on the table.

'Not at all. I'm Olivia, if you remember.' Olivia held out her hand.

Calvini shook Olivia's hand firmly.

'Ah, yes. Olivia with the perfect alibi. Girls' night out, I see.'

'Are you still working, Detective Inspector, or is this an off-duty call?' said Maya.

'Off-duty,' said Calvini sipping his beer. 'I've had a very busy day in Hazelton.'

'This seems a curious place to relax, Laurie,' said Maya, leaning towards Calvini, 'in the presence of the prime suspects.'

Calvini returned her gaze, then turned to Lisa.

'That's a smart suit. Very distinctive.'

'It's Vivienne Westwood,' Tasmin said.

'Have any of you ever had been to Hazelton? Beautiful place,' Calvini continued.

There was a pause before Lisa replied.

'Yes, it's lovely. I'd love to go on holiday there.'

'I've had a very productive day there,' Calvini said. 'Do you know the guy over there?' He pointed to Dave Dawson, who was deep in conversation with Janet of The Dispossessed, but raised his head as Calvini gesticulated and nodded. 'It's best to give him a wide berth.'

'We do,' said Tasmin. 'He was talking to us before. He was very interested in Lisa.'

'It's always best to talk to the police about what you know, rather than the press,' the detective said.

'I knew he was more than a casual well-wisher,' said Lisa.

'Dave Dawson's more likely to screw up an investigation than solve it. He has a way of being very creative with his newspaper stories, but he's always very careful to attribute his quotes to sources. Now that's caused a few people some trouble over the years. Especially when they had no idea they'd even been talking to the press, or should I say the gutter press.'

'Lisa said nothing,' said Tasmin.

'Lisa, always so careful with her choice of words,' said Calvini, looking at her. 'It's amazing how, after the initial shock of a major crime, people suddenly remember the most important details that can really move an inquiry on. Sometimes they're loath to come forward, because they're reluctant to explain why they have just remembered. But, believe me, it's quite common.

'So, if you remember anything else, don't worry about calling me.'

Love that girl

DI Calvini held a plastic bag in front of Rob's face.

'Does this key look familiar?'

Rob slumped back in his chair in the MedTime staffroom. He should have told them before they found out. They must have analysed the webcam by now. When Calvini had asked for a quick chat, Rob was expecting five minutes to go over old ground. Now he realised he was going to have to answer questions for a lot longer before the detective was satisfied.

'There're a lot of your fingerprints in that house. Would you like to tell me how they got there?'

'I'm sure you've seen the webcam.'

'Yes, we have. It looks like you've been there a few times, both with and without Ms Clarkson. Did you use this key on the night of the murder?'

'What? No, of course not. We only used it before because we – I mean, I – thought Judith had self-harmed. She hadn't. I was hoping the webcam had recorded the murder. I mean … so that it would prove I hadn't done it, and you would catch the murderer.'

'Unfortunately not. Coincidentally, there was no recording of that night. Or perhaps that was deliberate.' Calvini picked up another bag. 'Do you recognise this?'

'It looks like a business card.' Rob could feel himself reddening.

'Would you like to tell me why it was in your pocket and has Denise Carvel's blood smeared on it?'

'I don't know.'

'Are you protecting Ms Clarkson? Or perhaps you know our procedures and expected it to be found, which would deliberately incriminate her. After all, you were furious with her that night. You'd just split up.'

'This is incredible. I'd never do that. I love Lisa. You think I framed her? I can't think of anything more ridiculous.' Rob got up and paced the room, scowling at the detective. 'I remember very little of that night, except finding the body. That face will stay with me until the day I die. I don't know why I did what I did. Why I went there, I mean.'

~

'DI Sex on Legs is in again, Lisa. Do you think he's here to see Andy again?' said Tasmin, peering through the office greenery as Lisa returned from a meeting.

'No, he's here to see me. I asked to see him.'

'Oh my God. What have you remembered?' Tasmin could barely contain her astonishment.

'I'll explain later. I think DI Calvini might think I should talk to him first.'

'Rob's phoned. He tried to get through to you while you were with Andy. He says they've watched the webcam.' Tasmin searched Lisa's face for a reaction, but found none. 'And found your card.'

'Well, Lisa, thank you very much for your honesty about why you went to Hazelton. You rightly concluded, following your 'sleuthing', that Denise Carvel had taken the name of Judith Crayvern by deed poll.'

'Thank you, sir.'

'You left quite an impression on Mr Oliver.'

'Mr Oliver?'

'He was a golfing partner of Martin Crayvern and a friend of Denise. You met him on your visit to Hazelton in the coach park.'

Lisa looked puzzled.

'Oh, the coach driver. Yes, he liked Denise. I couldn't get my head round that.'

'I know you find it difficult to believe, Lisa, but there seem to be a lot of people who liked her, who were quite sympathetic to her.'

'Well, not her work colleagues.' Lisa could see her own work colleagues circulating outside the frosted glass of the interview room. She wondered what they were thinking about her. 'The ones in the museum.'

'Even some of her museum colleagues.'

Lisa frowned.

255

'Well, not Marsha and Paula. They hated her.'

'Why do you say that?' Calvini leaned forward.

As Lisa related her conversations with the museum staff she noticed that the detective was not wearing a wedding ring.

Probably wedded to his job and divorced for being such an aloof, sceptical prick. Vain too, with those good looks.

'And why did you hate her, Lisa?'

Calvini remained motionless at the other side of the interview table, looking at a spot on the wall above Lisa's head. She rested her chin on her cupped hand, then took it away, twisting her handkerchief.

'I didn't hate her, but she was the arch manipulator. She infiltrated every aspect of my life, and of the lives of others, I suspect.' Lisa told the detective how she had been introduced to the widow, Judith, in The Sun by Keith, and how the woman had subsequently inveigled her way into her life by contriving coincidental meetings.

'So Lisa, what you seem to be telling me today is that she was stalking you and that this attention was unwanted. Despite this, you quite willingly accepted gifts from her and socialised with her, even on Valentine's Day, when your boyfriend would have preferred to have been alone with you.'

'What? It was just the once. I was just celebrating my new job. The other time I was celebrating Keith's birthday. We had to go for Keith's sake. Really I had nothing to do with her socially, apart from the quiz.'

'Then why were your fingerprints in Judith's kitchen, on her pictures, on the stairs, and in her bedroom – even in her refuse bins? But, tell me first, just what were you doing going into her bedroom?'

'I can explain. Rob was worried. We were worried. The anniversary of Martin's death was approaching and Rob thought she might have tried to commit suicide, because she had been so down, so fragile, he said. We went in her house to find her. Rob knew where her spare key was.'

Fuck, that doesn't sound good.

'Very convenient. You know, I began wondering if Rob had a thing with Judith, but now I'm not so sure that's true. But he's most

256

definitely in the grip of someone. Now who's that? Maya?'

'What? There's nothing between Rob and Maya.'

'No, I think that someone is you. Which is why he tried to hide your bloodstained business card. Now I'm thinking that maybe the person who had the affair was you.'

Lisa groaned.

Fuck, fuck, fuck. He thinks I'm a lesbian and it's a crime of passion.

Friday evening

'Yes, Maya, that's what he said. He really thinks Fake Judith and I were lovers. So I had to tell him, straight, exactly what I thought of her,' Lisa said, circling her living room and gesticulating with her right arm.

'Oh, dear. Was that wise? Maybe that was what he hoped you would do, you know. Provoke you into revealing the depth of your feelings.'

'It's not funny,' Lisa said.

'Well, one good thing is that he thinks you're innocent, Rob,' Lisa said.

Rob shrugged.

'I wouldn't bet on it. Smart-arse Calvini is making no signs that he's getting off my back yet. Who can blame him with the evidence he's got? Breaking and entering her house, and me finding her body?'

Late Saturday afternoon

'I'm hoping that's the last time,' said Rob, as he got in the front passenger seat of Keith's cab. 'Though God knows when I get my phone back. You know, I don't even know the old dear's phone number. That's what technology does to you. Makes you so dependent that you can't even call up your own mother without it.'

'Do you want to?'

'To be honest, no. What do I say? I found a friend's body and now I seem to be prime suspect in a murder investigation? It's best if I say nothing. She'd be a bit surprised if I rang her, anyway. She usually calls Heather, but they aren't speaking at the moment. She

257

doesn't think Karl is good enough for her. Might have a point there.'
Rob grinned.

'You're not close, then?' Keith glanced in the wing mirror and edged out. 'Lisa's?'

Rob nodded.

'Close enough. We just don't live in each other's pockets.'

'You're really the prime suspect?'

'I think I was. Not surprising, really. They have to start somewhere. Why not with the gibbering idiot who found her? But I think they've almost eliminated me from their inquiries. It's amazing what you forget. Things keep coming back, and I wonder why I hadn't already mentioned it. Then, 'cause I didn't, it makes me look like I'm being evasive.'

'What do the cops keep asking you?'

'Timings. Why I was there.'

'Why were you there?' Keith said, glancing at Rob.

'I don't know. That is the truth and no one is ever satisfied with that answer, but I really don't know. I don't think there has to be a rational explanation for everything you do in life. If I'd been a bit earlier I might have seen her killer, or even saved her. Then everyone would have said it was fate, or luck. I'd be a hero. As I was a few minutes too late I'm a suspect. It's my bad luck, and hers. But there was no reason. No one ever understands that, though.'

'I think I do.'

'Eh?'

'I once deceived my Sandra. You know, with another woman, like. Once. I don't know why. It was an impulse. Because I could. There was no reason. I regretted it immediately. I never thought she'd find out but she did.'

'What did she say?'

'I don't know. I only found out after she died. She'd told my daughter. I found a letter from her down the side of the sofa. Now I just wonder who told my Sandra,' he said, squeezing the wheel.

'Does it matter? Did Sandra forgive you?'

'I guess she did. She never let me know that she knew.'

'Then forget it. That's what she wanted. You need to keep the happy memories, not make up bad ones.' Rob gripped Keith's shoulder. 'I can tell you, they come along when you least expect it. A few weeks ago I was thinking that Lisa was the one. I was going to ask her to shack up with me. This week she tells me I'm not committed to her, I'm wondering if I might be charged with murder, and I'm not even sure she's convinced I'm innocent.'

'Everyone has their ups and downs. Lisa's besotted with you. You can tell by the way she looks at you.' There was silence as the cab pulled to a halt between two lines of parked cars.

'Do you think she suffered? Judith, I mean.' Keith's voice quavered.

'I don't know. But I think someone meant her to. Look, I'll just grab Lisa and we'll be here in five. We're going to Parkers' bar to meet the city's leading art critics.'

'Who?'

'Taz, Jeremy, and Maya. I could do with some light relief.'

~

'They'll be looking for a motive. Sex is the obvious one. A crime of passion. She certainly evoked emotion,' said Maya.

'Was she sexually attacked, though? I thought she'd had her throat cut,' said Jeremy, pocketing the Hockney exhibition brochure that Tasmin had pushed across the bar table.

'I don't know. I think Lisa thinks they might suspect her,' said Tasmin. 'So that would rule out sex.'

'Not necessarily,' said Jeremy. 'You need to keep an open mind, Taz. Not that I was suggesting that Lisa and Judith ...'

Maya laughed.

'I can't even allow my mind to go there.'

'It's just that sex attacks need not be heterosexual sex attacks, if you get my drift,' Jeremy added.

'I think the only thing they suspect Lisa of now is deliberate forgetfulness,' Maya said. 'DI Calvini must be quite annoyed that she waited so long to tell him about her sleuthing in Hazelton. I think revenge is the most likely motive, though. Judith/Denise seems to have made a few enemies over her lifetime – which, I guess, is why she changed her name.'

259

'That story is just amazing. And Lisa knew, but no one believed her,' said Tasmin.

'I believed her,' said Maya. 'I just didn't see where it was leading.'

'Now,' said Tasmin, 'if it was revenge, for blackmail, say – perhaps Denise knew who really killed Judith – then the whole thing would have been planned. The murderer would have known she was walking back from The Sun and lain in wait for her. A calculated killer. I hope none of us know them, because if they think we are suspicious they could strike again.'

'Money,' said Jeremy. 'The love of money is the root of all evil. Greed. Who are the main beneficiaries from her death? That will be what the police are working on. It could be a robbery by a vagrant for drugs money or something bigger. Who inherits?'

'Her sister, I guess, but she's in Australia. Maybe she took out a contract. Now that might be hard to prove. Oh, here's Rob.' Tasmin leaped to her feet and embraced Rob, then Lisa.

'Are you free, Rob? Have they let you have your mobile back?' Tasmin said.

'Well, I think they have asked me everything they could, again and again and again. No mobile, though. I've got the feeling they think I hadn't the time to do it.'

'They can tell the time of death, can't they? I'm not sure how accurate they are,' said Jeremy. 'Lisa, sit here. I'll get another chair.'

'I'm not sure she was dead when I found her. So I don't know how relevant that would be,' Rob said.

'It must have been so horrible, Rob,' said Tasmin, shuddering.

'It's a picture I can't get out of my mind. I just keep thinking if I had been a bit earlier I might have saved her.'

'You could have been killed,' said Lisa. 'I'd rather it was her than you. Not that I wanted anyone to die,' she added hastily, as her friends turned to look at her. 'But if anyone had to die I would rather it was her than Rob. Sorry.'

'I think you are making a very credible case that you and the lady formerly known as Judith were not lovers.' Maya said. Lisa glowered at her. 'Don't overdo it, though.' Maya winked. 'Have you got a solicitor, Rob?'

'No. I did wonder about that yesterday, but they cost a bomb,' Rob said. 'Calvini pushes it. He came in the shop for a "chat". The next minute he threw all sorts at me. I think he was happy enough in the end. Then today he said he just wanted me to come into the cop shop to clear up some identification issues. He started to ask me about when I worked in Barcelona. He had a business card of mine from then with the telephone number of NatWest Bank on it. All neatly presented in an evidence bag. I presume my fingerprints were on it.'

'That's what Judith said. That she met you in Barcelona,' Tasmin said.

'That's right, Inspector Browne, and I still don't remember,' Rob said.

'What about you, Lisa? Have you got a solicitor?' Jeremy asked.

'God, no. Don't you just need one when they arrest you? Well, I asked to see DI Calvini myself. I mean, we've been voluntarily helping with their inquiries. We are innocent.'

'I think they prefer it when there's no solicitor present. So they can ask what they want,' Maya said. 'That's not in your interests, though.'

'This is a uni friend of mine,' Jeremy said, taking a business card from his wallet. 'He's a criminal lawyer. Take it, Rob. You never know when you might need it.'

'Have you got two?' Maya said. 'You never know. Lisa might need one too.'

261

Say it isn't so

'The newspapers seem to have lost interest already,' Tasmin said, draining her glass. 'All the stories are about that footballer who was stabbed by his girlfriend.'

'Robbed of some of her fifteen minutes of fame,' said Lisa. 'She would be most annoyed.'

'Well, I guess even Judith can't compete with two A-list celebs,' Jeremy said.

'Are soap star actresses A-list?' Tasmin said.

'If you murder your very rich boyfriend, most definitely,' said Jeremy. 'Look over there. Seems like Dawson's still interested.'

'You all right if I join you?' Keith said, looking anxiously at Lisa. 'You aren't going to have too many in the team?'

'Of course not, Keith,' said Lisa. 'This is your team. There's just the five of us. Olivia's away and Maya's gone to a fencing class. Rob's held up, but he's on his way.'

'We decided it was best to call ourselves Game, Set, and Match, as Prime Suspects didn't sound very appropriate. I bet Rob won't be keen on the name, though,' Tasmin said.

'He never is,' said Lisa. 'His fault for being late. You're going to have to start the picture round without me. I need to go to the loo.'

Both doors of the toilet cubicles were closed. Lisa brushed the tangles out of her hair as she waited and was closely examining her eye make-up in the mirror above the basins when one door opened. She turned quickly but caught only a flash of black leisurewear retreating into the cubicle as the door slammed shut again.

Lisa shuffled awkwardly, then heard a toilet flush. The other door opened and she dashed in, briefly exchanging smiles with Janet of The Dispossessed.

'Thanks. I'm desperate,' Lisa said. 'See you later.'

When Lisa left the ladies' toilets were empty. She was about to wander through the bar when the quizmaster made an announcement.

'I'd like your respectful attention, please, Ladies and Gents.'

262

Lisa stopped as the customers responded by turning towards the bar and setting their pens down.

'As you know, a terrible thing happened last week. Judith was murdered after leaving here. Tragic. She'd just won the quiz, as well.' The quizmaster coughed. 'We're going to have a minute's silence for her, like they do at football matches. If you don't know who Judith Crayvern was, she was the looker with the blonde hair. That's right, Keith, looked a bit like Michelle Pfeiffer. Classy lady.

'One more word. Our boys in blue – no, not the football team, Brian – are here again tonight, so if anyone has remembered anything since last week you'll find a friendly copper you can talk to. Now let's pay us respects to the beautiful lady we knew as Judith.'

Respects, Lisa thought scornfully. Lisa was not unhappy that Denise was dead. In fact she was pleased. The feeling surprised and shocked her. She knew she shouldn't feel that way, but she did, despite all the dark uncertainty that hung over her and Rob's future.

As silence descended Lisa noticed Dave Dawson was propped against the bar, scanning the customers. She followed his eyes, wondering if all the policemen were in uniform or if they had infiltrated the quiz with plain-clothes detectives. She couldn't really imagine there would be any point in that.

She looked round. Most of the faces were familiar: The Dispossessed, Dead Ringers, The Terminators, various teams of students. Beside The Terminators' table was a woman in dark leisure clothes, not someone Lisa recognised. She didn't seem to belong to any team. Lisa looked a bit closer. The woman was wearing a baseball cap, which shaded her eyes. A blue blouse peeked out under the cuffs and V-neck of a black fleece. She was studying a pen, which she twirled round her fingers, as those nearby bowed their heads. Lisa couldn't help but think it was someone familiar.

~

Rob had texted Lisa to tell her he was on his way but the bus was labouring through the city traffic. He scrunched his headphones into his coat pocket. No music had ever been composed that could help him make sense of the situation he was in. When Calvini had called

263

round to say he had some news Rob had been relieved for a brief moment. He had thought that maybe they had picked someone up and Calvini was going to tell him that his role in helping with police inquiries was at an end.

'Just how much do you think Mrs Crayvern was worth?' Calvini had asked as he sat opposite Rob in the empty travel shop.

'I really don't know.' Rob had flexed his fingers, trying to channel the anger he felt into his extremities away from his tongue. He was beginning to detest Laurie Calvini. But he was wise to his tactics now. Best to say nothing.

'That house is worth a few bob. Then there's her investment properties, the student flats. Must be going on for nine hundred grand, don't you think?' Calvini crossed his leg over his knee and leaned back in the comfortable chair usually occupied by customers. He waited.

'Yes, if you say so.' Rob felt like he'd just failed a television panel show where the competitor was not supposed to say 'yes' or 'no'. He focused on a large poster of Sitges on the wall opposite.

'And her shares.'

'I know nothing about any shares.'

'Well, I'd say we're talking well over a million.'

Rob said nothing.

'So how does it feel to be a millionaire, Robert?'

'I don't understand what you're talking about.'

'We finally found the will today. She's left almost everything to you.'

'What? Why would she do that?' Rob said. Calvini's grey eyes bored into him. The detective might as well have had a bubble containing the words 'The prime suspect has a motive' hanging over his head.

Rob had locked up as soon as Calvini had left and walked towards the bus stop. He had slouched into the first seat he saw on the crowded bus, one prioritised for the elderly and disabled. He had been oblivious to the piercing stares of an older woman whose dense body mass lurched and wobbled uncomfortably to the rhythm of the bus as she hung on to a strap. Christ. He was supposed to be starting

264

his new job soon. He had everything he had wanted a week ago. The chance to make his life on his own terms. Lisa. The money was a poisoned chalice. It could lock him away, end his life.

The bus juddered to a halt at a red light and the woman fell forward, her shoulder bag scraping past Rob's cheek. He studied the shops at Three Lane Ends. Sometimes everything looked so down at heel, so worn out. Not just the buildings, but the people as well. Perhaps he should leave it all behind, leave the city, and spend a carefree year in Europe, a different girl who didn't matter in every city. A girl who couldn't hurt him. When he had most needed Lisa she hadn't been there. As much as he wanted to, he couldn't forget that.

~

'That went well,' said Keith to Lisa as she sat down. 'I suggested it to Bernice before.'

'Good idea. It was very moving,' Lisa said. 'Hi, Rob, I was getting worried. What is it?'

'I'll tell you later, Lise. This isn't the place. I promise. Right, guys, sorry I'm late. Any questions you need help on?' said Rob, joining the table.

'In a tarot deck,' said Keith, slowly deciphering his notes, 'what is the tenth card of the major arcana? I said it was The Sun.'

'Crikey,' said Rob. 'I haven't a clue. Let's go with that.'

'We had a choice,' said Tasmin. 'The wheel of fortune or the hanged man were the others.'

'Maybe The Sun's too obvious,' said Jeremy.

'Not the hanged man,' said Rob. 'That's tempting fate.'

'The Sun it is, then,' said Lisa, glancing at Rob. She could not wait for the quiz to end so she could find out what was troubling him. He looked like the sword of Damocles was hanging over his head.

Lisa and Rob were leaving the pub through the front door, followed by Tasmin and Jeremy. The smell of the day's stale smoke wafted over them as they passed through the porch. Blue lights were spinning in the car park.

'Whoa, Maya will be disappointed she's not here. It's DI Sex on Legs,' said Tasmin. 'How do you do, DI Calvini?'

Calvini approached the group, followed by two uniformed officers. He stood in front of Rob, ignoring Tasmin.

'Robert Granville, I am arresting you on suspicion of the murder of Judith Crayvern. You do not have to say anything.'

'This can't be happening,' said Lisa.

'But it may harm your defence if you do not mention when questioned something which you later rely on in court. Anything you do say may be given in evidence.'

'No,' said Rob. 'You've got the wrong man. You're wasting time when you could be looking for a murderer.'

'Rob's innocent,' said Lisa, grabbing Calvini's sleeve. 'He wouldn't hurt anyone. You have it all wrong.' A group of customers edged out of the front door, jostling with each other to witness the seemingly final act of their crowded week of drama. Calvini glared at Lisa and pulled his arm away. One of the policemen handcuffed Rob and led him to the police car. Lisa followed.

'Jeremy's friend … Remember the card,' she called to Rob. 'Don't worry, I'll get you out.' But how would she get him out? Just how?

'He's arrested Rob?' said Maya, flinging her sports bag against the wall. It landed with a thud. 'How can he? What game's he playing?'

'Rob had something to tell me. He was going to tell me after the quiz. He looked really pensive in the pub, as if he knew what was going to happen. Damn Judith. Damn Denise.'

'Judith? Denise? It's not her who's the problem. Don't you think if you had just let things be that poor woman might still be alive? What can of worms did you open sleuthing in Hazelton, Lisa? Maybe none of this would have happened.'

'What are you talking about?

'Did you tell them Denise had taken Judith's name? Did you?'

'Maya, arguing isn't going to get Rob out. That's the only think that's important to me. They must know he didn't do it. He'd have her blood on all his clothes.' Lisa rummaged for her mobile which was squashed under Maya's bag. 'So much for DI Sex on Legs. I'm going to bed.'

'You did, didn't you? You told them,' Maya said, as Lisa slammed the door.

Damn Maya. Lisa threw a paperback over the end of the bed. It was pointless trying to read it. She imagined Rob in a jail, locked up with all the shite in the universe. His good looks would be a curse in prison. She had to get him out. If Laurie Calvini was so hopeless at his job she would have to do it for him. She must tackle the investigation methodically. It was usually someone the victim knew. She made a mental list of suspects and motives.

Keith: unrequited love, no alibi. But how could it be Keith?

Jeremy: crime of passion, but he wasn't really the passionate sort. Tasmin was his alibi.

Brian Cordon: sex, but he was in the pub.

Val Cordon: jealousy, but ditto alibi.

Andy had taken her side. He was enamoured of her, but surely it was no more than that? Who else? She added Tasmin and Maya to the list. If Taz was guilty then Jeremy would have to lie for her. Unlikely. He was far too correct. Maya actually had the time to do it and had no alibi. What motive could she have beyond being sick and tired of hearing Lisa bitching about Fake Judith? Why was she even considering Maya?

She kicked a leg out over the top of the duvet. What if Maya was right? What if her sleuthing had triggered something, that it was someone from Hazelton? Calvini had gone there on the second day, so he must have investigated all possible suspects. He'd met the coach driver, Mr Oliver, and the staff in the museum. The coach driver had liked her. Why would he suddenly decide to murder Denise Carvel? How would he even know where she was?

Calvini had been very interested in her views on Paula and Marsha. She went over her visit to the museum. The business card. She had given one of the women her business card. She had told her that Denise was now living as Judith Crayvern. Shit. She thought for a long time. Only the receptionist was there at the time. Was that Paula or Marsha? She had even told her that Denise went to The Sun. Shit. She remembered the worn cuff of the receptionist's blue shirt.

267

The stranger in the pub. That was her. The blue collar underneath the fleece was part of Hazelton Museum's uniform. Why the fuck had Calvini arrested Rob, when he'd already met the prime suspect at the museum?

(What's the story)
morning glory?

Lisa woke with a jolt and a sensation she had never experienced before. She felt as if all her energy was about to be sucked into a dark tunnel, into oblivion. She switched on the light, breathless with terror. Everything looked the same: the wardrobe, her clothes scattered on the floor, the paperback splayed half-open. She looked in the wardrobe mirror. Unruly hair, pale face, hazel eyes. She was still very much alive.

She pressed her face against the cold mirror. Was that what they call the night terrors? The feeling that all your energy is seeping into a dark vortex, that you are facing the end? She placed a hand over her heart. It was beating fiercely. She sprayed a mist of perfume over her neck and inhaled the calming scent as she sat on her bed pondering her options. She heard Maya leave. No goodbyes this morning.

Fifteen minutes later she grabbed her quilted jacket and hat. Maya would doubtless disapprove of her plans. Lisa texted her anyway so at least someone knew where she was going, although she had no idea what she was going to do when she got there. That was down to fate.

Lisa slowly wandered past the museum reception desk several times but saw no one she recognised. She wandered from the bright natural light of the main hall into the enclosed space that housed the ancient Egyptian collection. The kohled eyes of statesmen and pharaohs of thousands of years ago stared back at her as she peered through the glass exhibits cases. She wondered if they had all been dead when their vital organs had been ceremoniously extracted to prepare their mortal bodies for the afterlife. When she had come to the museum before she had masked her nerves behind her smart suit. Then she had known the purpose of her visit. Now she was not sure what to do.

She stopped in front of a display of knives. The copper glinted in the spotlights. The tools of the embalmer. Lethal weapons. She started as she saw a reflection in the glass case. She turned. Dave Dawson was standing beside her, a fraction too close. He was sucking on a mint that failed to disguise the stale smoke that clung to his clothes.

'Now, I could ask you what you were doing here. But I guess that's a question you could ask me. How about a coffee and we can both share?' he said.

Lisa scrutinised Calvini's adversary. *Your enemy is my enemy.* She had to get Rob out. Maybe Dawson had the answer.

~

The staffroom was a chaotic repository for out-of-date magazines and used plastic vending machine cups. It would exude the unsavoury aroma of stale tuna sandwiches and perspiration until the cleaner completed her last chore of the day and sprayed a lengthy squirt of vanilla air freshener around the room. Paula adjusted her hair as she looked in the vanity mirror then painted her lips a dark pink. Her blue eyes twinkled back at her. Dancing eyes. She smiled. Martin had always said she had a lovely smile.

She had known the police would be round to make inquiries. She was right. It hadn't taken them more than a day to work out they hadn't got the body of Judith Crayvern but of Denise Carvel.

Paula had been prepared for the detective's questions. There had been no sense in attracting attention to herself by saying what she had really thought of Denise. She had been very economical with her words, professing to remember only a little about her esteemed manager. The business card weighed heavily on her mind. She could not find it. Everything else had been accounted for. She stared at her reflection in the mirror as she tidied her hair.

Denise's arrival at the museum had shattered her dreams and had ensured that Paula's night of passion with Martin would remain a dream. Just when she had been sure that she was about to embark on the great love affair of her life, Martin had begun to share his confidences with Denise. He had been beguiled by her. He was spellbound. He had eyes for no one else after she arrived. Bitch. She stabbed the tail of her comb over her scalp to define her parting, wincing as she pressed too hard. And now that journalist was back, asking questions. She guessed the detective wouldn't be far behind. She placed her handbag in her locker, then walked out into the museum foyer. As she did so she caught a glimpse of the backs of Dave Dawson and Lisa Clarkson walking into the cafe.

From the shadows beside the vending machine Paula watched them settle down with their beakers of coffee, then she quietly slipped into the back of the cafe. Going back to The Sun had been a mistake. It had uncovered a hornets' nest. She certainly hadn't expected to see that scumbag journalist again. She had been beside herself with joy as she watched Lisa's boyfriend being handcuffed and taken to the police car. It wouldn't have surprised her if she had whooped with delight. She didn't think she had, but the last few days had been so stressful she could not be sure. That must have been when Dawson had recognised her. She had thought Lisa hadn't seen her, but here she was.

Now she had two inconvenient strangers to deal with. Dave Dawson certainly wasn't bashful. This morning he had asked her outright why she had been in The Sun. She was still locking her car when he had confronted her. She had denied it, but she could tell he didn't believe her. It was the way he licked his top lip with his tongue. Like a toad flicking its tongue out to catch a fly.

'Why are you interested in Denise Carvel, Lisa?' Dawson said. His words echoed round the small cafe, bouncing off the bare wooden floors. They faced a large window that overlooked budding woodlands and wilting daffodils.

'Because I know my boyfriend isn't a murderer. Why are you here?' Lisa's instinctive revulsion about sharing a table with one of the gutter press had diminished when she realised that he might be on the track of the real killer, but her feelings of goodwill dissipated as she listened to him.

'I'm always on the lookout for a story. Sex and violence always sells. It's better with a twist, though. What do you make of it all,

271

Lisa?'

'Denise was the lover of the museum director. Did you know that?'

'Sex among the sarcophagus, or is it sarcophagi? No, that doesn't sound as good. That's no reason to be murdered, though.'

'People resented her. Maybe enough to kill her. She was manipulative. She twisted things.'

'Such as?'

'Well, she stole Judith's identity. She was a fake. Everything about her was fake.'

'Why do you think she did that?'

Lisa shrugged.

'People like stories they can relate to and fantasise about, especially older women. They're no different to men, really. Sex with a toy boy, especially an educated one ... Now that's a story with legs, don't you think?' Dawson raised an eyebrow.

'Martin wasn't ...'

'It seems your Rob spent a bit of time round at Judith's, according to her neighbours. Are you denying he was having an affair?'

'Of course I am.' Lisa flushed as Dawson made a note in a small spiral-topped pad.

'Wasn't he a holiday rep? I bet there're lots of girls around with stories to tell. After all he's quite a hunk, so the women in The Sun tell me anyway.'

She should have said nothing. She could see the news story now: *Girlfriend Denies Accused Was Murder Victim's Stud.*

That would not go down well at MedTime, or at Bergers. Rob would be beside himself. Maya would say, 'I told you so.' Tasmin would look at her like a betrayed puppy. She had to get Dawson on to a different story, one that didn't involve Rob. Preferably one that led to Paula.

'Why are you here? All the other hacks are off following the footballer story. Why do you think the deal's here?' she said.

'That story's covered to exhaustion. I just had a hunch. Paula, the receptionist, was in The Sun last night. She was behaving suspiciously. Perhaps she was just delighted that someone was arrested for murdering her former colleague, of course. I saw her this morning but she denied being there. No surprise.'

'I saw her last night, too. She's my prime suspect.'

'Motive?'

'I think Denise murdered the real Judith Crayvern. Why Paula might want to kill Denise I really don't know.'

'Why would Denise kill Judith?'

'Jealousy. Envy.' Lisa shrugged. 'Because she could.'

'You know how to kill a story. Good thing you didn't decide to follow my profession. The police at the time seemed satisfied. Suicide, not murder, was a rumour then, or so they tell me at the local rag.'

'That's ridiculous. No one would plan a suicide there. I'll show you where it happened,' said Lisa. 'Are you on? We can go in our own cars.'

Into the valley

The sun blistered a hole through the blanket of cloud, burnishing the ridge on the opposite side of the lake and silhouetting the windblown trees along the top. Below the water shimmered. Lisa and Dawson sat on the bench dedicated to Lydia Bignall, surveying the view. A patchwork of verdant fields stretched across the hills. Birdsong merged with the bleating of fattening lambs.

'So what's the story?' Dawson sealed his roll-up cigarette, tapped each end on his tobacco tin, then lit it.

Lisa related her meeting with Mr Bignall and demonstrated how it was not possible to see the bridge from the memorial seat, so it was possible that there had been someone else near the River Hazel that day. As she related her theory she realised she had no evidence at all. The case was totally flimsy. It just meant her case that Denise was at the river was possible, but not even probable. How keen she had been to incriminate Denise without any evidence. She glanced at the messages on her mobile. Nothing from Maya. She texted.

Dawson took a drag of his roll-up.

'Let's go down and have a look at your "crime scene".' He tweaked his fingers in the air, two mordant inverted commas.

'How did you know Denise?' Dawson said, as they marched briskly through the pines, which soared skywards like timber steeples. The cawing of the rooks penetrated the heavy silence.

'How did you know Denise Carvel?' repeated Dawson, panting as he tried to keep up with her.

'You aren't very fit, are you? I'd give those roll-ups a miss if you want a long and healthy life.'

'This is a two-way deal, love. I help you, you help me. So was Rob just her friend?'

'We were members of the same quiz team, that's all. Keith was her friend.'

'Yes, he certainly had the hots for her. Why do you think the police arrested Rob not Keith?'

'Why do you do this job? You just splice bits of gossip together to make a fairy tale. The truth doesn't come into it. It's all fake. You're an intelligent guy. How do you sleep at night?'

'Money. Mouths to feed. What do you do, Lisa?'

'Aren't these trees magnificent?' she said, gazing upwards as they crested a small hill, then descended once more.

'Advertising, isn't it?' Dawson asked, sharply. 'An honourable profession, indeed. Nothing fake about it at all.'

Lisa continued in silence as they left the woods and walked along the riverbank. Newly unfurled fronds of spring green adorned the silver branches of the gnarled trees that arched along the sparkling River Hazel.

'We're one and the same, you and me. Presenting images and stories in the way our paymasters want us to. You'll see it one day,' Dawson said.

'Look, this is the bridge,' Lisa said, 'where Judith died, the real Judith, in this shallow water. That's the remains of the old bridge near where Martin died.'

'You can die in a few inches of water, if you're unlucky,' said Dawson. 'Why do you think Denise is a murderer?'

'When I came here two weeks ago Paula said she had been behaving suspiciously on the day Judith died, and she stole Judith's cat.'

'What motive do you think Paula had for saying that?'

Lisa shrugged.

'She didn't like her.'

'Exactly. She could even have been deflecting suspicion from herself. Listen, there's no story here. Readers don't like babbling brooks and silly accidents. Tsunamis, sex, and violence. That's more like it. A cat-stealing glamour puss. Cat Woman? Maybe. Tragic widows having sex with younger men, then getting their throats cut. Now that's a story that sells.'

'Paula knew that Denise was living as Judith and that she went to The Sun quiz,' Lisa said.

'How come?'

'I told her.'

Dawson dragged on his cigarette slowly.

'Tell me, Lisa. How do you sleep at night? Have you told DI Calvini?'

'Not that bit,' said Lisa, blinking as the tobacco smoke irritated her eyes. 'He's convinced it's Rob who's the prime suspect.'

'I can see you're determined not to tell me why,' said Dawson. 'Right, I'll see you later. I have to earn my living and I can only do that if people talk to me. I'm heading back to the museum to find out what they really think about Cat Woman.'

Lisa watched the journalist retrace the path until he disappeared into the pine plantation. She turned and ambled to the crown of the bridge, holding on to the handrail as her trainers slipped on the damp wood. The river foamed over jagged rocks, rushing relentlessly into the depths of the lake's head, metres away. A robin hopped along the edge of the bank then disappeared into the shadows. Lisa felt hollow, empty. Calvini had told her to keep away from Dawson. She should have taken all the information she knew to the police or Jeremy's solicitor friend.

The robin reappeared, its scarlet breast revealing its rocky perch, a worm wriggling in its beak. Lisa looked into the shallows. Clear, pure water bubbled around the stones. She was just an amateur punching way above her weight. She had wanted to cast Denise as a murderer, incriminate her without evidence. But Denise was just an unhappy, lonely woman with a liking for her boyfriend. Who could blame her for that? A jay flew across her line of vision, handsome in its sienna coat and turquoise-patterned plumage. Who was Judith anyway? For all Lisa knew she could be worse than Denise.

A slight rustle whispered through the tops of the trees. The infant leaves, fresh and green as the spring, quivered, suspicious of the breeze. Soon every leaf was moving. Above, dark clouds swept across the white strata and obscured the meek sun. Rain splattered on the path and bounced into the river. Birds screamed and chattered in the foliage, like monkeys in a rainforest.

Lisa hurried back into the woods, slowing as she walked uphill, her feet sinking into the pine needles. It was soon silent except for the occasional cracking of small, fallen branches. Even the funereal cawing of the rooks had stopped. She was cocooned among the pines, inhaling their cedar scent, seeing the world through their

276

dismal light.

The fierce howl, as savage as a wild animal's, stopped Lisa in her tracks. The cry began again, but lower, whimpering with fright. The fear she had felt in her sleep returned, enveloping her body. She continued to walk, more deliberately, carefully. She crested the path.

Then, as it dipped into a shallow valley, she nearly trod on the shivering body of Dave Dawson. Crimson blood oozed through his right hand, which he held over his trembling belly. The other hand, like a white claw, was stretched awkwardly on the carpet of needles. A cigarette burned nearby, its rancid smoke rising upwards, blending with the bitter scent of bark. His eyes were open. His mouth was gaping, contorted with terror. She knelt closer, then reeled back as he gurgled and bile dripped from his mouth.

Lisa took off her quilted jacket. She wasn't sure if it was best to keep him warm or stem the flow of blood. She decided to put her wool hat over the wound, gingerly moving his bloody hand to complete the task. She dropped his hand back on top of her hat, pressing it firmly to try and stop the bleeding, and covered his shoulders with her jacket. She tried to roll him on to his side, but abandoned the manoeuvre as he groaned. Instead she fashioned a pillow out of pine needles and cones to support his head.

'Don't worry. I'll get help. It will be all right.'

But would it? The killer had struck only minutes ago. She slowly turned round, scanning the hill below her. There was no sign of anyone. The cawing of a bird broke through the silence like crunching glass.

She put her ear to Dawson's mouth as he mumbled.

'Paula,' he said.

'She did this?'

'Yeah. Tell Sarah I …'

'What do you want to tell Sarah, Dave? What?' Lisa leaned forward. His face was set like an unhappy gargoyle. She felt his wrist. She could detect a faint tremor. She got up and walked slowly forward. She could see the path ahead as it dipped then climbed again. As rays of light penetrated the pine canopy, Lisa caught a gleam of steel to her right.

Paula had found the expression on Denise's face especially pleasing as she had yanked her hair and twisted her head around. She had made her look into her eyes. She had relished the look of complete surprise and horror. No, terror.

The cuts had been surprisingly easy to make. How fragile her skin and bones had been. Revenge had been served cold and sweet. It had given her great satisfaction.

There had almost been a glitch in The Sun car park. She had just taken off her blood-sprayed outerwear when a customer had passed by with his dog. A witness. The little dog had started sniffing around her feet but she had managed to keep her head. That was what she must do now.

After leaving The Sun she had thrown the bloody evidence into a field and then watched a television programme on catch-up TV that she could always claim she had watched live. It was not much of an alibi, but it was the best she could come up with. Tim was on nights and her son was out with his girlfriend, so no one could dispute it. She had opened up the museum early in the morning and given the ancient copper dissecting knife a good clean before she had returned it to the exhibition case. No one at the museum suspected a thing.

But last night she had made a mistake. She had returned to the scene of the crime and drawn attention to herself. Now things were definitely problematic, but the situation was not impossible to save. Self-preservation was the priority now.

Killing Dawson had not been easy. She had really had to push the knife in and twist it round before he fell down. For a moment she thought he might push her over. She had intended to hide Dawson's body in the woods. He might not be reported as missing for a few days. But Lisa as well. That was a bigger problem.

Paula had been prepared to kill her last night – she had even bought a kitchen knife in Sainsbury's for the purpose – but when the police arrested Robert Granville she decided there was no need. How wrong she had been.

Paula hid behind the trunk of the tree and chewed a chocolate eclair as she contemplated how she was going to stop Lisa getting back to her car. That was her priority. Disposing of the bodies was secondary. She turned over the kitchen knife in her latex-gloved

278

hands. Surprise was on her side. That was her main weapon now.

Lisa started as she saw the metal gleaming menacingly below. Paula. It had to be her. The woman was powerful, but she was surely no match over the distance it would take her to run to the car park. Then what? Get in the car. Lock it. Phone for help. No, get away first. She checked her car keys in her back pocket. If necessary she could poke at her eyes. Gouge them out, if need be. Like Paula had tried to do to Dave Dawson's stomach.

Go. She sprinted through the woods, taking deep gulps of air as she made the steep climb near the top of the plantation and out into open countryside. Raindrops pelted down, stinging her skin and softening the ground. The muscles in her legs tightened, unwilling to provide the firepower she needed to propel her safely to the finishing line. Her lungs burned.

She looked over to the hillock, hoping to see Mr Bignall, but it was empty. The rain fell in curtains, turning the dirt path to orange mud, churning the gravel. Fresh new streams poured down the hillside. She clambered through the lime green moss alongside the cascading path, mimicking the sharp hand movements of a sprinter while her feet clumsily thrust her slowly forward. Through the gloom she could see the yellow arrow on the signpost which pointed towards the gate and the car park, as if beckoning her to safety. Her lungs were tight, unable to inhale more than shallow gulps of air. She looked behind. Paula was lumbering up the hill, red blood staining her blue blouse, a knife glinting in her hand. Beyond, the ridge merged with its own shadow, melding into the lake.

She could do it. No, she would do it. She would make it to the car. As she tried to push her calves forward, the spongy moss pulled her into the earth. Not far. Paula was way behind. She would do it.

Something whistled past her cheek, so close to her ear she could feel the rippling air. She dropped heavily into the soggy marsh. She felt like she had been shot in her left leg. A stone bounced near her head. She had to get up and move. She scrambled into a crouching position to protect her head and took a step forward with her right leg. But, as she put her weight on her left knee, it crumbled beneath her. She could hear Paula panting behind her. Another stone flew

279

past. She pulled herself up again and hopped on her right leg.

She could see the gate. She pulled her keys out of her pocket. As she hopped forward Paula bore down on her like a rugby scrum half, pulling her legs from under her. Lisa yelped, kicking wildly.

Attract attention. There might be someone around. This is not going to be the end.

She was going to save Rob. She was not going to die. Not when the person who would hear her last words was Paula.

'Help me,' she screamed. 'Help me. Murder!' As Lisa yelled she jammed her elbow into Paula's ribs, winding her, and managed to pull herself free. She must get the knife. She twisted round. The sweet smell of caramel assaulted her nostrils. She looked into the ice-blue eyes, sunken behind gold-rimmed spectacles, and smashed them with her car keys. The receptionist's head jarred backwards as Lisa tried to grasp her hand and take the knife.

'Bitch.' Paula choked, her head thrusting forward, splattering drops of blood, which clung to the lenses of her glasses.

'Why?' Lisa gasped. 'Why … did … you … kill … her?'

'Interfering bitch,' Paula spat. 'Like you.'

Lisa could see the blade was about to strike her fingers. Her hand was frozen. She willed it to move.

Move.

The knife flew away. She gasped in surprise and looked up to see the comforting yellow luminous waistcoat of a policeman.

'He's down there. Dave Dawson. She tried to kill him in the woods.' Lisa stood up, grabbing the policeman's arm. She looked at Paula, who was now restrained by two police officers, her hair stuck to her face, cuts bleeding over her eyes.

Lisa watched as Paula was handcuffed and dragged up the path towards the car park. Whatever Denise had done, she didn't deserve to die like she had. She certainly wasn't as guilty as Paula.

'Lisa, are you all right?' DI Calvini was standing at the wooden gate under a large umbrella. Lisa was surprised how pleased she was to see a man she had cursed for most of the previous night.

'Fine. Just my leg. She tried to stone me. She's knifed Dawson. It looks bad.'

'Did she hit your head?'

'No, just my calf. Felled me.'

'We'll take a statement first, if that's OK with you, and then get you checked out. The lads will get Dawson. You probably want to know that we released Rob without charge this morning. You're certainly full of surprises, Lisa. I wasn't expecting to see you in Hazelton today. Not until Maya called, anyway.'

Fool (if you think it's over)

'I don't want you to think badly of me, like, but The Dispossessed have asked me to join them,' said Keith, taking a sip of a half pint of Guinness.

'Traitor,' said Rob.

Keith flinched.

'Only joking, Keith. You and Bea will make a formidable team with Janet and Clive. We'll have a job beating you.' Rob patted Keith's arm.

'Did they really think you'd done it, Rob?' said Tasmin, joining her friends' table. Jeremy and Olivia followed.

'It certainly felt like it,' Rob said. 'I thought they'd discounted me. Then, when they discovered the will, they had a pretty compelling motive. But my solicitor – he was great, by the way, Jeremy, thanks – made sure the cops spoke to Judith's solicitor. He only got back from holiday on Wednesday. He remembered that Judith had said it would be a big surprise for me, although she didn't expect it would be for a long time. By then the cops were already on their way to Hazelton, anyway.

'Drinks again, Lisa? What about you, Livvie? Can I get you a farewell drink?'

'Please, Rob. Sauvignon Blanc would be super,' Olivia said, as she sat down next to Lisa.

'You can buy the next one, Liv, to celebrate my new high-powered job,' Rob called as he walked to the bar.

'Can you drive, Lisa?' Olivia said, distracting her colleague from a conversation with Maya.

'Yah, just about. I thought I'd pulled a muscle but it's just badly bruised. I'm going to get back to that gym. It was only when I had to run for my life that I realised how unfit I was. They say you can pull that little bit extra out if your life depends on it, but my extra went halfway up that hill. Thank God it's all over.'

'Now that the investigation's over and Paula's behind bars,' said

Maya, 'do you think there is any professional or ethical reason why I can't contact Laurie Calvini?'

'Yes, me,' said Tasmin, feigning disapproval, then moving closer to Jeremy.

'Don't be greedy, Taz. I'm serious. I'd like to find out about police work. I could quite see myself as a detective,' said Maya, as Lisa looked at her inquisitively. 'He's not married. I checked.'

'It was hard luck for Dave Dawson,' said Jeremy.

'I'm sure someone must be sad for him,' said Tasmin.

'His last words were, "Tell Sarah I—", but I don't think the police know who Sarah is. It's not his wife or his kid. I'd love to know who she is so I could tell her she was the last person on his mind.'

'I hope you aren't going to go to the funeral and try to find her,' said Maya. 'That could open a whole new can of worms. I know you think he was going to say, "I love you", but that might not be true at all.'

'Yes, not something his wife should ever know about,' Jeremy said. 'Interesting that he suspected Paula. He was pretty much on the ball. Pity he'd chosen crime reporting, not investigating. He might have made a good detective,' said Jeremy.

'Why did the police suspect her?' said Tasmin. 'You were lucky, Lisa. You might have been killed if they'd not arrived in time.'

'I think Paula became a suspect because she'd said positive things about Denise when everyone else knew she hated her,' Lisa said. 'I saw Marsha later and she said there were records of disciplinary and grievance procedures between the pair. Marsha thought Paula had been behaving oddly the day after the murder, turning up early for work and volunteering to do some conservation work in the Egyptology department that she had always hated. So she called DI Calvini again. Her colleague Helen had thought the same and called the police as well. Forensics have taken the Egyptian knives away, so I guess they think the murder weapon's there.'

'I thought you were crazy, going up there sleuthing again, Lisa,' said Maya. 'That's why I called Laurie Calvini, but he was already there.'

'I've had some very good news this week,' Keith said, to no one

283

in particular, but making eye contact with Maya, who was nearest to him. 'My daughter Jennie's having a baby and they're moving back up here in a few months' time. They've had an offer on their flat. They just need a house now.'

'Oh, Keith, that's fab news,' said Maya.

Lisa immediately thought about 23 Willow Tree Avenue being vacant. Rob now owned it but he hadn't mentioned moving into it, or what he was going to do with it. The prospect of living there seemed ghoulish. She felt sorry for Judith. Yes, she really did feel sorry for Judith. No one deserved to die like that. Like Rob said, if she wanted to be called Judith let's at least do that for her.

'That's good news, Keith. A whole new chapter in your life.'

'Brilliant, Keith. You deserve it, sweetie,' said Tasmin. 'Lisa, are you coming to Livvie's farewell bash tomorrow lunchtime?'

'I'll pop in. I'm seeing someone for lunch, though. It's been arranged for over a week, so I can't change it.' Lisa said, relieved that Maya was engaged in conversation with Keith. It was probably best that Maya had no inkling that she was lunching with James or she would be questioning Lisa's motives. But she just wanted closure, to get him out of her system. It was odd, though. James seemed to be acting like she was the one who had contacted him, not the other way round.

'Christ,' said Lisa, sitting up sharply in her seat, arching her back like a cat.

'What is it? You look like you've seen a ghost,' Maya said.

'Judith. I swear I saw Judith.'

Maya looked over to where Lisa was pointing.

'That girl next to Rob with the blonde hair?'

'The one he's chatting to?' said Keith. 'Oh, she's just passing through. Now you mention it, she does look like a younger version of Judith. She's not from round here. She's an Aussie, from Brisbane.'

284

EPILOGUE

Make you feel my love

Three years earlier

Judith walked steadily along the narrow gravel path. The mud from the puddles left by the previous night's rain splattered her hiking boots. After a few minutes the path climbed abruptly, winding round a grassy hillock to a wooden bench placed on its crown. She sat down.

The landscape she surveyed was a pallid imitation of its summer self. The grass was barely green, its energy sapped during the cold, dark winter days. Fields, scattered with bleating sheep and lambs, tumbled down the hills towards the lakefront before disappearing behind small plantations of pine trees. The water was high, swollen by the previous night's rainfall, which the river had carried from the uplands. Silver ripples shimmered across the surface of the grey lake.

As she stood up she glanced at the barely legible inscription on the back of the bench. It was in the memory of a walker, long since deceased and almost forgotten, who had loved this view. She caught sight of the blonde wood of a new bridge through a gap in the trees. A couple of ducks bobbed up and down on the river, their yellow beaks and viridescent heads occasionally disappearing into the greyness. It was not always such a tranquil landscape. She shivered.

She reflected that the view the long-dead walker had admired would have included the river and the bridge. The view from the seat was quite different. Even the creation of the memorial had changed the nature of the place. She wondered how many acts were performed in the name of remembering the dead that misrepresented the reality of their lives. She set off again, her thoughts returning to the past as she descended towards the line of trees.

The feeble light, which filtered through the high branches of the conifers, picked out the faint contours of a footpath almost hidden by a soft carpet of pine needles. Judith pressed on, the gloom reflecting her mood. She thought back to the funeral almost two years ago. She had been dreading the service but had felt she owed it to Martin to ensure it was a celebration of his life. He was popular and well respected, so it had not been difficult to find colleagues and friends who were willing to prepare a eulogy. She had selected the music herself: *Libera Me*, which she remembered had been so moving at Princess Diana's funeral, *Abide with Me*, which had been played at her father's interment, and *Love Divine*, which she had chosen for their wedding ceremony. She remembered little of the service, just lots of nameless people offering sympathy, giving her hugs. It had, however, been surprisingly comforting.

What a waste. Dying trying to save a dog. She did not think Martin was particularly fond of dogs. Although, now she thought about it, she was not sure if he had ever expressed his views either way. She was losing him. She could not remember things about him any longer. Just like his scent, her memory of him was diminishing too.

A fir cone, breaking free from the web of dark green branches high above, thudded as it hit the ground, awakening her from her thoughts. A jackdaw cawed eerily nearby. Ahead the river glistened beyond the edge of the pine plantation.

She increased her pace. As she was about to emerge from the half-light she felt she was being watched.

Get a grip, she told herself. *You're letting your imagination take control again.* She wrinkled her nose. Cedar was caught in the air under the canopy of the branches. And jasmine. And amber. Perfume. It was a familiar scent, one that Martin had liked. She turned round. Just feet away, under a tree, a figure in a red jacket was watching her.

'What are you doing here?' Denise said.

Judith vaguely remembered seeing Denise at an exhibition launch. Petite, intense, quite striking. Strangely familiar, as well. She remembered Martin saying that they did not get on. Her sister had told her Denise was at the funeral, but she could not really remember her. She also recalled her sister telling her not to worry about what people were saying. She had been taken aback. She didn't know

286

people were saying anything. Her sister had continued to tell her, anyway.

'People like to gossip, muckrake. It's currency for people with shallow lives. It's a way to make themselves important,' she had said. 'Just ignore them. The facts are that Martin tried to rescue a dog. The owner of the dog was someone Martin worked with. It was just a coincidence they both happened to be there at the same time.'

Judith had agreed, not really registering what her sister was saying. Words that once seemed to make no sense at all now seemed to have new meaning.

'I beg your pardon,' Judith replied, walking on. 'What am I doing here? I think that is a question for you to answer.'

Denise moved on to the riverside path, making Judith face her. She brushed strands of her long blonde hair from her face with a delicate hand.

'This was our special place. We wanted to be together. We would have been if it wasn't for you,' Denise said.

'Don't be ridiculous. This was *our* favourite place. He was my husband. We loved each other. He was mine,' Judith said.

Denise stared back. Her face impassive, cold.

'"My husband?" You didn't own him. You don't know what love is. You never understood him. You made his life a misery. You never listened to what he wanted. It was all about you. He loved me. He wanted me. You had nothing in common.'

'You're talking nonsense. You are completely deluded, lady. He would never have left me.'

'He wanted to. If you'd not become ill.'

'Me, ill?'

'One of your tricks.'

'I've never needed any tricks to keep him. I've never been ill.'

'He died trying to save me.'

'He died trying to save your dog.'

'For me. My dog died. I didn't.'

'What a pity.' Judith stepped forward. 'He'd be alive today, if not for you and your damned dog. Get out of my life, Denise. You're not welcome in it.'

'You never gave Martin what he wanted. What he needed. Yes,

287

he cared for you. Like a sister, like an old glove or – or a slipper. Not like a lover.'

Judith raised her hand and hit Denise smartly across the face.

Denise did not move.

'I lost everything that day. Everything that I loved, that was a comfort, that adored me. You can't hurt me. You can't take my memories away,' Denise said.

'There's only one Mrs Martin Crayvern and that's me, Judith Crayvern. You're nobody, just a colleague he once tried to help, to his eternal regret.'

Judith moved forward. Denise moved sharply away and, turning her back, started walking away down the muddy path. Denise turned as she heard a sharp cry. At first she couldn't see Judith. She seemed to have disappeared. She retraced her steps and saw her at the bottom of the bank. Denise slowly crept forward. Judith's face was submerged. The waters of the rock pool lapped gently over Judith's shoulders but her knapsack, still secure on her back, was above the waterline. Her legs, spread on the riverbank, were completely dry. Denise peered closer. She thought she could see small bubbles of air rising through the water by Judith's head, but she wondered if she was imagining it. Then she saw Judith twitch her fingers.

Denise considered her choices. She could pull Judith from the river, or she could let fate take its course and continue walking back to the car park, just as she had intended, or—she picked up a stone and caressed it between her palms.

She took aim, then let the full weight of her hatred and jealousy crash onto the back of Judith's head. A blackbird, perched on the wooden rail of the bridge, hopped towards her, singing a merry tune, as she tossed the stone into the burbling waters of the River Hazel.

That beady eye. Always looking. Judging. Sneakily stealing a glance. Singing a cocky little tune. Piercing the peace. Always watching. Knowing. Telling. Feathers like death.

Libera me

Dies irae, dies illa calamitatis et miseriae; dies magna et amara valde

Requiem aeternam, dona eis, Domine, et lux perpetua luceat eis

Libera me, Domine, de morte aeterna in die illa tremenda

Libera me, Domine, quando coeli movendi sunt et terra; dum veneris judicare saeclum per ignem

Libera me, Domine, de morte aeterna in die illa tremenda

Libera me.

The day of wrath, that day of calamity and misery; a great and bitter day, indeed

Grant them eternal rest, O Lord, and may perpetual light shine upon them

Deliver me, Lord, from eternal death on that awful day

Deliver me, O Lord, when the heavens and the earth shall be moved; when you will come to judge the world by fire

Deliver me, Lord, from eternal death on that awful day

Deliver me.

Acknowledgements

Laurie Taylor could easily pack out a lecture theatre at 9.15 in the morning. This was not a talent shared by all his colleagues, I seem to recall. It was during one of his presentations that I came across Erving Goffman's book *The Presentation of Self in Everyday Life*. Goffman's analysis of social life as a dramatic performance remains compelling, and his ideas underpin *Deluded*.

Thanks to Jenny Mayhew, Jackie Roy and Nicholas Royle of Manchester Metropolitan University's Masters programme in Creative Writing and the talented writers in my workshop, especially Karin Hala – gone too soon – who believed in my characters and helped me believe, too.

Thanks also to Dad, family, friends, neighbours, and the occasional tradesman whose interest in the progress of *Deluded* propelled me over the finishing line to publication. A special mention must also go to Barbara, Gordon, Janet, Jerry, Julie, Kieron, Mike, and Nick, who were brave enough to read my manuscript in progress, and for their encouragement.

And, finally, thanks to all the musicians who have played on the soundtrack to my life.

About the author

Lynn Steinson grew up in Preston and is a graduate of the University of York. She has had several professional roles including teacher, management consultant and marketing communications manager. She has worked in Essex, Liverpool, Chester and Manchester, where she now lives. More of her writing can be found on her blog– www.lynnsteinson.com

Printed in Great Britain
by Amazon